THE TENNIS PLAYER FROM BERMUDA

The TENNIS PLAYER *From* BERMUDA

FIONA HODGKIN

Matador
9 Priory Business Park
Kibworth Beauchamp
Leicestershire LE8 0RX, UK
Tel: (+44) 116 279 2299
Fax: (+44) 116 279 2277
Email: books@troubador.co.uk
Web: www.troubador.co.uk/matador

ISBN 978 1780882 215

British Library Cataloguing in Publication Data.
A catalogue record for this book is available from the British Library.

Typeset in Garamond by Troubador Publishing Ltd
Printed and bound in the UK by TJ International, Padstow, Cornwall

Matador is an imprint of Troubador Publishing Ltd

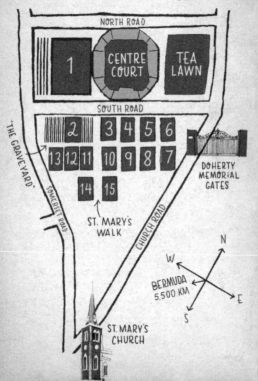

PART ONE

BERMUDA

I tossed the tennis ball high and out, cocked my wooden racket deep behind my shoulder, went up on my toes, whipped the racket forward, slammed the ball and ran toward the net.

Rachel Martin – *Mrs* Martin to someone my age – returned my service with her forehand, hard and low, to my feet.

I was already into the deuce service court alongside my father, and I bent down, so low my right knee was almost on the clay, and half volleyed, a bit too high, but angled away from Mrs Martin toward her husband, who was her mixed doubles partner. Usually, I would hit to the woman in mixed doubles, but Mrs Martin was a much stronger player than her husband. Earlier that summer, she had been a finalist in the Bermuda ladies' singles championship match. So when I could, I hit to Mr Martin.

He got his racket on it, just barely, and hit to my father in the ad service court, but I yelled "Mine!" and backhanded a hard volley straight down the centerline between the Martins. Our point.

3

Father bent his head down beside my cheek. "Rachel's forehand is so good. Why serve to it? It's match point, let's be careful," he said quietly. I didn't tell him what I thought, which was that I could volley her returns from either wing easily. He would regard that as cheeky. Instead, I smoothed down my tennis skirt and whispered, "I'll go down the middle to Mr Martin."

I went back to the baseline. I saw Father line up a bit closer to the far side. He was trying to fool the Martins into thinking that I would go wide again. I didn't bounce the white ball. Mrs Martin felt that bouncing the ball before serving was an affectation and had told me not to do it. I just set up, tossed, served, and ran forward. My serve hit the tape on the service line exactly and skidded a bit before coming up. Mr Martin bobbled his return and hit a lob, high but not deep.

"Mine!" I yelled. I backed up a few steps, set up, left index finger picking out the ball against the Bermuda sky, right elbow up, racket head brushing my back, kicked my left leg out for balance, and swung hard – what Bud Collins would call a 'skyhook.' The ball went fast down the line between the Martins. Neither of them got near it.

Game, set, and match to Dr. Hodgkin and his daughter, Fiona. I was 18, and that summer I was the ladies' singles tennis champion of Bermuda.

My parents both loved tennis and played often, usually at the Coral Beach & Tennis Club on South Road, but they were not what today we would call 'tennis parents.' I was their only child, and they began teaching me to play when I was perhaps five or six. The thought of pushing me to play tennis would not have entered their minds. I never had a paid coach; my parents would have felt that paying for a coach was unsporting and Not Done. Still, I loved tennis from the start. I just wasn't good. Father and I would play as mixed doubles partners on weekends and have great fun. When I served, even though I would hit a child's puffball over the net, Father would yell, "Come up, come up! Don't stay back!"

In July of 1957, I had just turned 14, and on my own I entered a girls' tournament at Coral Beach. I had never played in a tournament before. I knew all the girls who had entered, and perhaps one of my friends said she would enter if I would as well. In any event, I entered.

Private autos had been legal in Bermuda since just after the second war, but my parents, like many Bermuda families, did not own an auto until the mid-1960s or so. We rode pedal bikes, or took the ferries or the bus when we moved around. So my friends and I cycled to Coral Beach on a Saturday morning for the tournament, with our rackets in the baskets of our bikes.

I played two matches in the morning and won both. The Club served us lunch – cheese sandwiches and Coca-Cola – on the terrace above the courts along South Road. Then, after lunch, I was to play Sara Martin.

Sara was further along in puberty than me – I was quite envious of her – and larger and stronger. I didn't know this at the time, but Sara's mother, Rachel Martin, had played at Wimbledon in 1939, the last Wimbledon before the war. As a 14-year-old in Bermuda in 1957, it's possible I hadn't yet heard of Wimbledon.

Sara blasted me off the court. I would serve and run to the net, and Sara would easily hit the ball past me. She won 6-0, 6-0. Sara went ahead to play two more matches and win the girls' side of the tournament. Her mother had taught her to play tennis well.

Later that afternoon, I was sitting on a metal folding chair in the ladies' dressing room at Coral Beach. I had my head in my hands. I was sobbing because I couldn't bear losing. Mrs Martin walked into the dressing room, looking for me.

"Miss Hodgkin, why are you crying?" I looked up at her but couldn't answer. She was wearing a simple, white tennis dress that looked so old it was almost ragged. Just above her left breast, a small, faded Bermuda flag was sewn onto the dress.

"Your father has ruined your game by making you play mixed doubles with him. Come to the net, that's all you do."

I was still sobbing. "I like playing with Father."

"In singles, you must stay close to the service line. Don't come to the net unless the ball lands quite short."

"I like coming to the net."

Mrs Martin snorted. "You don't have the service to support a serve and volley game. You have to stay back."

I kept sobbing.

"Stand up," she said. She reached down and took hold of my arm. "We're going down to the courts."

She marched me down the steps to the lower courts. No one else was there; the tournament was over. The only bicycles leaning against the wall were Mrs Martin's and mine. She picked a tennis ball up off the court.

"Toss this," she said.

"I don't have my racket."

"I didn't ask you to hit it. I want you to toss it."

I tossed the ball, and it landed at my feet.

"Pathetic. It went straight over your head."

She reached under her tennis dress and pulled out a ball she had tucked into her tennis knickers. She raised her left arm with the ball in her hand, and when her arm was fully extended, she simply opened her fingers and let the ball's momentum carry it up. The ball went up about two meters and landed well out into the court.

"Like that," she said.

"But I can't – " She interrupted. "Toss it."

I did.

"Better. Again." I tossed another ball. "Higher. Farther out." I tossed again. "Better."

"But I can't hit it that high and out!"

She glared at me. She must dislike me, I thought, but I had no idea why.

"If you want to follow your serve in, you'll have to toss the ball high and out, and then extend your arm to hit it. You're not strong enough to do it any other way. Now try tossing it high and out and then hitting it."

I found my racket. I stood at the baseline. The sky was the blue that you see only in Bermuda. There was a farmer in a horse-drawn cart, slowly moving along South Road. Other than the hooves of the farmer's horse clopping on the road, and the barely audible waves landing on Coral Beach far behind me, the court was silent. Mrs Martin looked grimly at me. I set up, took the white ball and tossed it.

I drew my feet together and whipped my arm forward and out. I pulled the racket through as hard as I could and hit the ball with all my weight. The ball skidded on the tape of the service line of the opposite service court and then hit the concrete block wall at the back of the court, just under South Road. It ricocheted high in the air and finally landed back in the court. I turned to look at Mrs Martin.

She looked back at me for a few moments. It was as though I had confirmed something bad about myself that she had already suspected, but I had no idea what it could be.

"Like that," she said finally. She said nothing more, turned on her heel, took her bike and left.

I was alone on the courts. I gathered about twenty balls that I found on the courts and practiced my serve until dusk came. Then I rode my bike home.

A week or so later, Mrs Martin called Mother and arranged to play tennis with me one afternoon. Over the next four years, until I left the island for college at Smith, we played tennis with one another four or five times a week, and more often during school holidays, but she usually arranged these meetings through Mother.

Mrs Martin was careful to avoid any appearance that she was coaching me; that was Not Done. For boys on a football or cricket team, yes. For a young lady like me playing tennis, no.

But she was coaching me, though her style of coaching was unorthodox. She cared nothing for drills or exercises. We warmed up – she called it 'knocking up' – for ten minutes, and then we played a match. After a year or so, I would sometimes win one of the first two sets and then we would play out three sets.

She cared little about the form of my strokes, whether I was using an Eastern grip or was simply hanging on the racket handle any way I could. Occasionally, she would reach over the net and twist my racket in my hand, or bend my elbow up and say, "Like that."

She was reserved and quiet, and I eventually realized that she was extremely shy. She spoke little and had almost no sense of humor. She took the game of tennis with a deadly seriousness.

The first time we played, I either hit the ball into the net or made some other error, and I said out loud, "Oh, no!" At the next changeover, she was drying her hands with a towel when she said softly, "Never speak or make an unnecessary noise during play. It is unfairly distracting to your opponent."

I slowly learned that what fascinated her was strategy, although she never would have used that word. During one changeover, she asked, "Why did you lose that last point?"

She had made a backhand winner that she hit so hard any

full-grown, accomplished player would have struggled to reach and return. I had no chance whatsoever. "Your shot was too good."

"No." She picked up a ball by pinching it between her tennis shoe and her racket head, popping it up into the air and catching it with her left hand. She tossed it into the court. It landed just beyond the service line and about half a meter inside the sideline. "That's where your shot landed." She popped up another ball and then tossed it. The ball bounced exactly on the baseline. "If your shot had landed there, my return probably wouldn't have been a winner. I would have returned the ball, certainly." She looked at the court, and I could sense that she was replaying her shot in her mind. "Possibly a winner. But unlikely."

"You mean I lost because my shot was too short?"

"In part. But why was it short?"

"I should have hit it harder."

"No. Where were you when you hit the ball?"

I pointed in the general direction of the deuce service box on my side of the court. "There." I had no idea where I had been in the box.

"No." She popped up another ball and threw it softly into the deuce box. It bounced precisely on the centerline two meters back from the net. "You were there. Let's resume play."

I had already learned it was useless to ask her to explain.

One rainy afternoon, when we couldn't play tennis, I walked over to Mrs Martin's house and knocked on the screen door to her kitchen. She let me in, made me a cup of tea and sat at her kitchen table. I sat beside her. Mrs Martin took out a scrap of paper and a pencil and began drawing a rough diagram of a tennis court, with lines showing the paths a ball might follow.

"After being struck by the racket, the ball gradually begins to slow," Mrs Martin said. "But it slows at a faster rate before it goes over the net."

"Why?"

"Air resistance is proportional to the square of the speed of the ball. There's much more air resistance when the ball is traveling faster."

"Oh."

She sat quietly looking at her drawing of a court.

I asked, "What if I put topspin on the ball?" I had just learned how to make the ball spin, and I had been experimenting with this new skill.

"Because of the Magnus effect, topspin makes the ball curve sharply down to the court."

"Oh." I had no idea what she was talking about.

"A ball that spins in the direction of its travel creates a whirlpool of air and is forced downward. Isaac Newton realized this in 1672 while he was watching tennis at Trinity College, Cambridge. Real tennis, of course. Lawn tennis wasn't invented until the 1870s."

I'd never heard of 'real tennis', which later I learned had been played on enclosed courts for centuries.

For that matter, I'd barely heard of Isaac Newton.

She continued. "The spin of the ball affects its trajectory, not its speed. Until it bounces."

"What about after it bounces?"

Mrs Martin shrugged. "Depends on the court. On grass, there's not much friction between the ball and the grass, so the bounce doesn't slow the ball much. On clay, there's more friction and the ball slows more. Grass is a fast court, clay is a slow court."

"With topspin, I feel the ball doesn't slow after the bounce."

"It slows, usually. Just not as much as a ball hit flat, without spin."

"Why not?"

"When a ball hits the court, friction slows the bottom of the ball but not the top, so the ball begins to spin in the direction of its travel. But a ball hit with topspin is already spinning in that direction. So friction converts less of the speed of the ball into spin."

I was fascinated. "How do you know all this?"

"I thought about it a great deal when I was your age."

"Oh."

She took the scrap of paper on which she had drawn a court and drew an 'X' on the ad court baseline, right at the corner with the sideline.

"That's you."

Then she drew two lines, one following the ad court sideline, across the net, and down the deuce court sideline of the opposite court, and the second going crosscourt over the net to the ad court baseline.

"You would hit down the sideline," she said, pointing to the first line, "when your opponent is out of position. Here. Or here." She drew two 'Os,' one on the ad side of the baseline, the other in the ad service court. "From these positions, your opponent might not reach a down the line shot."

Then Mrs Martin asked, "Where would you hit when your opponent is well positioned?"

"I know!" I practically yelled. "I would hit crosscourt, and I know why, too. Father told me. The net is lower in the center, and a crosscourt ball goes over the center of the net."

She snorted. "Incorrect."

I was crestfallen.

"Miss Hodgkin, I spoke without thinking. I did not mean to sound as though I was contradicting your father."

"It's all right. But the net *is* lower in the center. Doesn't that make it an easier shot?"

"Which of the two lines I've drawn is longer? Down the line? Or crosscourt?"

I put my finger on the crosscourt line.

"Correct. It's longer by more than a meter, but both crosscourt segments are longer. The segment before the line intersects the net is longer, as is the segment after the intersection."

I was mystified.

"Over which segment does the ball slow at a faster rate?"

I put my finger on the segment before the intersection with the net.

"Correct. So you're hitting the ball a longer distance, and it's slowing at a faster rate before it reaches the net."

She paused. "When I was your age, I spent weeks at Coral Beach, on the court by myself, hitting balls and thinking about this problem. The net is lower in the center, which is an advantage to hitting crosscourt, but this advantage is basically negated by the greater force and the wider angle of attack needed to make the ball travel a longer distance and still clear the net."

"So I should hit down the line?"

"No, not when your opponent is well positioned. You were correct to say that crosscourt is the proper shot in that situation. It just doesn't have anything to do with the height of the net."

"So why do I hit crosscourt?"

"Because the second segment of the crosscourt line is also longer."

"You mean the segment after the net?"

"Correct."

"Why does that matter?"

"Because a longer line crosses a larger area." She put her finger on her drawing. "Look at all this space in the ad court you have to make a crosscourt shot."

"So I should hit crosscourt to just within the lines?"

"No."

"Father told me to aim about half a meter inside the lines, to be safe."

"I told Sara the same," Mrs Martin said. "But I want you to aim for the outer edge of the line. Not the line itself – the outer edge."

"Why?"

Mrs Martin had a pained expression on her face; I worried that something must be wrong.

Finally, quietly, she answered. "Because you are one of only two girls I've ever seen with the natural ability to hit the exact outer edge of the line, almost every time."

After I had played tennis with Mrs Martin for a year or so, I asked Mother about Mrs Martin's tennis career.

"Go ask your father, he knows about it."

I found Father in our sitting room, where we spent most of our time together as a family in our house – 'Midpoint,' it had been named for 200 years or so. There was no air conditioning in private homes in Bermuda at that time, and the sitting room was the coolest part of our house. The incredibly thick masonry walls and our water tank, which collected rainwater from our whitewashed limestone roof, kept it cool. The water tank was just underneath the sitting room and acted as a passive and quite effective cooling system. As in most old Bermuda homes, the plaster ceiling simply followed the inside pitch of the roof, creating the famous Bermuda tray ceiling.

From the windows on the north side of the sitting room we had a spectacular view of Hamilton Harbour below us, which no doubt is why Midpoint had been built in precisely that spot.

Mother and Father kept the back issues of their medical journals stacked on the floor of the sitting room. When Father decided he needed to see an article from an issue of *The Lancet* from a year or so year earlier, he would try to slide it gently out of the stack, but usually the entire stack would come crashing to the floor. In her favorite chair, Mother spent evenings writing notes in her patients' medical charts, which she kept in neat piles on the floor.

Father said, "Rachel? She was an honor for Bermuda in tennis, before the war. When she played overseas, she would sew a small Bermuda flag on her dress, just above her left breast. That pleased us all."

He thought for a moment. "Rachel was invited to play at Wimbledon in '39, the last championships before the war.

She was only about 19 then. Rachel went all the way to the final. She lost in a long match with Alice Marble. It was a chilly, rainy day. Early July, but you know London weather. Rachel pulled on a sweater during the match, but she couldn't have been comfortable. She wasn't used to the cold."

"How do you know it was cold?"

"I was there. I had just begun my medical internship at Guy's Hospital in London, and Rachel found me a ticket for the players' box. I got the afternoon off from hospital and took the Tube to Southfields. Rachel had no family in London except me" – Father and Mrs Martin were cousins – "and I thought I should be there for her. I sat beside Teach Tennant, Marble's coach. Teach is probably the greatest tennis coach ever, except for Rachel."

"What happened in the match?"

"It lasted from two in the afternoon until it was almost dark. They suspended play, twice, I think, for rain. Difficult conditions. I can't recall the score, but the last two sets went to extra games. Rachel played so well. She held off several championship points in the third set before she lost. She came close to winning. If the third set had gone on a few more minutes, the umpire would have had to suspend the match for darkness.

"It started to rain again, hard, just after Marble won. Rachel was just standing there, beside the umpire's chair, in the rain. I went down to the court, but a Coldstream Guardsman stopped me. I told him I was a physician, and he let me through. I walked over to her in the rain. She was crying. The groundskeepers had taken down the net and were pulling the tarp over the court. I told Rachel we needed to get out of the rain, and I led her over to the players' entrance to Centre Court, just under the Royal Box. Teach was just coming back out. She was looking for Rachel. Teach took Rachel to the ladies' dressing room.

"The London newspapers were full of it the next morning. Everyone in Bermuda was proud of Rachel. After the war, Rachel and Derek" – Mrs Martin's husband – "moved to London for some years because of his position with Butterfield's" – Butterfield's was our bank in Hamilton – "but by then she had her family and she never went back to international competition."

The next morning, Mrs Martin and I played at Coral Beach, and afterwards I asked, "Did you learn to play tennis here?"

"No. These courts weren't laid down until after the war." We were on one of the upper courts. "I learned on the lower courts, down by South Road."

"Who taught you?"

"My parents."

"But you must have had someone who showed you to play well."

"Miss Hodgkin, you just lost our match 6-2, 6-1. Why are we discussing the ancient history of tennis in Bermuda? Why not think through why you lost?"

"I apologize."

She snorted. "Don't apologize. Win."

"It's just that I know you played at Wimbledon, and I wanted to know more about that. How it happened. How you learned. That's all."

I was ready to cry. I was still a child, really. She never meant to hurt me, but she could be mean.

She cocked her head to one side. She was thinking. "The

only person who can tell you anything about playing tennis is yourself. All the fancy people who say they can teach you how to be a tennis champion are wrong, and most of the things they tell you are wrong. You'll have to find out by yourself. There's no other way."

She walked away toward her bicycle.

"I know you had to play the final in the cold. And it was raining." I wiped my eyes with the sleeve of my tennis dress.

She turned and stared at me. "You've been talking to your father. It was cold and rainy on Centre Court that afternoon." She left.

When I was 16, my parents and I were invited to a Christmas party at the Martins' home, and there I saw an old book on a table: *Match Play and the Spin of the Ball,* by William T. Tilden. It would be an understatement to say that this book had been thoroughly read. It looked as though the dog had been after it. On the flyleaf was scrawled, "To Rachel, with admiration. Bill." I started reading the book but quickly closed it, because I could see that almost every page carried Mrs Martin's handwritten notes in the margins.

I found Tilden's book in the Bermuda library, took it home and neglected my schoolwork for one evening to read it cover to cover.

The next day, before we played, I said to Mrs Martin, "I saw a book at your house by William Tilden. I checked it out of the library. He says that a baseline player with a good return of service will usually defeat a serve and volley player."

She nodded. "Big Bill thought a strong return would more often than not pass a player at the net."

"You knew him?"

She nodded again. "I met him at the Australian championships at Kooyong. Just before the war."

After a moment, she said, "Big Bill went to Berlin, to the Rot-Weiss Club, to coach the German Davis Cup team. In 1937. Before I knew him. He regretted going to Berlin. At least, I hope so."

"What's the 'Rot-Weiss Club'?"

She didn't answer; she was in a reverie.

"Was he right about baseline players? That they defeat serve and volley players?"

She snapped back to the present. "Miss Hodgkin, are we going to devote the entire afternoon to chatting about Bill's various theories?" She tossed her old wooden racket onto the court.

"Rough or smooth?" She meant that I should call whether the knots in the gut would land 'rough' – meaning that the side with the gut sticking out of the knots would point up – or 'smooth.'

At a changeover, while she was drying her hands, I asked, "Should I switch and start staying on the baseline?"

"No."

"You think I'm too small."

"No. There are women baseline players with your stature who play effectively. You would have to play with intelligence from the baseline, but you do play intelligently." This was one of Mrs Martin's rare compliments.

"So why shouldn't I think about switching to the baseline?"

19

She thought for a moment. "The baseline and the net each has advantages, but the principal advantage of playing from the baseline is time. Compared to the net, you have an additional half-second, maybe less, at the baseline to plan your shot."

She seemed to regard an additional half-second as the tennis equivalent of a long weekend in the country. "Let's resume play."

For once I had to have an answer, and I put my hand on her arm. "Please tell me what you mean."

"At the net, you can't plan. There's no time. You rely on instinct and confidence. A player at the net with good instincts and confidence may have been easy for Big Bill to pass, but not so easy for the rest of us. But confidence is essential at the net."

I felt I was the least confident person on the planet. I was a small, awkward teenage girl. "Am I confident? Do you think I'm confident?"

She cocked her head to one side. "Your mother, and both your grandmothers, are medical doctors. I'm certain that during their medical training, and after, they were made to feel unwelcome because they are women in a male profession. They cared not the slightest. Each of them had confidence in herself."

She paused. "You may have some of their confidence. Let's resume play."

I won the Bermuda girls' singles championship in both 1958 and 1959, both times against older girls, and both times easily.

But Mrs Martin did not come to watch my matches. That might have been misconstrued by some as coaching. Everyone knew she played tennis with me, but she wanted to make it appear that we merely played an occasional social game together, which was nonsense and everyone knew it.

She may not have admitted even to herself that we had a complicated, intense, private, and competitive relationship with one another. I don't mean to suggest that it was in any way inappropriate by today's standards; it wasn't, but I depended on her, and in some way I'm sure she wouldn't admit, and may not have even realized, she depended on me.

But I wasn't sure, and now decades later I'm still not sure, whether at that time she liked me.

I owe her so much and today, while she is quite elderly, and I am in my late 60s, we are close friends. I shop for her groceries, and we walk together slowly on quiet lanes in Paget and chat about our families. But when I was a girl it was as though she felt obligated to show me the way I might become a champion – even though she was plainly reluctant to do so. For what possible reason, I couldn't imagine.

We never talked about it.

She rarely talked about anything.

But we both knew we were watching sand flowing down through an hourglass.

For years, she won 6-0, 6-0, every time. Then it was often 6-2, 6-2. Later it was 6-4, 6-4, and a few times 6-4, 4-6, 6-4.

It was only a matter of time. But I had never defeated her.

JUNE 1960
FIRST ROUND LADIES' SINGLES TOURNAMENT
TENNIS STADIUM
MONTPELIER ROAD
BERMUDA

There were no rules about entering either the Bermuda girls' tournament or the main tournament. Most young ladies played in the girls' tournament until they went away for university to England or the States, and then they either stopped playing altogether or moved to the main tournament. There was no set age limit. You entered the tournament in which you wanted to play. In June 1960, I entered myself in the main tournament. Only after I had entered did I learn that the youngest, unseeded player was always paired in the first round with the top seeded player, who in 1960 was the defending champion, Mrs Martin. That meant I would play her in the first round.

At the time, this seemed a horrible mistake. Looking back, though, I'm not sure it was a mistake. It may have given me the career in tennis I had.

Mother's response was simple: "You must withdraw from the tournament." I said no. Father, the diplomat, asked for a word with me alone.

He began by calling me 'sweetheart,' which was his

softening up move. It usually worked. But it didn't this time. I said I was staying in the tournament.

"Fiona, Rachel is a tennis player with an international reputation. She is extremely competitive. I've known her all her life. She cares for you, a great deal, but you must understand if you challenge her in public competition she will crush you. And she'll be entirely justified. No one will criticize her in the slightest."

"I will play her and win."

"Fiona, Rachel is undoubtedly the best tennis player to ever live on this island. You must be realistic."

"I will win."

"I'm sure you will win over her, some day, and maybe some day soon. But not this year. Wait until you're 18, next year. Play her then."

"I'm playing her next week." And that was that.

After my brief first round match, the Hodgkin family and Mrs Martin met in the ladies' dressing room in the tennis stadium near Hamilton. It was highly unusual for Father to be in the ladies' dressing room, but the lady players, under the circumstances, all decided to be somewhere else until this particular meeting of parents, child, and defending champion had ended.

I was not merely crying; it would be more accurate to call it uncontrolled wailing.

Mrs Martin, after she won the match, 6-1, 6-0, had been furious and brutal. She called me a coward in front of my parents – who had not come to my defense. It is possible that, contrary to her bedrock principles, Mrs Martin had given me the only game I won in order to encourage me. If so, it hadn't worked.

In the dressing room, Mrs Martin was still angry and even more specific in her accounting of my shortcomings.

"You capitulated in the second set. You failed to even try. Why bother walking out onto the court?"

"I couldn't win," I said through my tears.

"How the devil do you know?" she snapped. "The match isn't over until the last point is played. You gave up."

"I just want you to play tennis with me, still. I have to play with you."

"I can't play with a coward."

"I'm not a coward."

"You have the skill. You're intelligent on the court. But you don't have the character to win. You're weak."

And then her *coup de grâce*: "You'll never be a champion."

I wailed.

Mother interrupted. "I think we should talk about whether Fiona should continue playing tennis at all. Perhaps another sport would be better for her."

Mrs Martin was a little calmer now. She had never called me by my Christian name, at least not since I was a baby. But now she turned to me and said, "I think that is something only Fiona can decide."

She said good day to my parents and walked out.

I didn't play tennis for a month. I worked for Mother and Grandfather filing their patients' charts. I talked to no one. I was humiliated, and everyone on Bermuda knew it. I was miserable. In the late afternoons, I would cycle to some deserted beach and sit on the sand watching the Atlantic. I thought about leaving Bermuda; we had plenty of relatives in both the States and England with whom I could live.

Finally, one Saturday afternoon, I put on a tennis dress, took my racket, and cycled to the Martins' home, but they were not there. I went to Coral Beach and found the Martins playing mixed doubles with another couple. I waited until they came off the court, and then approached Mrs Martin and asked if I might have a word.

"Of course," she said and sat down in a wooden chair.

I sat in a chair next to her.

I said, "Perhaps you're tired after your match."

"It was a social doubles match. It wasn't tiring."

"Would you be willing to play a match with me?"

"Certainly. Let me go to the dressing room and wash my face. I'll meet you on one of the upper courts."

It lasted almost three hours. By the second set, all the players on the other courts had abandoned play to watch our match. I'm sure the older tennis players watching us were thinking, "This is an important match for Bermuda."

She was so strong and hit her groundstrokes so hard that I thought, 'What could she possibly have been like when she was younger?' I took the first set 14-12; there were no 'tie-breaks' in those days – we'd never heard the phrase 'tie-break' in tennis scoring.

She fought every point of the second set, but by then she was tired. She should have put this match off until Sunday morning, when she would have been fresh. Then she could have pulled out the second set. But we both knew this was it. She was desperate to break my service early in the second set; she hit every ball viciously hard. This was her only chance. If the second set went into extra games, she would fade.

I was 17; she must have in her early 40s then. She knew I could play all afternoon and until it was dark. She had to break me, get this set behind her, and then the third set – well, she would deal with the third set when she got there. But she didn't have the chance.

With the games 6-all on her serve, she drove a backhand long, only by a few centimeters but still long, and made it my advantage in the game. I won the game, breaking her serve. I looked across the net at her; we both knew it was over. She still fought every point; she tried to get the break back; she would never concede. But I kept the break. Finally, I took the second set and the match.

I had beaten her. Not in competition. Not yet. And not when she was fresh. But I had beaten her.

When I came to the net to shake hands, she refused my hand.

Instead, with perhaps 30 people watching us from the sidelines, with the net between us, she put her arms around me, pulled my head to her chest and kissed the top of my head. "You're wonderful; I'm so proud of you," she whispered. I felt her tears falling on my forehead.

SATURDAY, 1 JULY 1961
MY EIGHTEENTH BIRTHDAY
LADIES' SINGLES CHAMPIONSHIP FINAL
TENNIS STADIUM
MONTPELIER ROAD
BERMUDA

The next year, I met Mrs Martin in the finals of the Bermuda ladies' singles championship in the old tennis stadium outside Hamilton. She, as the defending champion, was seeded first; I was seeded second. Every seat was filled, and spectators spilled out onto the sides of the court. She served first, and I took her first serve of the match and hit it for a winner back down the line – the ball just barely touched the baseline and then bounced off the back wall and hung in the air for seconds before it finally landed back in the court.

I wanted everyone there to remember this match forever.

It was a hot Bermuda day, but I felt so cold my hands were shaking between points. I fired volleys to her forehand just to show that I could catch her shot with my racket, drain the ball's terrific kinetic energy with my hand and forearm, and then sharply angle my volley softly into her service box for a clear winner.

I served ace after ace and volleyed winner after winner; I

took service game after service game at love. I hit only for the outer edges of the lines; I took ferocious, insane chances and came out on top each time. In the second set, I started following in my return of her first serve to volley winners.

I wanted to crush her, and I wanted everyone in Bermuda to watch me do it. She fought back; she would never give up; but I overwhelmed her.

Ahead 4-love in the second set, I lunged to volley one of her shots, got too far out over my feet, fell, hit the court, and lacerated the distal surface of my left elbow. I was bleeding, and suddenly there was blood all over the side of my tennis dress. I walked to the sideline and found a towel to stanch the blood. I looked up and saw Father starting down the steps of the bleachers toward the court.

"No, Father. Stay where you are," I called loudly.

The chair umpire, George Michaels, said from the chair, "Miss Hodgkin, perhaps Doctor Hodgkin or Doctor Wilson should look at your arm before you resume play." My mother used her maiden name, Wilson, in her medical practice – which was practically a scandal in those days.

"Mr Michaels, I am ready to play now." I picked up my racket and walked back to the baseline. Mrs Martin, across the net, was expressionless.

It was over in 34 minutes. 6-1, 6-0.

I walked to the net, shook hands with Mrs Martin, and went to pick up a towel to hold to my elbow. Mrs Martin said nothing to me. The spectators, even my parents, were silent. There was no applause. I didn't care. I knew the spectators thought I hadn't been sporting.

It was one thing to win a match handily. That would be acceptable. It was quite another for a young girl like me to appear to dominate an older, respected player. That was Not Done. To make it even worse, I had played with an obvious grim fury. I knew Mother and Father would disapprove.

But I had won; I was the champion; that was all I cared about.

Mr Michaels fussily arranged a small table on the court with the two cheap pewter plates that were the prizes for the finalist and the champion. Mrs Martin and I stood side by side. I was still holding a towel to my elbow. Mrs Martin walked forward and brushed past Mr Collins, who was attempting to award her the finalist plate. Instead, she walked to the center of the court, folded her arms over her chest, and looked out at the spectators.

Everyone in the stadium, still silent, stood up together at once. In Bermuda, in those days, this was a mark of immense respect.

As a teenager – back then she was 'Miss Rachel Outerbridge' – she had sailed on a steamship to Australia by herself. She was determined to become an unbeatable tennis machine, but she had almost no money. During her first week in Melbourne, she lived, homesick and lonely, in a decrepit rooming house in St. Kilda, ate only cheap Greek bread, drank tap water, and rode the No. 16 tram down Glenferries Road to Kooyong.

But when she played in the second round of the Australian championship on the lawns at Kooyong, Nell Hopman watched. Nell had just won her own second round match. Nell turned to her husband. "Who *is* that girl? What's that flag on her dress?"

That afternoon, Nell and Harry found a wealthy family in the Toorak neighborhood to take in Rachel. For her first two days with that family, Rachel told me decades later, all she had done was eat.

And Nell, being Nell, had taken Rachel's pocketbook without asking, rummaged around in it and – just as Nell expected – found no money. So she had the Lawn Tennis Association of Victoria give Rachel some spending money. This is what Rachel told me she remembered most: that the LTAV had given her money for her pocketbook.

Rachel was the youngest Australian ladies' singles champion until Margaret Smith, two decades later. An old black and white photograph of Rachel, taken just after she defeated Nell in the final, shows a shy young girl clutching her racket to her chest. The framed photo still hangs in the members' bar in the Kooyong clubhouse.

The news that Rachel had won the championship at Kooyong flashed to Bermuda in the middle of the night, and the next morning all Bermuda was on Front Street, cheering. Her anxious parents sent her a telegram congratulating her but urging her to come home to Bermuda.

She could afford to send only a one-word telegram in reply: WIMBLEDON.

I thought, 'What would she have done for Bermuda in tennis if the war hadn't come?' I think everyone else there that day had the same thought.

Mrs Martin turned away from the spectators, and Mr Michaels, relieved that she was finally going to accept her finalist plate, picked it up from the table.

"George, will you kindly forget those silly plates?"

She walked back to where I was standing. I tensed, expecting she might slap me across the face. Instead, she gently put her arm around my shoulders and walked with me back onto the court. I stood there with my hand holding the towel against my left elbow, with bloodstains on my dress, and Mrs Martin's arm around me. The crowd was completely silent.

Mrs Martin was at least four inches taller than I. She leaned her head down and kissed my cheek.

Then she said, loudly enough for everyone to hear, "Miss Hodgkin, that match was quite well played. Bermuda should be proud of you. I am."

The whole stadium suddenly exploded with cheers. My parents forgot themselves to such an extent that they actually hugged one another in public and began yelling together, "Fiona! Fiona!" Everyone took up crying out my name.

Mrs Martin turned to me and said quietly, "Now we need to ask one of your parents to look after your arm."

From today's perspective, my application to enter Smith College appears ridiculously simple. It consisted of a brief letter in late 1960 from Mother to Thomas Mendenhall, the then President of Smith, noting that I, Miss Fiona Alice Ashburton Hodgkin, of Paget, Bermuda, would be 18 years of age on July 1, 1961; that I was the granddaughter of Fiona Alice Wilson, née Ashburton, M.D., Smith class of 1912; that I was the daughter of herself, Fiona Alice Ashburton Hodgkin, née Wilson, M.D., Smith class of 1935; and that I would appreciate the opportunity to matriculate at Smith in the fall of 1961.

Mother, perhaps unnecessarily, added that I would pursue a pre-medical course of study at Smith.

Professor Mendenhall replied in an equally short letter to Mother stating merely that I would room in Emerson House (where Mother had lived), that classes would begin on Tuesday, September 5, 1961, and finally, that Mother would receive the college's statement for my fees and tuition.

And that was that.

Bermuda families, even today, are frugal. We are so

isolated, and much more so then than now. I was not surprised when Mother, who was helping me pack for Smith, lugged out storage boxes of her own winter clothes from Smith for me to take to Northampton. The clothes were outlandish and hideous. The winter boots were enormous, the sweaters incredibly thick; I could not imagine what it would be like to wear them. I had never seen snow except in cinemas and photographs. I did know what snow was: it was white and cold.

The day before I left Bermuda to fly to New York on my way to Smith, I went to see Mrs Martin. She was hanging her family's laundry to dry on a line in their garden. She saw me getting off my bicycle, and she put down the laundry and waited for me to walk through the garden to where she was standing.

"I leave tomorrow. I came to say goodbye – and to thank you."

"I appreciate you coming to see me."

She didn't say anything more. I waited and finally said, "Could we sit down?"

We sat down on the grass. She took my hand and held it. I was happy just sitting with her.

After a minute, she said, "You play at a level that, in a few years, will give you a place in international competition."

"You did as well."

"A long time ago."

"I want to do as well as I can at tennis."

"You want to win Wimbledon."

She was exactly right. "I can't expect it to happen for me."

She snorted. "We spent years on tennis courts so you could predict you can't win?"

"You didn't win."

"I didn't. I wanted to."

"But the weather was terrible, and you were all alone in England."

"I wasn't alone. I was with a young man. A German tennis player from Berlin." She hesitated. "I met him at Kooyong."

"You were seeing him?"

"Well, 'seeing him' is the polite way of saying what I was doing. The evening before I played Alice, he broke up with me. I never saw him again."

She stopped. I thought this was all she would say, but then she started again: "Later, I heard we shot down his bomber over the Channel in the Battle of Britain. He drowned."

She paused for a long time. "Or so I heard."

"Why did he break up with you?" I couldn't help asking, but I had crossed a line. This man broke up with her the evening before her Wimbledon final? I was dumbfounded.

"It made no difference. My match with Alice would have turned out the same anyway."

"How can you know that?"

She didn't answer. She leaned over, put her arm around me, and pulled my head against her chest, with her hand holding my head to her.

She held me for a few moments. "It's tomorrow, then?"

"Yes."

She stood and brushed off her skirt. She didn't say goodbye. She turned and went back to her laundry, and I took my bicycle and went home.

SEPTEMBER 1961
SMITH COLLEGE
NORTHAMPTON, MASSACHUSETTS

I loved Smith, but I had never been away from my parents before. Although they went home to England on holiday every three or four years, they always took me along. I say they went 'home' to England because that's what they would say, but both of them were born in Bermuda. Both of my grandfathers were born in Bermuda as well. And Mother's mother was an American. As a child, I began calling her 'American Grandmother.' Only Father's mother had been born in England. Naturally, I called her 'English Grandmother.'

I was terribly homesick for Bermuda.

In the 1880s, Smith had been one of the first American colleges to have a tennis team, and tennis had been a fad among Smith students. The Upper Campus had been covered with grass courts with narrow strips of fabric for the lines, which were held down to the grass by – what else? – hairpins.

The first day of practice for the Smith tennis team was

several days after classes began in September. I was a few minutes late to practice because my chemistry laboratory ran long, and when I got to the courts, about eight young ladies, from first years to seniors, were already running in a circle on one side of the court while a young man standing on the opposite service line – the team's coach, I learned – was feeding them balls from a large basket. He must have told the girls to hit the balls deep, because they didn't seem to be hitting the balls back to him. Instead, they were spraying the balls all over the court.

The coach kept calling out, "Good! Good shot! Keep at it!"

This was a different approach to tennis than that employed by Mrs Martin.

He caught sight of me in my tennis dress, waved his arm, and yelled, "Hi! Come join in!"

I dutifully inserted myself into the circle of girls. But when my turn came, the coach accidentally fed me a ball that nicked the net cord and then dropped softly into my side of the court close to the net. It bounced up only 10 centimeters or so.

I was already there. Both my right knee and the lower rim of my racket grazed the court surface as I half-volleyed the ball. I didn't try to do anything with it; I just flicked it over the net to the coach.

He looked at me for a moment, and then I returned to the circle of girls.

On my next turn, he hit the ball straight to me. I took two small steps back, swung my shoulders around so I was perpendicular to the net, took my racket back low, and hit the ball with heavy topspin. It flew a meter over the net but then fell sharply and just touched the baseline. I had hit the ball so hard that it drove itself halfway through one of the gaps in the chain-link fence at the back of the court.

The coach held up his hand to stop the circle of girls. "Can you do that again?"

"I think so."

The coach hit me a hard backhand, with a bit of backspin so that the ball, he thought, would bounce up at steeper angle than I expected. But I didn't bother letting it bounce. Instead, I closed in and volleyed his shot. I let my forearm recoil to drain most of the pace from the ball, which popped back over the net and landed at his feet.

The coach hit back a high, deep overhead.

I drifted back, used my left index finger to fix the ball as it fell back toward the court, and hit an overhead back to him.

He popped the ball up again, and I adjusted my position, set up, and again just hit the ball back to him.

This time he lobbed the ball high and to my backhand. I had to turn around so that I was facing my own baseline. I looked up at the ball, jumped, and swung over my shoulder. The ball landed at his feet.

The coach and I were both laughing. My Smith teammates were standing beside the court with their mouths open.

He hit another overhead high into the air over the court. Still laughing, I made a show of bouncing from one foot to the other as though I were trying to decide which direction to smash the ball. Finally, while the ball was still on its trajectory over the court, I pointed with my left hand and yelled, "Your ad court!"

I let the ball bounce. It went well above my head. I

smashed it. The coach had moved to his ad court and, though he lunged, the ball whipped past him. It barely nicked the outside of his ad court baseline.

He looked back at the fence. Now there were two balls stuck in it. The coach motioned for me to meet him at the net. "Are you an amateur? You can't play on the Smith team if you're a professional."

"I'm an amateur."

"I've never seen you before. You must be starting your first year."

"Yes."

"What's your name?"

"Fiona Hodgkin."

"Well, Fiona, you're playing in the number one position on the team. Come over to this side of the net and feed balls to your teammates. I'll move over there and help them with their ground strokes."

A minute later, I was standing beside the basket of balls and feeding them to my teammates. I was yelling, "Bend your knees! Good shot! Drop the racket head! Let's go, Smithies!"

MARCH 1962
SPRING HOLIDAY FROM SMITH
PAGET PARISH, BERMUDA

Smith kindly rearranged my classes to give me a full two weeks of spring holiday, and I took an airplane home from New York's Idlewild Airport. When I landed at Kindley Field, my parents were waiting for me; I was thrilled to see them. We took a taxi from the airport, and so I was quickly at Midpoint and back in my own room.

The next morning, I met Mrs Martin at Coral Beach for a tennis match. We embraced, and I said, "I missed you so much."

She said, "Let's knock up."

"Yes, but first I have to tell you about all the different drills we do in tennis practice; they're quite humorous." I said this just to hear her reaction.

She snorted. "After our match perhaps."

But it was wonderful to see her and to play against her again.

On my second evening at home, I was having tea with my parents, when Mother said that she had spoken that day by telephone with Mrs Pemberton in Tucker's Town, who said that her nephew, Mark Thakeham, was visiting from England for the school holiday.

"She's putting together a mixed doubles party for young people tomorrow afternoon, and she wanted to know if you could come join them."

Mrs Pemberton's home was called 'Tempest,' and it had a private grass tennis court, one of only two in Bermuda, at least to my knowledge. In the past several years, Mrs Pemberton had invited me to play there four or five times, and I had always accepted, just to have the experience of playing on grass. It is difficult, even if one is wealthy, to have a grass tennis court in Bermuda. Our climate is not well suited for it. Tennis players look at the beautiful greens on our golf courses and think, "This is the perfect place for a lawn tennis court."

The golf greens, though, support a few people each day who walk, slowly, across them to hit, gently, a small ball that rolls softly on the grass.

A tennis court has to put up with someone like me dragging a toe across the same foot of grass probably 80 times in a single match and then pounding along exactly the same path each time toward the net. Even in England, with consistently cool temperatures and plenty of rain, and as small as I am, I can damage a grass court in a single match.

In Bermuda? With inconsistent rainfall and hot temperatures? A grass court doesn't work well.

But, for all that, the grass court at Tempest was perfect and beautiful, probably because it was rarely played upon. It was for display, not tennis. Mrs Pemberton was not Bermudian, and she did not live in Bermuda. She was from England and stayed at Tempest only on holiday.

Father spoke up. "I served with Ralph Thakeham in the war. First-rate physician. First-rate officer, for that. Now a well-known senior medical consultant in London. He's 'Viscount Thakeham,' of course, but Ralph never uses the title. His patients call him just 'Doctor Thakeham.' He's the younger brother of our Mrs Pemberton in Tucker's Town. I hear good things about the young Mark Thakeham. He's fourth year medicine at Cambridge, and he played tennis for Cambridge."

My parents had been mixed doubles partners for many years, and they knew how to coordinate with one another. I recognized a planned, combined attack at the net. They must have discussed this in advance of raising it with me.

"I told Mother I would help in the clinic tomorrow."

"Oh, Fiona," Mother said. "You're home on holiday. Go to Tempest and enjoy yourself."

I said I would go, and Mother left the table to ring Mrs Pemberton.

I took the bus to the Mid-Ocean Club and then walked about 15 minutes to Tempest. I was met at the door by the housekeeper, who took me down to the grass court. The setting was beautiful, even by Bermuda standards, which in terms of natural beauty are about the highest in the world. The grass court was on the edge of a cliff, looking over the Atlantic to the southeast.

When you tossed the ball for your serve from the north end of the court, the last thing you saw before hitting the ball was the sharp horizon far out on the Atlantic. Looking exactly in that direction, there was nothing except the blue water of the Atlantic – and I mean *nothing* – between you and Antarctica, about 13,000 kilometers away.

In the other directions, the court was so well protected by Bermuda cedars and oleanders that the prevailing wind from the west usually didn't affect play. This grass court is still there today, and it must be one of the most spectacular tennis courts in the world.

It belongs to me, now.

I knew all the young people there except one, who I thought must be Mark Thakeham. There were seven people, plus me, evenly divided between girls and boys, so the plan must be for some ghastly round robin, mixed doubles play. I would rather have swallowed a lizard. I said my hellos to my friends, and Mrs Pemberton swooped down to introduce me to her nephew.

I realize how silly this sounds today, because my daughters roll their eyes when they hear me talk about it. But in 1962, in Bermuda, an 18-year-old girl like me could speak appropriately on a social basis with a young man she did not know only if and not until she had been introduced by an adult. I swear it's true.

Mrs Pemberton said, "Miss Hodgkin, may I introduce you to my nephew, Mark Thakeham?"

Mark said, "It's nice to meet you, Miss Hodgkin. I'm told you play tennis."

"Mr Thakeham, welcome to Bermuda. Have you been on our island before?"

"Never. I'm probably not the first person to say this is a beautiful place. So is it true that you play tennis?"

"I do play, Mr Thakeham, but not as well as I would wish."

Mark had strikingly good looks, with strawberry blond

hair, and that classic English complexion. He was attentive and polite, with an aristocratic English accent. He was plainly intelligent. He asked me about Smith – only approximately one percent of the members of Mark's social class in England at that time would have heard of Smith, so he must have been briefed on me in advance – and he asked what course of study I was pursuing.

"My parents are both physicians, and I hope to be one as well, and so I am what we in the States call 'pre-med.'"

"I am planning to be a physician myself, Miss Hodgkin. I think our fathers served together as doctors in the war."

"That is my understanding as well," I said.

Mark surprised me. When I said I wanted to be a physician, men reacted with derision and women at best were skeptical – this was 1962, remember. Even people who knew my mother and grandmothers, and therefore understood that my career in medicine had been decided the moment I was born, were still quite uncomfortable with the idea. Mark, though, seemed to feel that my plan to be a physician was nothing out of the ordinary.

But maybe he had been advised that this was just the way I was and to accept me on my own terms.

To me, this had the earmarks of a setup. Some people, including my parents, had apparently reached the conclusion that this toff and I should meet, and maybe one thing might lead to another.

"Mr Thakeham, I was told you played for Cambridge?"

"Yes, Miss Hodgkin." He laughed. "But understand that the university has only an informal team. It's just club play. I'm told you are a superb player, and you shouldn't expect much from me, I'm afraid."

"Mr Thakeham, I know we're planning to play some mixed doubles this afternoon, but would you consider playing a match of singles against me first?"

"I'll certainly play against you if you will please call me Mark."

"Then I hope you will call me Fiona." The social convention in Bermuda at the time was that, because we were close in age – Mark was about four years my senior – we could, by mutual agreement, decide to use our Christian names for one another.

So while the others were still chatting, and before the round robin, or whatever other awful scheme – probably something dispensing with advantage scoring – was organized, Mark and I walked out onto the beautiful grass and knocked up.

After a few minutes, I stopped, casually tossed my wooden Maxply racket onto the grass, and asked him, "rough or smooth?" Mark said "rough" and won, so he would have the first serve. I looked up to see where the sun was shining and decided I wanted to receive on the north end of the court.

Mark served, hard. It wasn't placed well – it bounced smack in the middle of my deuce service court – but all I could do was block his serve back. He came in on my weak return and blasted a forehand deep into my ad court. I wasn't anywhere near it. I felt as though I was playing mixed doubles, but without my male partner at the net to cut off shots like that.

As I walked over to the ad court, I told myself that Mark just wanted to show me how strong he was, and that now he would slow down. But no. His next serve was faster than his first, though again not well placed. I got my racket on it but made another weak return. Again, he hit a strong forehand crosscourt. I got to it, barely, but only clipped it with the rim of my racket. The ball glanced off into the oleanders.

My girlfriends were watching us and giggling. One of them called out, "Careful, Mr Thakeham. Our Fiona doesn't care to lose."

30-love. I went back to my deuce court. I was inwardly fuming. This time Mark's serve was well placed, right down the middle, and even harder. I hit it with my backhand, but late, so the ball popped up and floated over the net. Mark was waiting for it. He smashed it.

I motioned to him that I wanted to talk at the net.

"Mark," I said, "I'm about seven stone seven." I meant that I weighed 105 pounds. "I'll guess that you must be 13 stone. And you're fit. Have we established to your satisfaction that you're the more muscular player?"

He grinned. "You said you wanted to play singles."

I turned away from him. Over my shoulder, I said, "Not any longer."

As I walked off the court, he jumped over the net and took my arm.

"Fiona."

I shook his arm off. I regretted agreeing to come to this tennis party.

I went and sat down with my girlfriends. They had concocted a complex round robin mixed doubles format with games to five points, no ad scoring, one team serving all five points. The winning team then would sit out. It made no sense to me. Luckily, I was able to avoid being paired with Mark. I noticed that during the round robin his serves were good, but he didn't try to overpower anyone.

After tennis, the housekeeper served tea on the lawn beside the court. After we had tea, I looked at my watch. All the others lived in Tucker's Town or close by in St. George's parish, so they could bicycle home, but the last bus back to Hamilton left in half an hour, and I needed to be at the Mid-Ocean Club to catch it. I stood and said to the group that I needed to leave for the bus, and that I would go inside and thank Mrs Pemberton for inviting me.

Mark said, "Fiona, don't leave yet. I'm sure my aunt would loan me an auto to drive you home."

"Mark, that's kind of you, but my parents probably would prefer I took the bus." I left before he could reply.

When I walked into the sitting room in Midpoint, Mother was writing notes in the charts of patients she had seen that day, and Father was reading *The Lancet*.

Mother said, "Fiona, it's good to see you. Did you enjoy the party?"

"Yes, Mother." I sat down and picked up *Life* magazine.

I saw them glance at one another.

"Have you had your tea?" Mother asked.

"Yes, Mother. I had a good tea at Tempest."

Father said, "Sweetheart, did you meet young Mark Thakeham?"

"Yes, Father."

They glanced at one another again.

"Well?" Father asked.

I was leafing through the magazine. "I didn't care for him."

Mother bent over her charts, and Father went back to *The Lancet*.

After a minute or so, Father's curiosity got the better of him. "Why not?"

Mother glared at him, and he went back to the article on the new Sabin polio vaccine he was reading.

The next day, I was filing charts in the clinic Mother shared with my grandfather. One of my girlfriends, who had been at the tennis party the afternoon before, came in through the screen door of the clinic. She was agog about Mark.

"Fiona, after you left, he asked Mildred to go out with him. He borrowed a roadster from Mrs Pemberton and took Mildred to St. George's for pints at the White Horse."

"Good for her." Mildred was quite good looking. This boy was going to cut a wide swath in Bermuda in the two weeks he was upon us.

"Mark's father is Viscount Thakeham."

"So I've heard."

"You don't seem interested."

"I'm not," I said, slamming shut a file drawer of patient charts.

"Mark likes you."

"Why in heaven would you say that?"

"When you left just after tea, he kept asking us about you."

"Then why did Mildred go out with him?"

"Who wouldn't? He has use of an auto. He's cute. And his father's a viscount."

Later that afternoon, the screen door opened and then slammed shut.

"I'm sorry," Mark said. "I didn't know it would shut so quickly."

Then he said to me, "Hello, Fiona."

"Hello yourself." I turned back to my filing work.

Mother happened to come to my desk with several patient charts. "Fiona, take these home, will you? I need to write some notes in them this evening."

She noticed Mark. "May I help you?"

I said, "Mother, this is Mark Thakeham. Mark, this is my mother, Doctor Fiona Wilson."

They shook hands. Mother said, "Mr Thakeham, I've met your parents on two occasions in England. You're a medical student at Cambridge, I'm told."

"Yes, Doctor Wilson, I'm in my first clinical year."

Mother looked at Mark, and then at me.

"Well, I have patients waiting for me. Good luck in the clinic, Mr Thakeham."

Mark said, "Fiona." Then he stopped.

"Yes, Mark? I have work to do."

"Fiona, I apologize to you. I know I was rude to you when we played."

"Apology accepted. And thank you for coming to see me."

"Fiona, perhaps we could play tennis tomorrow?"

"I have a match already." I was meeting Mrs Martin at nine the next morning at Coral Beach. "Perhaps you might arrange to play with Mildred."

"Well, news must travel fast."

"It's a small island."

"You and I might play just a set after your match tomorrow? Or we could meet for lunch."

Now I felt that I was the one acting impolitely. After all, he was a visitor to Bermuda.

"My match is at Coral Beach. But I'll be finished by 10:30 or so. If you want, we could play after that. You'd have to come to Coral Beach. Do you know where it is?"

He didn't, but I showed him on a small tourist map.

The next morning, when Mark arrived at Coral Beach, I introduced him to Mrs Martin. She said to the two of us, "Would you young people mind if I watched a bit of your match?"

This was meant for Mark, not me, and Mark replied that he would welcome having her as a spectator. I hadn't explained to Mark who Mrs Martin was for me.

Then Mrs Martin said to us, "I take it your match will be merely social?" Translated into today's English from the language of early 1960s Bermuda social conventions, she was asking whether she might coach me while I played Mark.

I turned to Mark and asked, "Mark, would you mind if Mrs Martin spoke to me during our match? Please don't hesitate to say if it might distract you."

This bewildered Mark. "It wouldn't distract me in the slightest. Not a problem for me." So Mrs Martin sat on a bench beside the court, and we began our match.

Mark served softly to me in the first game. I noticed that Mrs Martin's forehead was furrowed, as though she were puzzled.

At the changeover, she said to Mark, "Are you intentionally backing off your serve?"

"Perhaps a bit."

"No. Hit the best serves you can."

He looked at me, and I shrugged.

In Mark's next service game, he began sending hard, fast serves over the net, and I either didn't get my racket on them or, at best, blocked them back.

Mrs Martin signaled that she wanted to stop play. She walked over to me. "Don't block his serve. Stroke through your return."

"I can't, at least not on his first service. He hits it too hard."

She snorted. "Nonsense. You'll play plenty of women in international competition with more effective serves than this young man. Don't give him any more lollipops."

This was her term for a soft return: a 'lollipop.' She didn't approve of lollipops.

I tried moving back well behind the baseline to return his first service. I glanced over and saw Mrs Martin shaking her head. She didn't approve of standing behind the baseline. On his next serve, I held my ground at the baseline. Mark had little control over his serve. He could make the ball land in the service box, and hard. Whether it went wide, straight down the middle, or directly into my body, was mostly a matter of chance. But the ball certainly came over the net fast.

Mark served to my deuce court. I saw the ball was going to be down the centre line, to my backhand. I took the throat of my racket in my left hand and pulled the racket well back and down. But his serve was so fast I connected with the ball late, probably just a few centimeters in front of me, and my return went wide and landed well out.

I looked over at Mrs Martin. She was nodding. I guessed what she was thinking: 'Better to try, and hit it out, than not to try at all.'

I walked across to my ad court for his next service. I set up on the baseline. Mark tossed and hit a remarkably fast serve, which again went straight down the middle. A beautiful serve. It kicked up above my shoulder. I took the ball with my forehand, above my shoulder, as hard as I could swing, and sent the ball crosscourt into his deuce court. I hit the return so hard and flat that Mark didn't get within a meter of it. A clear winner.

I looked over at Mrs Martin.

She said, "Like that."

No more lollipops.

Mrs Martin left for home after our first set, and then Mark and I played two more. That was a total of six sets for me that morning, and I was done in. I had to shower before lunch, so I pointed Mark in the direction of the balcony overlooking the Atlantic where we would have lunch, and I went to the dressing room.

My hair was wet when I arrived on the balcony and sat down with him. "I hope you don't mind my hair being wet. To dry it would delay lunch by probably an hour."

"Your hair looks beautiful wet."

I had no idea what to think about that.

The waiter came and we ordered. Mark began to ask, "Who on earth – "

I put my hand on his forearm to stop him in mid-sentence. "I should have warned you about Mrs Martin. But I had no idea she would stay to watch us play."

"Who is she?"

"Well, really, she's my coach, but since on Bermuda it's considered unsporting and Not Done for a young lady to have a tennis coach, Mrs Martin would never think of herself as my coach."

"What would she say she is?"

"She would say just that she and I play tennis together. She's my father's cousin, so we're related. She's a wonderful person and good to me, but she's a bit of a character. She reached the singles final at Wimbledon just before the war."

"Wimbledon? Can you beat her?"

"Yes. For years I couldn't, but now I haven't lost to her for a year or so. But her play is at an international level, still."

"How long has she been coaching you?"

"Well, longer than four years."

"How often do you play with her?"

"On spring holiday, we've had good luck with the weather, and so we've played every morning. She thinks the tennis coach at Smith has given me some bad habits, and she's trying to fix them in the short time before I go back to school."

"What bad habits?"

"She thinks the Smith coach is making me play more cautiously and to work the percentages. He's influenced by Jack Kramer a great deal."

"So Mrs Martin doesn't believe in playing the percentages?"

"No, she doesn't." I thought for a moment. "I think she believes in playing each point as though your life depends on winning it."

After lunch, we walked down the steep staircase to the beach, took off our shoes, and walked along Coral Beach together.

"This must be the most beautiful beach in the world," Mark said.

"Most people would say this isn't even the most beautiful beach in Bermuda."

"Which beach is the best?"

"Oh, probably one of the beaches farther along the South Shore. Warwick Long Bay is where I usually go to swim."

When we reached the end of the beach, we sat down on the rocks facing one another and talked for two solid hours. We compared notes about pre-med at Smith versus the medical course of study at Cambridge, and he warned me about how difficult he had found organic chemistry. I would be taking organic chemistry in the fall. Mark told me about his first clinical rotation in medical school, which was fascinating. Someone must have taught Mark to make conversation: he expressed an interest in me, a girl, which was just about unheard of in my limited experience with boys. And he seemed to take what I said seriously. I couldn't recall any boy ever taking me seriously.

By the time we walked back to the staircase, and climbed up to the balcony, it was almost four o'clock. Mark said, "May I drive you home?"

"No, I have my bicycle here."

Mark waited a moment. I was looking at him. He said, "Perhaps this is a bit forward of me, since we've seen each other today. But might I see you again tomorrow?"

I didn't reply.

He said, "We could arrange something without Mrs Martin."

I didn't reply.

"I haven't seen much of the island."

"Oh, I don't know. You've explored the pub in St. George's."

He grimaced. I knew I had been a shrew, so I said, "We could go to Gibbs Hill Lighthouse tomorrow. It's one of my favorite places. We can take the bus from Hamilton."

"I've been using a roadster that belongs to my aunt. I could pick you up and drive you there."

"Mrs Pemberton owns a roadster? I'd be surprised if she can drive."

"She can't."

"Why does she have a roadster, then?"

"She and my father have an interest in British Motor. MG is part of British Motor. Aunt and Father thought having one of the MG roadsters in Bermuda would spark interest in MG autos here."

"It hasn't worked."

"Unfortunately, you seem correct in that."

"I'll make us a picnic lunch. If you could pick me up at home at, say, noon, we could go to Gibbs Hill Lighthouse and climb to the top to see the view. Then we could have lunch on the lawn there."

"That sounds perfect. Where do you live?"

The next morning saw pouring rain all over Bermuda, so the Gibbs Hill expedition was off the calendar. I worked in Mother's clinic, but in the early afternoon Mrs Pemberton rang Mother and invited me to tea later at Tempest. She offered to have Mark come collect me, but Mother declined. I could easily take the bus.

I sat on the bus on the slow ride in the rain to Tucker's Town telling myself not to become attached to Mark. He was probably bored to distraction staying at Tempest with his aunt. He couldn't possibly like me. He was an exceptionally handsome boy; no doubt he had his pick of girls. He was probably just fitting me in between visits with Mildred.

But when I got off the bus at the Mid-Ocean Club, Mark was standing there waiting in the rain under an umbrella. Despite the talk I had given myself on the bus, I thought it unlikely a boy would wait in the rain for a girl unless he liked her at least a bit. I had my own umbrella, but while we walked to Tempest, Mark put his arm around my shoulders and held his umbrella over both of us.

While we were having tea, the rain cleared, and the evening became clear. Typical Bermuda weather; it often changes back and forth between rain and bright blue sky several times a day. Again, I was bumping up against the time for the last bus back toward Paget from the Mid-Ocean Club, but, once again, Mark offered to drive me home. This time, I accepted and asked his aunt if I might use her telephone to ring my parents to tell them I would be home later than the last bus.

It was still quite light when we drove off from Tempest in the MG; Mark had the hood down. We swept along South Road past what must be some of the most perfect ocean views in the world.

When we drove past Knapton Point, I said to Mark over the wind, "Do you want to stop and see Spanish Rock?"

"What is it?"

"It's a flat rock above the Atlantic. A sailor carved some letters, a cross, and the year 1543 into it. We've always called it 'Spanish Rock,' but someone in Portugal now says the sailor was probably Portuguese. Perhaps we should call it 'Portuguese Rock' instead."

"Is it authentic?"

"You mean, was it really carved in 1543? I don't know, but the first settlers in Bermuda saw the carving, so it's been there a long time. The person who carved it must have been one of the first people on Bermuda. Do you want to see it?"

"Certainly. Where is it?"

"Just ahead, at Spittal Pond. Turn off here to the left."

Mark turned and brought the MG to a stop in a cloud of gravel dust at the entrance for Spittal Pond. We walked down a steep, rough path and then along a sandy track beside the pond. I told Mark, "The pond isn't really fresh water. It's a bit salty. We don't have much fresh water on Bermuda, except the rain water we collect on our roofs. Let's go this way, to the left." We hiked up a hill through thick brush to the top, where we had a spectacular view of the Atlantic waves crashing against the rocks of the South Shore and sending salt spray up almost to where we were standing.

"Down there," I said, pointing for Mark.

We scrambled down through the brush to a large, flat rock overlooking the waves. The rock was defaced all over with carvings. I said, "An American thought the carving, I mean the one from 1543, was going to be eroded away, so he made a plaster mold of the carving, and then covered it with a bronze impression. That was sixty years or so ago."

I stood looking out at the Atlantic.

Mark asked, out of the blue, "Were you homesick when you were in the States?"

"Terribly homesick. All the snow was a shock to me. And I missed my parents. I grew up in Bermuda, it was all I knew until I went away to the States. Well, I'd been to England several times but always with my parents."

Then I asked, "Did you grow up in London?"

"No. Not really. I spent most of my time before I went off to Harrow at our country house in Hampshire. We have a dairy farm there. When my father joined the Royal Navy at the start of the war, he moved Mother and me, and my nanny, to our country house. I had just been born, actually, so I don't have any memory of it."

"Do your parents live in Hampshire?"

"Well, Father's medical practice is in London, and we have a home in Hyde Park Gate. But it was bombed in

October 1940, during the Blitz, and we couldn't live there again until I was about 10 or so. Father couldn't get a license for the building materials right after the war. But finally he was able to have it all put right. Mother and Father still live there. They spend long weekends in Hampshire during the summer."

Mark looked down at Spanish rock and pointed to the bronze impression. "This must be the bronze cover?"

"Yes," I said. The impression showed a crude R and a P, with a cross and the year 1543. "This fellow in Portugal thinks the R and the P stand for the King of Portugal, and that the sailor who carved it was claiming the island for his King."

We turned away from the rock, went as close to the edge of the cliff as I was willing to go, and looked down into the impossibly clear, blue water, with waves blasting against the rocks.

It was getting on to dusk. We walked back to the sandy track toward the MG, and Mark took my hand in his as we were walking. Once we reached the roadster, he said, "You'd better tell me again how to get to your home, because I'm lost."

I pointed him back onto South Road. He made the turn into our lane and pulled over in front of Midpoint. He jumped out and opened the door for me.

"Fiona?"

"Yes, Mark?"

"We had talked about a picnic, before the rain came. Are you still willing to stand me for a picnic? Perhaps tomorrow?"

"Yes. At Gibbs Hill. I'll make a lunch for us. When will you collect me?"

We agreed on noon. He reached behind my head and

tugged gently on my ponytail to tease me, then jumped into the driver's seat and roared off.

It was almost dark. I stood there for a moment in front of Midpoint. Mark hadn't tried to kiss me goodnight, and I couldn't decide whether I was relieved or disappointed.

MARCH 1962
SPRING HOLIDAY FROM SMITH
GIBBS HILL LIGHTHOUSE
SOUTHAMPTON PARISH, BERMUDA

There was a bowl of Bermuda fish chowder in our refrigerator, which our housekeeper had made the day before, and it had been delicious when my parents and I had it last night. I took the left over chowder and poured it equally into two glass jars. And spoons. Then I made sandwiches with Irish cheese, the year's first lettuce from our garden, and Portuguese bread our housekeeper had baked. What else? A thermos of coffee. Then I baked oatmeal cookies, and wrapped them in two cloth napkins to keep them warm. Finally, an old sheet from the bottom of Mother's linen closet. I put all of this in a flower basket that Mother used to collect cut flowers in our garden. Then I sat down and waited for Mark to collect me.

When he did, I walked out with my basket, and he said, "Fiona, you're a beautiful girl."

I was startled; no one other than my parents and grandparents had ever said anything remotely like this to me. I didn't get compliments often, or really even at all. My figure was athletic and boyish, and even at age 18 my breasts were small. My parents liked me to keep my hair long. It was straight and light brown, and since I was a small girl it had hung down to the small of my back.

I loved hearing him say that I was beautiful. I said, "I'll give you exactly 15 minutes to stop talking nonsense like that." He laughed.

It was a perfect Bermuda morning after yesterday's rain, and Mark had the hood on the MG down. We drove along Middle Road and pulled alongside the road near Gibbs Hill.

"Let's take the basket and leave it at the foot of the lighthouse," I said. "We'll climb the stairs to the top and then have lunch."

As a girl, I must have climbed to the top of the lighthouse dozens of times – 185 steps up each time. As we went up the steep, narrow staircase, Mark said from behind me, "Now I know how you came to be so fit, if this is your idea of a pleasant way to spend a morning."

I laughed. "When I'm here by myself, I usually run up the stairs."

"Why am I not surprised?"

The view from the top was terrific. We could see most of the island, and the Atlantic on three sides of the island. It was such a clear morning that we could pick out on the horizon the tiny fishing boats that sailed out of St. George's.

"When was this built?" Mark asked.

"Every school child in Bermuda knows that the lighthouse gave its first light the night of May 1, 1846. The iron column of the lighthouse was made in England and then bolted together here."

Later, we walked to the edge of the tiny lawn below the lighthouse to a spot where there was a bit of shade. I spread out the sheet on the grass, sat down on it, smoothed out my skirt, and began pulling food from the basket. Mark sat down across from me. We ate and talked. We finished the chowder and sandwiches, and I poured him a cup of coffee.

"I hope you don't take milk. I entirely forgot milk. I never drank coffee until I got to Smith, but tea isn't easy to find in the States, so I started drinking coffee."

We talked for a long time, and then he leaned toward me and drew his finger across my left cheek. I just looked at him, with my hands on my skirt in my lap. I was totally naïve, but even I realized what was about to happen.

I had been kissed only once. That had been after a mixer at Smith – a 'mixer' being a chaperoned party with boys imported from nearby colleges. I liked that boy well enough, but he had not the slightest idea of what he was about. I had the sense that Mark was going to be different, and he was.

He put his hand under my chin, lifted my face up slightly, and kissed me. I didn't kiss him back, but only because I was so clueless that I didn't know I was supposed to respond to him. He pulled back and shifted himself on the sheet so that he was sitting beside me. He picked up my hands and put my arms around his neck.

"It's customary," he said, "for a girl to show some sign she likes being kissed. If she does."

I laughed. "What sign would you like?"

He kissed me again, and finally I tumbled to the idea that this activity demanded joint participation. But I said, "This is crazy. We're out in the open. A taxi full of tourists could show up anytime." He smiled and kissed me again. The potential for the arrival of tourists bothered him not a wit.

Then he put his hand gently under my breast. I

immediately jerked back and brushed his hand away. Nothing like that had ever happened to me.

"Are you all right?" he asked.

"Yes, of course. You startled me, that's all."

He put his arms around my shoulders and pulled me to him. I put my face against his chest. I liked being there. After a moment, he lifted my face and kissed me, and then he put his hand back on my breast. I clamped my hand around his, but I didn't move his hand away.

"Mark, I like that, but it makes me uncomfortable."

I was sending mixed messages here, since I kept my hand on his, but I was new at all this. He slowly moved his hand away but not before squeezing me, gently. I had never felt anything like that before. It was amazing. I buried my face in his chest again, with my arms still around him, where I was prepared to remain as long as possible. Tourists or no tourists.

He drove me home. It was late afternoon. We stood beside the MG, talking and holding hands, for so long that Mother finally came along walking home from the clinic, in her long, white lab coat.

I dropped Mark's hand.

Mother said, "Hello, Mr Thakeham. What have you young people been doing this afternoon?"

I answered quickly to avoid the possibility that Mark might say something not appropriate. "I took Mark to see Gibbs Hill, and we had a picnic lunch at the lighthouse. He's just brought me home."

Mother looked up at the sky to see where the sun was

over the horizon toward Dockyard. I could tell she was thinking that our picnic seemed to have lasted quite a long time, but she didn't raise the issue.

Instead, she invited Mark to come for tea the next afternoon, said goodbye to him, and went inside to begin making tea for Father.

When I walked into Midpoint, I went to the kitchen to help Mother. For a minute or so, she was silent.

Finally, she said, "I thought you didn't care for Mark Thakeham."

"I've changed my mind."

MARCH 1962
SPRING HOLIDAY FROM SMITH
'TEMPEST'
TUCKER'S TOWN, BERMUDA

Mark and I played three hard sets on the grass court at Tempest, then we changed into our swimsuits and dived into the salt water pool. His aunt was shopping in Hamilton and the housekeeper was off, so we had everything to ourselves.

I was sitting beside the pool with my legs in the water when Mark came up for air just in front of me. He folded his arms over my knees, and I leaned over and kissed the top of his head. He looked up at me and suggested that we go inside the house, to his room, and become lovers.

A week before I had not even known he existed, and now instead of slapping him, which is what I ought to have done, I found myself thinking that he had come up with a thrilling, fascinating, and frightening idea.

But good judgment got the better of me.

"We're going to do no such thing. Put it out of your mind." With that, I placed my hand on top of his head, pushed him off my knees, and played at holding him under water for a second or so before releasing him.

He came up for air, then pulled himself up on the side of

the pool and sat beside me. "I can't get it out of my mind, and I don't think you can either."

He was right about my part of that, at least.

"What's in my mind is my business. I have a question for you: have you ever slept with a girl?"

"That's certainly a personal question."

"Mark, you just asked me to sleep with you in the same tone of voice you might use to ask if I take milk in my tea. I think I'm entitled to ask a personal question."

He smiled ruefully. "Well, yes, I have slept with a girl before."

"More than one? How many?"

"Another personal question."

"Answer it honestly, and I'll leave off personal questions, at least for awhile."

"Two or three, I suppose."

I didn't think he was exaggerating. If anything, I thought he was minimizing the truth to make himself look less of a philanderer in my eyes. I took 'two or three, I suppose' to mean 'four or five.'

"I'm not adding myself to your list. But I do think we need to get you and your English complexion out of the Bermuda sun."

I stood up, reached down to take his hands and helped him stand. Then I led him over to a chaise longue on the grass that was in the shade of a large tree. We stretched out beside one another, and he put his arm around me.

After a few minutes, he reached up and pulled down the shoulder strap of my bathing suit and uncovered one of my breasts. I held my breath for a moment. He took my breast in his hand and then kissed me there, and the feeling was so wonderful that it frightened me. I put my hand on the back of his head and wove my fingers through his hair. We stayed like that for a minute or so, then I pulled my strap back up onto my shoulder. He didn't resist; he just reached over and playfully tugged at my ponytail.

We didn't talk while we were on the longue together; we may have even dozed for a bit. But Mark and I were expected at Midpoint for tea, so finally we got up and went to change into our clothes – separately.

After tea, Mother and I washed the dishes while Father and Mark went into the living room. There Father poured a Black Seal rum for himself, plus one for Mark. This was unusual; my parents normally didn't drink alcohol because of the risk that one of them might be called to hospital unexpectedly. But now Father and Mark, who were both Cambridge men, sat down with their rum and began seriously debating the Tories versus Labour.

"Macmillan is fundamentally sound," Father said.

"If Gaitskell steps down, though," Mark replied, "and Labour is led by Wilson, then Macmillan will have a tussle on his hands."

Mother and I, in the kitchen, laughed softly to ourselves while listening to them. Neither of them had a clue about politics. Mother leaned over to me and whispered, "Where *do* we find these silly men?"

It was thrilling for me to have her treat me, almost, as an equal.

MARCH 1962
SPRING HOLIDAY FROM SMITH
AMERICAN GRANDMOTHER

The day before Mark left Bermuda for England, English Grandmother gave a formal ladies' lunch in my honor at her home, which was less than 20 meters or so from Midpoint. The two houses had shared a garden for – well, for longer than anyone in Bermuda could remember.

English Grandmother's lunch was the reason I wasn't having a goodbye lunch somewhere else with Mark.

American Grandmother's idea of a formal ladies' lunch in my honor would have been to walk with me down to Hamilton Harbour and buy a freshly grilled fish, wrapped in newspaper, from one of the fishermen. Then she and I would sit down on the seawall around the harbour and dangle our feet in the water while we picked the fish apart with our fingers and ate it.

To American Grandmother, when I was young, this would be an opportunity to teach me the names of the bones in the foot, or the muscles in the hand, or how to take my pulse. Aside from her family, American Grandmother was interested only in medicine: she didn't garden, she sewed and mended only when essential, her house looked as though a hurricane had just passed through, and she was a truly terrible cook.

But she was an extraordinary physician.

When she was a girl in Massachusetts, she told me, somehow she had heard about Mary Elizabeth Garrett of Baltimore, who, in the early 1890s, had given a large share of the money needed to start the Johns Hopkins School of Medicine. In doing so, Garrett had extracted the painful promise from the Hopkins trustees (all male, of course) that women would be admitted to the medical school 'on the same terms as men.' American Grandmother couldn't recall how or when she had heard Garrett's story, but she had instantly decided to become a doctor.

I gather her parents (my great-grandparents) were at first amused that young Fiona wanted to attend medical school. When American Grandmother excelled at chemistry at Smith, they were less amused, and in 1912, when she was accepted at the Johns Hopkins School of Medicine, they were horrified – which bothered American Grandmother not the slightest.

American Grandmother became one of the first researchers to explore the biochemical basis of the menstrual cycle. In 1915, in her third year of medical school, she published a groundbreaking paper in *The Boston Medical & Surgical Journal* – then, as now, one of the leading medical journals, although today it is known as *The New England Journal of Medicine*.

For a woman medical student in 1915, life didn't get better than that.

I have an old, yellowed reprint of her paper: 'Ovulation and the Luteinizing Factor. Ashburton FA. From the Johns Hopkins School of Medicine.' In the paper, she explained how she had drawn a blood sample from a "human female volunteer" each day of the volunteer's cycle.

"How did you find a volunteer?" I asked.

"It was me!" she laughed. "By the third week, my left arm looked like a pincushion from all the needle sticks!"

No doubt she had a great future in medical research ahead of her at Hopkins, but she happened to visit Bermuda on holiday, where, by chance, she met a young doctor, who would become my grandfather. Apparently without a backward glance, American Grandmother chucked her career at Hopkins to marry him and practice general medicine on Point Finger Road in Bermuda. (Good for me, since otherwise I wouldn't be here to tell you this story.)

I once asked her why she had done it. At the time I asked, my daughters were her great-granddaughters. Without hesitating, she replied, "Because your grandfather was quite sexually attractive."

As the ladies' lunch in my honor was at long last drawing to a close, I heard the roar of Mark's MG pulling up in front of Midpoint. I quickly kissed Mother, then American Grandmother, and finally English Grandmother.

"I have to leave," I told them.

MARCH 1962
SPRING HOLIDAY FROM SMITH
MID-OCEAN CLUB BEACH, BERMUDA

Earlier that spring, I had gone to Boston with four of my
friends from Smith – all of us were in Emerson House – on
a shopping expedition. I bought several sensible knickers and
two nice blouses, and then, under the influence of my friends,
a two-piece swimsuit. Certainly not a bikini, but at least it had
a separate top and bottom. Today, none of my
granddaughters would consent to be seen even dead in this
swimsuit. It was quite modest, and they could easily make
three of their bikinis out of one of this swimsuit. But for me,
then, it was daring.

I had never worn the swimsuit outside the fitting room
of the store in Boston, and I seriously doubted Mother would
let me out of the house wearing it. I had stuffed the swimsuit
into my beach bag with a couple of towels so Mother wouldn't
see it. I would change at the Mid-Ocean Club.

Mark and I had the beach entirely to ourselves that
weekday afternoon. By the time I emerged from the dressing
room, still tugging at the edges of the swimsuit trying to make
sure it was covering everything that absolutely had to be
covered, Mark was already on the beach. He turned around

and was dazzled. He took my hand, and we walked toward the ocean.

"What have I done to deserve this amazing swimsuit?" he asked.

"Don't get any ideas. I don't want you trying to remove any part of it."

"There aren't many parts to remove. One would have to be selective."

I laughed. "That makes it easy; just stay away from it."

"I would never do anything improper with your swimsuit."

"Excuse me? What exactly happened at Tempest?"

"I don't recall any objection made to my conduct."

"Perhaps not, but today, behave yourself."

We dived into the water, which at that time of year was still cold, and we splashed one another. I swam toward the reef, and Mark swam up beside me; he was a strong swimmer. Eventually, we turned around and swam back to the beach. We walked up toward the wildly jumbled rocks at the top of the beach, and Mark spread a towel on the sand for us. I sat down and ran my hands through my ponytail to squeeze out the salt water.

Mark sat down beside me, put his arm around me, and then spread another towel on top of us, which felt warm and comfortable.

He kissed me, and all I could think about was that he would leave tomorrow. How many thousands of kilometers away would he be? I'd probably never see him again.

Mark reached below me, put his hand under my bottom, lifted me up, and dropped me between his legs, so that I was leaning back against his chest. I was scared at first, but then I found that leaning back against him, with his arms folded around me, was quite nice. I closed my eyes, and if I could have stayed like that for a long time, that would have been fine with me. Mark tucked the towel around me.

Then I was shocked when he pushed his hand under the front of the bottom of my swimsuit. I instantly went rigid, and I kept my eyes shut, but I didn't say 'No,' and I didn't grab his hand. But I did clamp my legs together.

He whispered, "I'm just going to touch you, don't worry, that's all."

After a moment he said, "Fiona, this won't work unless you move your legs apart, just a bit."

I spread my legs maybe a centimeter.

He laughed. "Fiona, it just can't happen unless I can put my hand between your legs. I promise you it will be all right. I'm only going to touch you; nothing more."

I spread my legs just a bit more. Mark touched me, lightly, but it felt like a small electric shock. I yelped, grabbed his hand, twisted away from him, and gasped for breath. He held me for a moment, and kissed me on the top of my head.

"Fiona," he said, pulling me back against his chest again. "It might be more comfortable for both of us if you took off the bottom of your swimsuit."

"I'm not going to do that."

"Fiona. Lift yourself up and pull off the bottom. It will be easier that way."

I was frightened, but I wanted him to touch me. "Don't look at me."

"I won't," he lied happily.

I pulled the towel back over me, reached down, and took off the bottom of my suit. I thought, 'I must be crazy to do this.'

I leaned back against him, holding the towel around me, and kept my eyes shut. He began touching me, gently, and it was instantly clear that he knew exactly what to do. At the end I cried out so loudly that I probably alerted everyone in Tucker's Town that I was there with Mark.

That moment, Mark could have made love to me without a word of protest from my side. Instead – to give the devil his due – he just held me for a minute or so, and then he stood up. He folded my legs so that they were in the shade of the rocks and out of the Bermuda sun. He put the towel over me and leaned over and kissed me on my forehead. I still had my eyes shut.

Then he walked down to the Atlantic and dove in. Mark, thoughtfully, was going for a swim so that I could have a few minutes alone to pull myself together.

When he came back, dripping wet, I had reassembled my swimsuit, and I was sitting with my back against the rocks. If that was just Mark touching me, what on earth would it be like to make love to him? He sat down beside me and put his arm over my shoulders.

I said, "I should have made love to you yesterday. You'll be on your way to England tomorrow, and I'll kick myself for not going to bed with you. But I'm so scared of making love."

"You're scared? What about me the first time? You think I wasn't scared?"

"Why would you have been scared? I would have thought it would be the girl who would be scared."

"I was scared out of my wits because I had no idea of how it was supposed to be done. And the young lady – it was her first time, as well – was absolutely no help. She kept saying, 'Mark, what *are* you trying to do?'" He said this mimicking a girl's higher pitched voice, with a slight accent I couldn't place.

I had to laugh at him.

Mark went on. "It was a complete embarrassment for me, and I'm sure the young lady wished she had picked someone experienced to sleep with for the first time. You know how I touched your clitoris just now?"

I'm sure my face turned red, but I nodded. I've subsequently found that in matters of human anatomy medical students are carelessly blunt.

"Well, my first time, I didn't know there *was* a clitoris. No idea."

"You seemed to have learned all about it."

He laughed. "Is that a compliment?"

I smiled. "Yes, it is. Was she your girlfriend? I mean, the person you slept with the first time."

"Yes."

"She must not still be your girlfriend, because you told me you've been with more than one girl."

"No, we broke up" – he stopped to think – "in the summer of 1959."

"Why did you break up?"

He shrugged. "She wanted to see someone else. But she's still a good friend of mine. I hope you'll meet her some day."

Meeting Mark's first lover was not going to be high on my list of social priorities, but I didn't tell him that. Then I had an uncomfortable thought. "Do you have a girlfriend now?"

"Not in England."

I didn't like the qualified sound of that answer. "Do you have a girlfriend somewhere else?"

"I seem to have acquired one in Bermuda."

I was so pleased I practically glowed.

After that, we walked along the beach together. Mark put his arm around my waist and, in a proprietary sort of way, tucked his thumb under the waistband of my swimsuit bottom.

The day Mark was leaving Bermuda, I was working for Mother and Grandfather in the clinic. Mark was having lunch with his aunt in Hamilton, and her driver was going to take him to Kindley Field later that afternoon. Mark said he would stop at the clinic after lunch to say goodbye. When I saw him pull up in front of the clinic and park the MG on Point Finger Road, I promised myself that I absolutely would not cry.

I smoothed my skirt down, checked the mirror to make sure my ponytail was neatly tied back, and walked outside. There couldn't be a more public spot in Bermuda. Mother's clinic was just across the street from hospital, and people were everywhere. Not the ideal place for goodbyes. Mark got out of the MG and put his arms around my shoulders. I put my arms around his waist, and we kissed. I was making myself the talk of Point Finger Road.

I said, "We'll never see each other again." I was keeping my promise to myself not to cry, but it was a close thing.

"Certainly we'll see each other again."

I leaned my forehead against his chest. "Doubtful. I'll be in the States, and you'll be in England."

"Not doubtful." He lifted up my chin with his hand and smiled at me. "I promise you we'll see each other again."

With that, he kissed me a final time, pulled lightly on my ponytail, got in the MG, and drove off. I stood there alone and disconsolate.

Mother came through the door of the clinic in her white lab coat with her stethoscope hanging out of the pocket. I expected her to scold me for making a spectacle of myself in public. Instead, she stood beside me and said quietly, "I know exactly how you feel."

Then she took me by the hand, led me back inside and began making me a cup of tea. I started crying. "You said you know how I feel. What did you do?"

"There's nothing to do. You put one foot in front of another." She handed me a tissue and kissed me on my forehead. "Now, stop crying. I have patients waiting for me, and you have work to do."

Three weeks after I returned to Smith from spring holiday, Mother wrote me a letter that I received on a Thursday evening, when I arrived back at Emerson House from tennis practice.

This was unusual; Mother and I wrote one another every Sunday afternoon. This was a tradition that Mother and American Grandmother had started when Mother began at Smith, and Mother and I had decided to continue it. It took the mail about a week to travel in either direction from Bermuda. So normally I received a letter from Mother on Monday or Tuesday, which she had written on Sunday the week before – usually with a quick note from Father at the end of her letter. But I had already received a letter from her earlier that week, and now here was a second letter. I was a little concerned, though if anything were seriously wrong she would have telephoned me. A telephone call was not easy, and it was expensive, but occasionally we would speak by telephone.

I opened the letter and got incredibly wonderful news. Mark's mother, Lady Thakeham, had written Mother to invite me to London for the season of parties in June, and Mother was asking me if I wanted to accept.

Actually, Lady Thakeham's invitation was to just one party, which the Thakehams were giving for Mark's younger sister, Catherine. Lady Thakeham, though, told Mother that, once it became known that I would be in London, I would likely receive invitations to many other parties. Mother said in her letter to me that this was certainly true. I would need an escort, but Lady Thakeham said that Mark would be willing to escort me unless I had some other young man in mind. (Reading this, I knew that Mark, as a joke on me, had suggested to his Mother that I might prefer someone other than him as an escort.)

Mother also told me that Lady Thakeham had invited me to stay with them, but she also knew that I had family in London, and that I might prefer to be with my own family, and if so that was completely agreeable. (Since my London relatives were elderly great aunts, this would be an easy choice.) Finally, Mrs Thakeham had said that she understood I was interested in tennis, and since Wimbledon would be on during June, it might be possible to find tickets for Centre Court one or two afternoons during the fortnight.

Mother went on to say in her letter that, if I wanted to accept the invitation, Father would have to make my travel plans and establish credit for me at the Butterfield's bank office in London, that she would have to reply to Mrs Thakeham, and she and I together would have to think about my clothes for the parties. So, if I wanted to accept, it might be best for me to telephone home.

There was one telephone in Emerson House, down in the front hallway, and I was dialing the international operator about two seconds after finishing this extraordinary letter.

The best part was that, obviously, Mark had put his mother up to this scheme and must have done so promptly after returning to London. I had not heard from Mark since we parted in Bermuda. He had asked for my address at Smith, and I had given it to him, but I pointedly did not ask for his address. Not having a letter from him in three weeks, I had almost decided he simply didn't want to write me. Now, it seemed, he had done something better than write; he had arranged to keep his promise that we would see one another again.

The invitation also solved an unspoken but real problem in the Hodgkin household, which was that at some point I would have to make an appearance at the London season. Both Mother and English Grandmother had done so.

I was about to turn 19, and our English relatives would expect that this year, or next, or at the latest when I was 21, I would spend the season in London, going to parties and perhaps finding a husband from a good English family. Back in the 1930s, American Grandmother had taken Mother to the season; that must have been an interesting cultural clash. But I couldn't go to the season alone. That was Not Done, and it was always difficult for Mother and Father to close their clinics and leave for England on holiday.

I finally was able to ring our home in Paget, and Father answered. When he heard me on the line, he said, "I told your mother that you were far too busy with your studies to run off to London for the month of June." And we both laughed.

When Mother came on, she seemed most concerned about my clothes, which surprised me. Mother normally cared little about clothes, and, in any event, I had plenty of nice things. But she said, "Fiona, you have no idea about the season." And she was right about that. So Mother wrote Lady Thakeham, thanked her for the kind invitation, and said I was pleased to accept.

And that was that.

Smith for me that spring was a blur of chemistry labs, calculus, and tennis. I received a letter from Mark, which pleased me a great deal. It was just a page and a half of scribbled comments about his clinical work in medical school, but just after his signature, he added a postscript: "Heard that my mother has invited you to stay with us in June; what a coincidence given that you and I just met in Bermuda a few weeks ago; hope you can accept."

MAY 1962
EXHIBITION MATCH WITH CLAIRE KERSHAW
LONGWOOD CRICKET CLUB
CHESTNUT HILL, MASSACHUSETTS

By the end of April, I was ranked number one in singles tennis among girl college students in New England. My ranking led to an invitation for me to play early in May in a ladies' tournament one weekend at the Longwood Cricket Club, on grass. Longwood was in Chestnut Hill near Boston. I arranged to stay with my cousins in Boston for that weekend, and late Friday after my classes, I took a Greyhound coach to Boston. There would be three rounds on Saturday, and then the final would be on Sunday morning.

But there was a surprise: when I arrived at Longwood Saturday morning, I learned that, on Sunday afternoon, the winner would play an exhibition match against Claire Kershaw. I recognized that name instantly. Kershaw had won the singles championship at Wimbledon in 1960 and 1961. I had seen her only in newspaper photographs. She had been 25 and recently married when she won Wimbledon her first time. Now Kershaw must be close to 27.

At the end of 1961, Lance Tingay, the tennis correspondent of London's *Daily Telegraph* newspaper, had ranked Kershaw the number one woman player in his World Rankings. Before the objective, computerized rankings began in 1973, Tingay's World Rankings in the *Daily Telegraph* were considered authoritative.

I asked the referee what Mrs Kershaw was doing here, and he told me that she was on a tour of America before defending her championship at Wimbledon.

When I was handed the draw, I saw that I knew most of the players. I had beaten all the ones I knew, and I had been seeded number one. With luck, tomorrow afternoon I would play the defending Wimbledon champion. My knees went weak as I thought about it. I didn't lose a set on Saturday; I can't recall how many games I lost but not many.

When I went home to my cousins late that afternoon, I was trembling. I could barely talk. All I could think about was playing Kershaw.

'Please don't let it rain on Sunday afternoon,' I thought. I wolfed down dinner and went straight to bed, where I tried to force myself to sleep.

Sunday morning in the final, I played an older woman I didn't know. She was a good club player but not at all a threat. I tried to keep it interesting for the spectators, but mainly I wanted to keep myself as fresh as possible to play Kershaw. After winning the final, I went to the showers and turned on the hot water. I was always amazed by the amount of water, and especially hot water, that was taken for granted in the States. In Bermuda, we had only rainwater, and we heated little of it.

There was a buffet lunch in the Longwood clubhouse before the exhibition match with a crowd of people, all there to watch Kershaw play. I got myself a salad and sat down at table with the tournament referee; I knew no one else. The players I knew had lost the day before and gone home.

A young woman sat down with us. Her hair was so blond it was almost silver; she kept it brushed back and held in place with a simple barrette. Her face was lovely, with large, pale blue eyes, and an impish grin. Her elegant white tennis dress had a matchbox skirt, with narrow, light blue ruffles on the seams. On the hem was embroidered in tiny blue script, 'Teddy Tinling.'

She wore a thin, plain gold wedding band but no other jewelry, not even earrings, and, unusual for that time, no makeup. Well, perhaps there was a trace of cream on her cheeks to ward off the sun. But nothing else.

She wasn't a large woman, but when she made even a simple movement – reaching for the pepper shaker, for example – it was impossible to miss the muscular power behind her limbs. Still, she was quite feminine.

The way she chatted with the referee was so friendly and outgoing that she might have been mistaken for an American, except that her upper class English accent gave her away. This, it dawned on me, was Claire Kershaw, and the idea that I was sitting at the same table with someone who had won Wimbledon – twice – was just incredible to me.

The referee turned to me. "Well, here's your opponent this afternoon!"

Kershaw stood up and reached out her hand. "I'm Claire."

I shook her hand. "I'm Fiona Hodgkin."

Claire burst into a smile. "I thought it might be you when I saw you just now! Fiona, I've heard so much about you!"

How could a Wimbledon champion possibly have heard of me? I was bewildered. But then a group of ladies descended on Claire for autographs and photographs, and I didn't have the chance to talk to her again before our match. In those days, tennis outfits for ladies in the States (and Bermuda, for that matter) were usually shapeless dresses, or blouses with pleated skirts that, unfortunately, tended to emphasize the hips. Claire's carefully tailored dress with its blue ruffles was a sensation at Longwood that afternoon.

Once we were on the court, Claire casually tossed her racket onto the grass. I called it smooth and won the serve. Once we began playing, it was obvious to me that, as they say in the States, I wasn't in Kansas anymore. Claire played effortlessly, with complete grace, and her style was perfectly balanced between the baseline and the net.

She put huge topspin on the ball with each groundstroke, and the ball would sail a meter over the net before dropping like a rock. I practically had to scrape her shots off the grass. She was patient, consistent, and happy for each point to go on until, at last, she would hit a winner.

And she was casual. She chatted with the spectators on the changeovers. Claire knew how to warm up the crowd and charm everyone. She wanted to entertain the spectators; that was the whole point of this match. Claire wasn't even taking it seriously. I was there only as a foil, so she could delight the crowd, which infuriated me. I was not about to roll over for this show.

Today, I know the custom that often governs exhibition matches, which is that they don't go to three sets. The matches aren't fixed. It's just that the player who wins the first set usually then, by convention, wins the second set, so that both players can catch the late afternoon flight out of wherever the exhibition is played. And the second set often features trick shots to amaze the crowd. At the time, no one had explained any of this to me – and it might not have made any difference even if someone had.

I lost the first set 6-4, because I made two stupid errors when I was serving in the seventh game with the games even at three apiece. Claire took advantage of these errors to break me and then take the set. I decided I wasn't going to let that happen again.

Early in the second set, on Claire's serve, I took up my usual spot a meter from the net. Claire hit a beautiful passing shot down my ad court line. I lunged for it, caught it with my backhand, punched it back crosscourt to her ad court corner, and drifted toward the centerline. Claire reached my shot and hit a topspin forehand that made the ball drop over the net right at my feet. I half-volleyed it back; I was so low to the grass that I found myself looking *up* at the net cord. Claire sent up a deep lob. I ran back, with no time to set up, jumped, and smashed the ball. It wasn't pretty, but it got the job done. Claire got only the rim of her racket on the ball, and it ricocheted into the crowd.

This put me ahead in the score, 30-15, and I went on to break Claire's serve.

At the next changeover, she wasn't chatting with the spectators. This was all business now. Claire had no intention of going three sets in an exhibition match with an unknown teenager from nowhere. But that's what happened. She couldn't get the break back, and I took the second set.

In the third set, I came to the net on almost every point and punched volleys into the corners of Claire's court. But, on my serve, I hit a forehand volley that went wide, and she went ahead in the game. That was all she needed; if you gave her the slightest opening, she would make the most of it. She won the third set 8-6, and so the match, but only by making an enormous effort.

The crowd was sophisticated enough to know this wasn't the match they were supposed to see, and this was confirmed at the net when Claire shook my hand but then put her arms around me and hugged me over the net. Claire was emotional; she whispered straight into my ear, "You're everything I heard you were."

A few minutes later in the dressing room, Claire sat down beside me. She hadn't taken a shower yet; she was toweling the sweat off her arms. She said, "That third set was something. Great for the Longwood members to see a real match."

"I'm sure you gave me the second set to make it interesting."

She laughed. "I didn't give you anything. My plan was to take the second set, sign a few autographs, and head back to my hotel."

Then Claire said, "Rachel Martin told me about you."

I was astonished. "Do you know Mrs Martin?"

"Rachel was my coach for four years or so when I was a teenager."

"That couldn't be! She and I listened together to the BBC shortwave broadcast of the final last year at Wimbledon when you won. She didn't say she knew you."

"We're certainly talking about the same lady. Only Rachel would not think to mention that."

"How did Mrs Martin become your coach?"

"She and her husband spent the weekend at my parents' country house when I was, I guess, 14. Her husband worked in the City for a few years in the '40s and early '50s. We have an old grass court, and Rachel watched me play with my brother. After we finished, she asked my mother if she could play with me. We played a couple of times that weekend. After that, Rachel arranged with Mother to play with me in London maybe four or five times a week. Sometimes we played on grass at Queen's. Other times on a covered wood court."

I felt a chill. This was so much like what had happened after I served for Mrs Martin the first time. I remembered something Mrs Martin had said to me years ago: I was one of only two girls she had seen who could hit the outside edge of the lines exactly, almost every time.

Claire Kershaw must be the other girl.

Claire went on. "I had never been especially keen on tennis, because I disliked all the drills."

"But Mrs Martin doesn't use drills."

"That's right. No drills. By the time she went home to Bermuda, I was wild for tennis, and then my parents found another coach for me. I didn't like that coach and dropped him after a couple of months. Never had a coach again. But Rachel and I still play together whenever she's in London."

"How did she tell you about me?"

"Rachel and I exchange letters two or three times a year, and last Christmas I mentioned in my note to her that I was going to tour the States in the spring. She wrote back a long letter and asked me to make a point of watching you play, which I planned to do while I'm here. But I didn't know I would wind up watching you from across the net."

"What did she say about me?"

"She said that you have a bad case of the serves and volleys. Was she ever right about that!"

Claire laughed but then paused. "Rachel also said that you might win Wimbledon within the next four or five years. After this afternoon, I think she might be right about that as well. Rachel says that what you need is experience in international competition. You need to get out of Bermuda and out of college competition, in other words."

I was stunned; I couldn't speak.

'So," Claire asked. "What are your plans?"

"Both my parents are physicians, and I hope to go to medical school."

"Good for you! But, actually, I meant more where are you going to play this summer?"

"I don't have any plans to play this summer. I'm going to be in London for the season. My boyfriend is English, and his family invited me to stay with them in London. Did you ever do the season?" I could tell by her accent that she was from a family that would have made certain she was at the season.

"I did, the same year I made my first appearance at Wimbledon. That was 1956. I met my husband, Richard, at a party that season, although it took us years to get married. Because of my tennis, I didn't drink at the parties. I'm probably the only person ever to get through the season sober!" She laughed.

"When did you get married?"

"In 1960. This year will probably be my last Wimbledon. I've been there six times so far. I'd love to win again before I give up competition."

"Do you think you'll win?"

"I have to get past Margaret Smith first. She hasn't yet won the singles at Wimbledon. Lucky for me, last year

Margaret lost in the fifth round to Christine Truman. But now the London bookies are giving highwaymen's odds of six to four on Margaret to win the singles this year. I've played her three times in competition, all three times on grass, and I lost twice. I lost to her at Kooyong just a few months ago."

"Why would you give up competition?"

"I want to have a family. I could still compete after I have children; I know some women who do. I talked to Kay Menzies about it."

"Who is she?"

Claire stared at me in disbelief. "Kay Stammers Menzies. The best English woman player before and after the war. Older than me but a good friend. She had her family during the war, then led our Wightman Cup team."

"Oh."

"But I don't think I want to keep playing if I can have a baby. Too much travel, for one thing." Claire leaned over to me and said softly, "Richard and I are already trying to have a baby. I thought that, even if I were lucky enough to get pregnant, Wimbledon would be so early for me that being pregnant wouldn't make any difference."

"Won't you miss tennis?"

"No, not if I can have a family."

I was silent. It was hard for me to imagine giving up tennis, I mean in competition.

Claire knew what I was thinking. "Fiona, do you know what I did after I won the final in 1960? I went out with Richard, my brother, and my parents and celebrated at the Wimbledon Ball. But we went home quite early because I was tired."

She laughed. "Actually, we were *both* tired. Richard claims it's much harder to watch a Wimbledon final than to play in one. And then, Sunday morning, I woke up and boiled him an egg and made tea for his breakfast. It was the same as always. I had gotten what I had wanted for years, but everything was just the same. I mean, there's all this, now." She smiled. "Exhibition matches with girls from Bermuda. But nothing really changed. I won't miss it."

She thought for a moment. "I want a family now."

Then she changed the subject. "Tell me about this boyfriend."

"I only met him a month or so ago. He came to Bermuda to visit his aunt there on holiday, and I was set up with him."

"Set up?"

I thought that maybe I had used an exclusively American expression. "I just mean that apparently it had been arranged that I should meet him."

"I know what 'set up' means. I'm not a dinosaur. How were you set up?"

"I don't know exactly, but his father and my father served together in the war, in the Royal Navy, and they're friends. I had the feeling that everyone had decided I should meet him. When I did, then my parents basically let me see him whenever I wanted, which was all the time. That's unheard of for them."

"You must like him."

"A great deal."

"Did you sleep with him?"

"Claire!"

"Yes, yes, it's a personal question, I shouldn't ask, it's private, I'm awful. What's the answer?"

"No. But maybe I should have."

"Have you ever slept with anyone?'

"No."

"Well, as soon as you're on the international tennis circuit, the men players will fix that, for sure, and quickly." Claire said this bitterly.

"Did you sleep with anyone before your husband?"

She shook her head ruefully. "Fiona, I was already on the circuit, and by myself, when I was your age. By the time Richard finally got around to proposing to me, I had gone through most of the men on the circuit and was about to start in on the Wimbledon ball boys."

Then she asked, "What's this boyfriend like?"

"He's good looking. He's a medical student at Cambridge, so he's older than me."

"So he doesn't push you into things? He must not, or you'd already have been in his bed."

I nodded. "Well, I seem to do almost anything he asks. But I don't think he pushes me, at least not too much. He's about right, I mean in the way he treats me." I smiled. "Claire, he's wonderful."

She laughed. "We'll see about that."

Then Claire switched subjects again. "Fiona, will I offend you if I say something about your game?"

"I'd want to hear anything you say about my game."

"There were only two important games in our match. The two games when I broke you."

"Yes."

"If you had won either of those games, we'd probably still be out there, or maybe you would have won by now. You think so?"

"Yes."

"You know what I think? You got behind in the score on your serve, and you got impatient. Because you were impatient, you made mistakes. I don't mean to lecture you, I hate it when people do that to me, but that's what I think."

"I know what you're saying. You're right."

"You play so quickly on your serve. I know where that comes from. Rachel plays so quickly. Play has to be continuous, sure. But still, you usually serve less than 10 seconds after the previous point. Slow down, catch your breath, think, plan the next point."

At that time, the Rules of Lawn Tennis required play to be "continuous," including between points, so the server wasn't given time to reach for a towel or bounce the ball endlessly before serving. It wasn't until 1979 that the server would be allowed 30 seconds (later cut to 20 seconds) to serve. So, in 1962, play in international competition was much faster than today.

Claire smiled. "I'm not going to tell you to bounce the ball on the court while you're taking your time. I know that's against Rachel's rules."

"But to serve quickly can put pressure on your opponent."

"Maybe. Maybe a few women feel the pressure. For most of them, though, it's like trying to put pressure on a rock. They don't care, and it doesn't affect them."

Now I switched subjects. "Were you serious when you said I might win someday at Wimbledon?"

"There's so much that's pure luck, good or bad. The weather can be terrible. We always say we should re-schedule Wimbledon and hold it in the summer!'"

I frowned. "Wimbledon is in the summer."

Claire sighed. "It's a joke, Fiona."

"Oh."

"You can wake up one morning sick. Or you can wake up one morning with your period and feel awful. An opponent can have a great day. You can have a bad day. It's two long weeks. Unless you have a bye for the first round, it's six matches in a row just to get to the final. It's exhausting, it really is exhausting. Anything can happen. And you know Centre Court."

When she said this, I thought, 'No, I don't know Centre Court, but I plan to learn all about it.'

"It all happens so quickly, and then it's over. All that matters is who wins the last point. So you never know." She stopped for a moment. "But, yes, I think you might win Wimbledon. For one reason: you're extraordinary at the net."

She paused again, thinking. "You may be one of the best ever at the net. That's what Rachel thinks, and maybe she's right. But it's too soon to know. Maybe you'll collapse in international competition. Rachel is worried about that, because you've been cooped up in Bermuda and at college in the States. You certainly take too many chances. That's Rachel's influence, to go all out. She's never liked being cautious. But still – the question is how you'll do in international competition."

We heard a knock on the door, and Claire yelled, "Come in!"

The club steward poked his head through the door. "Claire, could we ask you to come back out on the court for some photographs with the members?"

"Yes, I'll be right there." Claire turned to me, smiled, and held up her index finger. "Be careful what you wish for!" She walked to the door, stopped for a moment, then turned around to me.

"Fiona, you're an amateur; am I right about that?"

"Of course."

"Have you ever played in a tournament where a professional was also playing?" She was referring to the ridiculous rules that governed whether a player could be considered an 'amateur.' Even if you had merely played in the same tournament with a professional, you could be disqualified from amateur competition.

"No. Last year I saw Pancho Gonzales beat Frank Sedgman, when Jack Kramer brought them to Bermuda. My parents took me to see them play. But I didn't even meet them. I've never played with a professional."

"You'll be in London the week of June 18?"

"Yes. I'll be at the season."

She walked back to the bench and sat down beside me. "You could play at Roehampton that week. If I could get you an invitation, would you play?"

"Yes, I'm sure I would enjoy it." I had never heard of Roehampton. I had no idea what Claire was talking about.

"The draw is probably already set. Everyone fights for an invitation. The LTA would have to submit an entry form for you. That's all right, they probably consider Bermuda to be part of Great Britain. Don't get your hopes up; I doubt I can make it happen. Tomorrow morning I'll send the Committee a telegram about you. But remember, every woman in tennis wants to be at Roehampton. I'll do my best. Will you give me your address?"

I pulled my notepad from my pocketbook, tore off a page, wrote my address at Smith, and handed the page to her.

She got up and walked to the door to go have her photograph taken with the Longwood members.

"Claire, what is the 'LTA'?"

She turned and stared at me. "The Lawn Tennis Association. They run amateur tennis in Britain. I don't really know how they submit the forms. They do it for me, I guess, more or less automatically."

"They might submit a form for me? To where?"

Claire laughed. "To the All England Club, silly. For Wimbledon."

I sat staring at Claire with my mouth hanging open.

It finally dawned on Claire that I wasn't conversant with the process for selecting the qualifiers for the singles draw at Wimbledon. "Fiona, Roehampton is the week before Wimbledon. It's the qualifying competition. That's how I qualified for Wimbledon, my first time. The All England Lawn Tennis Club Committee of Management, in its infinite wisdom, and after consulting with the Referee, Colonel Legg, may invite you to play at Roehampton. There are three rounds at Roehampton. It's brutal."

She laughed again. I had the sense that Claire had enjoyed Roehampton thoroughly.

"The women who win all three rounds get unseeded spots in the Wimbledon draw." She leaned over and kissed my cheek. "I'll send the Committee a telegram first thing in the morning. I'll tell them to see what you can do. But they probably won't listen to me."

Claire left for photographs with the Longwood members.

To me, then, Wimbledon was merely a shimmering dream. I had seen it only in smudged black and white newspaper photographs showing legendary players, like

Angela Mortimer and Maria Bueno, on Centre Court. I had heard matches at Wimbledon only over crackling, short wave BBC radio broadcasts: *"Crosscourt. Point to Miss Mortimer. Good show by the girl from Devon."*

I sat on the dressing room bench, trying to breath slowly. I might, just possibly, have a path to Wimbledon.

MAY 1962
SMITH COLLEGE
EMERSON HOUSE
NORTHAMPTON, MASSACHUSETTS

Two weeks after I played Claire at Longwood, I was at Smith waiting for an afternoon chemistry lab to get started, when a girl from Emerson House came in and told me that I had received a telegram. She had seen it when she had gone back to the house for lunch. I instantly cut the lab, ran as fast as I could along the path under the trees back to the house, burst through the door, found my telegram on the front hall table, and tore it open.

WESTERN UNION

FIONA HODGKIN
    CONFIRM SOONEST ENTRY JUNE 18 QUALIFYING
ROEHAMPTON STOP CONFIRM AMATEUR STATUS STOP

THE COMMITTEE
ALL ENGLAND LAWN TENNIS CLUB

I screamed at the top of my lungs, "YES! YES!" I was jumping up and down in the hallway.

The house matron came out of the kitchen. "Fiona, a young man must have proposed to you. That's the only thing that could make you so happy. Congratulations!"

Mother was Not Pleased.

I had written her immediately with the news about Roehampton, told her I had accepted the Committee's invitation by a reply telegram, and generally made it clear that this was the most wonderful thing that could have happened.

It never entered my mind that Mother would not see it that way.

She telephoned me during dinner one night at Emerson House. "Fiona," she began coldly. "By agreeing to play tennis in London, you've put yourself and me in an awkward position. Lady Thakeham is likely to feel, and would be justified in feeling, that we have taken advantage of her invitation in order to have you enter a tennis tournament."

I had not thought about this, and I regret to say Mother was correct on this point.

"Also," Mother continued, "this isn't a step you should have taken without discussing it first with your father and me. I'm unhappy that you did this on your own."

I had never thought to talk with Mother about this; I had been too excited. Again, unfortunately, she was in the right about this.

"I think you need to withdraw from this tournament in London."

I hesitated and then decided on a strategic retreat. "Mother, you're exactly right, and I apologize to you and

Father. I was excited about this, and I acted without thinking. But the tournament will only be a day, at most two. I'm sure I'll lose in the first or second round. It won't interfere with anything I'm doing with the Thakehams."

She had anticipated my retreat. "No. I talked with Rachel Martin today, who is as surprised as I am. But she tells me not to count on your losing. She expects you'll be in it until the end, or near the end."

Thanks a lot, Mrs Martin, for all your help here; you can't be bothered to tell me that I'm any good, but you seem to advertise me widely to everyone else.

"Mother," I said, "I do apologize, but I will write a letter to Lady Thakeham tonight, a long, polite letter, and mail it in the morning. I'll tell her I did this without asking you, which I sincerely regret, and I'll promise her Roehampton won't interfere with the season. And if it does, I'll simply withdraw. I'll tell her I had no idea about this tournament when you accepted her invitation to stay with them, which is true."

When I said this to Mother, I thought that what I should really do tonight is a calculus problem set, but I put that aside for the moment. The important thing was to hang onto my place at Roehampton. Mother was entirely capable of saying simply that I wasn't playing tennis in London. That would be that. If she decided I shouldn't play at Roehampton, it would be hard, probably impossible, to change her mind. I doubted I could persuade Father to take my side on this.

But I had one major psychological advantage over Mother, which is that I was her only child. I have no idea why my parents didn't have more children; they certainly didn't seem to have the slightest difficulty having me, and they both loved children. But I was their only child, and that meant, in my experience, that neither of them could be angry or upset at me for long. I could tell Mother was at least a bit mollified by my apology.

So I went at Mother again. "I'll write Lady Thakeham tonight, and I promise you I'll make it right with her, and while I'm in London I'll behave so that she will be happy to have had me visit."

Mother said, "Fiona, will you write me tonight and tell me you've written Mark's mother?"

"Yes, Mother."

"And you'll apologize to her?"

"Yes, Mother, I will."

"And you'll tell her you'll withdraw from this tournament if it interferes in any way with your obligations to her family?"

"I will say that explicitly to her."

"Then please do so. And, Fiona, you really must talk with us before you decide on something like this."

"Yes, Mother, I will."

And so we told one another that we loved each other and said goodbye.

Roehampton and Lady Thakeham didn't turn out exactly the way I promised Mother they would.

When I told Claire I was going to write this story of my tennis career and how I met my husband, she wasn't enthusiastic. She and I are both old now – I'm in my late 60s, and Claire is almost 76. It had happened so long ago, why go back into all that? That was Claire's thinking.

Claire had published her own tennis autobiography soon after she first won Wimbledon in 1960. An autobiography was one of the few accepted ways for a successful amateur to make money from tennis. But Claire hadn't written a single word of that book – except for the preface. She wrote the preface herself.

Claire explained in the preface that, when she had told her husband, Richard, about her plan to include the louche details of her love affairs with men players when she was a single girl on the international tennis circuit, Richard objected. Then, Claire wrote, Richard engaged a young literary lady from a good English family to ghostwrite a proper tennis autobiography for Claire.

The ghostwriter, naturally, asked to interview Claire, and so Claire had invited her over to the flat. In her preface, Claire wrote: "She was an aspiring novelist; she was charming; she preferred Earl Grey tea; she knew nothing about tennis."

Claire's tennis autobiography had been a runaway best seller in England.

I was in London to give a paper at a pediatric medical conference, and I was staying with Claire and Richard. At breakfast, I asked Claire if she'd kept a copy of the telegram she had sent to the Committee about me in 1962.

"No, I didn't. I just scribbled something down on a Western Union message pad in the hotel in Boston that morning. I didn't think to keep a copy."

"You must remember what you said about me to the Committee."

"No, I don't. Anyway, it's a mistake, this idea of writing it all down."

I persisted. I had decided to write my story, and I was going to do it.

Finally, Claire said, " The All England Club hasn't thrown anything away, ever. So they'll have my telegram. Just speak with the Club's Secretary."

That morning I rang the Club. The Secretary said, "It's Doctor Hodgkin, isn't it?"

"Yes. I regret that you and I haven't been introduced. But if you please. There was a telegram in 1962, about me. If it still exists, may I see it?"

"A telegram?"

"To the Committee of Management," I said. "From Claire. I mean, from Mrs Richard Kershaw. About me."

The Secretary told me to come around to the Club, and he would meet me at Gate 5. We would see, he said, if the telegram could be found in the files.

I took the Tube to Southfields and walked under my umbrella in the rain down Church Road. I hadn't been to Wimbledon in many years, and all the new gates confused me. But surely the 'Gate 5' the Secretary directed me to must be the old South East Gate, the main entrance to the Club?

Good to his word, the Secretary was standing at the gate under an umbrella.

"Where are the Doherty Gates?" I asked.

"Oh, they're down at the south end of the ground now. Have been since 2006."

The Doherty Memorial Gates, made of black wrought iron, with the letters 'A.E.L.T.C.' in bright gold leaf, had stood at the South East Gate since 1931. They had been given to the Club by Rev. W. V. Doherty in memory of his brothers, Reggie and Laurie, who between them had won Wimbledon nine times – Laurie won five times in a row, 1902 to1906. The Committee approved the design of the Gates in October 1930, and they had been bolted to the masonry gateposts the next year.

"Why in heaven would the Doherty Gates be moved?"

"My dear Doctor Hodgkin, the lorries, of course."

"The lorries?"

"When Centre Court was rebuilt. For the new retractable roof. The construction lorries were too wide for the old gates."

"But no one ever goes to the south end of the ground! No one would see the gates."

"Oh, the Committee put quite a nice little plaque down there. In the wall beside them."

Once we were in his office, the Secretary summoned a young clerk. "Simon, we want a telegram from 1962, it will likely be on an old Post Office Telegram form, probably quite short, telegrams were expensive. From Mrs Richard Kershaw to the Committee."

I interjected. "She may have signed the telegram 'Claire Kershaw,' or even just 'Claire.'"

"Just so," the Secretary said. "Off you go, then, Simon."

The Secretary suggested that I wait in the members' buffet in the Millennium Building, on the other side of Centre Court, while Simon conducted his search.

In September, on a chilly, rainy London day, the buffet was as cold and closed as a tomb. The lone attendant gave me a cup of tea, and I took it out on the covered balcony, which had a view of the outer grass courts and, in the distance, on a hill, in the mist, the old spire of St. Mary's Church.

On a sunny day during the Championships, this balcony would be a splendid spot from which to see the milling crowds, the brilliant green grass, the tennis players fighting to stay in the draw, and the blooming hydrangea. Now, though, the nets were down, the umpires' chairs gone, the hydrangea pruned back to the old wood, and the only sign of life was a single groundskeeper wearing a yellow rain slicker who appeared to be merely looking forlornly down at the grass.

I stood there, lost in thought.

Simon, the young clerk, appeared after about an hour. He coughed, politely, to gain my attention. I turned around.

"Doctor, is this possibly the telegram for which you are looking?"

I went back inside the buffet and sat down at a table. The telegram was crinkled, and I held it down with my fingers spread to flatten it. The strips of type that had been pasted onto the form were peeling off.

Post Office Telegram

THE COMMITTEE
ALL ENGLAND LAWN TENNIS CLUB

DEAR DARLING BOYS STOP YESTERDAY EXHIBITION
MATCH LONGWOOD BOSTON GRASS FIONA HODGKIN
18 YEARS BERMUDA AMATEUR SINGLES CHAMPION STOP
COACH AMATEUR RACHEL OUTERBRIDGE 1939 SINGLES
FINALIST STOP FH SWEET YOUNG BALL OF ENERGY
STOP YOU MUST LIST FH FOR ROEHAMPTON STOP FH
ADDRESS   EMERSON   HOUSE   SMITH   COLLEGE
NORTHAMPTON MASS US STOP I PROMISE TO SLEEP
WITH EACH OF YOU UPON RETURN ENGLAND STOP
SEPARATELY OF COURSE STOP

The telegram was signed with a single word: CLAIRE.

I burst out laughing, which startled Simon. In 1962, the
members of the Committee were all men, with an average
age of probably 75. (The first woman on the Committee
would be Virginia Wade, but that wouldn't happen until
1982.) In their dreams, the Committee members no doubt
wished the beautiful Claire actually meant to sleep with
them.

But they had obediently put me down for Roehampton.

In the rain, under my umbrella, I walked back to Gate 5.
The young security guards at the gate wore bright orange
jackets and had coiled wires from their radios running under
their collars to earphones. They must have been told who I
was or, more accurately, who I had been before they were
born, because they quietly stepped aside as I approached.

I stood at the gate for a moment, looking across Church Road at the Wimbledon golf course.

Then, instead of turning left, back to Southfields, I turned right and walked toward to the point where Church Road met Somerset Road, at the south end of the Club's ground.

I wanted to say hello to my poor old friends, the Doherty Memorial Gates.

The day before my flight to London, Mother was helping me pack. We were going to have a family dinner that evening with my grandparents to say goodbye for a month.

While we were in my room, surrounded by piles of clothes, Mother said, "Fiona, during the season in London, many young people drink too much at the parties and do not conduct themselves well; in fact, quite badly sometimes. Drinking is a risk for girls – I mean drinking alcohol."

I was glad she had cleared that up for me.

"Your father and I are sending you off for the season because we can count on you to show good judgment and to conduct yourself well. Can we rely on you?"

"Yes, Mother." I predicted to myself what was coming next. Mark Thakeham. And I was right.

"I know you like Mark a great deal. And he seems to like you. Maybe over the next few years you'll have a friendship that's important to both of you. If that happens, all well and good. But Mark is four years older than you, and I'm confident he's sexually experienced. Perhaps quite so."

She was right about that, I thought.

"You, I take it, are not sexually experienced?"

"Uh, well, not very."

She sighed. "I meant my question to ask whether you've had sexual intercourse." She had been a physician for a long time and didn't shy away from biological facts.

"No."

Mother looked at me. "But something close to it, I think," she said.

I said nothing.

Mother arched her eyebrow. "Well?"

"Mark touched me once." I dreaded telling her what I was talking about, but to my surprise she seemed to know exactly what I meant.

"And that's all?"

"Mark said he would just touch me, nothing more. That's all he did."

"Well, good for you, Mark Thakeham," Mother said softly. She sounded a bit surprised at the show of at least partially responsible conduct from this quarter.

Then she asked, "Do you plan to sleep with him while you're in England?"

I hesitated. "I don't think so."

"Good. I don't want you to. Fiona, I know how tiresome it is at your age to have adults always saying that you're too young to do this or that, but here you really are too young. I want you to wait."

"I won't sleep with him while I'm in London."

"Good."

"But maybe someday?"

"Fiona, if in two or three years you decide this is what is right for you, and you protect yourself with a contraceptive, then go straight ahead. But when you decide to start, do it on your terms, not on Mark's terms, or on some other boy's terms. And not now."

"I promise that's what I'll do."

"Good. So I don't need to take you to the clinic in the morning and fit you with a diaphragm. Am I right about that?"

"I don't need a diaphragm," I almost whispered.

The idea of having Mother fit me with a diaphragm made the blood drain from my face. I knew about contraception because, a year or so earlier, while I was on a walk in Paget with American Grandmother, she had told me, in great and embarrassingly graphic detail, how to use a diaphragm. Then, having built up a full head of steam on the subject of human reproduction, American Grandmother had gone on to explain the biochemistry of the menstrual cycle.

It was extremely interesting, and when I had arrived at Smith I found, to my surprise, that I was far better informed that most of my classmates.

"And when the time comes," Mother said, "don't hesitate to ask me for help with a contraceptive. Or ask American Grandmother, if you feel more comfortable talking to her."

We both laughed; we knew that if I so much as said the word 'sex' to American Grandmother, she'd have me on her examining table within five minutes.

Mother said, "Now, which of these tennis dresses do you want to pack?"

"How old were you when you married?"

Mother did not like the implication behind this question in the slightest. "I was 27, almost 28, so nine years or so older than you are now. I was a medical doctor in practice. Your father was serving on a Royal Navy destroyer in the war, and I knew I would be lucky to see him again."

"Were you sexually experienced then?"

"That's an impudent question, and I shouldn't answer it. But I will. You've been honest with me, and so I should be honest with you. Yes, but only with your father. While I was in medical school, I decided it was time I should take him to bed."

Mother chuckled but almost just to herself. "When I did, I couldn't tell whether he was more surprised or thrilled."

She paused, probably thinking that she shouldn't make this sound to be so much fun. "But I protected myself. Contraceptives were difficult to obtain in the States, but I went to the Baltimore Birth Control Clinic, where there were five women physicians. One of them fitted me with a diaphragm. When I said I was a medical student at Hopkins, she told me to get to work in the clinic. This was the Depression; almost no one had money, but I replied, 'Oh, no, I can pay for the diaphragm; I don't need to work to pay the fee.' The doctor said, 'You don't understand. We need the help.' So I volunteered three evenings a week at the clinic."

"But how did you see Father? You were in the States, and Father was in medical school at Cambridge."

She smiled. "We found ways to meet twice a year or so. And for the two days we were together after our wedding, before his destroyer left Bermuda, I didn't use a contraceptive. I wanted to have his child, and I did."

She reached over, took my chin in her hand, and playfully waggled my head. "Obviously."

"Now," she said with relief, "back to packing."

My flight to London did not depart until the evening, so early the next morning I played a match against Mrs Martin and won in two sets.

Afterward, she sat down on a bench beside the court. She was thinking, with her head cocked to one side.

After a few moments, she told me to sit down. Then she said, almost in a whisper, "I didn't mean for Claire to arrange for you to play at Roehampton, not this year anyway. She's so headstrong. I wouldn't have written her about you if I'd thought she would do this. You should wait one or two years. Not now."

"Are they that much better than I am?"

"No. But most of them are older and more experienced. It will be different than anything you've done, and harder. Much harder."

"How old were you?"

We both knew that in June 1939 she had been my age now.

"Yes, but I had played in international competition before. I knew what it is like."

"I played Claire."

She shook her head. "In an exhibition, not competition."

"You think I can't win."

"No. I think you might win. But this year, when you're so young, winning will take so much it will change you. Maybe not for the better. Especially because you'll have to do it alone."

It dawned on me that she was thinking of herself. "Did that happen to you?"

She nodded.

I thought for a moment. "And maybe Claire as well?"

"Claire had a difficult time on the circuit. I wasn't there to help her. I couldn't leave my family."

"You can't imagine how much I want this."

"I know exactly how much you want it. But go to the parties for the London season, watch some matches at Roehampton and Wimbledon, come home to Bermuda, and then we'll prepare for next year. Now is too early."

"I have to do this."

"You'll be a long way from home. I won't be there to help you." Mrs Martin was speaking so softly I could barely hear her.

She straightened up. "I'll talk to your parents and suggest you take time off from college to play at Kooyong this winter. I might even be able to come with you. Then next year you'll have experience with international competition."

The odds that my parents would agree to my taking time off from Smith to play tennis in Australia were vanishingly small. I put both my hands around her left hand and held it.

"I have to do this now. I know I can win. I won't let anything happen to me."

She used my Christian name. "Fiona, I haven't prepared you for this. It's my fault. I know I'm difficult. I'm weak. I haven't helped you. Now you're going to play at Roehampton, and I haven't shown you what it's going to be like."

She began crying.

I put my arms around her; she was so important to me. "Rachel, that's nonsense. You've done everything for me. Look, I love tennis. This is what I want. And if I can get it, the only reason is you. Please stop crying, because if you don't stop, then I'll start crying."

She had her head on my shoulder. "I've been terrible for you. I haven't taught you anything you'll need."

"Rachel, stop. You've always told me that you can't show me what I need, that I have to find it by myself."

She nodded. Then she wiped her eyes with the back of her hand, stood, and walked to her bicycle. She lifted something wrapped in tissue out of the basket. She came back to me.

"I want you to have this." She held it out to me.

I took off the tissue. It was an old tennis sweater. A long time ago, it had been white, but now it had faded to beige. There were narrow navy and green borders at the neck and cuffs. The cuffs and the hem were coming a bit unraveled. Over the left breast was embroidered 'KOOYONG,' and just below that were crossed tennis rackets and 'EST. 1892.'

"Nell and Harry Hopman gave me this sweater. I wore it in my third set against Alice on Centre Court."

"Rachel, you shouldn't give this to me."

"It can be chilly in London in June. I'll feel better if I know you have something warm to wear."

"Claire is bound to see me wearing this. She might feel you could have given her your sweater."

"Claire will understand." Rachel paused. "She's probably known since she played you at Longwood."

I had no idea what Rachel meant.

I held the sweater to my chest. Rachel leaned over and kissed me on top of my head. "Good luck, Fiona."

She walked back to her bicycle and left me alone on the court. It happened to be the same court where I had served for her the first time, years before. I sat on the bench thinking for several minutes. Then I got up and bicycled home. Neither of my parents was there; we had called a taxi to Kindley Field for five o'clock. Now it wasn't even yet noon; I was all packed. I still had time.

First I put Rachel's sweater into one of my suitcases. Then I left Midpoint and walked down to the dock at Lower Ferry and waited for the ferry across the harbour to Hamilton.

Once I got off the ferry near Albuoys Point, I began looking in the shops on Front Street that catered to tourists and the passengers on ships calling at Hamilton. It took me 20 minutes or so to find what I wanted. In a small, dark shop, there was a bin of miniature cloth flags glued to short sticks of wood, a bit longer than a matchstick. I think these little flags were meant to be stuck in the tops of cakes for celebrations.

I was taking five tennis dresses to London; I bought five of the small flags. These flags had the Union Jack in one corner, with a coat of arms showing a shipwreck and a lion, all against a bright red field.

They were the flag of Bermuda.

On the ferry back to Lower Ferry, I stood at the railing

looking out at the blue water and the Bermuda fitted dinghies with their triangular sails racing across the Great Sound. I had lived almost my entire life beside this harbour. Now I was going to sew these flags onto my tennis dresses, just above my left breast. I was determined, one way or another, whatever it took, to win all three rounds at Roehampton – and qualify for the Wimbledon draw.

Whatever it took.

PART TWO

LONDON

MONDAY, 11 JUNE 1962
16 HYDE PARK GATE
KENSINGTON
LONDON, ENGLAND

When I came through the barriers after passport control and
customs at Heathrow, I was clutching just my tennis rackets,
a paperback copy of Vera Brittain's *Testament of Youth* I had
read on the flight, and my pocketbook. I had checked as
baggage everything else. I was groggy and rumpled after the
bumpy 10 hour flight from Bermuda, which had been on a
BOAC turboprop aircraft, not a jet. There had been a time
when I thought I'd never see Mark again, but now he was
standing right there, on the other side of the barricade. I didn't
have to go to him; he jumped over the barricade and hugged
me.

And then he kissed me.

Originally, the Thakeham family was Dutch and certainly not
named 'Thakeham.' Mark's ancestor, Marcellus ter' Joopt,
came to England with William of Orange at the time of the
English Revolution in 1688. ter' Joopt amassed a large fortune

after arriving in England – how exactly isn't known – and then retired to Hampshire with a young bride from an aristocratic English family.

ter' Joopt sensed that his Dutch name might not be ideal for an upwardly mobile family in England. He noticed that the house he had purchased in Hampshire, which was called 'Thakeham House,' had a perfectly good English name. And for good reason: the house had been built a 100 years before by one of Queen Elizabeth's courtiers.

So, one day, ter' Joopt simply changed his name to 'Thakeham,' and the next day, William made him the first Viscount Thakeham

Basically, my boyfriend had been named after a house.

For longer than a hundred years, the Thakeham family was content in Hampshire. Dutch thriftiness and industry ran in the family – the Thakehams conserved and increased their fortune. No drunken, gambling wastrels in this family. Mostly, the men were physicians.

In about 1830, the sixth Viscount Thakeham decided to build a fashionable London residence (though he retained Thakeham House). The Campden Charities were then attempting to develop Hyde Park Gate just south of Kensington Palace, and Viscount Thakeham bought a lot and built an unusual, red brick, L-shaped house that was now entirely overgrown with Boston ivy. The front door was an arched lattice of frosted glass and wood.

Hyde Park Gate is actually two streets, side by side, with the same name. The more famous street is to the east, with the house where Virginia Woolf was born, and the house where Winston Churchill died. Generations of London cabbies have called the other street, just to the west, the

'Frying Pan,' because it leads to a circular drive around a small sylvan park surrounded by a rustic wooden fence. The street looks like a frying pan.

The Frying Pan always has a London bobby casually standing at the entrance on Kensington Road, because several of the greatest families in England, including Mark's, make their London homes there.

It was to 16 Hyde Park Gate that Mark took me after I landed at Heathrow.

We were met at the door by a slender, middle-aged lady who said, "Miss Hodgkin. I've heard so much about you from Mark. I'm Myrtle Hanson. Mark, bring Miss Hodgkin's luggage upstairs. I'm putting her in the second rear bedroom."

The three of us climbed a magnificent curved staircase with a wrought-iron balustrade with the initial 'T' worked into the intricate design.

"Here you are," Miss Hanson said. "I thought you'd be comfortable here because this bedroom has its own bath and a nice view of the rear gardens."

We were in a large, airy room with two tall windows. Mark dropped two of my bags and went back downstairs for the third.

"When I first came through the front door, I thought you were Lady Thakeham."

Miss Hanson laughed but in a friendly way. "I was the nursery nurse for Mark from the time he was born and then the same for Catherine. Now I'm the housekeeper."

Mark returned with my third bag, dropped it, and dropped himself into a side chair in the bedroom.

Miss Hanson said, "Mark, your services are no longer required here. Miss Hodgkin has had a long flight and needs to rest before lunch."

He started to say something, but Miss Hanson cut him off. "Goodbye, Mark."

Mark gave me a rueful smile and left the room. I gathered Miss Hanson was more than a housekeeper.

Miss Hanson said, "Young Janet works for me, and she'll be here in a minute with a pot of tea for you. Then she'll unpack your bags and put away your clothes. You should wash your face and stretch out on the bed for some rest. Janet won't bother you. If you're tired, you may have lunch here in your room whenever you want, or Mark will be having lunch downstairs in an hour or so. Suit yourself."

She walked over to the side of the large bed and pointed to two small buttons on a brass plate set into the wall. The brass was highly polished.

"There used to be markings to show which button was which, but the markings wore away with the polishing before I got here."

I had the impression that, if Miss Hanson had been around then, the polishing would have been done more carefully.

She went on. "So, you just have to remember. The button on the left brings Janet until about nine o'clock in the evening. On Thursdays, her day off, it will be one of my other girls. The button on the right brings me, any time of day or night."

"I'm sure I won't call. I won't need anything."

"How old are you?"

"I'm 18. I'll be 19 on July 1."

Miss Hanson smiled. "You're a long way from your parents. Don't hesitate to call me." She left.

I learned later that, when Miss Hanson was 18, she had placed an advert in the magazine *The Lady*, seeking a position as a nursery nurse. She was engaged by Lady Thakeham, who was then expecting Mark. During the war, Miss Hanson worked in the dairy at Thakeham House, with Mark toddling along after her. Now, she managed both 16 Hyde Park Gate and Thakeham House, including the dairy, which, over the years, she had built into a large and profitable business for the family. Miss Hanson was regularly brought in by Doctor Thakeham to consult on the family's financial affairs – unlike Lady Thakeham, who was consulted only on the new wallpaper for the front hall.

Mark told me that once at Harrow he had been struggling a bit with mathematics, no doubt because of the competing demands of cricket. Miss Hanson taught herself basic calculus in a week and then began taking the Tube to the Harrow-on-the-Hill stop each weekday afternoon for a month. She would meet Mark in a tea shop, where she drilled him on equations for an hour. Mark no longer struggled in math.

I put my head on the pillow and was quickly asleep. I didn't even hear Janet unpacking my bags. I slept for two hours.

I met Lady Thakeham that afternoon at tea, which was in a long, narrow conservatory that extended out from the house into the rear garden. There were glass doors on each side that opened onto the garden. With the doors opened, I felt that we were practically outside, but with protection from the rain and the (occasional) sun.

Mark leaned over his mother and playfully kissed her on top of her exquisitely coiffed hair.

"Mark, please don't. You'll muss my hair."

Then she turned to me. "You must be Miss Hodgkin, child. Thomas Hodgkin's daughter. How kind of you to visit us from Bermuda." She said 'Bermuda' in the way that some people might say 'Antarctica.'

I was wary of her from the start. I said, "My parents and I appreciate your invitation to me."

"We are pleased to have you. And thank you for your kind letter to me about your plans for tennis."

Mark said, "Fiona's plans for tennis? We're going to Wimbledon for an afternoon the first week of the fortnight. Do we have tickets? Should I ring the Club?"

"Miss Hodgkin plans to play tennis for a day while she is with us. She wrote me a nice letter with all the details."

I hadn't written to Mark about Roehampton, mainly because he had been quite stingy in writing to me. So I had reciprocated. Now I thought that perhaps I should have prepared him in advance.

I hesitated. "Well, it may be for a day or possibly a few days."

Lady Thakeham, I sensed, knew that she had an opportunity to trap me, and she took it. "Miss Hodgkin, dear, where is it again you've been invited to play one afternoon?"

"The Bank of England Sports Grounds at Roehampton."

Mark was tucking into a crumpet when I said this, and he choked slightly. "Roehampton? You've been invited to play at Roehampton?"

Lady Thakeham smiled icily.

Mark managed to control his choking. "Fiona, did you say you're going to play at Roehampton?"

"Yes, I did."

"You mean the qualifying round for Wimbledon?"

"Yes."

"You're not serious," he said with a laugh.

"Mark," I said, maybe a little sharply, "I don't care for your tone. The Committee invited me to play at Roehampton. I wrote your mother about the invitation. I'm going to play the first round, and we'll see what we see."

"You could not possibly both compete at Roehampton and attend the season."

Lady Thakeham beamed.

"Claire Kershaw did."

"How do you know?"

"She told me."

"You know Kershaw?"

I was a mere colonial from Antarctica – excuse me, Bermuda – but I'd had enough. "Mark," I said stiffly, "I know Claire quite well." Perhaps this was stretching things a bit. "She was kind enough to find me a place in the qualifying round at Roehampton. I told Lady Thakeham in my letter that Roehampton would in no way interfere with my social obligations during the season. I was entirely sincere."

Again, stretching things a bit.

Mark was about to say something, but Lady Thakeham stopped him. "That's all settled, then," she said. "We should discuss our social obligations this week." She pulled open her datebook.

"Tomorrow, the Wilsons have invited Miss Hodgkin and

Catherine for tea" – the Wilsons were my cousins – "and that evening is the party for Marjorie Boynton at the Savoy. Wednesday, Catherine is giving a luncheon at Simpsons in the Strand for Miss Hodgkin, and then, my dear, that afternoon you have invited 12 young ladies here for tea. Don't be concerned, I've already arranged the details and sent invitations to your guests. That evening dinner is with the Ralstons, we'll return home to dress for the party for Alice Herbert, but I've promised Catherine that we will leave by one in the morning and have breakfast at the party for Harriet Rutherford – Lady Thornton asked Catherine if we could come. Thursday, lunch is at Claridge's with the Alstons, then tea with Mary Matthews, dinner with Lord Hawthorn at the Inner Temple, home to dress, then a dance at Grosvenor House for Hope McAllister. Friday, my dear, you and Catherine have invited 15 young ladies to an informal lunch here, then tea is with Anne Gofford and her parents. We're invited to dinner at White's by Lord Wilberforce, Princess Margaret will be there, so you'll want to dress especially well, and then there will be Mary Sanford's party, but we'll leave by midnight or so to have an early breakfast with Lady Crawford and her daughters."

I was stunned. Maybe Mark was onto something when he said I couldn't both attend the season and play at Roehampton. "Should I be writing this down?"

"No, dear child, there's no need. I will see that Harold takes you and Catherine to everything." I had no idea who 'Harold' might be. Lady Thakeham smiled, closed her datebook, excused herself, and swept from the room.

Mark was chuckling. "I told you."

"Maybe it's busy just this week."

"Next week is *worse.*"

Miss Hanson came into the conservatory. "There is a telegram for Miss Hodgkin."

Mark looked at me quizzically. I opened the telegram:

POST OFFICE TELEGRAM

RECEIVED LONG LETTER RACHEL TELLING ME
EXACTLY HOW TO PREPARE YOU FOR ROEHAMPTON
STOP SHE APPEARS TO THINK I KNOW NOTHING ABOUT
TENNIS STOP WE HAVE A LOT OF WORK TO DO STOP
MEET ROEHAMPTON 11 TUESDAY MORNING STOP

CLAIRE

Mark held out his hand for the telegram. This was rude of him, but I obediently handed it over.

"So you do know Claire Kershaw. How does Kershaw come to know Rachel?"

"Rachel was her coach back in the late 1940s. They're friends."

Mark didn't say anything. He simply held the telegram in his fingers.

Finally, I said, "Mark, tomorrow I'll need to spend some time practicing with Claire."

"I can't be with you next week for the qualifying round," Claire said. "Eastbourne invited me to play there next week and sent along a nice packet for my expenses. So you'll be on your own."

We were standing in the Secretary's old, cluttered office in the clubhouse at Roehampton while credentials were checked, green eyeshades adjusted, papers stapled, applications stamped, notices issued, and procedures followed.

If Claire hadn't been with me, none of the Roehampton staff would have believed that I was actually on the Committee's list of players invited to compete in the qualifying round. But Claire navigated the system for me, and I finally received an impressive pass with the word PLAYER splashed across it in red ink. With this pass hanging around my neck, I could come and go at Roehampton as I pleased, get tea at no charge, and even try to schedule practice time on the courts.

Practice time wasn't a problem as long as I was with Claire. She politely asked the referee, Mr Soames, if she and I might have the use of a court for three hours or so. "Certainly, Mrs Kershaw. Which court would you prefer?" Two

Wimbledon singles championships carry definite privileges in the world of tennis.

When I first practiced with Claire, it was immediately apparent that she'd been coached by Rachel. Claire knocked up for 10 minutes and then threw her racket out onto the grass. "Rough or smooth?" she asked. Just like Rachel, she thought the best practice was to play a match.

On a changeover in our second set, I drank a cup of water with Claire beside me. She said quietly, "In my service game just now, at 30-15, just before I tossed the ball for my serve, you looked up at two people walking on the path from the clubhouse.

I couldn't recall. "Did I?"

"Yes. I won the point. And the game."

"Well, if I looked away, it was just a quick glance."

"You won't win, at least not at Roehampton, if you let your mind wander during a point, even for a half-second. Pull a curtain around the court in your mind so that it's just you and the other girl. If Rachel were here, you might glance at her, quickly, just for reassurance. But she won't be here. You'll be by yourself."

I was a bit shaken by Claire's lecture.

When we finally finished practicing, we walked back to the Roehampton clubhouse. Claire asked, "How's the season going? Found a potential husband yet?"

"My first party is tonight, but Lady Thakeham read me my schedule yesterday at tea, and I can't believe it. I don't have clothes for half the parties I'm attending this week, much less next week. How did you manage both the season and qualifying at Roehampton?"

Claire laughed. "It wasn't easy. But I had only my own

mother to deal with, and I didn't have a boyfriend. Well, maybe I did, but not someone I cared about. So it was easier for me. Are you buying new clothes?"

"Before I left home, Mother told me to go to shopping in London and buy an evening gown. I asked her for a budget, and she said, 'Use your judgment, but don't spend too much.' Which isn't helpful. How much does a gown cost?"

"Between £2 on Saturday morning in Portobello Road and £2,000 any day in New Bond Street. Somewhere in that range."

"That's about as helpful as what Mother told me. Where should I go to buy a gown?"

"Let's go shopping together, tomorrow. We'll practice early and then look for a gown. You should find one that will make people talk about you."

"I don't want people to talk about me."

"But that's the whole point of the season."

"We'll start with Teddy," Claire said. "He doesn't design many evening gowns now, but let's see what he might have on offer for you."

"Who's Teddy?"

"Teddy Tinling. In the 1930s, a girl couldn't go to the season without at least a couple of Tinling gowns in her closet. After the war, Teddy mostly gave up on gowns because of the utility restrictions on clothes. He started designing tennis kit instead."

Claire was driving her white Alfa Romeo roadster with the hood down. She suddenly swerved to avoid hitting a young man who was crossing Ken High. Claire turned halfway around in the driver's seat and blew him a kiss as we roared down the busy street at about 120 kph.

"Maureen Connolly asked Teddy to make her wedding dress when she finally married Norman, and I did the same when I married Richard. But his main line now is tennis dresses."

She changed down to third gear as we whipped around the Wellington Arch and shot into Piccadilly. Claire's favorite speed in the Alfa was as fast as it could go.

I was desperately hanging onto a leather strap on the door. "Who in heaven taught you to drive? Or did you just teach yourself?"

"My brother taught me. He taught himself. He bumped into a few things at first, but then he got the hang of it. Now he races autos in his spare time."

Just off Berkeley Square in Mayfair, she found a tiny parking spot and wedged in the Alfa. Then she led me to a narrow townhouse, where she didn't bother knocking on the door. She walked in and called, "Teddy, it's me."

I gathered from this entrance that Claire was well known in the Tinling establishment.

From the back of the shop stepped the tallest person I'd ever seen. I guessed he was in his early 50s. His head was shaved entirely bald, and he was wearing a yellow shirt with an open collar, trousers with vertical mauve and white stripes, and white patent leather shoes. The effect was dizzying.

He and Claire embraced and kissed one another. He said, "Claire, *ma chérie*, you remind me so much of Suzanne. We should take *Le Train Bleu* to Cannes tonight. Together. Alone. The two of us."

Claire linked her arm with his. "I don't remind you of Suzanne in the slightest, but Cannes might be interesting. After Wimbledon perhaps. Now I need you to find a gown for my friend from Bermuda."

"Suzanne?" I asked, brightly.

Tinling glanced at Claire with one eyebrow raised.

Claire said, "My friend is young. But nice. Once you get to know her."

Tinling was skeptical.

"Teddy, please meet Miss Fiona Hodgkin. She's going to

play at Roehampton. You remember Rachel Outerbridge, Teddy."

Tinling nodded.

"Rachel coaches this girl."

This, I could tell, moved me up several notches in Tinling's estimation.

Claire turned to me. "Fiona, this is Lieutenant-Colonel Cuthbert Collingwood Tinling. Known to his friends, with one exception, as 'Teddy.'"

Teddy bowed slightly to me.

"The exception," Claire said dryly, "is Bud Collins, who calls Teddy 'The Leaning Tower of Pizazz.'"

I held out my hand to Teddy, but instead of shaking hands, he leaned forward and kissed my hand. "My dear Fiona, how delightful to meet you," he murmured.

Claire pointed to an old photo that hung on the wall. "Teddy is taller than even Bill Tilden was, and he's got a photo to prove it."

The photo showed a young Teddy, with a full head of slicked-down hair, beside Bill Tilden, who was wearing a trench coat and holding two rackets. Teddy was slightly the taller of the two.

"The verdict," Teddy said, "Tilden 1.8 meters; Tinling 1.9 meters. Actually, I think the measurement of me was wrong. I'm two meters. Claire, I must show you what I've made for Maria Bueno."

With a flourish, Teddy picked up from a cutting table a white tennis dress. The skirt had a pink lining so bright anyone who saw it would feel faint.

"I call this 'Italian Pink,'" Teddy said.

"Teddy, Maria's dress is lovely, but have you lost your

mind? If that dress makes an appearance on Centre Court, the Committee will have your head mounted on the Doherty Gates, as a warning to others."

"You've yet to see the matching panties."

"Don't show them to me. I want to be able to tell the Committee truthfully that I knew nothing about the panties."

"There's nothing in the rules or on the entry form that prohibits colour on ladies' tennis dresses."

"What about the sign in the ladies' upper dressing room?"

"It's gone. I took it down last week." He fished around in the fabric scraps on the table and finally held up a small, faded handwritten sign: '*Competitors are Expected to Wear White Clothing.*'

I asked, "How could you take down a sign that was in a ladies' dressing room?"

Claire explained. "Kay Menzies always wore Teddy's dresses, but one afternoon she couldn't get her zipper up. Mrs Ward tried but couldn't get it up either."

"Who's Mrs Ward?"

Teddy said, "She's the attendant for the upper dressing room. Been there since Worple Road, probably."

"So Teddy was in the hallway, banging on the door and yelling for Kay to get onto Centre Court. Finally, Teddy barges through the door, gets Kay's zipper up in one second, and hustles her out to the waiting room."

I looked at Teddy in shock. "You went into the ladies' dressing room?"

Teddy made an elaborate courtier's bow, with his incredibly long arms outstretched.

Claire said, "Maybe a couple of girls had to wrap towels around themselves. But the world didn't come to an end.

Since then, Teddy comes and goes as he pleases. He doesn't even knock. He makes all the tennis kit, so it's convenient to have him around."

I picked up the handwritten sign that Teddy had taken from the dressing room. "Why was there a sign like this in the first place?"

It must be hard to look sheepish when you're two meters tall, but Teddy did.

Claire said, "The sign was thumbtacked to the wall in 1949. Just before *l'affaire* Gussy Moran."

"But it had nothing to do with Gussy," Teddy objected.

"I know. It was the pink and blue hems you sewed on the dresses for Joy Gannon and Betty Hilton in '48."

Claire turned to me. "The Committee think they've fixed the 'Tinling Problem' with the sign in the dressing room when BOOM!" Claire flung her hands out to mimic an explosion. "Gussy Moran appears at Hurlingham the day before Wimbledon wearing panties on which Teddy had sewn lace around the bottom."

"Did anyone notice?" I asked.

They both looked at me as though I had just arrived from Mars.

"Everyone noticed," Claire said. "Including the photographers from *Life* magazine, who were all on their stomachs trying to get photos of the panties. The newspapers issued special editions on sightings of the lace panties. Teddy, what was it Louis Greig said about all this?"

"Sir Louis told the newspapers, 'Wimbledon needs no panties for its popularity.'"

"Sir Louis?" I asked.

"At the time," Teddy said, "Sir Louis was the Chairman

of the All England Club. I regret to say he has since gone to his reward in heaven, where I have it on good authority all white attire is required."

Minutes later, I found myself in only my knickers, standing in the middle of the room. I had my arms wrapped resolutely around my small bust. Teddy, Claire, and Mrs Hogan, Teddy's long time assistant, were unconcerned by my obvious embarrassment at being practically naked in front of them.

Teddy gave Claire a look that I could tell meant, 'Where did you find this girl?'

"Fiona," Claire said. "Please. Drop your arms. Teddy needs to fit a gown for you. In the unlikely event Teddy is overcome by lust, Mrs Hogan and I will protect you."

Reluctantly, I dropped my arms, and the three of them regarded my boyish figure.

Teddy said, "This young lady needs a gown cut with considerable décolletage."

Claire, who is well endowed in the bust department, was dubious. "Teddy, are you sure? Fiona doesn't have much décolletage to work with."

"Perhaps, but this girl reminds me of what Billy Wilder – Claire, you know, the movie director – said about Audrey Hepburn when he first met her."

"What was that?"

"'This girl, singlehanded, may make bosoms a thing of the past.'"

All three of them chuckled. I snapped my arms back around my chest.

At Teddy's direction, Mrs Hogan disappeared into the back of the shop and returned with a black, strapless, floor-length gown, which the three of them pulled over my head. Teddy and Mrs Hogan began sticking pins into the gown and occasionally, by accident, into me, while they fitted the gown.

They led me over to a floor length mirror. The gown was about five times more sophisticated and revealing than any dress I'd ever worn, and about 10 times more expensive. If the goal was to make people talk about me, this gown would make that happen. I instantly loved the gown.

After I wrote Teddy a bank draft on Butterfield's for an outrageous amount of money, Claire drove me back to Hyde Park Gate.

"You and Teddy were talking about Suzanne. Does she work for Teddy?"

Claire made a racing change and swung into Kensington Road. "Teddy meant Suzanne Lenglen. She won Wimbledon six times. Five times in a row, 1919 to 1923. She had jaundice in 1924, but she won again in 1925."

Claire narrowly missed swiping a bus.

"In 1919, Suzanne appeared on the old Centre Court on Worple Road in a short dress – and get this! – no corset."

"Well," I said, "she certainly couldn't play tennis wearing a corset."

"Think again. Suzanne was the first girl to play on Centre Court without wearing a corset. It was so shocking and immoral that everyone had to come watch her!" Claire laughed. "The Committee were scandalized, but they decided to build a bigger Centre Court on Church Road so more paying spectators could come see Suzanne."

Claire slowed slightly so I could wave to the bobby at the entrance to Hyde Park Gate to let him know I belonged there. "Bunny Ryan was Suzanne's doubles partner. They won the last match ever played on the old Centre Court. The BBC interviewed Bunny a month or so ago, and Bunny said every English tennis girl should kneel down and thank Suzanne for getting rid of corsets!"

"Did Teddy know Suzanne?"

Claire started to say something but then stopped. I wasn't a member of the informal Wimbledon family. Maybe I would be in a few years but not now. Not yet.

"Yes, Teddy knew Suzanne. Quite well."

That night, Harold drove Mark and me back from Miss Rutherford's breakfast after two in the morning. My Tinling gown wouldn't be ready for several days, but in any event I had half decided to save it for Catherine's party, which would be the Wednesday during the first week of Wimbledon. So I wore a party dress that dated from my days as a Bermuda teenage schoolgirl.

Until that evening, I had no idea that my parents were well known, and well liked, in London. Several couples I met said, "You're the daughter of Fiona and Tom, aren't you? It's wonderful to have you in London. You must come for tea next Tuesday." And they seemed sincere. Mark and I danced together, and I was quite aware that there were many girls watching who were envious of me.

Still, even at two in the morning, Mark felt that we had left breakfast a bit early, and I had been the one to suggest we say our goodbyes. I was tired. Mark was in the middle of a hospital rotation in London, but in those days medical school rotations, at least in England, and especially during the season, were relaxed affairs, not at all the frenetic, 18-hour-a-day marathons that they became just in time for me to start my own medical rotations.

If it didn't rain, I was meeting Claire at Roehampton to practice at 11 the next morning, or rather *that* morning, and I wanted to go straight to sleep. I had learned that practice with Claire was so exhausting that it made practice with Rachel seem like time spent reading a mystery novel at the beach. Claire was *serious*.

But I sensed my boyfriend was unhappy with me, and so I sat him down on a sofa in Dr. Thakeham's study and gave him the type of kiss that I hoped would make him feel better. It did, but it also made him feel that the idea of me going straight to sleep was premature.

"We should spend some time alone," Mark said. It was true that, since I had arrived, most of my time had been spent on tennis, and when Mark and I were together, we had been in the company of other people.

"Yes, definitely," I said. "But not tonight. I'm tired, and I'm meeting Claire at Roehampton in the morning."

"Fiona, is this friendship you have with Kershaw a bit too much of a good thing, do you think?"

I was taken aback by this. I had known Claire only a short time – two months, perhaps. She was older than me by almost eight years. I didn't think of her as my 'friend.' I was thrilled even to know her. I hadn't thought of it before Mark asked, but I suppose I had assumed that Claire was looking after me merely because Rachel had asked her to do so.

"I can't imagine that it's too much of a good thing. Claire's been very helpful to me. Rachel thinks highly of Claire."

Mark was astute enough to know that Rachel's endorsement was, for me, the final word on the subject.

"It just seems that tennis and Claire Kershaw have taken over your visit to London."

He was right about that. I leaned over and gave him another kiss. "Mark, my tennis this year is just a trial run. Some day, I hope to play at Wimbledon – and I hope you'll be there to watch. Let me have some fun at tennis this year, and I promise I'll be a good girlfriend for you."

He kissed me and put his hand on my breast.

I laughed and kissed him back. "Within reasonable limits."

"Fiona, everyone here is sound asleep. Let's go upstairs to my room, or the room you're staying in, and make love."

"Mark, I'm only 18 – "

"Almost 19," he said.

"Almost 19," I agreed.

"Fiona, I will take good care of you. I promise," Mark said.

"Mark, I know you would take care of me, but making love would be a big step, and I'm not ready to take it. At least, not tonight."

To give the devil his due, Mark took this in good spirit. He stood up and held out his hands. I put my hands in his, and he pulled me gently up from the sofa. I was so tired that I appreciated his help. And we went off to bed – separately.

In retrospect, I know I wasn't fair to Mark. I should have been straightforward with him, but I wasn't. I should have said, 'Look, Mark, I'm going to qualify for Wimbledon this week. I don't care what it takes – season or no season. Whatever it takes. Incidentally, I promised Mother I wouldn't sleep with you while I'm in London.'

The question in my mind now is, if I had been straightforward, and I had told Mark exactly the truth, would my life have turned out any differently?

For all my bold talk to myself about getting through the qualifying rounds, on the first morning of Roehampton, I was nervous and uncertain. My first match was scheduled for noon, but I learned that, at Roehampton, with so many matches to complete in only four days, and with London's usual rainy June weather – well, the 'schedule' was just a guess at which matches would be played, on which court, and when.

So, after delays, and rain, and mix-ups about courts, my first match in international competition started, not at noon, but after six that evening on a grass court that even the chair umpire said, charitably, was "damp."

Mark was at Roehampton to encourage me, but I knew that evening was a party at White's for his cousin, Jennifer Pemberton. I didn't have to be told that, for Mark, this was a party at which he absolutely had to appear. If my first round match finished in an hour, we could get to Hyde Park Gate, dress, and still arrive at Jennifer's party fashionably late.

My first round opponent was a Polish girl, Anastazja Banaszynski. In the dressing room, for six long hours, she tried to be friendly to me, but she spoke little English, and my Polish was non-existent. But I admired her. I kept thinking, 'How much courage must it take to come to England, without speaking the language well, I'm sure with almost no money, and from a Communist country, to play in the qualifying round?'

Anastazja had qualified for Wimbledon the year before at Roehampton, and I'm sure she was disappointed to have to try and qualify again. She had lost in the first round of Wimbledon in 1961. If she had been trounced by Claire on Ladies' Day on Centre Court, that would have been one thing. (Claire, in fact, had never played her.) But Anastazja had lost, in straight sets, on one of the outer courts to another unknown player.

The Committee had not invited her into the draw for 1962, but they had offered her another chance to qualify at Roehampton. Now I watched her in the dressing room. She weighed at least half again as much as me, and she was far stronger. But I guessed – correctly, as it turned out – that she could not match me in speed. I expected she could hit the ball incredibly hard, but, if I could get it back, and away from her, she wouldn't be dashing around the court and hitting a return. The court, though, with the weather we'd had that day, would be slippery – not good for me.

You cannot imagine the relief associated with the call at long, long last: "Miss Banaszynski, Miss Hodgkin, you're wanted on court, please." We walked together past the long line of 12 grass courts; we were to play on the far court. We knocked up, and then I tossed my racket down on the grass. Anastazja called 'rough' and won. She didn't know the difference in English between 'rough' and 'smooth,' but she had memorized the word 'rough.' When she called the toss in England, she always called 'rough.'

Anastazja served first. It went straight past me; her serve was unbelievably fast. I crossed to my ad court and set up again to receive. She served. I got my racket on it but just barely. The ball hit the rim of my racket and went wildly wide into the next court, where it disrupted play and forced the women there to play a let – in a match that, I'm sure, meant everything to each of them. This was the lowest form of poor play; I knew everyone was looking at me and thinking, 'What's this teenager from nowhere doing at Roehampton?' I went back to the deuce court. I was asking myself whether I should be at Roehampton.

Anastazja won the first game at love. I couldn't remember the last time I had lost a game at love. Then I served for the first time. Anastazja had a problem with my serve as well; she couldn't tell where I was going to place it, and even when she was able to return my serve, I was already at the net to cut off her return. She wasn't fast enough to get to my volley, most times.

With the games in the first set at 8-9, on my serve, the rain started. It was already close to eight o'clock. "Play is suspended," the umpire called while he was heaving his considerable bulk out of the chair. The courts at Roehampton had no tarps to cover them. The rain fell straight onto the grass. I rushed for cover and found Mark. He kissed me in front of half the tennis world – and I kissed him back.

At least I had a boyfriend.

Anastazja had seen me kiss Mark. Once we were in the dressing room, and drying off, she said, "You – " Then she stopped, trying to think of the English word. She pointed to the door of the dressing room.

"You mean my boyfriend?"

She smiled. "Yes. Boyfriend. He – " She stopped. She couldn't think of the word, but she made an 'OK' sign by touching her right thumb to the tip of her index finger.

I tried to think what she meant. "Good? Good looking?"

"Yes! Boyfriend good looking."

I laughed and put my arms around her. For the next hour, we did our best to talk to one another, and, despite our language difficulties, we became friends. Then Mr Soames knocked on the dressing room door. "We're resuming play, girls. Five minutes."

When I walked back out onto the court, I couldn't believe he had decided to resume play. The rain had stopped, but the grass was soaked. Maybe 20 minutes of daylight remained. At the rate Anastazja and I were going, we wouldn't even finish the first set before dark. To cap things off, the temperature had dropped. It was chilly, and I reached in my kit, took out Rachel's sweater, and pulled it over my head.

The umpire called out, "First set. Miss Hodgkin to serve. The games are 8-9. The score is 15 all. Resume play."

So there was nothing for it but to set up and serve.

A few minutes later, Anastazja had taken the first set and had broken my serve in the second set. I had fallen to pieces. I was saved only by the umpire, who, finally, suspended play for darkness. I thought it was easily five minutes past the time the daylight had become too weak to permit play to continue. Then the rain started again.

I picked up my kit, my rackets, and my pocketbook and shuffled toward the clubhouse. Once inside, I stood off to the side, shivering. I did not feel well. Rachel's sweater was cotton, and now that it was damp, it did little to keep me warm.

I missed Claire, I missed Rachel, I missed Bermuda, and above all, I missed my parents. Mark was nowhere to be seen. What in heaven was I doing here?

Mr Soames was standing, holding a clipboard, in the middle of a clump of players, each of whom wanted to know when her match would resume on Tuesday? On which court? Would there be practice time Tuesday morning? He was unperturbed, and I had the impression that this wasn't the first time he'd faced a group of anxious tennis players.

Once the crowd dispersed, Mr Soames turned in my direction and walked over to me. "It's Fiona Hodgkin, isn't it? Are you all right?"

I tried to stop shivering but couldn't. "I'm fine." I was nearly in tears, and I must have looked like a drowned mouse.

Mr Soames glanced at his clipboard. "You're from Bermuda. Where are you staying in London?"

"In Hyde Park Gate. With friends of my family."

"How are you getting to their home tonight?"

"The Upper Richmond bus to East Putney and then the Tube."

It was a walk of a kilometer up Priory Lane to Upper Richmond Street, in the rain.

Mr Soames called, "Mr Raymond!"

One of the tournament stewards appeared at Mr Soames' elbow.

"Mr Raymond, this is Miss Hodgkin. Please arrange for her to be driven to Hyde Park Gate, now."

"Yes, sir," the steward replied.

"Miss Hodgkin, Mr Raymond will arrange for you to be collected by auto in the morning. We'll need you here by noon, so perhaps the auto should come for you by 11."

I thanked him – gratefully – and walked away with Mr Raymond.

I let myself into 16 Hyde Park Gate, walked into the study, and flopped down in an armchair. I leaned forward and put my head in my hands.

There was no way I could defeat Anastazja.

Harold had heard the door open, and he came into the study. "Miss Hodgkin, young Mark apologizes to you, but he has already left for Miss Pemberton's party. He asked that I drive you to White's as soon as you dress."

"Harold, I'm not feeling well."

"Doctor Thakeham is at Miss Pemberton's party – should I call him home to see you?"

"Harold, thank you. There's no need to bother Doctor Thakeham."

"May I make you a cup of tea?"

"Yes please. That would be kind of you."

Harold left the study. I started sobbing.

The Thakehams had only a single telephone, which was in the first floor pantry. I heard the telephone ring in the distance.

Harold returned. "Miss, the telephone rang for you."

I walked back to the pantry, still crying, and picked up the receiver.

"What happened today?" It was Claire, who didn't bother with saying hello. "The BBC said you're down a set."

"I can't win." I bit my lower lip in an effort to stop crying.

"Complete twaddle. Pull yourself together. Certainly you can win, and you will. Did you play any of the second set? The BBC didn't say."

"Yes. She broke me. Then play was suspended."

I sensed that even Claire was concerned by this news. But

she said, "Don't worry about it. Eat something and then go to bed. Then get the break back tomorrow and win."

"Harold says I'm supposed to go to a party."

"Who is Harold? Don't tell me you've met *another* boy."

"Harold is – " I hesitated. It dawned on me that I had no idea what Harold's position was in the Thakeham household.

Harold had come into the pantry with my cup of tea and overheard me. "I'm Doctor Thakeham's gentleman."

"Harold is Doctor Thakeham's gentleman," I told Claire.

"Fiona, you're at Roehampton, damn it, you're not a character in a P.G. Wodehouse novel. You're not going to a party tonight. Hit the ball where she isn't. Just do that 30 times, and you've won. A break is nothing. Play your own game, and she can't beat you."

I felt better after talking with Claire.

Harold's response to any problem, including a weeping female houseguest, was to call for Miss Hanson. She appeared, wearing a worn, blue bathrobe. Miss Hanson took one look at me and turned to Harold. "Miss Hodgkin is not going out tonight, Harold. You may as well go to White's now and wait there for Doctor and Lady Thakeham."

Miss Hanson took me by the hand and led me into the kitchen, where I'd never been. "Sit down at table. I'll make you a sandwich, and then I'll draw your bath. I want you asleep in your bed in half an hour."

I was alone at breakfast Tuesday morning. Mark either was still asleep or else he had already left for hospital. In any event, he didn't appear at breakfast. A young lady served me tea, toast, and a boiled egg, and Harold brought me the morning papers. At exactly 11, an auto from Roehampton was in front of 16 Hyde Park Gate.

The weather on Tuesday was still overcast, but it wasn't raining, and it didn't seem as though rain was imminent. It was warmer. Rachel's sweater stayed in my kit. When Anastazja and I knocked up at noon, the grass was nearly dry and less slippery than the evening before.

The umpire called the score: "The sets are 1-love in favor of Miss Banaszynski. Second set. Miss Banaszynski to serve. The games are 2-love. Play."

It wasn't even close. My volleys began to click, and Anastazja couldn't reach them; I just volleyed to where she wasn't. I took her break back early in the second set and then I broke her again. I won the second set easily. In the third set, Anastazja faded. I started taking even more chances at the net, and most of the time my gambles paid off.

There was no room between the courts for spectators, and there were hedges behind the fences at either end of the court. The only place for spectators was a grassy bank at the other end of the row of courts, closer to the clubhouse. I doubt anyone other than the umpire could see my match with Anastazja.

I took the third set. The umpire called, "8-10, 6-4, 6-3, Miss Hodgkin wins game, set, and match."

Anastazja was already at the net when I ran forward. I extended my hand but then saw she was on the verge of tears. I leaned over the net and hugged her. She put her head on my shoulder and began to sob.

I returned to Hyde Park Gate in time for tea, which was attended by 20 or so young ladies. The only ones I had met before were Catherine and two of my cousins on the Spencer side of my family. Several of the guests distinctly reminded me of Madeline Bassett, a humorous character in the P.G. Wodehouse 'Jeeves' novels.

I was in the second round at Roehampton.

Harold drove Mark and me to Brown's in the Bentley. Catherine and Lady Thakeham were going to another party, and Harold would return to Hyde Park Gate to collect them after he left us at Brown's. Mark was polite but distant.

I was thinking only of my second round match. When we had left home, the BBC was reporting that the two girls in my bracket were still battling it out on a court at Roehampton, even though it was almost dark. I would play the winner in the second round. Defeating Anastazja had given me a much-needed boost of confidence, but still I was so nervous about the second round that I was almost wringing my hands.

I knew how Claire would deal with the uncertainty. She would ignore it. 'There's nothing for you to do about it,' Claire would say. 'So why worry?' I tried not to worry but couldn't help it.

As Harold pulled the Bentley to a stop at Brown's, I worked at pulling myself together for my cousin's party. My dress was a long, pale green gown that had last seen service at a dinner dance at the Mid-Ocean Club years ago. I was certain Mother would receive letters from my relatives giving detailed, and critical, accounts of my dress and, most important, whether I had been seen talking with – or, better yet, dancing with – any good husband candidates. Harold came back and opened the door on my side, and I stepped out. Mark was already out of the Bentley, and he took my arm.

Mark was wearing white tie, and he looked dashing. We swept into Brown's side by side.

I was getting used to the routine of a party during the season. First, there were cocktails, conversation, and paying respects to the hosts. Then dancing. Finally, breakfast, always well past midnight. After breakfast, many of the young people would pile into autos and go off to a nightclub or café to finish the evening.

This schedule was a contrast with Bermuda, where the island is usually closed, locked, and asleep by 11 o'clock at the latest – *maybe* midnight during Cup Match, the two-day cricket meet each July between Somerset Parish and St. George's Parish, which originated as a celebration of the abolition of slavery in Bermuda. During Cup Match, everyone wears the colours of one team or the other – red and navy for Somerset, pale blue and dark blue for St. George's – and gambles at Crown & Anchor, while the entire island throws a huge party.

I had been surprised that Mark did not know as many of the guests at the parties we had attended together as I had expected.

"Not my crowd, now," he said. "Too young. My friends are going down from university and beginning to find places in the City or the FO" – he meant the Foreign Office – "or somewhere else in Whitehall. Most of them have already found the girl they want. No reason for them to attend the season."

"So why haven't you found the girl you want?" I couldn't help asking.

He didn't rise to the bait. "Medicine. I'm still in university." The medical course of study at Cambridge was five years; Mark had one more year to complete before he began his internship.

"But," he went on, "there are the nurses."

I rolled my eyes. "I hope you're trying to be humorous and simply failing."

"Not at all. The nurses are wonderful people."

"I'm sure you've made the acquaintance of many of them."

We made our way to our hosts. When I had been 12 or so, my parents and I had spent a long weekend with the Spencers at their house in Devon. The house was so large that I had been given my own room – during the English Civil War, a small army of Cavaliers had been quartered in this house, apparently quite comfortably – but after Elizabeth and I had played in the garden for two hours on Friday afternoon, we had decided to move me into her bedroom. Together we had a delightful weekend, of the flashlights-under-the-covers variety. I hadn't seen Elizabeth again until I arrived in London for the season, but we had exchanged Christmas cards for years, and we liked one another.

I said hello to Elizabeth's parents – I couldn't begin to explain how we were related, except that it was through English Grandmother – and they asked after my parents. I introduced Mark, and I could tell my relatives were impressed that a young colonial – me – had snared such a prize.

Later, after the dancing started, I lost track of Mark for a few minutes, but I saw Elizabeth talking with a young lady, a bit older than us. She was an exotic creature, in a stunning gown, with a figure that made me feel as though I was a Boy Scout. Her hair was dark, and swept up, and her eyes were a shade of green I don't think I'd ever seen before. I went over to Elizabeth, who introduced us. Her name was Margarite. She was Spanish, but her English was fluent, with only a slight accent.

Elizabeth was called away by her mother, and Margarite turned to me. "I see you are escorted by Mark."

"Mark Thakeham, yes," I said. "You must know Mark?"

"We know one another at university."

"You were at Cambridge, then?"

"I am at Cambridge. I went down last year, but now I'm a fellow at Trinity."

Even I knew that going straight from being an undergraduate to a fellowship at Trinity College wasn't something that happened every day, or even every decade.

"Are you in medicine? Is that how you know Mark?"

Margarite smiled. "No, I'm not in medicine. I could never stand the messy parts. I'm in mathematics."

The only other mathematics fellow of Trinity I could recall was Isaac Newton. Good thing I hadn't mentioned to Margarite how relieved I was to be finished with freshman calculus at Smith.

Now Mark reappeared at my side. Neither he nor Margarite said hello to one another. Instead, Mark put his hands on her shoulders, and they kissed one another on both cheeks. She murmured something into his ear, and Mark chuckled. I imagined that she had told him something about me, probably something witty, in a Cantabrigian way.

It dawned on me that Margarite and Mark had been lovers – perhaps, for all I knew, they still were.

Mark asked me, "Have you been introduced?"

"Yes. Elizabeth introduced me to Margarite."

Margarite said, "You two should be dancing."

"No," I said. I had the sense that Margarite did not have an escort for the evening. "Mark, you should dance with Margarite."

Mark did not require further encouragement. He took Margarite's arm and led her onto the dance floor. Before I could ask myself whether it had been a good idea to push them into dancing with one another, a young man I didn't know approached me and, after the usual nonsense about not having been properly introduced, asked me to dance – and he turned out to be quite an accomplished dancing partner.

Suddenly, it was one o'clock in the morning, and I needed to get to sleep, even though breakfast wouldn't be served for another hour or so. I found Mark and suggested we say our goodbyes.

"We really should stay for breakfast."

"I need to get some sleep, in case I get to play my second round tomorrow."

He wasn't pleased by this, I could tell. I said, "Mark, would it be rude for me to take a taxi home? Then you could stay for a bit longer, and we could see one another in the morning." To coat this pill, I gave him a kiss.

"You don't need a taxi. I'm sure Harold is waiting for us. He'll take you home, and I'll find my own way." Mark, I thought, had agreed to the idea of my leaving on my own more readily than I had expected.

So Mark walked me out of Brown's and, as predicted, Harold was waiting at the curb with the Bentley. Mark kissed me, turned around, and headed back to Elizabeth's party. I got in the Bentley, and Harold pulled away into the London traffic.

"Harold, did you by any – " I started but then stopped. I shouldn't give the Thakeham household even more reason to think my only concern was Roehampton.

"Yes, Miss, I did," Harold said. "Those two girls finished their match this evening in three sets. Your opponent will be the American. I think her family name is Johnson."

On Wednesday, it poured rain all day, relentlessly, across London. Not a single tennis ball was hit at Roehampton. I spent most of the day in the dressing room, which was crowded with girls. We had to be there in case the rain stopped and, somehow, the courts dried quickly enough for matches to begin. I tried not to be too obvious in looking around for my opponent, but finally one of the other girls said to me, "If you're looking for Charlotte Johnson, don't bother. She'll not be here."

"But we all have to be here."

The girl shrugged. "Johnson's parents have taken a flat in Fulham, close by. They've employed a former Roehampton steward to alert them by telephone if she's going to be called. Johnson can be here in 10 minutes. That way she doesn't have to wait in the dressing room for her match."

"Have you played Johnson?"

"Once, outside San Francisco, a year or so ago. I won in straight sets. But Charlotte's strong and, I think, getting better. Her coach is Teach Tennant."

"Tennant must be quite elderly."

"I suppose. But all the American girls, at least the ones from California, seem to want her as a coach."

At four o'clock that afternoon, I went to find Mr Soames, the referee.

"Mr Soames, I have a family tea at five. If it appears we're not going to play any matches today, might I be released?"

"I was just about to release everyone. Even if it stopped raining now – which seems unlikely – the grass wouldn't be sufficiently dry for any play this evening. Certainly, Miss Hodgkin, leave for your family tea."

I thanked him and walked back toward the dressing room. Then he called to me, "Miss Hodgkin!"

"Yes, Mr Soames?"

He was looking at his clipboard intently. "We may have drier weather tomorrow, Miss Hodgkin. If so, I'll have you and Miss Johnson out first. So please plan to be here well before 11 in the morning."

"I'll be here."

"If you win your second round, Miss Hodgkin, and if the weather holds dry, I'll have to set your third round for tomorrow afternoon. I'll try to give you a couple of hours rest, but I can't promise it."

"I'll be ready."

"You've attracted the Committee's attention, Miss Hodgkin."

I was startled to hear this. "Have I done something wrong?"

"The contrary, Miss Hodgkin. You defeated Miss Banaszynski. And under difficult conditions. The Committee expected you to lose."

I started to say something, but he cut me off. "Have a

good evening, Miss Hodgkin. Get a good night's sleep. I may give you a long day tomorrow." He turned away.

Catherine, Lady Thakeham, and I returned from tea around seven that evening. Lady Thakeham said, "You young ladies should rest and then dress for dinner at the Savoy. I've asked Harold to bring the auto around a bit after nine." I knew a formal dinner probably wouldn't conclude until midnight, perhaps later, and there might be cocktails at a café after dinner.

Catherine went upstairs to her room, and Lady Thakeham went into the drawing room and began removing her gloves. I followed her.

"Lady Thakeham, may I have a word?"

"Certainly, dear child."

"It's about Roehampton, Lady Thakeham. If the weather is better tomorrow, my second round match will be early, perhaps before noon. And if I'm lucky enough to win, then I'll have to play my third round match in the afternoon."

"Well, child, we're to be at Rebecca Hurst's home at five tomorrow for tea."

I hadn't thought of that engagement. I said, "I'm sure my match would end well before tea." I had no idea if this was true. For all I knew, my third round – if I got into the third round – might not even start until after five. But that wasn't my immediate problem.

"Lady Thakeham, because my match may be early tomorrow, I'd prefer to go to sleep early this evening. Do you think I might be excused from dinner?"

She stiffened. "Miss Hodgkin, our hosts are expecting us. And, without you, Mark would have no partner for dinner."

"I know, and I regret so much having to ask, but it's terribly important for me to play well in the morning."

Lady Thakeham was icy. "Miss Hodgkin, Mark is your escort for dinner, not me. You should discuss this with him."

She dropped her gloves on a side table and left me without another word.

Mark came home from his hospital rotation that evening after eight o'clock, and I raised the issue of my missing dinner with him in the front hallway as he was taking off his short medical student's lab coat.

He was silent for a moment and then said coldly, "Fiona, you should do as you think best. It makes no difference to me, and I doubt anyone at dinner would notice your absence."

He started up the staircase. I put my hand on his arm to stop him. "Mark. That's mean, and I think it's unfair."

He gently removed my hand from his arm. "I have to dress for dinner. Excuse me."

He went up the stairs.

I waited a moment and then went up to my own room. I didn't go to the Savoy for dinner.

Later, there was a sharp rap on my door. It was Miss Hanson. "You're reduced to sharing dinner with me in the kitchen. I've put out cold steak and kidney pie. Come along, you can't play tennis on an empty stomach."

We talked for a long time at the kitchen table over the cold pie, and we began calling one another by our Christian names. She asked me all about my plans for medical school and wanted to know how my mother and grandmothers had become physicians. I told Myrtle American Grandmother's story about Mary Elizabeth Garrett and the admission of women to the Johns Hopkins School of Medicine 'on the same terms as men.' She seemed fascinated.

I had the impression that Myrtle might have become a physician herself if this had been even remotely thinkable for her as an English working class girl in the late 1930s. But it wasn't, and so she became first the nursery nurse and then the manager and counselor for a great Dutch-English family.

I was alone when I walked out on the court at Roehampton for the second round. No spectators, no boyfriend, no chair umpire, and no Charlotte Johnson. There were no benches to sit on, so I simply stood beside the court holding my pocketbook and rackets. At least it was a beautiful day; I bent down and put the back of my hand on the grass. Not dry, but just damp. In a half an hour or so, it would be dry.

Finally the chair umpire arrived. He had brought the tennis balls for our match, but he wouldn't let me practice my serve until my opponent arrived. I hadn't hit a tennis ball since Tuesday afternoon. The umpire seemed unconcerned that Johnson wasn't on the court.

After 10 minutes had passed, I asked him, "Does my opponent plan to appear, do you think?"

The umpire shrugged and didn't answer.

Finally, Charlotte Johnson arrived with her parents. She was dressed in a Teddy Tinling creation, a white dress with a pale red belt at the waist. The hem of the dress was quite short in order to show her knickers, which had alternating stripes of different shades of white and beige. I felt out of place in my plain tennis dress from Trimingham's on Front Street with the small Bermuda flag I had inexpertly sewn onto the breast.

Johnson not only didn't speak to me, she ignored me completely.

I said to her, "I'm Fiona Hodgkin."

Johnson didn't reply.

"I heard that Teach Tennant is your coach."

No reply.

"I ask, you know, only because I've heard so much about Teach, and if she's here with you, I'd like to meet her."

This time, at least, I got a reply. "Miss Tennant no longer travels to tennis tournaments."

"Oh."

I regret to say I never met Teach. Father and Rachel knew her and, while I doubt either of them liked Teach, they respected her as a tennis coach.

We started to knock up, but the umpire stopped us. Johnson's parents were standing beside the umpire's chair, where they apparently planned to watch the match. The grass courts at Roehampton are directly next to one another, with no room for spectators. The umpire advised them to walk back to the grassy bank and watch the match from there. They weren't happy about this.

Once we began play, I could tell that Johnson wasn't a contender for qualifying. Don't get me wrong – all the players at Roehampton were world-class amateurs. And Johnson was in the second round, after all. But still – in the first point, on her serve, she hit a perfect, hard backhand from her baseline. She finished with her right arm straight, racket face just past perpendicular to the net, butt of the racket straight down toward the grass, weight balanced on her right foot, head held steady, topspin on the ball – all exactly correct.

Then she looked up and, surprised, saw me a meter behind the net, just in the middle of my ad service court. Whatever was I doing there? Her backhand came straight to me. The shock of it hitting my racket twisted my chest almost halfway around, but in doing so all the kinetic energy of her shot drained away. I dropped the ball into her deuce service court. She wasn't anywhere near it.

Her other strokes were as beautiful as her backhand, but she couldn't knit her strokes together. It was over in 50 minutes. Straight sets, 6-4, 6-2. At the net, Johnson didn't exactly refuse my offered handshake, but she just barely touched my hand. She didn't acknowledge the umpire at all but trudged off toward her parents. I reached up to shake the umpire's hand; we looked at one another; we both shrugged.

I knew what Rachel would have done if she'd seen Johnson's incredible strokes. Rachel would have found a way to use them to win tennis games. If Johnson had spent two years – maybe just one year – with Rachel, that backhand wouldn't have landed conveniently in my racket. Johnson wouldn't have been surprised to see me at the net, and her backhand would have drilled a small, precise hole in the air just under my right arm. I would have stood there watching the ball go past me.

There were lots of differences between Johnson and me – thank heaven! – but the important difference was that I had Rachel.

I was one match away from Wimbledon.

My opponent for the third round had been decided in another morning match, so I didn't have to wait to know whom I would play. The problem was finding an open court. Mr Soames told me that there was no chance we would have a court before three o'clock, so I left Roehampton, walked up Priory Lane, and ate lunch in a pub on Upper Richmond Street.

My opponent was going to be Martha Fellows. I had met her in the dressing room the first day of Roehampton, and she had surprised me by saying that Claire had mentioned me to her. Martha was about Claire's age, and they had played one another many times, including a match at Wimbledon – "Claire thrashed me!" Martha laughed. Martha was married – Claire had been one of her bridesmaids – and had a young son. She hadn't played tennis in international competition for several years. But now she was back.

If Martha wasn't enough of a problem, there was Rebecca Hurst's tea at five o'clock. My hope was that I could win my third round match in time to allow me to get to Hyde Park Gate, make myself presentable, and attend the tea. A three o'clock start held a shadow of a possibility that I could get to the tea. Three o'clock, unfortunately, came and went, with still no open court. The wait was nothing to Martha; she had waited for tennis courts many times before.

She brought her son – he was almost three – into the dressing room to show him off to the girls. Martha had him wearing a British sailor's suit, and each of us wanted to hold him, which was fine with him; he wasn't the least shy.

It was past five o'clock when Martha and I walked out onto the court where we would play our third round match. So much for tea at Rebecca Hurst's. I thought about placing a telephone call to Lady Thakeham to apologize, but I decided against it. It would probably just make everything worse rather than better.

Martha won the toss and her first service game. I dug in my heels and held my service. And so it went – each of us held her service more or less easily, and we traded games until, finally, on Martha's serve, with the games at 6 all, I got ahead in the count, 15-30. Then Martha, of all things, double-faulted, and I went ahead, 15-40. Unbelievably, though, I dropped the next two points; we went to deuce; and Martha pulled the game out of the fire. How could I have let her do that?

To make matters worse, she broke my service in the next game and took the first set, 8-6.

Wimbledon was slipping away from me. No – I had *thrown* Wimbledon away by not breaking her serve when I had the chance. I was furious with myself.

But at the first changeover in the second set, a remarkable thing happened: Martha got to the water tank before me, and she poured water into a paper cup. Then she handed it to me.

She said, so quietly the umpire couldn't hear, "Calm down. The first set isn't the match. The first set is over. Focus on this set." Then she walked to her baseline.

I stood there, watching her back with amazement. But I calmed down.

I had to make my volleys work against her – which they hadn't in the first set. Unless I hit a pure winner, which usually I didn't, Martha would simply put up a lob. Her lobs weren't perfect, and most of the time I could send them back, but then I'd be right where I started – or worse, I'd be smack in No Man's Land between the baseline and the service line.

Now I started punching my volleys harder, and deeper, and Martha began to wobble, just a bit. When she would serve wide, to keep me off the court, I started taking her serve on its rise from my service court and then rushing the net. Slowly, my game started to work better for me.

There was only one court between the court we were on and the grassy bank where spectators could sit. The match on the court closest to the bank had ended, and now the spectators were following our match.

At the changeovers, I could tell Martha was breathing hard. On her serve, I got ahead in the count, but she took the game to deuce. We were at deuce three times. Then, on my ad, Martha took my backhand volley on the rim of her racket, and the ball spun off the court.

I had broken her. The second set was basically over. In a few minutes, the sets were one all.

Martha got her second wind in the third set, and it took me extra games to beat her. But I did. We shook hands at the net, and she said, "Well played. Congratulations."

"Martha, thank you for calming me down at that changeover. I'll never forget it."

"Make it up by winning Wimbledon for me."

I laughed. "Well, that's not going to happen, not this year at least."

We were walking along opposite sides of the net to acknowledge the umpire. But Martha put her hand on my arm and stopped me. She looked at me seriously for a moment. Then she said softly, "I'm not so sure. You might go all the way."

When Harold came into the breakfast room with *The Times*, I practically snatched the newspaper out of his hands. I rifled through the pages searching for the ladies' draw at Wimbledon. I found the men's draw; I had almost forgotten that the other sex also played at Wimbledon. Then, the next page carried the headline:

The Ladies' Singles Championship Draw
Holder: Mrs Richard Kershaw

Just under the headline, in the first line of the draw I saw, in bold type:

Miss Margaret Smith (Australia) No. 1 Seed

This wasn't a surprise; Claire had known since she had lost the Australian Championship to Margaret Smith that probably Smith would be the top seed at Wimbledon. I looked down at the bottom of the page and found Claire's name:

Mrs Richard Kershaw (Great Britain) No. 2 Seed

I ran my finger up the players above Claire's name – I wasn't there. I was frantic; had there been a mistake? Without thinking, and for no reason, I simply assumed that I would be in Claire's bracket of the draw.

Then it dawned on me that maybe I was in Smith's side. The Committee, after all, simply pulled the names of the unseeded players out of an old cloth bag to establish the draw. I looked up at the top of the page under Smith's name. Finally I found, in a tiny letters, the most thrilling words I've ever seen in print:

MISS FIONA HODGKIN (BERMUDA) Q

The 'Q' meant Qualifier.

Unbelievably, incredibly, I was going to play in the Championships at Wimbledon.

And, I knew this wasn't likely, but it *might* happen – I could get to play a match on Centre Court.

Later that morning, Myrtle brought me a telegram:

POST OFFICE TELEGRAM

MEET SATURDAY 11 AM AELTC TO GET YOUR PASS AND PRACTICE COURT 8 STOP WILL PRACTICE SUNDAY HURLINGHAM STOP WHEN I PLAYED YOU LONGWOOD I KNEW YOU WOULD QUALIFY WIMBLEDON STOP

CLAIRE

Claire forgot to mention in her telegram that she had won the final at Eastbourne in straight sets.

I didn't see either Mark or Lady Thakeham during the day on Friday. I assumed that I was *persona non grata* with Lady Thakeham and probably with Mark as well, because I had missed both my social obligations the day before. If Mark had gone to the party last evening, he must have done so alone, without an escort. Given his tone with me Wednesday evening, when I had begged off dinner at the Savoy, I expected that I was in a deal of trouble with him.

I went out during the day and sent my parents a telegram telling them that I had qualified for Wimbledon. In the few words of a telegram, I tried to sound as though it was just a minor thing I had managed to do on the side, in between parties and teas.

That afternoon, Mark came home from hospital just before tea and, to my surprise, he took me in his arms and congratulated me on qualifying for Wimbledon. When I apologized for failing to appear the evening before, he said, "Oh, Fiona, you've qualified for Wimbledon. That's the important thing. I'm extraordinarily proud of you." He sounded sincere.

"I know I left you without an escort last night, and I'm sorry. I was being selfish."

"It wasn't a problem," he said cheerfully.

I didn't like the way he said my absence hadn't been a problem. "Did you go to the party?"

"Certainly. Margarite has been in London all this week. I rang her. She dressed at the last moment, and Harold collected her in the Bentley."

For a moment, I couldn't think what to say. Finally, I said, "Well, do you want me to go with you this evening?"

"Yes, if you would like. But it's your decision."

"Perhaps you'd prefer to go with Margarite again."

"Now, Fiona. Don't be that way. I told you in Bermuda that I'd broken up with Margarite several years ago."

At first, this bewildered me. I hadn't heard of Margarite until earlier that week. Then it dawned on me. "She was your first lover? You told me about making love to her, your first time?"

Consternation crossed his face. He must not have recalled that he had told me that the unnamed girl he broke up with several years before had been his first – and somewhat unhelpful – lover. He hadn't meant to permit me to deduce her identity.

"Don't worry," I assured him. "Your secrets are safe with me. But if you'd rather take Margarite tonight, please do so. It's not a problem for me."

But Mark said he wanted me to go with him, and we went. The party that evening was for a girl I hadn't met, Elsabeth Norton; it was at Grosvenor House (where the Thakehams were giving Catherine's party the next week); and it followed the formula with which I was now quite familiar. To my relief, Margarite wasn't there.

Mark wanted me to have a cocktail with him before the

dancing began, but I declined, which displeased him. But I was determined, for once, to stay out as late as Mark wanted, even though I was meeting Claire at the All England Club in the morning.

As Mark and I were dancing, I couldn't help asking him, "Did you and Margarite go anywhere after the party last night?"

Mark laughed. "Fiona Hodgkin, I think you're jealous of Margarite!"

I must have turned red in my face, and I tried to break away from him, but he held onto me. "Fiona, I'm teasing you. There's nothing between Margarite and me. We're only friends."

I relented, and remained in his arms, but I said, "I certainly don't mind either way."

"I'm sure that's true."

We didn't arrive back at Hyde Park Gate until almost three in the morning. Once we were in the front hallway, to my surprise, Mark simply picked me up in his arms and carried me into Dr. Thakeham's study, where he sat on the couch with me on his lap. I put my arms around his neck and kissed him. He reached up to my shoulder and pulled the strap of my gown down.

"Mark!" I practically hissed. "What are you doing? Anyone could walk in here."

This made no difference to Mark. He said, "There's really no reason for you to be in your gown. Let's take it off."

"Absolutely not."

He kissed me and pulled up the hem of my gown. This, I thought, was rapidly getting out of hand. I tried to make a joke of it. I pushed away from him, put my hands on either side of his face, kissed him, and smiled at him. "Behave yourself."

He was exasperated, but he did stop trying to undress me. "Fiona, really – "

I put my hand lightly over his mouth. "Let's sit here and kiss for a few more minutes, and then go off to our rooms – separately."

"Fiona, you know I want you, and I think you want me."

"You're certainly right that I want you, but that doesn't mean I'm going to sleep with you tonight."

He lifted me off his lap and sat me on the couch. He stood up and said, "Well, then. I'll see you in the morning. Do you plan to go to the dinner party tomorrow evening?"

I stood up as well. "Yes, I'd like to go to the party with you, but I don't want you to be upset with me."

"I'm not upset with you, but I'm certainly unaccustomed to having a girl repeatedly turn me down when I want to sleep with her."

He was incredibly arrogant to say this, and I was angry. "I'm sure Margarite didn't just say, 'OK, of course,' when you first tried to get her into your bed."

"No, she didn't say that. Actually, Margarite didn't say anything. She reached behind her neck and began unzipping her dress."

He turned and left me alone in the study.

SUNDAY, 24 JUNE 1962
HURLINGHAM CLUB
FULHAM, LONDON

When Claire arrived for our practice time Sunday morning at Hurlingham, I was already sitting on the bench beside our practice court. I must have looked awful, and I certainly *felt* awful. She put down her pocketbook and rackets and looked at me. "Are you all right?"

"No."

"I would never have guessed. Which bus ran over you?"

"Claire, don't make fun of me. I'm so ashamed of myself."

"You qualified for the Wimbledon draw. You did it on your own. So, what's there to be ashamed of? Every tennis player in the world would love to spend the Sunday before the fortnight at Hurlingham."

"Last night, Mark slept with me."

"Good! Finally! How was it?"

"Horrible. I was humiliated."

Now she knew I was serious. She sat down beside me and put her arm around me. "Tell me what happened."

"We were at a party, and I had three cocktails. I don't even know what was in them."

"Good preparation for the first round at Wimbledon."

"I know. I can't believe I drank cocktails. But Mark was drinking, and he said I should have one, and then another, and I wanted to please him."

"Have you had anything to drink before?"

"At Christmas dinner, my parents would always give me a glass of champagne."

"And that's it?"

"Yes."

"And last night you had *three* cocktails?"

"Yes. When we got back to Hyde Park Gate, I went upstairs and I was sick in the loo. I stretched out on the bed, and the room was spinning."

"I know the sensation well. Not pleasant."

"No, it isn't. But then Mark knocked on the door."

"Uh oh."

"He came in and got into bed with me."

"What did you say?"

"I told him to leave, that I was sick."

"I assume he ignored you."

"That's right. He was drunk. I told him to go away, to leave me alone, but I don't think he knew what I was saying."

"Well, he couldn't have been too drunk, if he did slept with you. But maybe he didn't, really."

"He was certainly drunk, but I think he did."

Claire was dubious, I could tell. "This boyfriend sounds like a real piece of work. When's your period?"

I looked at her. "Early this week, I hope."

"Did he spend the night with you?"

"No. He went back to his own room.

"So what did you do?"

I didn't say anything.

Claire said, "You cried into the pillow."

I didn't reply.

She shrugged. "That's what I used to do."

"I'm worried sick that I'm pregnant. But there's something worse," I said.

"After what you've told me already, I'm bracing myself for the 'something worse' part."

"I promised Mother I wouldn't sleep with Mark. And she even warned me about drinking. I don't think I've ever broken a promise to Mother before."

I started crying.

"Fiona, now this I wouldn't worry about. Your mother will care first about you, and then, maybe, about some promise you made. You told him to get out and leave you alone. What more could you have done? Hit him over the head with your tennis racket?"

She paused. "I tried that once, actually. It worked pretty well."

I still had tears on my face, but I had to laugh at her. Then I said, "There's something more."

"Fiona, the good thing is that you'll never forget the weekend before your first Wimbledon match. What 'more' could there possibly be?"

"I woke up this morning and went down to breakfast. Mark wasn't there, but Lady Thakeham was having breakfast, and I sat down with her."

Claire, who loved eating, nodded. "A good English breakfast is important for winning a match."

"She threw me out."

"She did what?"

"She said she thought I'd be more 'comfortable,' that's

the word she used, with one of my aunts until I had finished with my tennis. To make sure I didn't misunderstand her meaning, she said she would ask Miss Hanson to have one of the girls pack my bags while I was here practicing with you. I'm to pick up my bags later."

"What does the boyfriend have to say about this?"

"I didn't see Mark. I don't know where he was."

"This is a really lovely family you've found. Have you considered engaging some master criminal? For a price, you could ensure they're never heard from again."

"Claire, don't make fun of me. My aunts wouldn't let me wear a tennis dress, much less travel across London without a chaperone. I don't have anywhere to stay."

"Certainly you have a place to stay. You'll stay with us."

"No, I'm not going to do that. You're going to win Wimbledon again, and you're trying to get pregnant. The last thing you need is having me sleeping on your living room sofa. Where do the girls in the draw stay for the fortnight?"

"I don't know. I've always lived in London, so I've always stayed at my own flat. But Colonel Macaulay will know where the younger girls lodge."

"Who is he?"

"The Colonel is the Secretary of the All England Club; I'm sure he'll be here at Hurlingham today. Here's what we'll do: let's hit a few tennis balls, then we'll go to the buffet and have a late lunch. I'll find the Colonel and ask where you might lodge. I have the Alfa here, so I'll take you to pick up your bags at your boyfriend's place. Shall we set fire to it while we're there?"

I had to laugh. She was irrepressible.

Claire was the perfect practice partner for me – it meant that I was practicing against the best there was. Plus, being Claire's practice partner attracted attention to me in the newspapers. Claire could have had Margaret Smith, or anyone she wanted. While we knocked up on one of the Hurlingham courts, I watched Claire from across the net and thought she must be one of the most beautiful tennis stylists of all time. It was humbling to be hitting with her. 'I'm out of my depth here,' I thought.

Finally, even Claire was ready to quit. "Let's go get you some lunch," she said. We walked back toward the Hurlingham tea lawn together. Claire held her rackets and pocketbook in her right hand, and she had her left arm draped casually over my shoulders. Everyone was watching me walk off the court with the defending champion. I was still sick with worry about myself, but I was proud to be the practice partner of such a great tennis player.

The tea lawn was noisy and crowded with tennis players of both sexes, plus an array of guests. There was a outdoor buffet where food was served, but it took us some time to get to the food because everyone knew and liked Claire, so she stopped to chat with people, and she was kind enough to introduce me to them.

Claire embraced a large woman who, I thought, looked not much older than me. The two of them shared some private joke and chuckled. Claire said, "Margaret, let me introduce you to Fiona Hodgkin. Fiona, please meet my friend and formidable opponent, Margaret Smith."

Margaret took my hand in hers. She was surprisingly gentle, but she towered over me; she was a powerfully built woman. I think she and Christine Truman, who was a year or so older than Margaret, were the first women to 'train' for tennis by lifting weights.

The men in Australia had been weight training ever since 1938, when Harry Hopman wandered into a gym in Melbourne's Little Collins Street and met a weightlifter named Stan Nicholes. Hopman was then on his quest to bring the Davis Cup back to Australia, and he saw in Nicholes just the way to accomplish that goal. Harry was right, but the Davis Cup was only for men. Margaret and Christine, to their credit, had understood that weight training was just as important for girls as for the men – maybe more so.

But to tell you how unusual this was at the time, in Stan Nicholes' gym, there was no ladies' dressing room – Stan would have to guard the door to the men's dressing room while Margaret took a shower after her weight session.

Claire said, "Maggie, I think you're up right after my opening match on Ladies' Day."

"Can you believe it? I drew Moffitt, the girl from the States."

"Have you played Billie Jean? I haven't."

"No, I haven't either. How she plays so well wearing those eyeglasses, I can't imagine."

Margaret turned to me. "You and I are on the same side of the draw, so I hope we'll meet in the third round. If the weather holds up, and we stay on schedule, that'll be later this week."

"That couldn't be good for me," I laughed.

"Don't say that," Margaret told me. "Wimbledon is a surprising place. You'll do well."

Margaret and Claire knew that almost certainly they would meet in the final, two weeks from now.

"Enough, Maggie," Claire said. "I need to get some food into Fiona."

Claire and I went to the buffet, where I got a salad. Claire eyed it suspiciously. "Fiona, a rabbit couldn't survive on that." She turned to an older lady who was serving at the buffet.

"Evie," Claire said, "could we give this young lady some roast beef?"

"Certainly, Claire. And potatoes?"

"Definitely potatoes. Your son, I hope he's doing well? He's what now – 25?"

Evie beamed, because a Wimbledon champion had asked about her son. "He's 27, married, and I'm a grandmother, as of last Christmas."

"A grandmother? At your young age? It's a scandal!" Claire leaned across the buffet and whispered to Evie, who reached up, put her hand on Claire's cheek, and smiled. I guessed Claire had whispered that she, finally, was trying to start a family.

Then Evie, turning to business, put a huge slab of roast beef on my plate and enough potatoes to feed an army for three days.

This was more food than I could possibly eat. I turned to Claire to protest, but she said, "Don't worry, I'll eat anything left over," and we went to find a table.

"I hadn't thought about meeting Margaret Smith in a match," I said. Claire was busily eating most of my roast beef.

"Don't think about it. It wouldn't be until your third round. Don't think about anything but your first round match – which is Tuesday afternoon. Win the first round and then think about what comes next."

Claire, having almost finished my lunch, pushed her chair

back. "I'm going to find Colonel Macaulay and ask him where you should stay."

I worked on the food Claire had left me, and after 20 minutes she returned with a slip of paper in her hand.

"Sorry to be away so long. Had a talk about Bermuda with the Colonel."

"About Bermuda? Why?"

"He thinks Bermuda is part of Great Britain."

"He's not alone in that. But why were you talking about Bermuda?"

"Well, you should be assigned to the upper dressing room, with me. You're the champion of Bermuda. The dressing rooms are close together, and there's not much difference, but I'd rather have you with me."

"That would be wonderful. Is there a problem?"

"No, the Colonel finally agreed with me. He was just confused because the LTA ranks me the number one girl in Britain, so if Bermuda is part of Britain, you should be in the lower dressing room. The upper dressing room is just for seeded players and national champions. But now he thinks you should be assigned to the upper dressing room."

"More important." Claire spotted a piece of beef I hadn't eaten and speared it with a fork. "Where should you stay? Albert House, in Alwyne Road. It's just a rooming house for young ladies. Ten minute walk down Church Road from the Club. It's so close that the Club doesn't bother sending an auto for you. Three girls in the draw are staying there. The Colonel knows Mrs Brown, who manages the place, and he rang her. There's a room for you. Not fancy, but inexpensive. Agreeable?"

"Not fancy and inexpensive is good."

"Yes! Let's go collect your bags and bring them around to Albert House."

Claire drove the Alfa like a wild woman along Kensington Road, and at the turn into the Frying Pan I waved to the bobby standing guard.

In front of No. 16, Claire stopped the Alfa. "Let's get your bags."

I hesitated. "I don't want to see Mark. What if he's home?"

She looked over at me. "Why don't I go in myself and get the bags?"

I reached in my purse, took out my key to the house and gave it to Claire. "Could you leave this?"

Claire ran up the front steps, rang the bell, and Harold answered the door. A moment later, Myrtle appeared like a Royal Navy dreadnought steaming out of Scapa Flow.

"I knew nothing about this," she said. (I'm sure she was thinking, 'Or I would have put a stop to it.') "If I speak to Doctor Thakeham, I'm confident he will insist you remain with us."

I got out of the Alfa and hugged her, and she hugged me back.

"I'm fine. I've found a place to stay, in Wimbledon, close to the All England Club. It's better for me."

Claire and Harold emerged, Claire lugging one of my huge bags, and Harold struggling with the other two. They dropped my suitcases on the walkway beside the tiny Alfa Romeo.

Claire said, "Fiona, I go to Australia for two months in the winter to play in the run-up matches to their championship, but I take my rackets, my pocketbook, and one suitcase. A casket is smaller than any one of your bags."

Harold cleared his throat. "Ma'am," he said to Myrtle, "I don't expect that Miss Hodgkin's baggage will fit into this small roadster."

"Good thinking, Sherlock," Claire said dryly.

"Harold, put Miss Hodgkin's luggage in the Bentley and follow them to Wimbledon," Myrtle told him.

Myrtle turned to me. "Fiona, you will ring me if you change your mind about staying with us, or if you need anything. I want your word you will do so."

I agreed.

Harold loaded my bags into the Bentley, and he followed us to Albert House. I doubt that a Bentley had ever parked in front of Albert House to discharge a guest's luggage.

Albert House was a small, dark red brick house, with two front bays. A handwritten note was thumbtacked to the door: *"Do NOT Ring Bell After 9 At Night Or Before 7 In The Morning."*

Claire and Harold helped me carry the bags and my tennis things upstairs. My room was so small that the bags, tennis rackets, Claire, Harold, and I just about filled the room to the ceiling. Harold, I could tell, was dubious about my new living arrangements.

Claire shooed Harold out, but as he left he said to me, "Miss, please ring if you want me to come back and return you to Hyde Park Gate."

"Thank you and goodbye, Harold," Claire said.

Claire said to me, "Are you all right? Do you want me to stay with you?"

"I'm fine. You've been wonderful to me, Claire."

I was sitting on the edge of the bed, and Claire sat down beside me. "Fiona, listen to me. You have to eat a good dinner tonight, and you have to sleep well. Will you do both of those for me?"

"Yes, don't worry, Claire."

"We can't practice at the All England Club in the morning. Colonel Legg, the referee, gives all the courts to the men for practice on the first day."

The first Monday of the fortnight was only for the men players. Then the first Tuesday – 'Ladies' Day,' it was called – the women played, with the defending champion leading off on Centre Court. So my first round match, and Claire's second round match (she had a bye for the first round) would begin on Tuesday at two o'clock in the afternoon – 'precisely,' as the Intended Order of Play always stated.

The 'precisely' dated back to some of the earliest minutes of the Committee's meetings in the 1880s. The minutes always recorded that the meetings ended 'precisely' at 3:30. So the word 'precisely' had entered the Club's traditions. Until, of course, it had been blown away by American television, which couldn't begin a sporting event precisely on the hour – because when would the opening commercial advertisements be shown to the television audience?

Claire said, "I expect that if we ask Queen's Club politely, they'll give us a court for a couple of hours to practice. Let's meet there in the morning. Say, 11?"

"Yes. Where is Queen's Club?"

Claire thought for a moment. "You take the Tube from Wimbledon to Earl's Court. Change there to Piccadilly, then just one stop to Baron's Court. You can see Queen's just down Palliser Road when you come out."

She kissed my cheek and said goodbye.

I was alone. I took off my tennis shoes and stretched out

on the bed in my tennis dress. I was numb. I couldn't sleep, and so I just stared at the ceiling for a long time.

Then, I heard a loud knock. I got off the bed and unlocked the door. It was Mark, who was wearing a dinner jacket.

"Go away," I said, closing the door.

"Wait! Fiona! We're having dinner this evening at the Westons'."

"I'm not. How did you know where I'm staying?"

"Harold drove me here. May I talk to you for a moment? This is important."

"Go ahead and talk," I said, still standing in the doorway.

"May I come in?"

I stood aside and let him walk in.

"This is quite a nice place," he said after he had looked around the room. I assumed he was being facetious. I hated being in the same room with him.

"Fiona, Mother has told me what she said to you, and I'm sorry. I had no idea she would do such a thing."

I was certain Mark had known; that's why he had been absent from the house this morning. "It's not important. I'm better off here. Now leave."

"Fiona, we are expected at the Westons'. This is an important dinner for Catherine. You must be there." The Westons, I knew, were giving the dinner for Catherine and the Thakeham family as part of the celebrations leading to her big party that Wednesday night.

"I couldn't care less. I want you to leave now."

"Fiona," he began, but I cut him off. "Mark, it's humiliating for me to even be in the same room with you. The least you can do is go away and leave me alone."

"You're not upset about last night, are you?"

"You took advantage of me. It was horrible. I'm ashamed."

"Oh, Fiona, don't be that way. I didn't take advantage of you. I just had a bit too much to drink."

"Go away, now."

"I think we should wait to talk about this when you're not so upset."

I was determined not to cry. I hated him.

"Mark, if you don't leave now, I'm going downstairs to ask Mrs Brown to call a bobby."

"Fiona, I really must insist that you come with me this evening. Everyone is expecting you. It will be embarrassing if you're absent."

"Even if I were willing to go with you, which I'm not, I wouldn't go out this evening, because I'm going to practice with Claire in the morning."

He scoffed. "Look, you can't be serious about this. I mean, it's exciting that you made it to Wimbledon, and we're proud of you. I'm especially proud of you. But you said yourself this is just a trial run, this year. They've put you up against a top seeded player. You have to be realistic, you can't get past the first round. Eventually you'll win Wimbledon; I'm sure of it. But your first year, as a qualifier, you don't have a chance. I don't believe any lady qualifier has ever come close to winning. This is just for experience. You can't win. So why not come out tonight with me?"

The worst thing anyone could have said to me at that moment was that I couldn't win. I slapped him as hard as I could; he staggered and his cheek turned bright red where I had hit him.

"Get out," I yelled.

He turned and left.

I woke Monday morning and found I wasn't pregnant. It was like a huge stone had been suddenly lifted off my shoulders. I told myself not to cry, and I didn't. I had breakfast in a tea shop and then took the Tube to meet Claire at Queen's.

When I saw Claire parking the Alfa, I went over to her and said, "I'm not pregnant."

She smiled. "I didn't think you were. But I didn't tell you in case I might be wrong. Your boyfriend was drunk, wasn't he?"

"He's not my boyfriend. But he was quite drunk."

"Yes, well, I've seen that, plenty of times. And close up. They don't like to admit it, but when they're drunk, usually the most they can do is make matters unpleasant for the girl. They can't perform."

"What do you mean, 'can't perform'?"

Claire laughed. "Let's hope you don't have reason again to find out for yourself!"

Still laughing, she led me into the Queen's clubhouse, where she located the old groundskeeper in his tiny office. He was heating water in an electric kettle for tea.

The instant he caught sight of Claire, he said, "Absolutely not."

"I have a difficult draw on Ladies' Day," Claire said.

"I'm sure. Probably your Ladies' Day opponent is some hapless girl who's ranked number 10 in Mongolia."

"Tingay ranked me number 10 once."

"Yes, Lance did, back when you still wore your hair in pigtails and slept with your teddy bear under your arm."

Claire frowned. "I didn't have a teddy bear."

There was an ancient couch in the groundskeeper's office. The fabric was worn; the springs were poking out. The groundskeeper arched his eyebrow and pointed to the couch.

"A small, furry toy bear? You sound asleep after practicing with Rachel? Remember?"

Claire pouted, or pretended to. "Perhaps I did sleep with teddy."

"I'm not giving you a court. The grass is too worn from the tournament last week – in which you didn't compete. You, I noticed, were off somewhere else."

"Eastbourne paid my expenses. Queen's didn't."

"What expenses? Your flat is two stations on the Tube from here. We give you tea for free."

"I promise I'll never play at Eastbourne again. I'll always play Queen's the week before Wimbledon. If you'll let me practice today."

The groundskeeper snorted. "I don't believe you, but even if I did, the courts aren't in any condition for play."

She went over to him and kissed his cheek.

He shrugged.

Claire took his arm and hugged it to her right breast. She

stroked her finger slowly along his thin moustache. "Your moustache looks so dashing now that it's all gray."

"You've used that line with me before. It won't work."

I could tell his resolve was crumbling.

Still hugging his arm to her breast, Claire said, "Your wife is lucky to have such a vigorous man."

"I'll tell her you said so."

"Which court would you say is in the best condition?"

"Court 5 is probably the best of a bad lot," he grumbled.

"Good, I'll practice on Court 5."

Once we were on the court, and Claire was about to toss her racket and ask me to call it, I said, "Claire, was that appropriate? I mean, flirting with that older gentleman just now?"

"Fiona. Please. He loved every second of it. And we needed a practice court. Rough or smooth?"

TUESDAY, 26 JUNE 1962
COURT 14
LADIES' DAY FIRST ROUND MATCH
ALL ENGLAND CLUB WIMBLEDON

My first round match at Wimbledon was against a French woman, Michelle Lyon, who was seeded fifth. She was about 25, and 1962 was her fourth Wimbledon appearance. The year before, she had reached the quarterfinals at Wimbledon, and she had just played in the semifinals of the French championship at Roland Garros. Lance Tingay's World Rankings for 1961 had Michelle in the number six spot. Claire had played her twice, once on grass and once on clay, and had won both times.

"Michelle is more comfortable on clay than grass," Claire told me, "but her groundstrokes are strong. She's consistent. She's going to pass you at the net a few times. Just be steady. Don't get rattled."

"Can I beat her?"

"I'm sure you won't if you're asking questions like that. The question is *how* will you beat her."

"So how do I beat her?"

"You've only got one game. You attack the net. So, attack. But she'll have strong passing shots, and you'll just have to deal with them. And you can."

My match with Michelle was set for two o'clock on Court 14, which in 1962 was about as far away from Centre Court as it was possible to get and still be standing on a grass tennis court. (Today, the court known as Court 14 is just to the north of Centre Court, but in 1962 the ground north of Centre Court was beyond the Club's boundary.) Claire was playing the traditional opening ladies' match on Centre Court at the same time as my match with Michelle, so I was on my own. Claire had told me, though, that after her match she would come to Court 14 and hope to see the end of my match.

The first set went past in only 20 minutes or so; I lost 6-2.

I knew this was going to be a disaster. I would be out of Wimbledon in the first round. I cursed Mark for telling me I would lose; as much as I hated admitting it, I believed him. I absolutely had to pull myself together, right now, or Wimbledon would be over for me, quickly.

In the first game of the second set, I held my serve and played a couple of solid points at the net. Michelle won the first two points on her serve in the second game, but then I volleyed a ball back to her. It took a bad bounce on the grass in her deuce court, and her return went wide. So it was 30-15. Her first service went into the net.

This was my chance: I took her second serve on the rise, returned it down the line as hard as I could, and came in behind it. She got to the ball and hit it back crosscourt, but I caught it with my backhand and angled my volley short into her service court. There was no way Michelle could get to it. 30 all.

If I could just win the next two points, I would have broken her serve. I felt a little more confident; my volleys were working better for me now. Also, as I watched Michelle bouncing the ball, getting ready to serve, taking her time, I sensed she was thinking that she needed to get her first serve in, and hard, to keep me away from the net. I decided to take a chance: if she got her first serve in, and I could do anything with it at all, I would rush the net.

Michelle served. It was in. Beautifully placed wide but not hit that hard. I returned it down the line and came in. She had plenty of time to set up a passing shot. 'Probably she'll go crosscourt,' I thought, and I moved toward the centerline of the service court. No, she went back down the line, and her shot was the hardest she'd hit so far in the match. I lunged for the ball and volleyed it back. Then I slipped and hit the grass with a thud.

My volley wasn't the best, but at least it went deep and gave me a split second to jump back to my feet. Now she had to go crosscourt because I was at the net wide, and she did. But I caught the crosscourt shot and punched back a deep, hard volley. She had to lob.

I drifted back, picked out the ball against the sky with my finger and swung as hard as I could. Both my feet were off the grass when I made contact with the ball. Michelle charged for my smash and made it, but her return was wildly wide. My ad.

Michelle tried to do too much with her first serve and faulted. 'This is it,' I thought. She served a slice right into my body. I sidestepped, took it with my backhand, and started to run in behind it. But I stopped. I didn't have to come in. It was a winner. The games were 2-love. I had broken her serve.

The crowds that second day of Wimbledon were distracting because people were walking up and down on the narrow path between Courts 14 and 15 – 'St. Mary's Walk,' it had always been called, after the old church in the distance. It ran all the way through the outer courts to the covered gangway between Court 1 and Centre Court. Few of the spectators stopped to watch our match. It was a high seeded player against a qualifier nobody; it wouldn't last long and would be boring while it did. I did my best to pull a curtain around the court in my mind and focus on the game.

At the next changeover, I sensed that Michelle was concerned. She'd been in worse situations than this and pulled out wins. She was up a set, but still – concerned. My volleys were clicking now, my footwork was better, and, most important, I had forgotten that this was Wimbledon. Now it was just a tennis match that I had to win.

I cruised through the rest of the second set and took it 6-3. Now there was a crowd watching us – could this be a possible upset? And this unknown qualifier was from *where*? Bermuda?

Third set. Neither of us could break the other. We went to extra games. On my serve, I made two stupid mistakes and got behind in the score. It was love-30. Michelle smelled blood. She was experienced; she was going to make full use of this opportunity I'd just handed her on a platter. Two more points and she'd put her first round into a bag.

For once, I took my time getting ready to serve. I tossed the ball high and out, and swung through it with every bit of strength I could find. The instant my racket collided with the ball, I rushed the net.

But my serve was an ace, my first of the match. Michelle didn't get near it. 15-30.

On my next serve, I came in, and Michelle tried passing

me down the line. I got to the ball with plenty of time, but I punched it back and it went just long. Another careless mistake. 15-40. Two match points for Michelle.

I faulted on my first serve. Nerves. I decided to gamble on following my second serve in. I hit a good second serve and forced Michelle to try and pass me at net. Michelle hit her shot into the net.

One match point saved. 30-40. Michelle's ad.

Claire, meanwhile, had finished the demolition of her opponent on Centre Court. Now she was at Court 14 to watch the end of my match. The crowd made a path for her to the yellow rope along the side of the court; everyone knew Claire was my practice partner. The chair umpire noticed Claire's arrival and gave her a short, stern glance that meant 'no coaching.' So Claire stood there, arms folded over her chest, showing no emotion, and not applauding.

I had never been so glad to see someone in my whole life.

I served wide, to Michelle's backhand. She returned low, to my feet, but I made a good half-volley into her deuce service court. She ran up but couldn't reach it. Both match points saved. Deuce.

I won the deuce point and gained the advantage. I served, ran forward, caught her return on my racket and punched it back. She had to stretch to reach my volley, hit a weak return, and I put it away.

My game. The crowd roared with approval.

I lost the first two points on her serve. 30-love. But then she faulted on her first service. This was the wrong time to hand me a second serve. I got to the net, took her passing shot with my backhand, and angled it away from her. 30-15.

She took her time on her next serve, and it paid off. An ace, her third of the match. 40-15. I risked a glance at Claire, who had not a trace of emotion on her face. Suddenly what Mark had said Sunday evening, that I would lose, that I had no chance, came into my mind. I gritted my teeth; I was *not* going to lose this match.

Michelle served, and I took the ball on the rise, returned it down the line, and came to the net. She got to the ball easily and hit a beautiful crosscourt shot, which I cut off with a volley and sent back down the line. Again, Michelle reached the ball with plenty of time and fired a forehand straight back at me, hard. I caught it with my racket, let my hand and arm drain off the momentum from the ball, and angled it softy into the opposite service court. A stop volley. Michelle couldn't reach it. 40-30.

The crowd on St. Mary's Walk had grown.

Michelle put her first service into the net. The crowd gasped. Michelle seemed tired to me. She had to serve as hard as she could over and over just to try and force me to stay back, and now her serve began to fall off just a notch.

I stepped inside the baseline for her second service. She sliced the ball wide but not hard. I sent it back down the line. This time, she hit a sharply angled, perfect crosscourt shot that should have been a winner. But I raced across the court and hit the ball back crosscourt.

I was off the court when I hit the ball, and I slipped on the grass and fell on my backside. The crowd groaned. But at least I'd hit a good volley, and Michelle had to run to get it back. She was off the court as well, and she hit the ball down the line with her backhand.

I sprang to my feet; I could just get to the ball. I ran back across the court as fast as I could and volleyed the ball crosscourt. Now it was Michelle's turn to race across the court, which she did – Michelle was *fast*.

She had time to hit a groundstroke but she didn't; instead, she lobbed down the line. I was surprised. I wasn't in a good position to take this lob. I had to jump to reach it with my backhand. I angled my shot into the opposite service court.

This should have been a winner. But Michelle sprinted diagonally across the court and reached my ball. Amazing speed. She hit the ball crosscourt, but then slipped on the grass. Michelle didn't fall, but she did have to catch her balance rather than get back in position for my next shot. I knocked the ball with my backhand into the service court away from her.

Deuce. If I could just break Michelle's serve, I thought I could take the match.

I won the deuce point. My ad. Michelle took her time serving. She went down the middle, to my forehand. She'd had enough of my backhand for one afternoon. I took her serve on the rise and ripped the ball crosscourt, deep into her deuce court. She couldn't get to it. I had broken her. I would serve for the match.

The crowd cheered; even Claire decided it was permissible for her to yell "Fiona! Fiona!" Michelle, as a good sport, clapped her hand against her racket head in acknowledgement.

I was playing on autopilot. She took her time setting up to receive. I could tell she was struggling to make passing shots off my serve. I fell behind in the score, 15-30, because of a volley that went long. But I made it 30 all with a crosscourt volley, and then 40-30 after she lobbed one of my volleys, and her lob landed long.

Match point in my favor.

The crowd was hushed. I served and came in. She had to pass me. She went crosscourt, and by instinct I sidestepped and hit a backhand volley into the corner of her deuce court. She barely got to the ball and then hit another lob. She was tired. That's why I was getting all these defensive lobs.

I set up, found the ball in the sky with my finger, and whipped my racket through the air. Michelle didn't get near my smash.

Claire was jumping up and down yelling, "YES! YES!" I shook hands with Michelle and then with the chair umpire, who called, "Game, set, and match to Miss Hodgkin, 2-6, 6-3, 10-8."

I was in the second round of Wimbledon.

I shook hands with Michelle, gathered my rackets and pocketbook, walked off the court and slipped under the yellow rope where Claire was standing, or rather jumping. She hugged me. She was still yelling. "INCREDIBLE PLAY!"

There were people with cameras taking photographs of us, and several British reporters were asking me questions. Claire knew all the reporters, and she said to them, "Not now, boys. Fiona needs a bath and a cup of tea before she'll be fit to talk with the likes of you!"

Claire and I walked back along St. Mary's Walk to the upper dressing room. She had her arm draped over my shoulders. All she could talk about was my "spectacular" upset of the fifth seed; she didn't bother to mention her own victory on Centre Court.

"Claire?" I said softly.

"Yes?"

"I would have lost if you hadn't been there."

"Nonsense."

But I could tell Claire was pleased.

As we walked, Claire warned me not to talk with reporters, at least not unless I had plenty of time to think and was careful in what I said. "They'll twist anything you tell them."

"Do you talk to reporters?"

"I used to, all the time, but I haven't since I married Richard."

"Why not?"

"Richard prefers not to see me quoted in the newspapers."

"Why doesn't he want to see you quoted?"

"Well, I can understand his thinking. I'm his wife, and I'll be the mother of his children. He doesn't want to see me saying something outrageous that's been splashed across a newspaper."

Before we walked into the South West Hall of Centre Court, Claire turned her head to glance at the scoreboard that was against the stands for Courts 2 and 3.

She stopped instantly. "I almost can't believe it," she said in a whisper.

"What?"

She pointed at the scoreboard. "Billie Jean beat Margaret."

Results – Centre Court

Mrs R Kershaw (GB)   def Miss M Curzon (GB)   6-0 6-1
Miss BJ Moffitt (USA) def Miss M Smith (AUS)   1-6 6-3 7-5

I'd never seen Claire nonplussed, but she was now.

We went in the South West Hall and found Margaret, disconsolate, in the upper dressing room. Margret dominated the first set, which took all of 18 minutes. Billie Jean took the second set, but in the final set, Margaret had been serving for the match with the games at 5-3 – and the score was 30-15. She had been just two points away from winning. Billie Jean fought back to deuce, broke Margaret's serve, and finally walked off with the match.

Every girl in the dressing room knew what this meant. Barring another, equally incredible upset, Claire would be the holder of the championship for a third year.

When I got back to Albert House late Tuesday afternoon, I had one task that I dreaded. I hadn't told my parents that I wasn't staying with the Thakehams any longer and that I was by myself in a rooming house. Which of these two facts would be more upsetting to my parents, I wasn't sure. Probably Mother would be angry with me for leaving the Thakehams, and Father would be angry with me for staying by myself in a rooming house. I didn't know if Lady Thakeham had told them; maybe she would have felt obligated to do so. In any event, I needed to send them a telegram, and now.

Mrs Brown told me where to find the Post Office; it was close by, next to the Wimbledon Tube station. I walked there, took a telegram pad, and wrote:

POST OFFICE TELEGRAM

WIN TODAY THREE SETS OVER FIVE SEED FIRST ROUND STOP HAVE MOVED TO ALBERT HOUSE ALWYNE ROAD WIMBLEDON STOP HOMESICK AND LOVE YOU STOP FIONA.

The 'homesick and love you' part was certainly true. Part of me wanted to return to Bermuda immediately and never leave the island again.

But another part of me wanted to play in the second round at Wimbledon.

I handed in the telegram.

When I walked back to Albert House, Mrs Brown presented me with a dozen red roses, and an envelope, which just had been delivered. I had a bad feeling about this delivery.

"Mrs Brown, I don't have anywhere to put these roses in my room. Could we possibly find a vase for them and put them here on the counter? Then all your guests could enjoy them."

Mrs Brown readily accepted this added touch of class to Albert House, and we went back into the kitchen to find a vase. Albert House, I learned, was not well equipped with vases, but we did find an asparagus cooker. So we sliced the stems at an angle, put them in the asparagus cooker, added water, pushed the roses around a bit so they were shown to best advantage, and finally placed them on the counter in the reception room. Mrs Brown was pleased.

I went up to my room, dropped my rackets, pocket book and tennis kit on the floor, sat on the bed, and looked at the envelope. I recognized Mark's handwriting – 'Fiona Hodgkin, Albert House.' I really didn't want to open this envelope; I guessed the contents would be about Catherine's party tomorrow night. And once I opened it, I found I was right.

I threw Mark's note away just after reading it, and now, decades later, I can't recall exactly what he wrote. The gist was, as I expected, that I should attend Catherine's party with him, tomorrow night. And, to give the devil his due, he apologized for Saturday night. But most of the note was to the effect that I was expected at Catherine's party, and that he would appreciate it if I would come with him. He asked that I ring him and let him know.

I sat on the edge of the bed. I crumpled up Mark's note. On the one hand, I never wanted to set eyes on Mark again. On the other hand, Catherine's party was the reason Lady Thakeham had invited me to London. If I didn't attend Catherine's party, and Mother learned that I hadn't, which she would, she would be angry with me. She might well decide that I was withdrawing immediately from Wimbledon. If Father backed her up, and he probably would, that would be that.

So I needed to show my face at Catherine's party.

My second round match was set on Court 2 for Wednesday, following a men's match that started at two o'clock. The men should be finished by four o'clock, or five at the latest, unless there was a rain delay, or the men got involved in some extra game death march. If I were on the court by, say, five, my match would be over by seven, or, at the worst, eight. My match couldn't possibly go more than a few minutes past nine o'clock because of darkness. Catherine's party would begin at Grosvenor House in Mayfair at nine o'clock, but I wouldn't be considered late if I arrived by ten o'clock or so. I would come back to Albert House straight after my match, dress, and catch the Tube to Marble Arch.

I went downstairs. There was a telephone off the entryway. I put in the necessary coins and rang Hyde Park Gate. Harold answered the telephone in the pantry. "Harold, this is Fiona Hodgkin."

"Yes, Miss. I'm pleased to hear from you."

"Harold, may I speak with Mark?"

"Miss Hodgkin, young Mark is not in at present. I think he plans to return for tea. May I ask him to ring you then?"

"No, Harold. I don't have a telephone that is easy for me to answer. May I ask you to give him a message?"

"Certainly, Miss."

"Will you thank him for the roses he sent me?"

"Yes, Miss."

"Please tell Mark that I will attend Catherine's party tomorrow evening, but I will come by myself."

"Miss, should young Mark come collect you in his automobile? At what time?"

Harold was not grasping the idea of my coming to Catherine's party by myself. "No, Harold, I will take the Tube. The Marble Arch stop is close to Grosvenor House."

"Miss, let me ask Miss Hanson if I may come around in the Bentley and collect you at Albert House."

He really didn't get it. "Harold, is Miss Hanson there? May I speak with her?"

"Certainly."

After a moment, Myrtle came on the line. "Fiona? Are you doing well?"

"Yes, Myrtle, I'm fine."

"Wouldn't it be better to have Harold come bring you back to Hyde Park Gate? I would send one of my girls with him to pack your clothes. I would – " She paused. "I would satisfy Lady Thakeham. You needn't worry about her."

"Myrtle, I'm comfortable where I am. And I promise you I would ask if I needed you to help me. But I want to ask you a question: Would I be welcome at Catherine's party if I came alone, by myself?"

She instantly deduced what had happened. "Did Mark mistreat you?"

I didn't reply.

"Fiona, the truth, now."

I didn't reply.

"Your choices are to tell me, or for me to assume the worst, immediately find Mark, and strangle him."

"I drank too much last Saturday night. That was my fault. I think Mark took advantage of me after we came back to Hyde Park Gate."

She paused. "Are you all right?"

"Yes. I got my period yesterday morning."

"That's good, but that doesn't mean you're all right."

I didn't reply.

"I'll strangle Mark."

"No, Myrtle, leave Mark alone. It's over and done with between Mark and me."

I must tell you about Wimbledon and amateur tennis in 1962. Few people remember now; it was 50 years ago. And you can't understand this story about Claire and me, really, unless you know.

We were all amateurs then. That meant even Claire – the top woman player – could accept only her 'reasonable' travel and lodging expenses. If she ever accepted money for playing tennis, she would become a 'professional,' and professionals were barred from most tournaments, including Wimbledon.

When Claire won Wimbledon in 1960 and 1961, her prize each time was a voucher for £15. She could use the voucher for lodging and meals – or she could visit a bank and redeem the voucher for cash. Which is what Claire did. In case you're wondering, £15 in 1961 was worth about $300 in today's American dollars.

In 2011, when Petra Kvitova won Wimbledon, she took home £1.1 million (about $1.71 million). In cash.

Oh, I almost forgot. Claire also received a tiny replica of the sterling silver Rosewater Dish that has been presented to each ladies' singles champion since 1886 – and then promptly snatched back! Claire was allowed to hold the actual

Rosewater Dish for all of about five minutes, each time, just so the photographers could snap their photos. She put the replicas in the back of a closet in her parents' country house, along with her other trophies.

When I first met Claire, at Longwood, she was touring the private grass court clubs on the East Coast of the States – Westchester Country Club, Merion Cricket Club, Baltimore Country Club. Having a Wimbledon champion play an afternoon's exhibition match was a feather in the cap of each of these clubs. But none of them paid Claire to appear, because that would be paying Claire to play tennis. Instead, each club paid her a handsome *per diem* for her expenses, about half of which she saved and deposited in her father's bank in the City.

The French took a unique approach to the reasonable expenses of top amateurs. For playing at Roland Garros, Claire got *un forfait* for her expenses. A lump sum, that is, and the French tended to estimate 'reasonable expenses' in terms of how many paying spectators a player was likely to draw through the gates at Roland Garros. Claire was a tremendous draw, and consequently the French felt her reasonable expenses in staying in Paris certainly must be quite substantial. Another tidy amount deposited in her father's bank.

I've never asked Claire about her earnings from tennis (although if the shoe were on the other foot, Claire would demand to know my take down to the last shilling). But I'll guess she cleared about £2,000 each year when she was at her peak. That's about $40,000 in today's American dollars. Nothing to sneeze at, but an offer of $40,000 to one of the top women tennis stars today wouldn't even get her agent to return your voice mail message.

And for a nobody like me in 1962? You can forget my reasonable expenses. I was lucky the All England Club fed me lunch and gave me tea without charge – and I appreciated it!

Players in those days traveled without the entourages of coaches and others that are common today. There was no money to pay for an entourage. At most, a player might travel with a parent or a spouse. And in any event, 'coach' implied 'professional coach,' which was quite the gray area. The Committee was uncomfortable when Teach Tennant, who was a professional coach, came to Wimbledon with Alice Marble and later Maureen Connolly.

On Ladies' Day in 1952, Maureen – 'all tiny 17 years of her,' as Teddy Tinling said – marched into Colonel Macaulay's office; announced she was calling a press conference; and told the Colonel to assemble the sports journalists – immediately! She then told the journalists, in no uncertain terms, that Teach was no longer her coach. Maureen thought Teach had been saying that Maureen was injured and couldn't compete at Wimbledon. Maureen proceeded to win Wimbledon three times in a row – and the Grand Slam in 1953.

The Committee was pleased with the departure of a professional coach, if not with the idea of a press conference. But no one could decide which was more amazing: that an amateur tennis player had held a press conference, or that Teach would no longer be running Maureen's life.

In 1962, three of the major international tournaments were played at small, private grass court clubs: Kooyong, in Melbourne; Forest Hills, in New York City, and the All England Club. Only Roland Garros was owned by a national tennis organization. Today, Wimbledon – excuse me, I meant

'The Lawn Tennis Championships upon the lawns of the All England Club Wimbledon' – is the only 'major' played at a private club, and the only one played on grass.

In 1962, the ground of the All England Club was 13½ acres tucked into a small triangle between Somerset Road to the west and Church Road to the east. The Club had only 16 grass courts, including Centre Court.

Centre Court then wasn't at the center of the Club's ground; it was off on the north edge. So why was it called Centre Court? Because before 1922, when the All England Club was just off Worple Road in Wimbledon, the main court *had* been in the exact center of the ground, and it was logical to call it "Centre Court." When the Club moved to Church Road in 1922, but the new show court, with its 12-sided design by the architect Stanley Peach, was built on the north edge of the ground, it was still called, inevitably, "Centre Court."

This is England, right?

In 1967, the Club purchased 11 additional acres to the north of the original ground and eventually on that land built the new Court 1, the new Courts 14 to 19, and the new Aorangi Park practice courts. So now Centre Court is closer to the actual centre of the ground.

When I played at Wimbledon, the roof over the stands around Centre Court was lower by a meter (and the stands smaller by 1,000 seats) than it became after an expansion in 1979. Centre Court in 1962 was so small and enveloping that, when you played there, to see the sky you had to look basically straight up. The writer John McPhee once compared Centre Court in the 1960s to 'an Elizabethan theater,' like Shakespeare's Globe, and that's exactly how it felt. A player on court could speak to the chair umpire in a normal tone of voice and still be heard by most of the spectators. The sound of a ball hit hard by a racket – *THOCK!* – would echo under the low roof.

Margaret Smith, who was accustomed to the open, expansive stadium at Kooyong, which had space for two grass courts side by side, and no roof, said that Centre Court was like playing "on a postage stamp" (although maybe she was simply repeating something Tony Trabert had said years before).

The outside of Centre Court was draped in Boston ivy so thick you could barely see the building itself, and, once inside, you were in a labyrinth of dark, narrow corridors, some of which seemingly led nowhere, but one of which led, through a small waiting room and two swinging glass doors, onto Centre Court.

Even the grass was different in 1962. Back then, the Club's courts were planted with red fescue, mixed with a little Oregon browntop, which made for a soft, slippery, and unpredictable surface. In 2001, the All England Club re-turfed all the courts with pure rye grass, and a much firmer soil, which made the courts slower. The most noticeable effect of the new turf is on the bounce. The ball comes up much higher, partly because the soil is harder, and partly because rye grass, unlike fescue, grows in tufts and is stiffer than fescue. The ball is now about one tenth of a second slower over the 23.8 meters from one baseline to the other compared to when I played at Wimbledon in 1962.

The All England Club insists the 2001 change in the grass was made only to make the courts more durable. Maybe so. Some people say it was because American television wanted longer rallies. But it's interesting that Jack Kramer back in the 1970s predicted that the different court surfaces at the major tournaments would be changed to be more uniform in terms of speed. And the speed of the grass courts at the All England Club today seems similar to the composition courts at the Australian Open and the U.S. Open.

But if you ever want to play a set on the old, unpredictable, and fun Wimbledon grass, you can. Just pack your tennis whites and take the rail from Wimbledon station to Eastbourne – the trip is about an hour and a half. You can walk from the station to Devonshire Park. Ask the staff if you might play on Court 1. Why Court 1? Because early in 1997, the All England Club demolished its old Court 1, which since 1924 had been pushed up against Centre Court like a shed. Eastbourne asked – politely – if they might have the turf from old Court 1. And so 730 square meters of turf was carefully taken by lorry to Eastbourne and reverently planted on Eastbourne's Court 1 – it's still there!

I don't mean to sound so nostalgic for 1962. Professional 'open' tennis should have come to Wimbledon decades earlier than it did. The retractable roof over Centre Court, the new show courts 1, 2, and 3, and the practice courts in Aorangi Park, are welcome improvements. If American television needs longer rallies, and a longer time on the changeover for a commercial advertisement, so be it.

Still. Wimbledon in 1962 was a thrilling place for me. When I walked past the Doherty Memorial Gates, I would brush a fingertip lightly over the wrought iron. Maybe Laurie and Reggie would bring me good luck. The British military officer standing guard would say, "Good morning, Miss Hodgkin. Lovely weather today for a bit of tennis."

One morning, I was walking down Church Road in my tennis dress with its tiny Bermuda flag, with my pocketbook in my right hand and my rackets clutched under my left arm. When I excused myself and cut through The Queue of people standing in line since before dawn to buy tickets, I overheard one of them whisper to another, "She's the tennis player from Bermuda."

For an 18-year-old tennis player from Bermuda, life doesn't get better than that.

I was moving up in the world; my second round match would take place, not on one of the outer courts, but on Court 2, a show court nicknamed 'the Graveyard' – it was considered bad luck for a seeded player to have a match on Court 2 because over the years so many top players had been upset there. The BBC covered matches on Court 2 on television.

My opponent was an American, Mary Ann House, who was seeded eighth. Although she was just a year older than me, House had been on the tennis circuit for two years and had made a serious run at Kooyong that winter until Margaret eliminated her in the fifth round. Claire had never played House but had watched her match with Margaret at Kooyong. "It wasn't a walk in the park for Margaret," was Claire's assessment. House's play at Kooyong is probably what had gotten her such a high seeding at Wimbledon.

House and I sat together in the upper dressing room while the men played their match in the Graveyard. To be honest, I didn't care for House. She ignored me and gave me the impression that I had no business being in the upper dressing room. I tried once or twice to make conversation on some neutral topic, the food in the buffet, for example, with no success.

The men took forever. It was almost six o'clock before a callboy summoned House and me to Court 2.

I decided I would blow House off the court, and that's exactly what I did. It took 44 minutes. 6-4, 6-2.

I played so totally by instinct that I don't even recall much of the match. On House's serve at one game apiece in the second set, she hit a beautiful, sharply angled crosscourt passing shot that bounced exactly on my deuce court sideline. As usual, I was camped out at the net, and it certainly looked as though House had successfully passed me.

Still, I gave it a try. I *ran*. The ball was already way off the court when I managed to catch it with my racket. At full speed, I hit the ball with my forehand. I didn't have time to aim – I just hit the ball on the run as hard as I could and hoped for the best. I was so far off the court that, at the instant my racket struck the ball, my right foot tripped on the tarp that was rolled up at the edge of the grass, just along the first row of spectators, ready to be unrolled over the court in case of rain. My racket flew out of my hand, and I pinwheeled over the tarp and slammed into the spectators' barrier with my legs in the air.

I heard a collective gasp from the crowd and then cheers and applause. I landed in a position that was not modest for a young lady, and the BBC and several photographers captured it all on film. I rolled over, got up on all fours, reached back, and pulled my tennis dress down over my backside. I found myself looking straight at an older couple in the first row of spectators. The man leaned over. "Are you all right?"

I replied, "Did you see if my shot went in?" The spectators who heard me all laughed loudly.

There's no rule in tennis that the ball has to go *over* the net; the ball is still in play if it is hit *around* the net – provided it lands within the opponent's court. The point was replayed on television over and over, and I could see that the ball went wide of the net but then bounced just in the corner of House's ad court. The newspapers the next morning all ran an almost indecent photograph of me on my back with my legs splayed above me.

When I walked off the court, there were so many people crowded around me waiting for an autograph or a photograph that finally a Coldstream Guardsman led me back to the upper dressing room.

Claire was there, having just finished the demolition of another hapless, unseeded player on Centre Court. She asked, "How was Mary Ann?"

"Not a problem. Straight sets."

"I'm impressed. I was worried she might be a handful." Then Claire said, "Well, we have two days off." The Committee hadn't yet posted the Intended Order of Play for Thursday, but probably we wouldn't play our next matches until Saturday. "Let's bathe, find Richard and go out for dinner. Don't worry, I won't attack him until he and I are back home in our flat."

"I can't. I have to go to a party."

"I forgot! It's the season, and you're a young, unmarried lady looking for a husband!"

I laughed. "My current state of mind is to spend my life as a celibate spinster. No, this is a purely social obligation."

"Meaning?"

"This is the party for Mark's younger sister, Catherine. Her party is the reason I'm here in London for the season. Lady Thakeham invited me to come to Catherine's party. All the other invitations followed. Mother would – well, I don't know what she'd do if I skipped Catherine's party, but it wouldn't be good. She might make me withdraw from Wimbledon. Now I have to run because I need to get dressed."

"You'll be careful at the party, and after?"

"Yes, older sister, I'll be careful." I leaned over and kissed Claire's cheek. "Can we practice tomorrow morning?"

"I have Court 12 at 11." Another perquisite of being the holder: Claire decided when and where she would practice, as opposed to being told by the stewards whether she would be granted any practice time on a particular day. "Too early after a party for the season?"

"No, I'll be asleep in bed, alone, by midnight. See you at 11." I ran off to Albert House.

WEDNESDAY EVENING, 27 JUNE 1962
PARTY FOR LADY CATHERINE THAKEHAM
GROSVENOR HOUSE
MAYFAIR

I took the Tube from Wimbledon Park to Marble Arch, changing at Notting Hill Gate. I tell myself that I dazzled my fellow riders on the Tube that evening; I was wearing my new Tinling gown, and a small diamond necklace, which Mother had loaned me, and which reached down just to my décolletage – not that I had much décolletage to work with.

I had been eating so many meals with Claire, who was convinced that I should double my intake of food, that I had put on an extra kilo in weight. I worried I might not fit into the gown, but actually it fit better now than when Teddy had finished it.

I felt elegant and sophisticated, and I loved it. Several people on the Tube recognized me from the BBC's television coverage of my match and congratulated me.

Catherine's party was in the ballroom at Grosvenor House and breakfast was to be served at two o'clock in the morning. I planned, though, to stay just long enough to be polite, for which I thought about an hour would be sufficient. I would be civil to Mark and avoid hitting him again. I walked into the ballroom just before 10 o'clock. The dancing hadn't started yet, and the guests were standing around in groups, drinking.

A young man I didn't know turned to me as I entered the room, put his drink down on a table and began to applaud. He cheered, "Well Done!" Then others began applauding and cheering. They crowded around me, and someone called out, "Are you going to win Wimbledon?" Claire had told me how to answer *that* question, and I replied, "I'm only thinking about the next round."

One of the men in the crowd wore a formal Royal Marine uniform. He was tall, with blond hair, and I guessed he was about 30 years old. He walked toward me. "May I introduce myself? I'm John Fitzwilliam. I saw you play today."

"I'm Fiona Hodgkin. You saw the match on the telly?"

"No, I was there. My family has debentures for the first Wednesday. I was watching Claire Kershaw's match on Centre Court, but from the cheering your match on the Graveyard sounded exciting. So I went over to Court 2. Were you injured in your fall in the second set?"

I laughed. "No, not at all, except for my dignity." I reached out and tapped my finger on a small medal on his chest. It was a silver cross bearing the Royal Cypher – 'EIIR,' for Elizabeth II Regina. "What an interesting medal."

He looked at me quizzically. "Do you know the DSC?" He meant the Distinguished Service Cross, which Britain awards for gallantry in combat at sea.

"My father has one. He was a ship's surgeon in the Royal Navy in the war. I've only seen him wear the medal once or twice. He wore it when the Queen came to Bermuda in 1953. The Queen walked down Front Street, and we saw her. Father wears the ribbon sometimes. On Christmas Eve, usually."

"That's right, I've heard you're from Bermuda. Why was your father awarded the DSC?"

"I don't know. I asked him, and he told me he couldn't recall. But I don't think he was being truthful. For what service were you awarded the DSC?"

"I can't recall."

We both laughed.

"Are you on a ship?"

"No, usually not."

"Shore duty, then."

"No, not that, either. I'm a Captain in the Special Boat Section." This was, and is, Britain's elite, small, and secretive naval commando group.

I put my hand on his arm. "Captain Fitzwilliam," I started, but he stopped me.

"Please call me John."

"I will, if you will call me Fiona. But, John, I need to find the guest of honor and pay my respects."

"I do as well, but I don't know her. Will you introduce me?" He offered me his arm. I put my hand in the crook of his elbow, and we set off across the room. "How do you come to know the Thakehams?" he asked.

"My father and Catherine's father served together in the war, and they're friends. Lady Thakeham was kind enough to invite me to London for Catherine's party and for the whole season."

"So you must be staying with the Thakehams?"

"Not at the moment. How do you know the Thakehams?"

"I don't. My mother knows Lady Thakeham – I couldn't tell you how – and my parents were invited to Catherine's party. They're away in the country, and my mother insisted that I come instead. I'm too old for a party during the season, but Mother hopes I'll find a girl to marry." He laughed.

"Are you looking for a wife?"

"No, not at all. My career isn't compatible with marriage."

We arrived at the side of the room where the Thakeham family was standing in a row, saying hello to their guests. There was a short line, so John and I waited our turn. We came to Mark first, and I held John's arm to avoid the possibility that Mark might try to take my hand.

Mark turned to me and rubbed his left cheek. "Luckily the doctors were able to save my jaw."

"How regrettable. I hoped to inflict permanent disfigurement."

"You came close, though."

I felt John straightening out his left arm to drop my hand. He sensed he might be in a false position here, but I held on tight.

"John, may I introduce you to Mark Thakeham? Mark, this is Captain John Fitzwilliam."

Catherine was now free, and I kissed her cheek and gave her my congratulations. Lady and Doctor Thakeham were next, and I thanked Lady Thakeham for inviting me to Catherine's party.

"Miss Hodgkin, dear child, I've been so worried about you. You're in a hotel somewhere. That wasn't my intention."

"It's not a hotel. It's a rooming house."

Lady Thakeham was taken aback that I would be living in a rooming house, which had been my intent in telling her. "Dear, it would be much better for you to return to our home. I'll have Harold collect you tonight, after the party."

"I'm quite comfortable where I am, but thank you for the offer." I tried to say this in a tone of voice that would convey my intent to never set foot in her house again. I looked at John, whose arm I still had in a death grip. From his expression, I guessed he was thinking that I had an interesting relationship with our hosts.

"But your parents are coming. They'll be upset that you're not with your aunts, or with us."

"My parents? Where are they coming?"

"To London, of course. This Monday. I sent them a telegram telling them to stay with us, but your mother said in her telegram that they would be at Claridge's, so I imagine that's where they'll lodge."

"Why are they coming to London?"

John interjected, "To watch their daughter play at Wimbledon? No, that couldn't be it. It must be something else."

"Your mother said she had sent you a telegram to the address of your" – an aristocratic pause – "hotel." You haven't received it?"

"No," I said, but then I thought that I had rushed dressing for the party so quickly that there might have been a telegram at the desk, and that I missed it.

Lady Thakeham said, "Your parents are bringing a friend from Bermuda as well."

"A friend? Rachel Martin?"

"Oh, dear child, I can't recall a name. Someone from Bermuda."

Just then the music began. I had planned to make my exit before there was any dancing, but John asked me to dance with him. He put his arm around me on the dance floor and said, "Ah, yes. Sweetness and light in the Thakeham household, I think."

I laughed. "You don't know the half of it. But if my parents are coming to London, that's wonderful news."

"Not until Monday, though. So they'll miss your third round match?"

"Yes, let's hope I win. I don't want them to come all that way and then find out that I'm no longer in the draw."

"Oh, I think you'll win. You were impressive this afternoon. I wish I could come see you play. When's your next match?"

"I won't know until the morning, when they post the intended order of play, but probably not until Saturday. Are you on duty this weekend?"

"Not that I know, although when they want me to be on duty, they usually don't give me much advance notice."

"Then why can't you come? I'd like to have you there."

"The tickets for the middle Saturday are impossible. Except for the finals, it's the most popular day of the fortnight."

"I think I'm entitled to a guest ticket. If I could get one, would you come?"

He stopped dancing. He wasn't any good at dancing to begin with. "Yes, I would."

"Then I'll do my best to get a ticket. How may I reach you?"

He gave me a house number in Wilton Place, Belgravia. I asked, "You don't live in barracks?"

"No, it's quite a cushy job, actually. I come and go as I please, except when they want me to do something for them."

I shivered a bit listening to him say this.

It was well past 11, and I told John I needed to leave.

"Why so early?"

"I'm practicing tomorrow morning. I need to get to sleep."

"Yes, of course. I've heard that you practice with Claire Kershaw."

I smiled. "To be honest, I'm proud she would practice with me. Claire got me into the qualifying round, so I wouldn't be at Wimbledon in the first place without her. She's a wonderful person."

"I quite agree; Claire is wonderful."

I was a bit surprised by the way he said this. "Do you know Claire?"

"Claire is my sister."

The instant he said this I saw the resemblance between them; why hadn't I noticed it before? I was stunned.

"Claire told me to watch your match on Court 2, but I wanted to see her match on Centre Court. On one of the changeovers, she noticed me in our seats. She glared and gestured for me to get over to the Graveyard and see what was happening. We could all hear the cheering, so I went to see you play. I got to the Graveyard just in time to see your tumble. Quite an interesting way to see you for the first time."

Then he said, "Do you have an auto?"

"No, I'm taking the Tube."

"Let me drive you to your rooming house – I'm sorry, I mean your hotel." He smiled. "My auto isn't here at Grosvenor House, but it's in Wood's Mews, just around the corner. Before you say 'No,' I'll tell you I must insist. Claire wouldn't forgive me for allowing her practice partner to get home on the Tube."

"But I'm staying in Wimbledon, and you'll have to drive there and back."

"I'll survive the round trip. Shall we?" he said, offering me his arm.

His garage in Wood's Mews was so narrow that he had to back the auto out before I could get in. The auto was painted silver, with a blue cloth hood. It looked like an upside down bathtub, and the motor rasped as though it was out of breath. I'd never seen or heard one like this before.

"What is it?" I asked.

"It's a Porsche 356 Carrera from West Germany. I've only had it a year. I meant to race it when I got it, but I've been away on duty quite a bit recently, and I've only gotten to the track twice. Do you prefer the hood up or dropped? The wind might ruffle your hair."

"Let's keep the hood up."

He drove like a man possessed, weaving in and out of traffic. I said, "Now I know Claire wasn't joking when she said you taught yourself to drive."

We pulled to a stop in front of Albert House, and John got out to open the door for me – but I noticed he kept the motor running.

He said, "I must tell you that you're splendid in that gown. I hope I'll see you in your third round match." He shook my hand, said "Goodnight," and started to walk back around the Porsche. I was going in the door of Albert House.

"Fiona!" he called.

I turned around. "Yes, John?"

"If your third round match happens to be on Saturday, would that mean that you could have dinner with me tomorrow evening?"

I smiled. "Yes, it would mean that."

"Then I'll hope that the match isn't until Saturday. Will the order of play be in the news tomorrow?"

"It's always in *The Times* and *The Daily Telegraph*."

"If your third round is set for Saturday, I could pick you up here tomorrow at, say, seven?"

"I'll be here."

The order of play went up that morning. I would be on Court 2 again for my third round match, against an American girl, Anita Castro. But not until Saturday afternoon, which meant that I would be having dinner with John that evening.

After we practiced, I said to Claire casually, "I met your brother yesterday evening."

She looked surprised. "John? Where would you meet John?"

"I told you I was going to a party for Catherine Thakeham, Mark's sister. John was there, and he introduced himself to me."

Claire laughed. "Why would John be at a party? He's not exactly the party type."

"He said your mother wanted him to find a girl to marry."

"Mother's engaging in wishful thinking there. He's not getting married, at least not anytime soon."

"He told me his career isn't compatible with marriage."

She frowned. "I don't like it when John says things like that. I wish he'd resign his commission and find another job. Father has asked him to, twice, and offered to help him find a place in the City, but John just laughs."

"Claire, John asked me to dinner this evening."

That stopped Claire in her tracks. "Fiona, he's much older than you."

"It's just dinner."

"With John, I doubt it's ever just dinner."

"Well, he was a perfect gentleman last evening. He drove me back to Albert House."

We had to get off the court because two groundskeepers had arrived to prepare it for the afternoon's matches. Claire pointed out to them a small patch of grass just outside the sideline that she thought was still damp from the early morning dew. They went down on hands and knees and began patting the grass dry with cotton towels.

Claire took my arm, and we went along St. Mary's Walk toward Centre Court.

"Don't misunderstand me," Claire said. "I love John. I probably know him better than anyone else. But he dates a lot of girls. He's not interested in a relationship. I just don't want you to have your feelings hurt."

"I'm just going to have dinner with him. I doubt he has any interest in me."

"If he asked you to dinner, he's interested in you."

I was thrilled to hear her say this. "Do you really think he might like me?"

Claire rolled her eyes. "I can't believe this is happening. And in the middle of Wimbledon. If my brother throws you off your tennis game, I'll poison him. Just don't let him take you to bed until Wimbledon ends."

"I have no intention of going to bed with anyone."

Claire scoffed. "We'll see about that."

A schoolgirl in a blue jumper approached Claire and asked

for her autograph. The poor girl was so shy she could barely get the words out of her mouth. There was no 'security' for players then. A shy schoolgirl asking for an autograph was about the most dangerous thing that could happen at Wimbledon to a tennis celebrity like Claire.

To be honest, the girl wasn't as pretty as she could have made herself: her hair was curly and wild, and she was just a bit chubby – unusual for an English girl then.

Claire said, "How old are you?"

"I just turned 14."

"What's your name?"

"Edith Wright."

"Do you have a boyfriend?"

"Claire!" I said.

Claire said, "Edith, ignore Fiona. What's the answer?"

"No." Edith hesitated. "I'm not that pretty."

Claire turned to me. "What do you think, Fiona?"

"Edith's quite attractive. She might pull her hair back. Perhaps take up field hockey in school." I thought a season of field hockey would fix the chubbiness.

Claire handed her rackets to me, took Edith's head in her hands, and gently turned Edith's face this way and then that. Then Claire took Edith's hair and pushed it back from her face.

Claire said, "Edith has strikingly good looks. The boys will be after her in a year or so."

Edith glowed.

"Give me your programme," Claire said.

Claire turned Edith's programme to the ladies' singles draw. Printed at the top of the page was: "HOLDER: MRS R. KERSHAW." She wrote carefully on the page, "*To Edith Wright, who has a LETHAL forehand. Best Regards, Claire Kershaw.*"

Claire thought for a moment. Then she wrote on Edith's programme, "*LIBerty 6152.*"

Claire handed the programme back and pointed to the number. "Edith, listen to me. That's my telephone number. If you have any worries about boys, or anything else, ring me. I'll remember you, and we'll talk."

She said softly, "Yes, Mrs Kershaw."

"Edith, call me 'Claire.'"

Edith glowed. "Yes, Claire."

THURSDAY EVENING, 28 JUNE 1962
LONDON, ENGLAND

John said to me over the rasp of the Porsche's motor, "Do you like Syrian food?"

"We just don't get as much good Syrian food in Bermuda as I would like."

"Are you teasing me?"

"Yes, I'm teasing you. I've never had Syrian food and have no idea what it's like."

"Are you willing to try it?"

"Certainly."

We went to a small lane in Ludgate Hill, then up a dark flight of steps, and into a tiny restaurant. A young man appeared from the kitchen and greeted John in what I took to be Arabic, and John answered back in the same language. They kissed one another on each cheek. There was no menu, and after John consulted with the young man for several moments, he ordered for both of us. "Do you mind eating with your fingers?"

"Not at all. In Bermuda, we regard using knives and forks as bad form."

"More teasing."

The meal was served in a series of small dishes – all

delicious. John taught me the name of each dish and showed me how to eat with a small, folded piece of bread in my fingers. He took a tiny piece of lamb in a piece of bread, put one hand under my chin, and with his other hand fed me the lamb. He shared Claire's dry sense of humor but none of her rambunctiousness.

"Is the language you were speaking Arabic?"

"Yes. My friend here speaks some English, but he's more comfortable in Arabic."

"Where did you learn Arabic?"

"I read oriental languages at Christ Church, Oxford, before I went down and took my commission in the Royal Marines."

"Oh."

After dinner, we left the Porsche parked near the Embankment and went for a walk along the Thames. There was a bit of fog, and I looked up at the night sky over London.

John said, "Are you worried about rain? You don't play until Saturday."

"We're right on schedule; there's been no rain this week. If it rained tomorrow and delayed the order of play, it could set back my match on Saturday."

We walked along, and I asked him, "How did you join the Special Boat Section?"

"One of my senior officers in the Marines once casually asked me if I'd ever thought about the Section. I replied it would be something I'd be quite interested in doing. But I heard nothing further about it. Then, a few months later, I was on a ship that's in port, not in Britain. Somewhere else. I'm on shore one afternoon on leave, and this uncouth chap in blue jeans and a tee shirt approaches me. He says he's a

Captain in the Section, and I'm to come with him. I don't believe him, do I? He's got no identification. Well, that's not true. He showed me an expired driver's license from the States. But he sounds to me as though he's from East London – which he was, in fact.

"So he asks, of all things, if I want to come see his helicopter. I say, certainly, I'll come see his helicopter, which of course I assume doesn't exist. We drive an hour or so to an airfield and damned if he doesn't have a helicopter."

He stopped. "Excuse me, Fiona, I didn't mean to swear."

"I'll survive."

He went on. "The helicopter was a sleek machine, in fact. I thought either this fellow is in the SBS, or he's stolen this helicopter, one or the other." John laughed.

"Was he actually with the SBS?"

"It turns out I was right on both counts. Yes, he was a Captain in the Section, and, yes, he had stolen the helicopter. He'd also stolen the car we'd driven to the airfield."

"How did you know he'd stolen the helicopter?"

"Just then, three fellows arrived at the edge of the airfield in an auto. They opened fire on us with small arms. I asked him why anyone would be trying to kill us. He said he thought they wanted their helicopter back. He could be quite sensitive to the feelings of others, when the mood was upon him."

"What did you do?"

"We got in the helicopter, and he said that there was an Uzi in the cockpit."

John stopped again. "An Uzi is a light automatic weapon."

"Thanks for clearing that up for me."

"So I said, 'You fly, and I'll find the Uzi.'"

"He was a helicopter pilot?"

"Not really. The first time he ever piloted a helicopter was when he stole this one. He was what you might call a 'self-taught' helicopter pilot. He had particular problems with landing; he never could work out how it was supposed to be done. So he just would get within a few meters of the ground and kill the engine. His landings were a bit rough."

John laughed again and shook his head. "Quite a chap."

"He must be a friend of yours."

"He was. A close friend. He's dead now."

My blood ran cold. We walked along the Embankment for a minute or so. "Were you with him when he died?"

John didn't say anything. I sensed he was trying to decide whether he could tell me, but finally he said, "Yes." He paused. "I carried his body back."

He wanted to change the subject. He stopped and turned to face me. "Why do you wear your hair in a ponytail?"

"My parents want my hair kept long. They think it looks feminine long. I want it out of my face, for tennis. So, a ponytail."

He reached around my head and held my ponytail in his hand. "Do you mind?" Then he gently pulled off the band that held my hair back. "Shake your head."

I shook my head, and my hair flew around my face. He took my left hand and slipped my hair band onto my wrist. It occurred to me that somehow he knew how a girl would use the band to tie her hair back. Then he pushed his fingers gently through my hair. I felt faint. He put his hand under my chin and kissed me.

He finished kissing me. "Do you want to have a cup of tea at my flat? I live in the ground floor of my parents' house."

"A cup of tea would be perfect. Why do you live in your parents' ground floor?"

"Well, it's convenient. When I have to go away on duty, they look after my flat. I don't have to tell anyone else that I'm on duty, which is good."

"What about Claire?"

"Oh, our parents tell her I've gone away for a bit."

His parents' home was one of a long, curved row of identical, white townhouses on a private square in Belgravia. I've returned to this home many times in my life, and each time I think about that Thursday evening during the 1962 Championships.

The door to John's flat was down a winding staircase from the sidewalk. It led to a door under the entryway to the main house. There were flowers in boxes on the windowsills of the house. John unlocked the door, swung it open, and turned on the light. It was just two rooms, a sitting room and a bedroom, joined by a hallway in which there was an old kitchen. The flat was small and windowless, with a few pieces of furniture covered in English floral-print cloth.

"Don't blame me for the decorating," John said. "My mother had the flat fixed up when I came back to live in London a couple of years ago. Not my preference but, as I say, it's convenient."

I sat on a sofa in the sitting room. I had half expected that the promised cup of tea would not actually be offered, but John busied himself in the hallway kitchen putting together a tea tray. He carried it out and poured us each tea. I was permitted perhaps two sips before John took my cup away. He kissed me again, and I kissed him back. He pulled me onto his lap, and I put my arms around his neck.

John said, "Do you want to stay here tonight, or would you rather I drive you back to Albert House?" Direct, but the perfect gentleman. My decision; no pressure.

I had my face buried against his shoulder. "Here."

"Good." He stood up, with me cradled in his arms. He was incredibly strong; he might as well have been holding a pillow.

He was carrying me though the hallway kitchen when he asked, "How old are you?"

"I'll be 19 on Sunday." The hallway was narrow; he had to turn sideways to maneuver me through. My answer, I could tell, had given him pause. No doubt I was much younger than his other girlfriends.

"Fiona, have you done this before?"

I knew Claire was still skeptical about exactly what had happened with Mark, so I answered, "Maybe."

He roared with laughter, then put me down on my feet. We were standing in the kitchen hallway. I could tell he was worried he had hurt my feelings by laughing, and he had, just a bit. He kissed me, which made me feel better.

"Fiona, I'm sorry. I didn't mean to laugh. But most people would answer that question with a 'yes,' or 'no.' It's not a question that often elicits a 'maybe.'"

I didn't say anything. I put my arms around his waist and leaned my head against his chest. I sensed his next question would be on a subject that he normally wouldn't concern himself with but that now, as a gentleman, he would feel obliged to raise. And I was right.

"Fiona, do you have a way to take precautions?"

"No. But it's not a problem." My period had just ended; I didn't think I could get pregnant that night.

He didn't say anything for a moment. Then he said, "Look, I want you very much. But this isn't a good idea. Let's wait."

So we got back in the Porsche, and he drove me to Albert House. He opened the door of the 356 for me, and when I got out, he put his arms around me and kissed me.

"John, may I ring you tomorrow?"

"I hope you will."

"Give me your number, then," I said. He popped open the glove box of the 356 and found a scrap of paper. "Turn around," he told me. I turned around, and, using my back for support, he wrote out his number.

Then he kissed me again, said goodnight, and stepped over the door of the Porsche into the driver's seat. He didn't bother opening the door to get in. He waved at me, threw the 356 into gear and raced off.

Earlier in the week, the upper ladies' dressing room had been crowded all the time, with a constant babble of talk among the girls. Now the draw was much smaller. Each round sliced the draw in half. Claire and I were alone in the dressing room Friday morning.

Claire asked, "How was dinner?"

"Claire, I need a diaphragm. Can you help me?"

"I take it we're talking about my brother?"

"Yes."

"Yesterday you said you weren't going to sleep with anyone."

"I've changed my mind."

"It must have been quite a dinner. Fiona, I love John, but is this a good idea?"

"I know, I know. He has plenty of girls, he's older than me, I shouldn't fall for him, I'll get hurt."

"Well?"

"So I won't fall for him."

"I think you've fallen for him already."

"I've fallen for him already. Will you help me?"

"Did you sleep with him?"

"No, but only because we didn't want to until I can take what he calls 'precautions.' Or, more accurately, *he* didn't want to. I was prepared to be more flexible."

"See? I did teach my brother some things. Fiona, John is a good person, basically, but sometimes he toys with women. Maybe most of the time. He sees a lot of girls. A couple of them are movie actress types. He's not going to be interested in a relationship. And he's nine years or so older than you. I just think this is a bad idea for you to see him, much less sleep with him. I don't think you should get involved. I think you're going to get hurt."

I just looked at her.

"I'll ring my doctor now and see if I can get you an appointment today."

That afternoon, Claire took me to her gynecologist. She was sitting in the waiting room when I came out half an hour later. "Well?"

In reply, I opened my pocketbook and showed her the small blue plastic box inside. She embraced me.

"Excellent!" Then she said suspiciously, "Do you know how to use it?"

"Yes, my grandmother explained it all to me."

"Your grandmother told you how to use a diaphragm?"

"She's an unusual grandmother."

"I'll say."

When I got back to Albert House, I went to the telephone in the downstairs entryway and rang John. "May I come see you?"

"Are you at Albert House? Why don't I come get you?"

"No, I can easily take the Tube. The Friday afternoon traffic will be frightful."

"The Tube to Hyde Park Corner?"

"Yes."

"Come out the exit on Grosvenor Place. I'll wait for you there."

Two hours later I was in his bed.

I got up on my knees and whispered to John. "May I spend the night?"

John was dozing. "You're not going anywhere. You're staying close at hand and naked. I'll want you again later tonight."

I kissed him on his ear. "Now."

"Fiona, I am entitled to a break now and then. It's in my contract somewhere, I think."

I shook my head. My hair hung down over his face. "No."

"No? Don't you have an important tennis match tomorrow afternoon?"

"Yes, I have a match in the afternoon. And no, you're not entitled to a break." I kissed him again, and he reached up for me.

SATURDAY MORNING, 30 JUNE 1962
BELGRAVIA

We were sitting in bed with a tea tray John had made and reading the Saturday morning papers, which John had collected from his parents' front steps, when the telephone rang.

John picked up the receiver, listened for a moment, and said, "Claire, dear, what makes you think Fiona would be here?" Then he had to hold the receiver away from his ear. His sister was yelling at him over the telephone.

John held the receiver out to me. "Claire wants to speak with you."

Claire didn't begin with any pleasantries, like 'hello.' Instead, she said, "How much sleep did you get?"

I giggled.

Claire yelled, "I knew it. I can't believe John's done this. Let me talk to him."

I handed the receiver to John. "Your sister wants to talk to you."

"Claire, I wanted Fiona to get some sleep. This wasn't entirely my fault."

He had to hold the receiver away from his ear again. Claire said so loudly that I could hear: "Has she had breakfast? I mean, a real breakfast?"

"Well, I was just going to boil her an egg and perhaps make some toast."

He held the receiver away from his ear. I could hear Claire yelling, "A boiled egg? You couldn't boil an egg. You have no idea how to boil an egg."

"Yes, I do. You take a pot of water and – "

She cut him off. "You don't own a pot, much less do you have an egg. Let me speak to Fiona."

John handed me the receiver. "My sister wants to speak with you."

"Fiona, are you there?"

"Yes," I said meekly.

"Listen to me. I want my brother to take you to a tea shop, right now." She paused. "And I mean right now. No more fooling around. I want you to have a full English breakfast. Drink a lot of tea and water. Have John take you back to Albert House. Go to bed – alone. Ask Mrs Brown not to let you sleep past noon. Then I want to knock up at one o'clock sharp. We have Court 12. You'll be there? You're on the Graveyard at two o'clock. They'll call for you a bit before two so we'll have half an hour, maybe a little more, to practice."

"Yes, Claire. I'll meet you on Court 12."

"Fiona, this American girl, Castro – I've never played her, but she's not a lollipop. No one gets into the third round without being dangerous, extremely dangerous. You'll have to beat her. It could rain today. You might have rain delays. It could be a long day."

"I know. I'm fine. I can take her."

Claire softened her tone just a bit. "So, how was John?"

"Claire, he's sitting right here, so let's talk later. But he's a perfect gentleman. He took care of me."

"Good, I knew he would," she said, and rang off.

Claire had her own match on Centre court that afternoon to think about. Instead of worrying about herself, she was taking care of me.

With John listening, I didn't want to tell Claire that I was hopelessly in love with him.

There had been comments in the Saturday morning newspapers about the Committee's decision to set my third round match on Court 2, rather than on Centre Court, or perhaps at least Court 1.

I had been a bit disappointed when I had seen the order of play; I had hoped to play on Centre Court. The newspapers, to my surprise, commented that the Committee seemed to be trying to help me by keeping me away from the pressure and intensity of Centre Court. My third round opponent, Anita Castro, from Florida in the States, was in her third Wimbledon and had played twice on Centre Court. The bookies, according to the newspapers, were giving good odds in favor of Castro.

In the dressing room before the match, Castro was relaxed and friendly. The American girls I had met so far at Wimbledon had all been influenced by Teach Tennant, even those who had never met Teach. Teach felt strongly that a player should be hostile to opponents.

I said to Anita, "I thought Teach told the American girls not to chat with their opponents."

241

Anita laughed. "You mean the girls from the West Coast, from California."

"I thought it was everyone."

"No, Teach influences just the girls from the West Coast. I'm from Florida. Most girls in Florida have never heard of Teach."

Anita was a large, strong woman, and she played Jack Kramer's 'Big Game' – meaning that she served hard and rushed the net, looking for a quick volley winner.

I lacked the physical strength to play the Big Game. I had to serve spot on and then make a good approach shot off my opponent's return of my service. Everyone thought I took too many risks. But once you hit an approach shot, there's no going back. You can't stand there in No Man's Land, between the baseline and the service line. You have to go forward, into the service boxes, and take your chances. But when you go forward, you're stuck out in the open and vulnerable to a passing shot. You have only instinct to help you; there's no time to think.

Rachel had told me for years that my game, assuming I placed my serve well, depended on my getting into the correct position at the net. And this was a matter of centimeters. Six or so centimeters out of the correct tactical position, and I would miss the volley altogether, or the ball would ricochet off the edge of my racket into the stands.

There were dark storm clouds overhead when we went out on Court 2. I failed to concentrate in the first set and lost 6-2. Court 2 had been full at the start of the match, but I sensed the crowd had now decided that this was the end of my Wimbledon, and many of the spectators began to drift away. I had a sinking feeling that Anita was confident that she had this match in the bag.

In the first game of the second set, on my serve, Anita lunged for one of my volleys when, of all things, the hooks on her bra snapped, and she hit my shot into the net. Anita's bust was of a size that made the bra's demise immediately obvious to the spectators. Also, her bust made continuing play *sans* bra not an option.

Anita had a couple of spare rackets and a spare pair of tennis shoes. But a spare bra? No. The chair umpire – a man, naturally – had not previously been presented with this particular problem.

A lady in the crowd called out that she had a safety pin in her purse, if that would help. Technically, it violated the rules to accept the safety pin – spectators could offer no assistance to the players – but perhaps the rule hadn't been written with this situation in mind.

I turned to Anita, and we both started laughing. I went over to the stands, and the safety pin was passed down to me through several rows of spectators.

"Turn around," I said to Anita. "I think we can do this and still retain your modesty." I yanked her blouse out of the waistband of her tennis skirt and pulled it up in back. It took me a minute, but I got the back of her bra pinned together with the safety pin.

I said quietly to Anita, "Does that feel all right?"

"It feels great – thanks!"

The crowd started to applaud.

I picked up my racket and held it up in the air. "I think we should thank the lady who contributed the safety pin!" I said, loudly enough for all the spectators to hear.

The crowd stood and applauded even more.

The umpire – no doubt relieved that this feminine crisis

was over – said into the microphone, "Second set, first game, Miss Hodgkin to serve at 30-love."

He had awarded me the point.

Anita and I were still standing together, just behind the umpire's chair. I put my hand on her shoulder, leaned over, and said quietly, "I think we should play a let." I meant that we should replay the last point.

"That would be great. I'd appreciate that." Then she kissed my cheek.

We separated and walked back to our respective baselines.

I said to the umpire, "Anita and I have decided to play a let. The score is 15-love."

The umpire was taken aback and plainly concerned that I was taking over from him as the person in charge of this match.

The crowd roared its approval.

I held my serve, and then, in the second game, with Anita serving, the clouds opened and a heavy rain began. The groundskeepers ran to pull the tarp over the court, and Anita and I raced for the players' entrance.

When I made my way to the upper dressing room, John was standing at the door.

I kissed him quickly and asked, "How is Claire's match?"

"She's inside," he said, nodding toward the door. "She's just a game away. Easy for me to say, but I can't see that she's having any problem dealing with her opponent."

I kissed him again and pushed through the door.

The dressing room was crowded; all the matches in progress had been suspended at once because of the sudden rain.

Claire was sitting on a bench, and I sat down beside her.

I said to her, "You've almost won your match, John says."

"Yes, I don't think it'll be a problem – if we can resume play. I'd like to get this match over with. And you?"

"Not good. I dropped the first set, 6-2."

Claire stared at me. "What happened?"

"I wasn't paying attention. But I am now."

Anita was sitting just across from us. Mrs Ward had taken her bra and was sewing the hooks back on. Anita had a towel draped over her shoulders.

A rumor ran around the dressing room that it had stopped raining, and we would be called back onto the courts soon. Anita leaned over and said to me, "Fiona, I'm worried they'll call us back before my bra is fixed."

"Anita, I'm not playing until you're ready to play. The umpire can't default both of us."

I looked back at Claire, worried that she might think I shouldn't agree to a possible delay that might help my opponent. I whispered, "Was that all right to tell her?"

Claire shrugged. "Just fair play. Not worth winning otherwise."

The rumor was wrong. The rain delay ended up lasting longer than an hour, and then finally we were all called back to the courts.

Anita and I knocked up and resumed play on Anita's serve.

We played out the second set, and I was so focused that I didn't realize that Claire and John had found seats during one of the changeovers. I took the set at 10-8.

Third set; I finally noticed John and Claire in the stands. I held both thumbs up to ask, 'Did you win?' Claire smiled and held both her thumbs up. She was in the fifth round, or as we would say today, the quarterfinals. Or just 'the quarters.'

Anita and I were on serve in the tenth game of the third set when the rain began again, hard. I looked at my watch; it was almost eight o'clock. We ran to the players' entrance.

In the dressing room, Anita went to the loo, and Claire immediately took my shoulders in her hands. "How are you doing?"

"Claire, I'm exhausted," I whispered back.

"Fiona, she's exhausted too. You have to play out the third set. You'll win. You're so close."

Claire asked Mrs Ward for a cup of tea. When she brought it, Claire had to hold the cup to my lips. I couldn't even raise my hands.

I thought, 'How can I even play, much less win?'

Claire put her arm around my shoulder. She placed her lips close to my ear so she could talk to me privately. We were in a gray zone of the prohibition against coaching. "Fiona, you have to win before it's dark. You can't give her a day to rest."

"I can't play. I have to quit."

Claire took my chin in her hand. She shook my head, not hard, but not gently either. She spoke right into my ear so no one else would hear her. "You're a champion. Now's the time a champion proves who she is." Claire gave me another sip of tea. "Run her around."

"Claire, I've already – "

She cut me off. "Fiona," she whispered, "she's almost done in. Volley to one corner, make her run there, and then volley to the other corner. She's almost finished. But win before it gets dark. Don't give her a day to rest."

At half past eight, our chair umpire knocked on the door

of the dressing room. Mrs Ward answered the door, and the chair umpire asked, "May I speak with Miss Castro and Miss Hodgkin?"

We went outside the dressing room. The umpire said, "Well, Monday's going to be a train wreck of a schedule anyway with this rain. Colonel Legg just met with the Committee, and they'd like to finish your match this evening, if possible. It would make Monday a bit easier. It's not raining now, but clouds are so dark the light isn't perfect, I'll admit that. Colonel Legg told me that you'll both have to agree to play in the fading light. It's your right to have good light for play. If either of you don't want to play, well then, somehow we'll just do it on Monday."

There was never play at the All England Club on Sunday. This was to avoid disturbing the local churchgoers on their way to St. Mary's.

I looked at Anita. 'Claire's right,' I thought. 'She's even more done in than me.'

I reached over and put my hand on Anita's arm. "Anita, this is your decision. I'm happy playing now, but it's whatever you want to do."

Looking back on all the extraordinary things that happened to me at Wimbledon 50 years ago, what I remember best is Anita's reply that rainy evening.

She hugged me. "Let's play it out now, Fiona."

This, I knew, was her thanks to me for helping her earlier in the match. Anita was a sport. I had helped her. Now she would play even though I'm sure she knew she'd be better off waiting until Monday.

We went out on Court 2. The Committee's definition of 'not raining' was interesting, since in Bermuda we would have classified the weather on the court that evening as 'light drizzle.' The grass was slippery. Plus, it had suddenly turned quite chilly during the rain delay. Anita put on a cardigan, and I took out Rachel's old sweater and pulled it over my head, freed my ponytail from underneath the sweater, and walked out on the court.

There were five or six Australians in the stands, still in mourning over Margaret Smith's loss on Tuesday. When they saw 'KOOYONG' on my sweater, they were thrilled. From then on, I had a small but loud and boisterous cheering section.

I concentrated on making Anita run from corner to corner, over and over again, as Claire told me to, and it worked. After each point, I looked at the sky and the fading light. I had to win tonight and that meant winning quickly, before it became too dark.

But Anita was out of fuel. I could tell because she started hitting more crosscourt shots – she needed the additional margin of error a crosscourt shot provides.

I drilled down on my volleys.

I would have lost to Anita if the rain hadn't come. Or, probably, if Anita had elected to wait until Monday to finish the third set.

It was just luck.

But as it happened, minutes before the umpire would have had to suspend play for darkness, I broke Anita and then got a match point on my serve at 7-6. There were only a few spectators left in the stands on Court 2, including the Australians. John and Claire were there, both soaked to the skin, both shivering and both cheering for me.

What did I ever do to deserve these two people?

I tossed the ball, swung my racket and hit the ball down the center. Anita just reached it and hit a return. Not strong, but short and low. I reached the ball, bent so far down that my right knee was skidding on the wet grass. Out of the corner of my eye, I saw Anita shifting a bit toward the deuce court; she was guessing I'd go crosscourt. But I didn't. I flipped the ball over the net into the near ad court.

My point. My game. My match. One more minute, at most, and the umpire would have suspended play for darkness.

Now the umpire wanted nothing more than to get out of the cold and drizzle. He vacated the chair for cover as quickly as I've ever seen an umpire move. Anita and I embraced and then we stumbled toward the dressing room.

John was standing in the entryway, just under cover. I grabbed his shoulders and fainted. I went limp in his arms. Then Claire had her hands on my cheeks and was shaking me. "Fiona, wake up. Wake up."

I opened my eyes. The Australians had found us and announced their plan to carry me around on their shoulders in the rain. Claire told them, "Not tonight, boys. Fiona's knackered. Come back Monday, bring all your mates, and you can do whatever you like with her."

This satisfied the Australians, and they went off in search of beer.

Claire frowned. "Aussies can be so literal-minded sometimes. You might be a bit careful around them on Monday."

I said, "I'm going to be sick."

"Not here. The loo," Claire said.

There were photographers everywhere. Claire grabbed

me out of John's arms and hustled me to the ladies' loo just inside Centre Court. She took the back of my head and pushed me over the lavatory. I threw up.

I tried to straighten myself, but Claire said, "I don't think you're finished." I wasn't.

Finally, Claire took a paper towel, put water on it, and began cleaning off my face.

"Claire." I was choking, slightly.

"What?"

"Rachel told me not to play at Roehampton. I mean to try and qualify for Wimbledon. She said it would change me. Not for the better. That it would take too much. Is this what she meant?"

"She'll be here on Monday. Ask her yourself," Claire said, while she was wiping my face. But there was bitterness in Claire's voice.

I was in the fourth round.

SUNDAY, 1 JULY 1962
MY NINETEENTH BIRTHDAY
BELGRAVIA

I don't remember how Claire and John took me back to his flat. I don't recall anything about that evening after being sick in the loo. But I do recall waking up Sunday morning in John's bed.

"Happy birthday!" he said. "Would you like some tea?" He had made a tea tray, which he put down on the bed.

"I would love some tea. And I'm famished. Could we get breakfast somewhere?"

"Claire and Richard are on their way here. Claire just rang. They're going to stop and buy breakfast. I can't imagine why they think I couldn't just make breakfast for us."

"Could you?"

"No, not at all," he laughed.

I held out my arms to him and, to be honest, I deliberately let the sheet drop below my breasts. I almost couldn't believe that John would respond to me, but he did, and it was wonderful. He caressed me, and then reached under the bed and brought out a small package that had been gift-wrapped.

"This is for your birthday."

I tore open the wrapping. It was a cheap cloth wash bag

from Harrods. It had two small initials picked out on the corner: 'FH.'

I loved it. I still have it.

John said, "Well, if you're going to be hanging around the flat, I don't want your things in the loo getting mixed up with my own." Since John – like Father – used a regulation Royal Navy shaving kit for his razor, there was little risk of our things getting mixed up.

I put my arms around him and pulled him down to me.

Unfortunately, it turned out that Claire not only had a key to the flat, but that she didn't bother knocking when she entered – which she did at that moment, with Richard in tow, and with plenty of bagels, cream cheese, smoked salmon, red onions, and an almond coffee cake.

Claire said, "Would you two please stop for just a bit? You both have to eat sometime."

John's flat had no place for four people to have breakfast, so we trooped upstairs to the Fitzwilliam house to eat. On the way, we collected all the Sunday newspapers that had been delivered to the front steps. Claire made tea, and I spread out the bagels and other things on the kitchen table.

Then we sat around the table, ate, and read the newspapers. John was engrossed in *The Times Literary Supplement*. Claire was wearing her eyeglasses – which she never did in public – and she had her left arm draped over Richard's shoulders in a proprietary sort of way.

I was wearing a bathrobe that belonged to John, which was ridiculously big for me. I lifted my legs and put my feet on John's lap. He didn't raise his eyes from the *TLS*. Instead, he simply pulled my feet closer to him and squeezed my toes with his hand.

We were all quiet. It was an ordinary Sunday morning. Wimbledon didn't exist. Someone asked, "Is there more tea?" Someone else looked into the teapot. "No, I'll put the kettle on for more."

For just a moment, I allowed myself one wild, impossible thought: this would be a wonderful family into which to marry.

Later that day, John and I went for a walk in Belgravia Square Gardens, which is private. John took a small key out of his pocket to unlock the gate for us. It was a beautiful day after yesterday's rain, but still quite cool for the second day of July.

I said, "I have to go back to Albert House."

"Why?"

"I have no clean clothes. Mrs Ward looks after my tennis dresses, but I need to organize a laundry for my other things."

"Mother has a laundry room upstairs. You can use that. I'll drive you over to Albert House."

"John, I worry that I'm imposing on you at the flat. I'm sure you have other things to do than look after me. I'll stay at Albert House."

"You're sleeping at my flat. I want you available to me."

I liked the idea of being available to him; it made me feel feminine. "You're sure?"

"Don't be silly, Fiona. But I don't have the keys to the 356 with me. So we'll have to stop at the flat first before we head to Wood's Mews."

When we arrived at Albert House, there was a telegram for me from Mother and Father:

POST OFFICE TELEGRAM

ON BOARD THE SS OCEAN MONARCH BY WIRELESS

ARRIVE SOUTHAMPTON MONDAY AM LONDON PM STOP
CLARIDGES WILL SEND TO ALBERT HOUSE FOR YOUR
BAGGAGE STOP ALL TALK ON BOARD SHIP IS OF YOUR
WIMBLEDON WINS STOP LOVE MOTHER AND FATHER

I showed it to John. He said, "Do you think Claridge's will be delivering your things to my flat?"

"Doubtful."

There was one other item waiting for me. The Committee knew that several lady players stayed at Albert House, and so a steward that morning had hand-delivered copies of the Intended Order of Play for the next day.

I was to play on Centre Court Monday afternoon. At '2 pm precisely.'

MONDAY, 2 JULY 1962
CENTRE COURT
LADIES' FOURTH ROUND MATCH
ALL ENGLAND CLUB WIMBLEDON

Claire sat on the bench beside me in the dressing room. "I've played Dorothy many times." My opponent Monday afternoon was Dorothy Fielding.

Claire went on. "She's a good friend of mine. She's British, so the crowd might favor her." Claire chuckled to herself. "But remember what Jack Kramer once said: 'The British would pack Centre Court to watch two rabbits play tennis.' I don't think Dorothy will be a problem for you. I'll be in the players' box watching with John.

She kissed my cheek. "Good luck, Fiona."

She stood and left the dressing room. Three minutes later she came back through the door. "Fiona, do you have Rachel's sweater with you?"

"Yes, it's in my kit."

"Well, put it on before you walk out on Centre Court."

"It's warm. I don't need a sweater."

"The Australians are here, and I mean in force. They're cheering for you already, and I think they want to see that sweater. It's never good to disappoint Australians – they don't like disappointment."

"What are they cheering?"

"You'll find out. Just put on Rachel's sweater before you walk out. You can take it off after you knock up."

She took my hand, squeezed it gently and left again. I pulled on Rachel's sweater.

The callboy came, and Dorothy and I walked to the waiting room and then out onto Centre Court. I was met with a wall of noise from the Australians: "*AUSSIE! AUSSIE! AUSSIE! FI! FI! FI!*"

Over and over again. They were calling me 'Fi.' They yelled this cheer until the umpire finally asked them to be quiet.

My first match on Centre Court. I wasn't scared, exactly, but it was a big moment for me. It was a world away from the Graveyard. No one – not even Claire – was permitted to practice on Centre Court. During the first week of the Championships, I had asked Claire to knock up with me on Centre Court, just so I could see what it was like. Claire – who would do just about anything for me – shook her head. "I can't take you onto Centre Court. You have to wait for the Committee to schedule you to play there."

A tennis player's first Centre Court match, like for me that Monday afternoon? – well, that would always be the first time that player had ever set foot onto Centre Court.

Fred Perry said once that a player could see the ball better on Centre Court because the dark green sighting walls (which screened the tackle used to raise the tarp over Centre Court) and the low roof put the ball against a uniform, dim background. On most of the outer courts, the ball would pop up into the player's sight against a bright, sun-lit, multi-coloured expanse of spectators. Fred thought this difference made players in their first time on Centre Court think they had more time to swing their racket. He was right about that: it took me most of the first set against Dorothy to adjust my timing.

Centre Court was *quiet*. I would close in to the net, volley, and then stop and wait a half-second for Dorothy's attempt to pass me. Centre Court, in that instant, was so strangely tranquil – I loved that moment in each point. You're an actor on the stage of Shakespeare's Globe, with the audience waiting for your next line – *When we have match'd our rackets to these balls, we will in France (by God's grace) play a set.*

But then, Shakespeare in *Henry V* was speaking of real tennis.

In the third set, Dorothy and I were on service at 3-4, me to serve, and we changed ends. I waited for Dorothy to get a cup of water from the tank and then got myself a cup.

While I was drinking, I turned around to glance at John and Claire in the players' box. Claire was standing and hugging someone, but I couldn't see who it was. Then Claire pulled away; she had been hugging Rachel.

I yelled, "RACHEL!"

Rachel smiled at me, and gave me a slight wave, but she wasn't going to do anything that the umpire might consider coaching. Just then, Mother appeared in the gangway to the players' box, with Father just behind her.

I yelled again: "MOTHER! FATHER!"

Mother and Father waved, smiled, and called back, "Fiona!"

I was so excited to see them, and so proud that they could see me on Centre Court, that I pointed back to the court with my racket. "I'M PLAYING ON CENTRE COURT!" As though this wasn't entirely obvious.

A ripple of laughter went around Centre Court, and I heard even the umpire chuckling. There was a bit of cheering.

Then someone stood and began to applaud. In an instant, every spectator was standing and applauding.

The Australians took up their cheer: "*AUSSIE! AUSSIE! AUSSIE! FI! FI! FI!*"

The umpire felt this had gone quite far enough. "Quiet, please, ladies and gentlemen. The sets are one each. Games in the third set are 3-4. Miss Hodgkin to serve."

I held my service easily.

Dorothy served at 4 all. She went up 30-love quickly, but then I followed in her second service and hit a forehand volley winner. 30-15. I looked over at Rachel. She was impassive, with her hands folded in her lap. Dorothy hit a strong first service, which I could only block back, but then she took my shot and hit her return long.

30 all. I was two points away from breaking her serve.

Dorothy took her time preparing to serve. Another strong first service, but this time I took it with my backhand and hit my return as hard as I could. I thought it might float out, but it just touched the outer edge of the line. Dorothy got to it, but hit it back wide.

The umpire said, "Advantage Miss Hodgkin."

Dorothy put her first service into the net. 'Nerves,' I thought to myself. She hit a slice second service. I hit my return right down the line and came in. Dorothy hesitated for a fraction of a second. I was on the centerline of my service courts. Dorothy decided to go crosscourt, but I cut off the ball easily and put it softly into her ad court. She wasn't anywhere near it.

The games were 5-4. I was serving for the match.

I held my service easily; my match; I was in the fifth round.

I sprinted for the net, jumped over it, touched Dorothy's hand, and ran toward the players' box. Halfway there, I remembered the chair umpire, Mr Hewlett, so I turned around and ran back to the chair, reached up, and touched my racket to the toe of his shoe.

"Thanks! Well called," I said.

Then I tossed my racket in the general direction of my pocket book, spare rackets, and Rachel's old sweater, which were lying on the grass next to the umpire's chair, and ran straight toward the BBC television commentary booth. This was a little shed at court level just beside, and a bit below, the scoreboard. The BBC commentator, wearing a sweater and his old-fashioned headphones, saw me racing toward him and looked alarmed.

I was just trying to reach my parents in the players' box above the shed.

I stepped into the first row of spectators and reached up to climb onto the roof of the shed, but it was too high for me. One of the ladies in the first row put her hands under my backside and pushed. Father reached down and grabbed my right hand, while John grabbed my left. The lady spectator pushed, John and Father pulled, and I popped up on the roof of the shed.

From there, it was an easy step into the box.

Father hugged me. "Darling sweetheart," was all he said. I kissed Mother's cheek and then hugged Rachel. I was thrilled to see all three of them.

Claire said, "Solid, impressive play."

Rachel nodded. In the earlier rounds, Claire had been

exuberant about my wins. Now she was a bit more careful.

I guessed what Claire was thinking. By Thursday afternoon, barring rain delays, there would be only two ladies left in the draw. Claire would be one; some of the London bookies were beginning to give odds I would be the other.

John was standing back, on the other side of Claire. Without thinking that every pair of eyes in Centre Court was on me, I slipped past Claire, put my arms around John, and kissed him. I don't mean I pecked his cheek. I gave him a full, 220-volt kiss square on his lips.

The Centre Court crowd was agog over the kiss.

I took John's hand and turned back to face Mother and Father.

Mother's eyebrow was arched at the kiss I had given John.

Father was wearing his DSC ribbon on the lapel of his jacket, and John was wearing his on the left breast of his khaki uniform.

"Mother, Father, please meet Captain John Fitzwilliam of the Royal Marines. John is Claire's older brother."

Then I said, "John, please meet my parents, Doctor Thomas Hodgkin and Doctor Fiona Wilson."

The three of them shook hands. Father glanced at John's DSC ribbon and then looked at John. I could tell he was gauging how old John was.

Father pointed to the ribbon. "Suez Canal?"

John nodded. "You?"

Father shrugged. "U-Boat attack east of Gibraltar. Ship all on fire."

And that was that. Father and John were friends.

I sat on the edge of the bed in the room at Claridge's I was to share with Rachel. Mother was unpacking my clothes and putting them away, just as she did when we traveled when I was, say, 12. Rachel was downstairs having tea with Claire.

I knew that Mother was about to rake me over the coals for my behavior in the weeks since I had left Bermuda for London. I must have insulted the Thakeham family, after Lady Thakeham had been so kind to me. That's what Mother would say. I had been selfish. I had behaved completely contrary to the way I had promised her I would behave in London. And she would want to know what in heaven had happened with Mark?

Mother surprised me. She always did. She put the Tinling gown over Rachel's bed and told me that she would have the Claridge's staff brush it and then steam press it. "We dress for dinner on board the ship home, and you're old enough now to wear a gown like this for dinner. The other passengers will be amazed."

Then she said, "I take it you're seeing John Fitzwilliam?"

"Yes." Well, 'seeing' him was the polite word for what I was doing.

"Does he treat you well?"

"Quite well. He's a gentleman."

"That was my impression when I met him." She exercised her maternal prerogative: "Are you in love with him?"

"Yes. A great deal."

"Is he in love with you?"

"I don't know, Mother. Probably not. He likes me, but that's all. I'm about nine years younger than him. He may think I'm just a child."

"Are you protecting yourself?"

Other girls get to have mothers who would never think of questioning their daughters about sex and who instead assume their daughters simply aren't having sex. Me? No, I have to have for my mother a practical-minded physician who assumes that if her daughter is seeing a naval commando nine years her senior, sex probably enters into the equation.

"Yes. Claire took me to her gynecologist. But I don't want you to be angry with her for that. I asked her to."

"Since I would have done exactly the same for you if I had been here in London, I'd have a hard time becoming angry at Claire."

"Mother, I know I more or less broke a promise I made to you."

"I don't care about any promise you made. I care about whether you're safe, happy, and doing well."

That was exactly what Claire had said Mother would say.

Then Mother asked, "Are you careful?"

"Yes." I laughed a little. "John sets the pace, but he understands I need a minute or so."

I assumed she'd have no idea of what I was talking about, but instead she laughed as well. "Tell me about it."

I was amazed that she knew about these things, but apparently she did. She'd only slept with Father, she'd told me. Father set the pace the way John did? It didn't seem possible.

Then Mother said, "But if you're right about how he feels, that he's not in love, you need to be careful with your own feelings."

"I know."

"So, are you careful with your feelings?"

"No." I gave a rueful laugh. "I'm a mess."

"You're not a mess. You're a quite normal girl."

Mother held up one of my tennis dresses and frowned at it. I know I took five tennis dresses to England, and that sounds like a lot, but since I had arrived in London I had played tennis hard, almost every day, sometimes twice a day, and the tennis dresses, with the constant washing and pressing, were showing the wear and tear.

Teddy Tinling would have gladly – now that I was in the fifth round – given me fancy new tennis outfits for free, which I could accept and still remain an amateur. I knew, though, that Mother and Father wouldn't approve my accepting clothing, and especially not clothing that would, no doubt – Teddy being Teddy – include brightly coloured underpants and short skirts to show off the underpants.

Mother, still holding up the tennis dress, said, "Fiona, I think we need to go shopping for some new clothes for you."

Rachel and I were in our room when John rang that evening.

Rachel answered; she had known John since he was a teenage boy. Rachel replaced the receiver and said to me, "John's in the lobby. He wants you to come see him."

I got my pocketbook and walked over to the dresser. I opened a drawer slightly and pulled out a clean pair of knickers for the next morning and slipped them into my pocketbook. My washbag was in the loo in John's flat; I had everything I needed. I said, "Rachel – "

She cut me off. "You go with John. I'll think of something to tell your father." Rachel had been a teenage girl in love at Wimbledon herself. "But I want you to get a good night's sleep."

I laughed. "I'm not given much control over how much sleep I get!"

Rachel said simply, "John's waiting for you."

John wasn't in the lobby. He had parked the 356 on Brook Street in front of Claridge's. It was a clear evening in London; John had put the hood down. He was in his khaki summer uniform, with shorts and high socks. John was tanned and so fit that I could see the outlines of the muscles in his legs.

He was leaning against the 356, with his arms folded over his chest, chatting with a young London bobby. It sounded to me that they must have known one another in the Royal Marines.

I put my arms around him and kissed him. John opened the passenger door of the 356, and I got in.

The bobby said, "Captain, sir. That's a beautiful young lady you have there."

John said, "I entirely agree, Mike."

He jumped over the driver's door, started the Porsche and threw it in gear. With the motor rasping, we headed into the Mayfair traffic.

The next morning, probably at about the same time Rachel was telling Father that I had decided to spend the night at Claire's flat, I got out of John's bed, pulled on a pair of his boxer shorts, and a grey, cotton t-shirt with 'SBS' in black letters across the front. Both the shorts and the shirt were too big for me by at least twice; I had to hold up his boxers with my left hand.

I went into the hallway kitchen and tried to make tea for John on the huge, ancient cast iron gas stove. At one time, perhaps back in the Dark Ages, this stove must have served the entire house. It had all manner of strange valves and knobs. I turned one of the knobs, struck a match, and lit the burner. Flames shot up to the ceiling.

"John!" I yelled.

John ran into the kitchen and turned off the main valve. We both looked up at the ceiling, which now had scorch marks on it.

He said, "Put your hands up in the air."

I stuck my arms up. He pulled the t-shirt over my head. Without my hand to hold them up, the boxer shorts fell down around my ankles. John scooped me up and held me in his arms.

"There's only one thing you're any good for," he said with an air of weary resignation as he carried me back to bed.

"That's not true!"

"Oh, I forgot. You can also play tennis."

"Right," I said and buried my face in his shoulder.

The Times that morning had a photo of me on Centre Court that the photographer had taken *through* the tennis net. The top of my head was well below the net cord, though my ponytail was whipped above it. I was so low over my haunches that my left hand was down on the grass, probably to keep myself from sliding into the net. The ball was a white smear in the photo, and my eyes were locked onto it – I looked demented, to be honest. I didn't recall the point, but judging from the angle I was holding my racket, I must have been just flicking the ball over the net.

There was a caption under the photo:

THE BERMUDA SURGEON ARRIVES IN HER OPERATING ROOM

"I've invited Lady Thakeham to have tea with you and me this afternoon," Mother said to me.

I should have known this would happen. Mother had accepted the situation on the ground as she found it upon her arrival in London on Monday, but she would want to repair whatever damage I had done to the relations between the Thakehams and the Hodgkins.

"Mother, I – "

She interrupted. "We're not discussing it. Captain Fitzwilliam is not invited – even though I know it distresses you to be out of his sight for even five minutes. I asked Lady Thakeham to bring her son with her, if he can get out of hospital. "

"Oh, you didn't invite Mark!"

"We're not discussing it. We're going to have tea, we're going to be polite, and, if we've done anything for which we should apologize, that's what we're going to do."

"Mother – "

"Fiona Alice Ashburton Hodgkin, do you want me to ask your father to have a word with you?"

I didn't reply.

"I thought not," Mother said.

At tea, Mark did his level best to charm Mother and it worked. He complimented her frock, asked for advice on a difficult diagnosis he'd had that day in hospital, denied with a laugh her suggestion that I had been 'inattentive' as the Thakeham's guest and offered to pour her another cup of tea. "One more of these small éclairs, Doctor Wilson?" he asked, holding out a plate to her.

No female, not even one as practical as Mother, could resist him – except, apparently, me.

I was left to chat with Lady Thakeham. I would rather have swallowed a lizard.

After we finished our tea, Lady Thakeham and Mother went off to the ladies' loo together. Mark and I stood looking at one another in the lobby of Claridge's while we waited for them.

"I don't want you to hit me," Mark said cheerfully.

"I'm not going to hit you. I shouldn't have hit you and I apologize."

"Not at all. You were entirely justified. I didn't treat you well, which I regret very much. And I was certainly wrong when I said you would lose the first round at Wimbledon."

"Actually, your telling me that I'd lose helped me in my first round match. It made me so angry that I was determined to win. Anyway, the mistakes were all my own."

"Well, I'm proud of you. As is everyone."

"Thanks. I appreciate that a great deal."

"Fiona, perhaps before you return to Bermuda we could have dinner together."

"Mark, I can't. You're kind to make the offer. I'm sorry.

I'm seeing someone else, and I probably shouldn't go out with you for dinner."

Here I was stretching the nature of my relationship with John. I'm sure John would have been surprised to hear that I thought our relationship had any element of exclusivity.

At first, Mark was surprised. Then it dawned on him. "Is this the fellow who was the lucky recipient of the kiss?"

The newspapers had all printed photographs of me kissing John and had called it, in huge headlines, "THE KISS."

"I doubt he considers himself lucky, but yes, it's him."

Mother and Lady Thakeham now reappeared. Mark put his hands on my shoulders and leaned over and kissed my cheek. He pulled back and said, simply, "Friends?"

I smiled at him and replied, "Friends."

Then we shook hands, and I noticed that he held my hand with a gentle pressure just an instant longer than I might have expected.

Then Lady Thakeham put her hand in the crook of her son's arm and they swept out of Claridge's lobby.

An objective observer – Mother, perhaps – might have said that I was turning away a handsome and charming boy, close to my own age, who I liked and who shared and accepted my plans to become a physician. He was, after all, the scion of an old and aristocratic, not to mention wealthy, English family. His children would bear titles.

I had the impression that, if I wanted, in a few years it probably could be arranged for me to be Mark's wife and then the mother of his children. If I wanted, someday I could be mistress of 16 Hyde Park Gate and Thakeham House. If I wanted, Myrtle Hanson might agree to be my children's nursery nurse.

But I was giving Mark up in favor of an older man who never would be interested in an exclusive relationship with me – or so Claire said emphatically, and she knew her brother quite well. John himself had said nothing that could lead me to think otherwise.

So I was just fooling myself. But American Grandmother used to say that people are only biological organisms. They don't do what they should do; they do what they want to do.

THURSDAY EVENING, 5 JULY 1962
CLARIDGE'S
MAYFAIR

When John arrived at Claridge's in the 356, Rachel was waiting in the doorway, with her arms folded over her chest, and an unusually grim look on her face. I was beside her. There was a small crowd of tennis fans waiting for a glimpse of me, and there were news photographers with the same goal.

That afternoon, I had won my semifinal match. My win had created a wild sensation in the tennis world. I was the first lady qualifier to ever advance to the final.

Claire had also won her semifinal match that afternoon. She would be my opponent on Saturday.

John got out of the Porsche and opened the passenger door for me with a flourish.

Rachel said, "John Fitzwilliam, I want her back this evening. I want her to get a good night's sleep, both tonight and tomorrow night. Do you understand?"

John smiled. "Yes, Rachel, I'll bring her back tonight."

"This is serious, John. She's playing the final on Saturday afternoon. I'm sure Claire is at home, resting."

"Or something," I said.

Rachel went on. "I don't want Fiona out late, and I don't

want her to come back – " Rachel paused, trying to think of a polite term. "Tired. I don't want her tired."

John laughed. "Why isn't anyone ever worried about *me* being tired? But I promise – I won't bring her back tired."

I got in the Porsche, and we left with the motor rasping. I turned backwards and kneeled on the seat to look back at Rachel over the hood. I leaned my elbows down on the folded, blue hood, gave Rachel a huge grin and two thumbs up.

I couldn't believe that in less than two days I would play to win Wimbledon.

Rachel slowly put out her hands and gave me two thumbs up in return.

I looked back at her in surprise. I could tell from her face that she was sad. No – she wasn't just sad; she was about to begin crying.

She had wanted to win Wimbledon herself so much; she had come so close that July afternoon in 1939. But Rachel loved Claire. She probably realized the first time she saw Claire play that Claire could win Wimbledon for her.

I remembered the first time I served for Rachel in July 1957, when I was 14. I didn't know Claire existed.

But that same Saturday afternoon in 1957, Claire had lost a long, desperate final on Centre Court against Althea Gibson. At the moment I was serving for Rachel, Claire was back in her flat in London, crying. She was in Richard's arms and telling him that she worried she'd never win Wimbledon.

Then in 1960, at long last, she'd held up the Rosewater Dish on Centre Court for the first time.

After I served for Rachel, I didn't keep going to the net. Instead, I turned and glared at her with my mouth open. I wasn't crying anymore, and I wasn't scared. The ball I had served was still in the air above South Road, just beginning its arc back down onto the court.

Rachel looked back at me coldly. She had said only "Like that" and then left.

I was still kneeling backwards on the seat of the 356. John reached his left hand over to brace my back. "Careful," he said. Then he made a racing change down into third gear, and the Porsche howled off through the London traffic.

How could I not have understood? That afternoon in 1957, Rachel must have known that she would teach me to play tennis, that she'd never again tell me to stay back on the baseline. I had, or would have after years of work, the serve I needed to take me to the net.

Rachel had known that first afternoon. I had wondered why she seemed to dislike me, as though teaching me to be a champion was the most difficult thing she could do, but it was something she was obligated to carry out as best she possibly could. The irony was that Rachel had come to love me in the same way she loved Claire. That's why she had looked about to cry as I pulled away in my lover's Porsche.

Somehow, she'd known from that first serve at Coral Beach that, eventually, someday, I would play Claire for the Championship on Centre Court.

And I might win.

At breakfast, I sat beside Rachel, with Mother and Father across from us. Father was reading *The Times* intently. After a few minutes, he folded the paper to display a particular column and then pushed the paper across the table so that it was between Rachel and me. He took his fountain pen from his lapel pocket and used it to point to a headline in the paper:

AN ALL-MARTIN LADIES' FINAL AT WIMBLEDON

I looked at Rachel; she was as baffled as I was. We began to read the article together.

> Twenty-three years ago, on the eve of the war, this reporter, as a young man, covered for this newspaper perhaps the most thrilling ladies' singles final ever played at Wimbledon. An American, Miss Alice Marble, supported by her formidable coach, Miss Eleanor ('Teach') Tennant, defeated a teenage girl from the island of Bermuda, who was then known as Miss Rachel Outerbridge, 6-8, 12-10, 10-8.

The match was played under metaphorical clouds
of war (it was the last Wimbledon until 1946) and
real clouds of rain. There were two rain delays, the
first of half an hour and the second of almost two
hours, and the match was completed only late in the
evening as both twilight and drizzle fell on Centre
Court.

In the weeks before the final, the English public
had become well acquainted with Miss Outerbridge,
because she often had been romantically linked in the
society pages with the handsome, debonair, and
brilliant German player, Gerhardt von Schleicher,
from Berlin's famed Rot-Weiss tennis club and a
member of Germany's Davis Cup Team. The couple
had just quarreled, or so the society pages the
morning of the final said, over Miss Outerbridge's
strong and quite outspoken anti-Nazi stance.

My jaw dropped. Years before, Rachel had once mentioned
the Rot-Weiss club to me. I looked at her, but she was still
reading.

Although Miss Marble ultimately defeated Miss
Outerbridge, this reporter has not seen any other
tennis player with the electric energy and dynamic
play of Miss Outerbridge. That is, perhaps until now.
One of the lady finalists tomorrow is another teenage
girl from Bermuda, Miss Fiona Hodgkin. Miss
Hodgkin is slightly built but runs like the wind and
appears utterly fearless on Centre Court. She has
charmed the spectators at this year's Championships

with her good-natured humor, sportsmanship, and youthful insouciance.

I looked up. "Father, what does 'insouciance' mean?"

"He means you appear to be unconcerned. He's complimenting you, sweetheart."

Miss Hodgkin has won over the Wimbledon spectators by showing her allegiance to the tiny island she represents. She appears on Centre Court with the Bermuda flag sewn onto her tennis dress. Miss Outerbridge, this reporter recalls, wore the Bermuda flag on her dress as well.

"Why do they always say that Bermuda is a 'tiny' island?" I asked. "It's not as though it's a speck."

"It's just the English, dear," Mother said. "Their idea of a good-sized island is Australia."

Yesterday, in her semifinal match against Fancy Pants La Bueno (also known as Maria Esther Andion Bueno), Miss Hodgkin was unperturbed by the loud commotion on Centre Court each time Miss Bueno's short skirt flipped up to reveal her dazzling pink panties designed by the irrepressible Mr Tinling.

Miss Hodgkin plays a wild serve and volley game and accepts risks in making her shots that no doubt many more experienced players would avoid, but in doing so she makes her matches extremely exciting to watch. Indeed, Miss Hodgkin reminds this reporter of no one so much as Miss Outerbridge herself.

Perhaps this reporter should not be surprised, because Miss Hodgkin's amateur coach is Mrs Derek Martin – formerly known as Miss Rachel Outerbridge.

The other finalist is the defending ladies' champion, Mrs Richard Kershaw, who many tennis fans may still recall as Miss Claire Fitzwilliam. Mrs Kershaw is a classic English beauty. Few women tennis players of the top rank regularly appear on the covers of leading women's fashion magazines, as Mrs Kershaw did before her marriage.

I said to Rachel, "Is that true? Has Claire been on the cover of magazines?" Rachel snorted, didn't answer, and kept reading. I don't think Rachel kept track of the women's fashion magazines.

The talented Australian girl, Miss Margaret Smith, has challenged Mrs Kershaw recently, but in this Wimbledon Miss Smith was eliminated on Ladies' Day by the doughty American, Miss Billie Jean Moffitt. Mrs Kershaw has a clear path to her third Wimbledon championship.

There is, however, a delicious irony. This reporter has learned that Mrs Kershaw, when she was a teenager, was also coached by Mrs Derek Martin, and that Mrs Kershaw's interest in tennis, and her competitive spirit, began during her time spent with Mrs Martin.

So, on Saturday afternoon, the spectators on Centre Court will see two ladies battle for a championship for which they have both been prepared by the same coach.

It has been striking to this reporter during the Wimbledon fortnight that Mrs Kershaw and Miss Hodgkin are close friends, as well as tennis practice partners. Centre Court this past Monday afternoon was treated to a memorable kiss Miss Hodgkin gave a handsome Royal Marines officer, who happens to be Mrs Kershaw's brother.

'Oh, great,' I thought to myself. 'Mother will be pleased as punch that I've managed to get my private life into the newspapers again.'

Mrs Kershaw is stronger than Miss Hodgkin, far more experienced in international tennis competition, and has a game that is better balanced than that of the diminutive Bermudian girl. At the top level, however, tennis, to a greater degree than other sports, is more about character than skill or experience. Both these players have character that seems to have been shaped by their common coach, Mrs Derek Martin.

Saturday will be, as it were, an All-Martin final.

I was staring at Rachel, amazed. This was the most incredible story I'd ever read.

Rachel said, "Don't believe everything you read in the papers."

I planned from the start to include in this narrative Rachel's love affair with the tennis player who broke up with her the night before her Wimbledon final. It seemed to me to be part of my own story – even though I hadn't even been born until four years later. But to include Rachel's story I first had to worm the facts out of her.

I dug out my clipping of the old newspaper article that had been published the day before my Wimbledon final with Claire. The fellow who broke up with Rachel, this Gerhardt von Schleicher, had been a member of the German Davis Cup team. Bill Tilden had coached the German team. Rachel had met Tilden at Kooyong. Rachel had met von Schleicher at Kooyong.

I could put two and two together as well as the next pediatrician. Tilden probably introduced her to von Schleicher.

Now Rachel is elderly and frail but completely in command of her faculties. Let's face it – elderly people enjoy reminiscing. So on a recent May afternoon, I left my clinic, took my auto, collected Rachel, and drove her to the Bermuda

Rose Society Garden on Harbour Road, which I knew she appreciated. It's a beautiful place.

I took her walking cane from her and hooked it on the side of a bench in the garden. Then I took her arm and helped her sit down on the bench. She was anxious to make sure she could reach her cane, and I showed her where it was. There were Bermuda roses in bloom all around us.

I was subtle in the way I approached the subject of 1939. "Rachel, how did you meet Big Bill Tilden? What was he like?"

Rachel snorted, found her cane, slowly managed to stand, and walked, unsteadily, to a rose bush. It was a 'Mrs Dudley Cross.' She put her fingers around one of the stems, carefully, to avoid the thorns.

"I'm not telling you anything about Gerhardt."

Before the men's singles final that afternoon, Claire and I stood in a line inside the clubhouse entrance to Centre Court with the men's finalists, Rod Laver and Marty Mulligan. Colonel Macaulay was going to present us to the Queen, who was making her first visit to Wimbledon since 1957.

I was in my tennis dress, but Claire had put on a frock. Claire was known to be a Palace favorite, and she felt a frock might be more appropriate.

With us in line were my parents, and, at the end of the line, John. Colonel Macaulay escorted the Queen into the entrance and, one by one, presented us to her. The Queen stopped to talk with Claire for a few moments.

Colonel Macaulay said, "Your Majesty, this is young Miss Hodgkin, from Bermuda."

I dipped my knee. I was awestruck.

"Good luck tomorrow, Miss Hodgkin."

Colonel Macaulay and the Queen moved onto Father and Mother. The Queen greeted Father, and then the Colonel said, "Your Majesty, this is Mrs Hodgkin."

Mother curtsied.

"It's actually 'Doctor Wilson,' isn't it?" the Queen asked Mother.

I don't know who did research for the Palace, but the Palace must have been world class in this department.

"Yes, Your Majesty, I'm called 'Doctor Wilson' in my clinic."

"I'm told your daughter plans to become a medical doctor as well. You must be proud of her."

"Quite proud indeed, Your Majesty."

Colonel Macaulay turned to John. "Your Majesty, this is Captain Fitzwilliam, of the Royal Marines."

"Captain, we have met before."

"Yes, Your Majesty."

"When you were awarded your Distinguished Service Cross, I believe."

"Yes, Your Majesty."

The Queen smiled. "That was before you took up your" – the Queen paused – "current duties."

John grinned and bowed his head slightly. "Just as Your Majesty says."

The Queen looked back at Father. I sensed that she had meant to say something to Father that she had forgotten when greeting him. "Doctor Hodgkin, I understand that your DSC was awarded at sea."

"Yes, Your Majesty," Father replied. "I was lucky to be above water at the time."

Everyone, even the Queen, chuckled at this – except Mother. She shuddered at how close she and I had come to losing him.

Then the Queen said, "I know my father would have regretted not awarding it to you personally."

Father bowed slightly. "The King favored me with a letter soon after the war, Your Majesty."

I had never seen this letter or even heard of it. A letter from the King wouldn't have simply arrived in the post at Midpoint. The King's Governor General of Bermuda would have delivered it in person, and such a letter would have been the talk of Bermuda for weeks. The Governor General would have quietly implied to his friends over cards and Black Seal rum at the Royal Yacht Club on Hamilton Harbour that the Palace had consulted him directly in the matter. But I had been just a small child then.

"I knew he did," the Queen said.

She turned back to John and placed her hand on his arm. This was a sign of royal favor. "I'm told I can expect even more great things from you in future years, Captain."

I would have thought that neither of the Fitzwilliam siblings would ever be at a loss for words, but I could tell that John had no idea of what to say. So he was silent.

Then Colonel Macaulay led the Queen up to the Royal Box on Centre Court.

Claire and I had decided to practice on Court 14 during the men's final, since the reporters and photographers would be otherwise occupied watching the Queen, while Her Majesty watched Rod dismantle Marty in straight sets. Claire and I could practice in peace and quiet for once.

Claire had to visit the dressing room to change out of her frock – "I can't recall ever wearing a dress at Wimbledon," she said. John and I walked hand in hand to the outer courts. John was going to watch us practice, and then he was going to drive me back to his flat. With John driving his Porsche, we hoped we could evade the reporters.

John and I couldn't have tea out because of the reporters and photographers, so I planned to make him something to eat in his flat. This was risky; I desperately wanted John to like me, and I hoped to show him that at least I could make his tea. Unfortunately, I had inherited American Grandmother's inability to cook.

Claire appeared on the court, and we knocked up. She was about to toss her racket onto the grass when we saw Colonel Legg walking rapidly toward us on St. Mary's Walk. This was astonishing: for Colonel Legg to leave Centre Court during the final between Rod and Marty, especially with the Queen present, was unthinkable.

Claire and I both assumed that, for some unimaginable reason, he was coming to talk with us, but instead he went straight to John and spoke quietly. I couldn't hear what he said.

John turned and said to Claire and me, "Someone's trying to reach me by telephone. I'll be back in a few minutes." He waved to us and left with Colonel Legg.

Claire and I tried to play, but our hearts weren't in the game. Something was wrong, we both knew.

About 15 minutes later, John returned. He was trying to appear casual, but I could tell that he was in a hurry.

"What is it?" I asked.

"I have to leave now."

"Why?" Claire and I both asked at once.

"I have to go away for a bit."

Claire's face instantly turned ashen.

"Where are you going?" I asked.

"I don't know."

"You'll be back for our match tomorrow?"

John laughed. "No, Fiona, I'm going to miss your Wimbledon final. But you'll be in other Wimbledon finals, I'm sure of that."

Claire said nothing.

"But when will I see you again?" I insisted. I was thinking only of myself. I was just 19.

"Fiona, I don't know when we'll see each other again."

Claire said to John, "Tell her, you fool."

Then I knew what he was going to tell me. He was going to say that perhaps it would be better if we didn't plan to see one another again. He was going to break up with me.

John said nothing.

Claire said, "John. Tell Fiona. Now."

My knees were giving way. I started to faint.

John said, "I've fallen in love with you."

I was standing just in front of him. I put my left arm around his waist, then took my right hand and began fiddling with a button on his khaki uniform shirt. This was the only way I could avoid bursting into tears. I just managed to whisper, "I'm in love with you as well."

He put his arms around me.

Claire said, "Why don't I leave the two of you alone?"

John said to her, "Stay here with Fiona. I have to leave now."

"John," I said. I was looking at his chest, not his face. "When you come back, I may be in Bermuda, or in the States."

"I'll find you, wherever you are."

Claire said, "Are you two sure you don't want me to go somewhere else? This sounds as though it could get mushy."

John and I ignored her. We were kissing.

Then I said, "John, will you marry me?"

Claire said, "Fiona, you know, usually we wait for them to ask that."

John said, "I'm definitely going to marry you. Should I speak to your father?"

"No, my parents are old-fashioned, but I think they're past that. I'll talk to them."

John asked, "How many children do we want to have?"

"Two or three? I'm an only child, and I don't want to have just one."

"Three sound good to me," John said.

Claire said, "Children are expensive, keep that in mind. School fees. The nursery nurse. The weekend country house. Holidays at the sea." Claire looked at me. "Well, Bermuda, maybe you have the holidays at the sea included."

"Three would be perfect," I said.

Claire said, "The way you two go after one another, you should expect a minimum of three."

John looked at Claire. "Mother and Father need to know about this, and I'll be away."

"Fiona and I will tell them."

John took my chin in his hand gently and lifted my face so that we were looking at one another. "The moment I come back, we'll make love to celebrate our engagement."

"I won't think about anything else until then."

Claire said, "I *knew* this was going to get mushy!"

John laughed and kissed Claire on her cheek.

Then he kissed me quickly, just brushing my lips, and said

softly, "I love you." I clutched at him, but he broke away.

Then I watched him saunter down St. Mary's Walk.

As soon as he came to Court 3 and thought he was out of our sight, he broke into a dead run toward the auto park and the little silver Porsche 356.

Claire and I walked back to the dressing room without speaking. Once in the dressing room, we were alone. The draw now was down to just the two of us.

Claire said, "John's gone off like this perhaps half a dozen times since he joined the Section. He always comes back." Her face was still ashen.

I looked at her but said nothing.

"He has promised me, as his sister, that he always will be careful."

"Do you believe him?"

Claire grimaced. "No. I don't."

"Neither do I."

"But he always comes back. Don't worry."

Neither of us spoke for a minute. Then Claire said, "John told me that he's in love with you. But he didn't know how you felt." Claire shook her head and laughed softly to herself. "I said to him, 'What? Are you blind?' I told him he was a fool not to tell you."

"Claire, I want the Kershaw children and the Fitzwilliam children to grow up together."

"They'll be cousins. Certainly they'll grow up together. I told you that I met Rachel at my parents' house in the country. The tennis court there is old – it must date from before the first war. The lines have been picked out with chalk for so many years that the lines are raised like ridges above the court. The grass is rough; my parents don't take good care of it. That's where I first played with Rachel."

She laughed. "We'll turn Rachel loose on our children on that old tennis court."

She leaned over, kissed my cheek, and we embraced.

Claire said, "We're going to be sisters-in-law."

I gathered my rackets and my pocketbook and left the dressing room. As I walked down the hallway, I saw Richard Hawkins, the long time Chief Groundskeeper – this was a senior position in the complex All England Club hierarchy. Last Tuesday, Rachel had surprised me by stopping to talk with Hawkins; he had been a ball boy at her final with Alice Marble in 1939. Except for the war years, he had been at the All England Club ever since. He and his family lived in the Lodge beside Court 1.

Hawkins stepped aside for me and said, "Good day, Miss Hodgkin."

Twelve days before, no one at the All England Club had known me. I had been ignored. Claire had to show me where the buffet was, where the dressing room was, where the order of play was posted, and how to obtain a competitor's pass. The only reason I didn't have to stand in line to request a court for practice was that Claire simply announced when and where she preferred for us to practice.

Now this gentleman stepped aside for me.

I knew exactly what Claire would have said to him, so I decided to say the same thing.

"Mr Hawkins, may I call you 'Richard'?"

"Certainly, Miss Hodgkin."

"And I would be happy if you would call me 'Fiona.'"

He beamed. "Thank you, Fiona."

"Will you be here tomorrow, Richard?"

"Yes, of course, to look after Centre Court for your match with Claire. I'll be sitting on the court, to the side of the players' entryway. If you have any problem with Centre Court, just motion to me."

"Then I'll look forward to seeing you tomorrow, Richard."

"Good luck, Fiona."

I smiled at him and continued on my way down the hallway.

He called out to me. "Fiona!"

I turned to look at him. He said, "We haven't had any lady like you here since Claire first came to us."

"Thank you, Richard. You can't know how much it pleases me to hear you say that."

SATURDAY, 7 JULY 1962
ALL ENGLAND CLUB WIMBLEDON

Mother, Father, Rachel, and I walked out of Claridge's to the auto that was going to drive us to Wimbledon. The auto had a small pennant on its radiator in the colors of the All England Club – mauve and green. When we came out, we could see a huge crowd of fans, reporters, and photographers. There were five or six bobbies waiting to escort us to our automobile. Mother held my hand tightly. The crowd cheered wildly, and the bobbies linked arms to protect us while we walked the few steps to the auto.

Mother clutched Father's sleeve. "Tom, I don't like having our daughter exposed in this way."

"Let's get in the auto and be off, Fiona." He was speaking to Mother, not me. We got in the auto, with Father in the front and Mother, me, and Rachel in the rear. We would pack Claire and Richard in the rear as well; there were small jump seats.

The crowd was large and noisy. A bobby knocked on the side window where Father was sitting. Father rolled down the window. "Sir," the bobby said, and then saw the DSC ribbon on the lapel of Father's suit coat. He said "sir" again, meaning it this time. "We're going to use a siren to get you out of here. Is that agreeable, sir?"

Father said, "As you think best, officer."

We roared off behind a police auto with its siren blaring.

The fans and the press hadn't thought that the challenger would be giving the defending champion a lift to Wimbledon, so no one was waiting on the street in Knightsbridge where Claire and Richard lived. They were standing in front of their flat. Claire had her pocket book, tennis kit, and rackets; her blond hair was neatly held in place by her barrette; she was calm, relaxed, and confident.

She sat in the jump seat, leaned toward me and took my hands in hers.

We arrived at the Doherty Memorial Gates to a mob scene. There were dozens of people, both men and women, jumping and screaming, on Church Road just outside the gate, plus all the photographers. There must have been ten bobbies trying to keep the crowd back. I looked over at Mother; she was as unnerved as I. She was holding Father's arm tightly.

Rachel said, "Fiona, let's go." I didn't move. Claire took me by the arm, not gently, and pulled me out of the automobile, with Rachel following me. Two military officers snatched us and hustled us through the gates. I just managed to touch the iron of the gates with my fingers. I felt I had to brush the Doherty Gates, if for just an instant, to have even the slightest chance of winning Wimbledon.

Then the auto with Mother and Father pulled away, with the bobbies slamming the door as the automobile left.

I had no idea they would drive off. My parents, in an instant, were gone. I yelled, "No! Mother! Father!"

Rachel said to me, "Fiona, you'll see them in the players' box in an hour. Don't worry." Then Claire half-dragged me down South Road to the South West Entrance to Centre Court. Neither Rachel nor Claire seemed bothered by the wild scene.

Then it occurred to me; they both had done this before.

As if she could read my mind, Rachel turned to me and said quietly, "You wanted to be here. This is what it's like."

Colonel Macaulay had offered Claire to move me to the lower dressing room for the final, so that we each could have privacy, but Claire had declined. Claire sat me down on the bench in the dressing room, while Rachel asked Mrs Ward for tea.

We drank our tea in silence. Finally, the telephone rang. It was Colonel Legg asking us to come to the waiting room. The three of us stood.

Rachel turned to me. "Stay in the point you're playing. Don't think of anything else. Win each point one by one."

She put her hands on my shoulders. "Fiona, you'll win Wimbledon this afternoon if you make your volleys work for you." Then she kissed my cheek.

Rachel turned to Claire. "Put your first serve in, hard and wide. Fiona's inexperienced, but she's dangerous if she can rush the net."

Claire nodded.

Rachel paused. "Claire, Fiona will win Wimbledon someday, I'm sure of it. But don't let her win today. She's just 19, she's a finalist at Wimbledon; no one could want more than that."

Which was all Rachel had gotten for herself.

Then Rachel kissed Claire's cheek and left us.

I walked down the narrow, dark corridor, carrying my rackets and my pocketbook. Claire followed me. In the waiting room, Colonel Legg was holding two large bouquets of flowers, one from Colonel Macaulay for Claire and the other from himself for me.

Colonel Legg said to us quietly, "Are you girls all right? I was at El Alamein under Monty with the gent in the Ministry of Defence who rang for John yesterday. When he told me he needed to speak with John immediately – well, it's an open secret that John's a senior officer in the – " And then he stopped.

Claire had her arm around my shoulders. She said, "Colonel, we're worried, but we're fine. John will come back. He always does."

I nodded.

Claire kissed my cheek. "Good luck, Fiona."

"Good luck, Claire."

The stewards lined us up, me first, then Claire several steps behind me.

Colonel Legg said, "Well, girls, we'd better get on Centre Court."

The doors to Centre Court swung open and sunlight suddenly flooded the small waiting room.

Claire called, "Fiona?"

I turned to look at her. "Yes?"

"Let's give them a final they'll *never* forget."

"Definitely, Claire."

I walked out into the brilliant sunshine on Centre Court. Two people – Mother and Father – cheered for me. Even the Australians were waiting for Claire. When she walked out on the grass, the crowd roared and stood to applaud her. We turned together and dipped our knees for the Royal Box.

Minutes later, Mr Watson, the chair umpire, pulled the microphone over, turned to Claire, and said, "Mrs Kershaw, are you ready?"

Claire, confident and relaxed, called back, "Ready."

He turned to me. "Miss Hodgkin, are you ready?"

My heart was in my throat. "Ready."

Mr Watson picked up his stopwatch. "Mrs Kershaw to serve. Play."

PART THREE

CENTRE COURT

PART FOUR

CENTRE COURT

SATURDAY, 7 JULY 1962
TWO O'CLOCK IN THE AFTERNOON PRECISELY
CENTRE COURT – FIRST SET

Traditionally, the spectators on Centre Court tend to cheer for the older player, especially when the older player is popular. The younger player will have plenty of chances to win. The older player? Perhaps no more chances.

And Claire wasn't just popular. She was beautiful, and her face might as well have had 'Made In England' stamped on it. She was a perfect sport: whenever her opponent made a remarkable shot, Claire would raise the face of her racket into the air and tap the strings lightly with her fingertips in appreciation. Claire could make this simple gesture elegant. She never challenged line calls, but if her opponent challenged and there was even the slightest question about the correctness of the call, Claire would simply raise her racket in the air – meaning that she conceded the point.

The loss of even an important point was nothing compared to the roar of approval Claire would get from an English crowd. People would turn to one another and say, "That's our Claire!"

Before she was married, Claire had the incredible knack of saying to the press things that were just outrageous enough to make everyone chuckle and say, "That Claire!" but never outrageous enough to make anyone say, "Our Claire shouldn't have said that."

And then she married Richard at St. Margaret's in Westminster. The wedding photograph that was in all the newspapers showed Claire, stunning in Teddy Tinling's off-the-shoulder white gown with her silver hair swept up, pale blue eyes looking straight at the camera, and her usual impish grin, as though she'd just pulled off a piece of mischief. Richard, handsome in a morning coat, his head cocked to one side, holding an empty Waterford champagne flute in one hand, had her hand in his. Once she was married, she stopped talking to the press.

Popular? The English crowds *loved* her.

Her first serve went straight past me.

Claire held her serve in the first game; I won only a single point. Worse, in the second game, she broke my service at 15-game. In two games, I had won only two points. I was terrified. Probably Claire would defeat me in just 30 minutes. Claire was relaxed and in her element. She was hitting perfect passing shots effortlessly. After breaking me, she held her service again in the third game, although at least I made it to game-30.

I served in the fourth game with Claire ahead 3-love. I began to steady myself, just a bit, and got the score to 30-15. I served and headed for the net. Claire returned my serve straight down the line. I lunged with my backhand but only managed to get the top rim of my racket on the ball, making it ricochet off into the stands. I was too far out over my feet, and I fell to the grass.

Claire came up to the net as I was getting up. "Are you all right?"

"I'm fine. Thanks."

Then Claire held up her racket as though she was straightening a string. Her racket then happened to cover her face. Quietly, so that no one but me could hear, she said, "Slow down. Take more time before you serve."

"I know, I know," I said, equally quietly. I kept telling myself, 'slow down, slow down.'

The game was even at 30-all. We went to deuce, but I got the advantage. My serve into her ad service court was sharply angled and drew her wide. Claire's only sensible option was to go crosscourt, which she did, but I was there and cut off the shot with a backhand volley for a winner. I had held my serve, so Claire was to serve the fifth game, ahead 3-1. But at least I was on the scoreboard. Gradually, I was calming down, and my volley was beginning to work for me. Just a bit.

It was Claire's advantage in the fifth game. She served, I chipped my return to her feet, and she hit a hard shot down the line. I split stepped well inside the service line and just managed to catch her shot on my racket. I sent the ball back crosscourt but not hard or deep. Claire had no difficulty reaching it, and she hit a hard forehand to my backhand side. I raced across the court and volleyed her shot back into her ad service court. Again, I didn't manage to hit the ball hard, but my shot was sharply angled.

This time Claire had to run hard to get my ball, but she did, and she threw up a perfect lob over my head. I couldn't get it with an overhead, and I had to turn and run back to my baseline. I got there, barely, without time to turn around, so I swung at the ball while I was still facing away from the net.

The crowd gasped in surprise that I even got to Claire's lob.

My ball fell softly right in the middle of Claire's service court. She could do anything she wanted with it. I ran toward the net, which was a stupid thing to have done just then. She came up to the ball and hit a forehand viciously hard to my backhand side. I lunged for it and got the ball back across the net.

Now Claire and I were facing one another across the net, less than two meters apart. She volleyed my shot at the level of her waist; the ball didn't get anywhere near the grass.

I volleyed back.

The ball went across the net twice in a split second. The crowd held its breath.

Claire volleyed crosscourt, and I volleyed back. The ball had been across the net four times in, maybe, two seconds – *THOCK! THOCK! THOCK! THOCK!*

With the crowd silent, the sound of our rackets colliding with the ball echoed back and forth under the low roof of Centre Court.

Claire then lobbed far over my head, and I had to turn and run for my baseline. I got to the lob only by leaping out over my feet, and my only option was to hit the ball up as high as I could and hope it would land somewhere in Claire's court. Then I fell flat on my face and slid across the grass.

Claire probably thought the point was over. Now my high lob forced her to run back to her own baseline. The ball bounced right on the line. The crowd gasped again because I had gotten off the grass and, like a fool, run to the net, when I should have remained on the baseline to have any chance of staying in the point. My tennis dress had grass stains on it from sliding along the grass.

Claire set up for an overhead, but my lob took a bad

bounce on the line and didn't come up as high as Claire expected. She had to adjust in a fraction of a second and hit a weak shot at her shoulder level. I volleyed it back with my backhand. It was hard and deep to Claire's backhand. Claire hit another lob, but her skill failed her for once. Her lob was high but not deep.

Claire, me, the crowd, Rachel, everyone knew this incredible point was about to end.

I had all the time in the world to set up. Living dangerously, I didn't wait for the lob to fall far. I jumped so that I was well off the grass when my racket made contact with the ball, with my left leg out in the air for balance – a skyhook. I put every single ounce of me behind the racket. I've probably never hit a tennis ball that hard before or since. *THOCK!* The ball smashed into the sideline of Claire's ad court so hard the chalk puffed up and hung in the air for seconds. Claire wasn't anywhere close.

The crowd was on its feet, cheering. I looked over at the players' box. Mother had forgotten herself. She was standing and yelling, "FIONA! FIONA!" Then I turned to look at Claire. She was facing away from me, walking back to her baseline. But she was holding her racket face in the air and tapping her finger tips against the strings.

Deuce. Claire got back to ad and then held her serve. But I was feeling far more confident, and my volleys were clicking into place. I held my service easily in the sixth game, so the games were 4-2 in Claire's favor.

Mr Watson said, "New balls, please."

The ball boys who had been kneeling at the centre posts stood and went to the small Lightfoot refrigerator on Centre Court, removed two cans of new balls and rolled the new balls along the grass to the ball boys at the ends of the court.

On my serve in the eighth game, Claire took me to deuce twice, but I got the advantage and volleyed the ball crosscourt, just out of her reach. The games were 5-3 in Claire's favor, and she was to serve for the first set.

She held her service, and Mr Watson said, "First set to Mrs Kershaw, six games to three. Second set, Miss Hodgkin to serve."

One thing that makes tennis so fascinating to me is advantage scoring – meaning that a player must be two points ahead to win a game, and two games ahead to win a set. Some points are much more important than others. Take the first set in the final I played against Claire, for example. The most important point in the set was in the second game, on my serve, when Claire went ahead of me in the score and then broke my serve.

Now, this was before the advent of the tie-break at Wimbledon in 1971. In 1962, having been broken once by Claire, I would have to break Claire *twice* to win the set. I'd have to get Claire's break of my serve back and then break her again to win. And the server has such a large advantage. Neither player could win without breaking the other's serve.

I was down a set to Claire. I had to win the second set. I couldn't allow Claire to break my service. If she did, I'd probably lose the championship. I might be able to break Claire once, but could I break her twice? Doubtful. So I had to hold my service.

I served to Claire and followed my serve in to the net. Claire was a master of slyly waiting just that fraction of a second to force her opponent to commit to one side or the other and then firing the ball back to the side the opponent *didn't* pick. She could be diabolical. I came to the net in my ad service court. Claire smashed her return crosscourt to my deuce sideline. The instant I saw her begin her swing, I guessed what she would do, and I moved to my deuce side. Her return was perfect and would have bounced exactly on the deuce sideline, except that I was standing at the net to cut it off and send it back straight down the sideline. Claire ran hard, but she couldn't reach my shot. I held my service easily in the first game of the second set.

Then Claire and I traded games, one after another, 1-1, 2-1, 2-2, 3-2. In the sixth game, I took Claire to deuce four times and got the advantage twice. But both times, she won the point. Finally, she got the advantage and hit a perfect stop volley that fooled me. I gave it a try and ran for it, but it bounced twice before I arrived on the scene. Her game.

4-3, 4-4, 5-4, 5-5, 6-5, 6-6, 7-6, 7-7, 8-7. Just when I thought to myself that this could go on all afternoon, I looked at the scoreboard clock. Almost four o'clock. It *had* gone on most of the afternoon.

Then Claire served with the games at 8-9 in my favor. Her first serve was straight down the line, and I hit back a clear winner. She served again. She chipped my return directly to my feet as I came in. I half volleyed back – I was so low that my right knee and the bottom rim of my racket face were both touching the grass. Claire ran, caught my volley, and sent it right back. I volleyed to her deuce court, deep. Claire ran. I volleyed to her ad court, deep. Claire ran. But she didn't get to my volley. love-30. I was two points away from taking the second set.

Claire served. She could usually serve an ace when she needed to and that's what she did. I didn't get my racket on her serve. 15-30. I won the next point, but she won the two points after that. Deuce. I was furious at myself for losing those two points. Claire got the advantage twice, lost it twice, but then won on her third advantage. The games were tied at 9 apiece.

Then she broke my serve. 9-10 in her favor. The crowd was completely silent. Claire had her third Wimbledon singles championship in the palm of her hand. I was exhausted and on the verge of tears. I looked at Rachel and my parents. All three of them looked grim.

Serving for the match, Claire quickly got the score to 40-15. She had two championship points. Our match was almost over. I was falling apart.

I returned her serve and came in. Claire hit a passing shot straight down the line on my backhand side. I lunged for it and hit one of the best volleys I've ever hit – although I fell and hit the grass just after I struck the ball. Claire raced for the ball but got only the rim of her racket on it. The ball shot off into the row of photographers on the side of Centre Court.

My parents were standing and yelling, and – finally! – the Australians decided I needed some encouragement: "*AUSSIE! AUSSIE! AUSSIE! FI! FI! FI!*" Claire tapped her racket face with her fingers. Mr Watson turned and glared at the Australians and they slowly quieted down.

Ad in. Second championship point. Claire served hard,

straight at me. I returned wide to Claire's backhand, trying to push her off the court. I came in behind my return. Claire was pulling her racket back for a passing shot.

"*Fault!*"

Claire looked up in surprise and, instead of swinging her racket, caught my ball in her left hand. I stopped and turned to the linesman who had called Claire's serve out. He was pointing to the service line, meaning that he had called the serve long.

I turned back and called to Claire over the net. "It looked well in to me, Claire. I returned it. Let's play a let."

She motioned to me to meet her at the net. She put her hand on my shoulder and her head beside mine so that she could talk quietly.

"You don't want to play a let on championship point," she said. "It's never been done on Centre Court."

"Well, I don't know what else to do. Your serve was good. The call was late."

Mr Watson turned off his microphone, leaned over, and said to us, "Might I participate in your conversation?"

The spectators closest to the umpire's chair overheard him, chuckled, and turned to tell those further up in the stands what he had said.

Claire said, loudly enough for everyone to hear, "Just girl talk, Mr Watson. Party frocks and babies."

The crowd roared with laughter.

I backed away from Claire and said to Mr Watson, "Claire and I have decided to play a let. Her serve was clearly in. Claire has the advantage and first service."

"I call the score, Miss Hodgkin, not you," he said stiffly.

Claire said, "Well, call it then."

Mr Watson hesitated. "Advantage Mrs Kershaw, first service."

The crowd stood, applauded, and cheered.

Maybe everyone there realized that Claire and I didn't need a chair umpire. We were opponents, but we were best friends. We were going to be sisters-in-law. This match was just between us, and we were going to see it through by ourselves.

Mr Watson, as far as we cared, could have gotten up, gone home, and let us decide which of us would be the Wimbledon champion.

Claire served, again straight at me. I stepped back and ripped my forehand down the line into her deuce court. She got to the ball, barely – and hit it into the net.

Deuce. Both Claire's championship points gone.

I looked over the net and saw why Claire was such a great champion: she was relaxed and calm as she set up to serve to me at deuce. No looking back. It's just another tennis game at deuce. She was serving; she could pull it out.

But for once, she didn't. I won the deuce point, and then, on ad out, I won the game. The games were 10 apiece. We were back on serve.

I had never seen, or rather heard, staid Centre Court like this. Everyone was standing and cheering loudly; today, my granddaughters would say the place was *rocking*. The Australians were the loudest – they were taking full credit for getting me out of the deep hole I had dug for myself. Maybe they deserved it.

I held my serve. On the changeover, as we were drinking cups of water, Claire said quietly, "Well played, Fiona." As I was walking to my baseline, I glanced at the scoreboard just to the left and below the Royal Box.

PREVIOUS SETS					
6	Mrs R Kershaw	–	1	10	
1 2 3 4		SERVER	SETS	GAMES	POINTS
3	Miss F Hodgkin		0	11	

At two o'clock, when we had walked out onto Centre Court, the sky had been brilliantly clear, but gradually clouds had appeared, and now rain threatened. I knew I had to get this set into the bag before it rained. If Claire had a chance to rest, she would come back and win the championship in straight sets.

Claire took her time setting up to serve. Another ace. I walked across to my ad court. I was tired. I needed to put this set behind me. Claire served – and it went into the net. Second service.

"Fault!"

Claire had double-faulted. 15-all.

I won the next two points on volleys. 15-40.

Centre Court was dead silent. My lips were parched; I licked them.

Claire served, I returned and came in. She hit a passing shot, and the ball nicked the net cord and dropped on my side of the net. I lunged, hit the grass, just barely got my racket under the ball, and flipped it back over the net. I was face down on the grass. Claire ran but couldn't reach my stop volley.

The crowd roared.

Mr Watson said, "Second set to Miss Hodgkin, 12 games to 10. The sets are one all."

Then, as though we were in a theatre where everything happened on cue, torrents of rain came down. Richard Hawkins didn't give Mr Watson a chance to declare that play was suspended. He immediately signaled to his groundskeepers, and they leaped onto the court, tore down the net, and unfurled the huge tarp over Centre Court.

Claire grabbed my arm, and we ran to the players' entrance. In the dressing room, we slumped down on the bench together. We didn't say anything. Mrs Ward wheeled in a tea cart, and she poured cups of tea for us.

Claire took one or two sips. "This is beyond doubt the best cup of tea I've ever tasted." I agreed.

Mrs Ward said that, if either of us wanted to bathe or have a massage, we had to do so now. Colonel Legg had told her he expected the rain to last only a few minutes. Claire shook her head. Mrs Ward looked at me.

I said, "Mrs Ward, if I got into the bath now, I wouldn't get out until tomorrow."

I needed to change my tennis dress, but I could barely reach around to my back to reach the zipper. Mrs Ward helped me. I stepped out of the dress and handed it to her. I was embarrassed; my dress was soaked with sweat and covered in grass stains. Claire's white Tinling dress was immaculate. She didn't spend any time spread out on the grass. I found a clean dress in my kit.

I had forgotten that I had one white tennis ball tucked under my knickers. I dropped it out onto the floor.

Claire said, "I was wondering why the ball boys could find only five of the balls."

We sat in the dressing room for 15 minutes. We spoke a couple of times, but we mostly left one another alone. I was thinking about John; she probably was as well.

The rain stopped.

When we walked back out onto Centre Court, I turned and looked at the scoreboard.

PREVIOUS SETS		SERVER	SETS	GAMES	POINTS
6 10	Mrs R Kershaw		1	1	
1 2 3 4					
3 12	Miss F Hodgkin	–	0	1	

"Final set. Miss Hodgkin to serve. Resume play," Mr Watson said into his microphone.

I served and quickly went up 30-love. On my next serve, Claire chipped to my feet. It wasn't a difficult half volley, but I carelessly hit it too low. The ball hit the net cord and fell back into my court. 30-15. I served and faulted on my first serve. I saw Claire take one step into the court, even though she knew I usually wouldn't take anything off my second serve. I decided to teach her a lesson for stepping in, and I hit a hard second serve. But it went long.

My first double fault today. So much for trying to teach Claire a lesson.

The crowd gasped. Claire was at 30-30 on my serve.

I served, came in, and volleyed Claire's return for a winner. My advantage. I served and followed my serve in. Claire had been chipping her returns, but now she hit an incredibly hard return down the line. I watched the ball go past me from about a meter away. Deuce.

The crowd had gone completely silent. Everyone knew what was at stake: the next two points might well decide the championship. If Claire broke my serve, all she had to do was hold her own serve, and in a few games she'd be serving for the championship.

I lost the deuce point and then, on Claire's ad, I tried a risky stop volley that backfired on me. It landed too deep into the service court. Claire raced to the drop shot, made it, and passed me at the net.

The crowd was cheering for Claire; she'd broken my serve; they thought she just about had her third straight championship wrapped up.

Claire held her service, and then I served with the games love-2 in her favor. I held my service, Claire held her service, and so it went. In what seemed like no time, Claire was to serve for the championship, with the games at 5-3.

The crowd was silent. This was almost over. Claire had told me once how quickly things happened on Centre Court; now I knew what she meant.

I was scared. I looked over at Rachel, but she was

impassive. I looked at Mother.

Suddenly, Mother jumped to her feet and yelled as loudly as she could, "FIONA! BREAK HER SERVE!"

The crowd all laughed, but in a good-natured way, and then, all at once, they stood and cheered. Mr Watson looked around to make sure that Rachel wasn't saying anything.

Mother wasn't my coach and so was free, like any other spectator, to yell anything polite she wanted between points. Claire looked at Mother, lifted the face of her racket, and then, still looking at Mother, Claire smiled and lightly tapped the strings with her fingertips.

I thought, 'I am *not* going to lose this match.'

Claire served, and in few minutes we were at deuce. It went to her advantage, which was championship point, but I won the point, and we went back to deuce. Claire hit her first serve into the net, and then set up for her second serve. I returned it, hard, down the line, and came in. Claire hit crosscourt, but I cut it off for a winner. My advantage.

Claire served down the middle, a classic, beautiful Claire serve. I got my racket on it, just barely, at about my shoulder level, and hit it crosscourt into her ad court. But it wasn't a strong return. Any sane player would have stayed on the baseline, but I went to the net. Claire had plenty of time to decide what to do, and she had plenty of good options. She went down the line on my forehand side, trying to thread the needle between the sideline and my racket.

I caught her shot and volleyed it back crosscourt, so Claire had to chase it down, which she did, but I cut off her return with my backhand. She raced for the ball, but she was too late.

I had broken Claire's serve.

The games were now 4-5, with me to serve. If I held my serve, this set would be tied at five games apiece.

Claire had turned her back to me. She was looking at the strings on her racket and shaking her head. She had three championship points, two in the second set and the third just now, and she had lost all three.

I looked over at my parents; Mother and Father both gave me two thumbs up and huge smiles.

I held my serve. The games were tied 5 all. Claire held her serve, so the games were 6-5 in her favor, with me to serve. Claire and I changed ends and stopped for cups of water from the tank under the umpire's chair. Claire smiled and whispered, "Long afternoon." We usually weren't given much time on the changeover, and you could forget sitting down to rest. It would be 1975 before there were chairs for the players on the changeover.

But this changeover was one of those moments in a long tennis match where the crowd thinks, 'This isn't ending anytime soon. Best visit the tea lawn, stretch our legs, and get a cup of tea or a pint'. Many of the spectators took advantage of the changeover to leave their seats. Mr Watson recognized this fact of tennis life and allowed a bit of extra time for the changeover and the partial clearing of the stands.

I held and tied the games again 6-all.

It was past six o'clock. The first evening shadows were approaching Centre Court. Our match had started longer than four hours ago. I gave myself one moment to think about John while I pretended to look at the strings on my racket.

Then I put him out of my mind. I would think about John after I defeated his sister – or she defeated me. But not just yet.

Claire held her serve, and then I held my serve. The games were 7 apiece. Then the games became 8 apiece. Then 9 apiece.

I sensed that Claire's serves were slowing down just slightly. To win, I had to break her again. It was Claire's service. I knew that this was probably my only chance; I was exhausted. If I let this match last longer than a few more games, I would begin to crumble.

I knew the only way to break Claire, at this stage, was to make her run from one side of the court to the other. Over and over. If I could break her serve now, then I would be serving at 10-9. Then, if I held my serve, the match would be finished, and I would win.

Claire served. Yes, I had been right; her serve *was* slowing down. Not much, but maybe just enough. Claire was tired too.

I returned her serve to her ad court and charged the net. Claire ran to catch my return and, again, she made a safe crosscourt shot, which I volleyed back for a winner.

We went to deuce twice before I got the advantage. I set up to receive and looked across the court at Claire. She served, and I hit a solid return and came to the net. Claire hit a beautiful, sharply angled crosscourt shot that went under my forehand before bouncing on the sideline.

So back to deuce again. I had thrown away my ad point.

"*Out!*" A way late call.

There was a dull roar from the crowd; everyone knew the ball had landed in – except apparently the line judge. I looked at Mr Watson. "That was a late call. Did you see the shot?"

"Miss Hodgkin, I cannot overrule." In those days, the

chair umpire wasn't authorized to overrule, although sometimes an umpire would give a line judge such a withering stare that the judge would change the call.

I held my racket in the air. "I concede the point." I looked back pointedly at the line judge. "Claire's shot was well in."

The crowd roared its approval.

I looked at Claire. She had already moved back to her deuce court before I had conceded. She had known I would concede the point. Then she served an ace; I wasn't even close to it.

Ad in. She was about to escape one more time.

Then, suddenly, I felt a cramp in my right thigh. I rubbed it and looked at Rachel. She shrugged. Nothing to be done. I was finished if I began cramping badly.

I returned Claire's service, took the net and volleyed deep. She just got to my volley, but her shot was weak, and I simply put the ball away for a winner. My advantage again. I worried about the cramp in my thigh. It hurt, and I couldn't move well.

Claire served, and I hit my best return of the afternoon. A winner. I had broken her serve. The games were 10-9 in my favor. I would be serving for the championship.

But my cramp was getting worse. I looked at the scoreboard clock. Coming up on seven o'clock.

We had been on the court for hours. We had played 50 games of tennis. We were exhausted.

SATURDAY, 7 JULY 1962
SEVEN O'CLOCK IN THE EVENING
CENTRE COURT – THE CHAMPIONSHIP

I hadn't thought for years about the end of my match with Claire – or, more accurately, I hadn't recognized that I have little recollection of it. I know the final score, and I remember playing the first two sets, and most of the third set, but I can't recall the end.

I wrote to the Committee of Management to ask if there was a film of the final that day and, if so, might I have a copy. The Committee graciously replied that there was indeed a black and white film made by the BBC of its live television broadcast, and they enclosed a copy of the film on a DVD.

After I watched the DVD, I knew why I couldn't recall the ending. My head had hit the court twice within seconds, and hard both times. I probably suffered a slight concussion. It reminded me that, after I had finally gone to sleep that evening at Claridge's, Mother had woken me to ask if I felt at all nauseous. She had held my head in her hands and shined the bed table light into my eyes. Now I realize she was making certain my pupils hadn't dilated, which might indicate a serious concussion. But I was fine, except that I couldn't recall much about few, dramatic moments in my life.

317

I watched the DVD in our living room. My granddaughters watched with me. One of them asked, "Bermuda Grandmother, why was your racket so small? It looks like it's made of wood or something." Remarkably, I see myself on Centre Court, barely aged 19, in the third set. I'm serving for the championship.

On the film, I look confused. I push my hair out of my face – somehow my ponytail has come undone, and for some reason I haven't put it back in order. How could I even see to hit the ball? I reach down to rub my thigh. When the television camera focuses on me bending over my thigh, there's sweat dripping from my forehead.

Mr Watson is speaking into his microphone. "Deuce."

I serve. It goes over the net and into the service court, but that's about every good thing you could say about it. Claire, though, doesn't put it away. She makes a good return but not a winner. I'm out of position and off balance, and I hit my return shot into the net.

Mr Watson says, "Advantage, Mrs Kershaw."

Break point. If Claire breaks me now, I'm done for.

The film is grainy. I rub my thigh. I look as though I'm in pain from the cramp. I serve. Again, it isn't much of a serve, but at least it's in play. Claire is determined to win this point. She blasts her return down my deuce court sideline. I just get to her return and send it back down the same line. This time, Claire goes crosscourt. I'm on the centerline of my service courts, and with my backhand I catch her shot on my racket face and drop it into her deuce service court.

Mr Watson says, "Deuce."

On my first service, I fault. The crowd gasps. Giving Claire Kershaw a second serve is never a good idea. I set up.

I serve a wide, sharply angled serve to Claire's forehand. My serve pulls her off the court. I'm in my ad service court when her return comes over the net, and I volley it deep into her ad court. She runs but can't make it.

Mr Watson says, "Advantage, Miss Hodgkin."

Championship point. Centre Court is silent.

My serve is weak and poorly placed. It bounces in the center of her ad service court. She can do anything she wants with it. Still, I rush the net. Claire waits a fraction of a second for me to commit, and I drift slightly to my right, betting she'll go down my deuce sideline. Then she blasts the ball crosscourt.

I lunge wildly for the ball with my backhand and hit it back, barely. I get my ankles tangled together, and I fall on my back, outside the sideline. The back of my head hits the ground so hard it bounces off the grass.

My backhand shot goes over the net but it's a sitting duck for Claire. On the film, I see Claire set up perfectly: she has all the time in the world. She split-steps, takes a short, precise backswing, and hits the ball softly into my deuce service court. She's taking no chances. Just hit the ball far away from me. I'm flat on the grass off the court. I can tell what she's thinking: take away the championship point, get back to deuce, and then win this game.

I watch this part of the film over and over. I push up with my left hand; I still have my racket in my right hand. I'm on my feet as Claire's shot crosses over the net, but I'm so far off the court that I could chat with the spectators in the first row of seats – and her ball is heading to the other side of the court.

On the film, I see myself shifting my racket to my left hand. It's my only chance. I switch hands by instinct.

When Claire's ball bounces, it barely lifts off the grass into the air. I'm sprinting across Centre Court, and my right foot lands on the centerline just as the ball begins its downward trajectory.

I'm a meter away from the ball. There's nothing else I can do.

I launch myself into the air, push out my racket in my left hand and barely get it under the ball. I whip my left arm up, just as my forehead slams into the grass. The racket flies out of my hand.

My face skids on the grass, and now, watching it 50 years later, I can almost taste the grass, dirt, and blood. My nose is bleeding.

Claire has already turned away, heading back to the baseline. She thinks she's saved championship point; now she's at deuce; she's back in this game.

My shot goes over the net by a centimeter and falls onto Claire's court. The spectators jump to their feet with a huge roar. She hears the cheering, looks down, and sees the ball rolling past her across the grass. Her mouth is open. I know she's thinking, how? It's impossible that I could have gotten to her shot.

Looking at Claire's face on the film, I can see that she's devastated. But she drops her racket, jumps across the net, comes over to me, and kneels on the grass. I slowly get up onto my hands and knees, but I'm dazed, with blood dripping from my nose. Claire puts her arm over my shoulders, she says something into my ear, makes me sit up on my knees, and helps me stand up. She's pinching my nose with her fingers to stanch the bleeding, and she's saying something to me, but it's inaudible on the soundtrack, and I can't recall anything she said.

I've never asked Claire about this moment; it must have been terrible for her.

Mr Watson on the film begins the traditional recitation of the score: "3-6, 12-10, 11-9, Miss Hodgkin wins game, set, match, and" – here there's a slight pause for effect – "championship."

Claire leads me to Mr Watson's chair, where I reach up to shake his hand, tentatively, as if I'm still not sure where I am, and then Claire walks me to the water tank under the umpire's chair and pours me a cup of water.

Watching the film, I see I never shook hands with Claire, which, I'm sure, is unique in Wimbledon finals – although maybe it counts for a handshake when you would never have made it off Centre Court without your opponent's arm holding your shoulders tightly.

Claire finds a towel to hold against her face. It's not audible on the soundtrack, but now I can recall the sound of Claire crying softly, covered by the towel.

A ball boy hesitantly comes up and offers me a bottle of Robinson's Barley Water and a towel. I take both, sip some Robinson's, wipe off my face, and pinch my nose with the towel.

The film shows the players' box, with my parents and Rachel standing and applauding – they look so young! Then the camera pans down to me, and I suddenly use the remote control to freeze the film.

A news photographer had taken a shot of exactly this scene, and the photo was on the front pages of all the London Sunday papers the next morning. The photographer, later that summer, sent me a print of the photo, which I've kept on my dressing table ever since. It's still in a cheap, plastic frame I bought in Hamilton just before I returned to Smith that September. I've glanced at it most mornings of my adult life.

In the photo, my tennis dress, with its small Bermuda flag, is streaked with grass stains, dirt, and sweat. There are smears of blood and dirt still on my face; my hair is a tangled mess. I'm standing there holding the Robinson's bottle in the air pointed toward the players' box. I have a huge gamine smile on my face, and I'm looking straight at my parents and Rachel. It had been the greatest ladies' singles final ever.

I had won Wimbledon.

That evening, Mother vetoed for me the Wimbledon Ball at Grosvenor House, so Rod Laver, the gentlemen's champion, had to dance with Claire rather than me. To be honest, I didn't want to go to the Ball. Mother and Father had decided my nose wasn't broken, but already I had a bruise appearing on my face. Mother had held an ice pack on me for 15 minutes. All I wanted was to have a bath and tea in the room I shared with Rachel and go to sleep.

Claire rang before she left her flat for the Ball to see how I was feeling. We talked for a couple of minutes about our match. I held an ice pack to my face.

Claire asked, "Have you told your parents about you and John?"

"No. Not yet. I haven't had time."

"Well, you need to tell my parents. Before you sail for Bermuda." My parents and I were sailing for Hamilton from Southampton on Wednesday. Rachel was staying in England to visit her relatives in the Midlands.

Claire said, "Here's what we'll do. Tell your parents tomorrow. Then you and I will meet for lunch on Monday.

Let's go to The Goring, on Beeston Place. We can talk then."
Claire said this in a conspiratorial tone, as though we were
planning a bank robbery. "But tell your parents that my
parents want to have them for tea Monday afternoon. I'll
arrange that with Mother and Father. Then, during tea, you
can tell my parents."

I replied quietly, because Mother was still in the room.
"That sounds as though I, by myself, have to tell both sets of
parents."

"Well, you're the one who's engaged to John, after all."

So I agreed to Claire's plan.

Claridge's delivered a wonderfully full tea tray to our room,
and, wearing only my bathrobe, with my wet hair hanging
down my back and a nascent bruise on my nose, I stepped
outside into the hall to hold the door open for the lady who
was delivering the tea. I looked down the hall toward the lift
and saw a London bobby standing there. He was the same
bobby that John had been chatting with earlier in the week.
Even though I was wearing just the bathrobe, I let the door
to our room close and walked down the hall toward him.

"Good evening, Officer," I said. "I think we've met, but
my friend John Fitzwilliam failed to introduce us."

The bobby smiled. "Well, Miss, perhaps the Captain was
more interested in seeing you. Congratulations to you on your
win today."

"Thank you, and I'm glad to see you, but why are you here?"

"Just to make sure that anyone who gets off the lift
belongs here, that's all, Miss. Normal procedure for us. I'll be

here for a bit, and then one of my mates will take my place."

He meant he was there to protect my privacy.

"Officer, may I bring you a cup of tea?"

"That's not necessary, Miss."

"I'm bringing you a cup. Milk or lemon?"

"Milk, Miss, please."

I returned to the room, and Rachel opened the door for me. "Do we have an extra cup?" I asked.

"The lady brought two extra cups, for your parents, I expect."

I poured a cup of tea, put milk in it and said to Rachel, "I'll return in one moment."

I went back in the hall. I looked ridiculous barefoot, with wet hair, a bruise on my face, wearing nothing but my hotel bathrobe. I carried the cup of tea to the bobby. I could tell he was looking at my legs. I hoped he didn't realize or imagine that I was naked under the bathrobe. "Here you are."

"Thank you, Miss."

I started to go. He said, "Will Captain Fitzwilliam be here this evening?"

"John has been called away on duty."

"Just as you say, Miss," the bobby replied stoically. He knew what that meant.

I walked away.

"Miss!" the bobby called out.

I turned around.

"I served directly under Captain Fitzwilliam in the Royal Marines for the better part of two years. He was the finest officer in the Marines."

"Thank you, Officer. I'm happy to say he is my fiancé."

"Well, my congratulations to you both."

SUNDAY, 8 JULY 1962
AFTERNOON TEA AT CLARIDGE'S
MAYFAIR

Winning Wimbledon certainly increases the invitations a girl has to lunch and dinner dances. On Sunday, Mother fielded four invitations for me to have lunch on Monday, and I think five invitations for dinner dances on Tuesday evening. She turned them all down.

When I walked out of Claridge's, there were photographers, but my bobby friend would shoo them away when I came out. Father was approached by an American businessman who had plans for 'promoting' me in the States. Father's curt response was decidedly negative. I knew Mother and Father were proud of me, but I sensed that the attention now being paid to me at age 19 made them uneasy.

At tea that afternoon, my parents launched their coordinated attack. They said that my winning Wimbledon had been extraordinary, they were proud of me, but they hoped I wasn't going to forget my medical studies. Like the good mixed doubles partners they were, first one talked and then the other about my future and my responsibilities to Bermuda, but I cut them off in mid-sentence. I told them that I would be back at Smith in September to continue with pre-med.

I had gotten what I wanted from tennis.

I reached into my pocketbook and pulled out a telegram I had received the evening before. The author of the telegram suggested that, although I was an amateur, still there were certain financial arrangements that could be made, if need be, to induce me to compete at Forest Hills that August. I handed the telegram to Father. "May I ask you to reply to this for me?" He took the telegram in his hand.

"Mother, Father, there's something you should know." I don't know why it is, but the phrase 'there's something you should know' coming from a child instantly grabs the attention of parents.

They both looked at me intently. They weren't going to like this, not at all, and I dreaded telling them. I knew what they would say: 'What about medical school? Aren't you too young to make a decision like this? Isn't he a bit old for you? Have you had time to think about this carefully? You've only known him for a few days.' I didn't have any answers for those questions. I didn't have an engagement ring. I didn't even know where John was or when I would see him again. I was a pathetic excuse for an engaged daughter.

Anyway, I told them; I just blurted it out. "I'm engaged to be married to John Fitzwilliam."

In the middle of Sunday tea in the dining room of Claridge's, they both hugged me at once. They were from old, established English families, and they probably knew half the people having tea that afternoon at Claridge's. Knew? They were probably *related* to half the people at tea. But still, they forgot themselves. Mother started crying. Father said, "Darling, sweetheart."

Mother said, through her tears, "That is so wonderful."

Father said, "I hope the plan is to be married in Bermuda?"

Mother wiped her eyes. "We should have the wedding in the garden of Midpoint. That's where your father and I were married."

Father said, "Captain Fitzwilliam is perfect for you."

"Fiona, you should wear what you want, of course. If you want to wear my wedding dress, we still have it at home."

Mother's wedding dress had been English Grandmother's wedding dress in 1917, during the Great War. One afternoon in 1942, in the middle of another war, my two grandmothers had hurriedly altered the dress to fit Mother. I can imagine English Grandmother that afternoon watching the sweeping, wild loops of thread American Grandmother was using to stitch the dress back together. English Grandmother probably said dryly, "Fiona, dear, we're all so pleased that you didn't let William Halsted talk you into becoming a surgeon." After my parents' marriage, the dress had spent two decades in a humid Bermuda closet, ripe with mildew.

It was not, shall we say, a Teddy Tinling wedding gown.

"Mother, I plan to wear your dress when I marry John."

She began crying again. Father put his arm around me. "In a few years, several grandchildren would be welcome additions to the family."

As planned, I met Claire in Beeston Place for lunch on Monday. She simply left the white Alfa with its hood down, smack in front of The Goring, handed the keys to the doorman, and kissed his cheek.

"Darling young man," she said to him. He looked to be around 70. "You will take care of my Alfa?"

"Certainly, Claire," he replied, tipping his bowler.

She took my arm and whispered, "Now I'm *sure* I'm pregnant!"

I giggled.

A press photographer standing across Beeston Place caught this scene, with Claire speaking to me and me giggling. A morning newspaper the next day ran this photo on its front page under the caption, 'WIMBLEDON FOES CHATTER IN BELGRAVIA!'

We walked out on the hotel's veranda, looking over the gardens, and took a table. I ordered a plate of cucumber and salmon sandwiches for myself, all of which Claire proceeded to eat. After lunch, we went to her parents' home to prepare tea; she had told her mother not to worry about tea, that Claire and I would take care of it.

For Immediate Release

The Association has received an inquiry from the United States Lawn Tennis Association in regard to whether arrangements could be made for Mrs Richard Kershaw and Miss Fiona Hodgkin to enter the United States National Championships upon the lawns at Forest Hills in New York City. In light of the intense public interest in a potential re-match between Mrs Kershaw and Miss Hodgkin, and the continued speculation in the sporting press, the Association has concluded to issue this statement in reply to the inquiry.

Mrs Kershaw has advised the Association that she and her husband are expecting their first child, and therefore she will not be in a position to compete at Forest Hills.

Dr. Thomas Hodgkin, D.S.C., father of Miss Hodgkin, has advised the Association that his daughter's pre-medical studies at college will cause her to limit her tennis competition to collegiate matches in the New England area of the United States. Consequently, Miss Hodgkin will not compete at Forest Hills.

* * * * *

After our Wimbledon final, neither Claire nor I ever played tennis in international competition again.

PART FOUR

ST. MARGARET'S

OCTOBER 1962
ST. MARGARET'S
WESTMINSTER
LONDON, ENGLAND

October came, and I was back at Smith as a sophomore pre-med student immersed in organic chemistry. I had told the tennis coach that I would still play on the team, but that I no longer wished to play in the number one position. I said that my chemistry classes and labs would prevent me from giving the tennis team the time it deserved if I remained in the first position. This was half true. If I could have left the team altogether without disappointing my teammates, the coach, and Smith generally, I would have done so. But for Smith to have a Wimbledon champion on the team was sensational, so I played.

By late October, Claire and her parents had still heard nothing from or about John. I had been sick with worry about him, but slowly, in my heart, I came to feel John was dead. Otherwise, by then, he would have come back to find me. One day, I walked back to Emerson house through the New England fall afternoon and found a telegram addressed to me from London on the hall table. I picked it up and walked back outside to read it.

There was a bench about a hundred meters from the house, under a small copse of trees, and I walked to the bench and sat down. There were the red and gold leaves that New England trees produce in the fall on the ground, and there was a slight breeze that blew the leaves around my ankles. I looked at the telegram envelope for probably 20 minutes before I opened it. I knew exactly what the telegram would say.

WESTERN UNION

LEARNED TODAY JOHN DID NOT SURVIVE STOP HIS REMAINS NOT RECOVERED STOP NO OTHER INFORMATION STOP SERVICE ST MARGARETS NEXT WEEK STOP COME LONDON SOONEST STOP

LOVE CLAIRE.

I didn't cry. I was numb with sadness. Although I've led a happy, privileged life, and, after a long time, I finally said goodbye to John, even today a part of me has never left that bench under the trees, where I sat mourning him.

I went back inside my house and made the arrangements to make an international call to my parents. I sat down while I waited for the call to go through and held the telegram between my fingers. When the call came through, I picked up the receiver. Mother spoke first. She was crying. "Fiona, we know. Claire sent Rachel a telegram."

"Claire has asked me to come to London." I knew this would be a large expense for my parents, and going to London would take me away from Smith for at least a week, perhaps longer.

Father said, "You have to go to London. I'll make your flight arrangements in the morning. Flying from Boston probably would be best."

It was too late that day to send a telegram from Northampton, but in the morning I cut an English class and walked into town, where I sent Claire a telegram.

POST OFFICE TELEGRAM

ON MY WAY LONDON STOP LOVE FIONA

Claire met me at Heathrow. She was visibly pregnant. We embraced, and I asked, "Tell me how you feel?"

"Tired and nauseated. The baby has moved in and completely taken over. I wanted to be this way?" We half laughed and half cried.

I stayed with Claire's parents. The day after I arrived, Claire and I undertook the task of clearing out John's flat. There were few personal things there; maybe, I thought, he had deliberately kept his life simple, at least until he met me. Out of the corner of my eye, I saw Claire discreetly pull a pair of lady's knickers from John's laundry and put them in her pocket.

"Claire, you look exhausted. Sit down, and I'll make you a cup of tea." John had shown me how to operate the huge stove to make tea.

Claire sat on the couch without protest. When the tea was ready, I handed her a cup. "May I have the knickers?"

"What knickers?"

"Claire, they're mine."

"Oh," she said. "I was just concerned that – " She

stopped, reached into her pocket, and handed them to me. "You and John must have been quite compatible in bed."

"Yes, quite compatible, in all ways."

I got myself a cup of tea and sat down beside Claire. She said sadly, "We'll never be sisters-in-law."

I nodded.

"When I was a girl," Claire said, "I looked up to John. I followed him around, at least when he would let me. But I always wanted a sister. I wanted someone to talk to."

She didn't say anything for a moment. "I don't remember the Blitz well. This house wasn't hit directly. It was damaged, but we could stay here. We were lucky. One night, Mother and Father told John and me that the next day the two of us would be leaving for Canada, for Quebec City, on the St. Lawrence. Father had a business friend there. He and his wife were going to take us in. Mother and Father worried about the sea travel, but they must have decided it was worth the risk to get us to Canada. Father had gotten us passes for a train to Liverpool the next morning – that wasn't easy to arrange. John and I were going to go by ourselves. Father started to explain to John how to get us from the train to the ship in Liverpool."

"I never knew you and John were evacuated to Canada."

"We weren't."

"Why not?"

"John told Father, 'I won't leave London while the King is here, you and Mother are here, and we're being bombed.' Father said to him, 'Son, this is the best thing for you and your sister.' But John said, 'Father, I'll run away, live in the Tube, and take Claire with me.' Mother started crying and saying that we had to leave, how could we question our parents. But Father looked at John and said, 'If you stay here, you and Claire both could be killed.'"

There were tears steaming down Claire's face. She wiped them away with her palm. "John told Father, 'I won't leave London, and Claire won't either.' Mother was saying we would have to leave the next day, but Father motioned to her with his hand. He looked at me: 'Do you know what your brother is saying?' I didn't, but I told him, 'I'm staying with John.'"

"So you didn't go to Canada?"

She shrugged. "All four of us stayed in this house. We weren't evacuated. We lived here, on the ground floor, for awhile."

She looked around. "This used to be a coal bin, before Mother had the flat made for John."

Then she changed the subject. "Fiona, you and I could decide to be sisters."

I said, "Yes."

I put my arms around her, and we held one another. We talked for a long time, and finally she fell asleep on my shoulder. I lowered her head onto a pillow on the couch, stood up, got the blanket from the bed I had shared with John and gently covered her with it.

The day before the memorial service, an equerry from Buckingham Palace arrived with a letter and a small wooden box. The letter was from the Queen, in her handwriting. She had awarded John the Victoria Cross posthumously "for exceptional valor in defending the realm." The VC was in the box. Legend had it that the VC medals were struck from the barrels of canon used in the Crimean War.

I saw John's father open the box, glance at the medal, close the box, and shove it onto the mantelpiece. It's still there today. I don't think it has ever been moved or maybe even touched.

The memorial service was full of military men, many tennis players, and friends of Claire and her parents. There were also a half dozen or so men in dark business suits, but none of them seemed to have a name. Just before the service began, Prime Minister Macmillan slipped into a pew in the back of St. Margaret's. Claire asked me to read the twenty-third psalm, which I did.

As I walked out after the service, I saw Mark Thakeham, who had left the church and was waiting just outside.

"Hello, Fiona. I know you cared about him. My condolences."

"Mark, thank you for coming to the service. It's thoughtful of you."

"I saw in *The Times* obit that he was awarded a VC. For 'defending the realm,' without any more detail."

"Yes. Maybe some of the people here today know what happened to John, but I don't."

The brief obit in *The Times* had also said that it was "rumored" in Whitehall that John had been one of the senior officers of the secretive Special Boat Section. It said he was survived by his parents and by his sister, Claire Fitzwilliam Kershaw, who had been the 1960 and 1961 Wimbledon ladies' champion – and that his "frequent companion" had been the 1962 Wimbledon ladies' champion, Miss Fiona Hodgkin, of Paget, Bermuda. The newspapers didn't know we had been engaged.

"Are you going to stay in London?" Mark asked.

"No. Claire asked me to stay here and transfer from Smith to University College. She wants me in London. I've thought about it, but I've decided to go back to Smith. I've already been away from my classes for a week and a day. I need to get back to Smith. I leave tomorrow for the States. But I've promised Claire I'll come back to help when she has her baby."

Then I asked him, "How is medical school?"

"I go on rounds and, after a resident presents a patient, I'm occasionally asked for my diagnosis. I give it and everyone chuckles. Then the consultant gives the correct diagnosis. So it's going as expected, I suppose. You're taking organic, I recall?"

"Yes, and, as you said, it's rough. But it is interesting. I hope I haven't gotten too far behind."

"I never had the opportunity to congratulate you on Wimbledon."

"Well, now it seems like a very long time ago, but I guess it actually was only last summer."

We stood looking at one another for a few moments. Finally, he reached out, and we shook hands. His hand lingered on mine for just a second longer than would be customary.

"Well, again, my condolences to you. Keep in touch."

"Certainly," I said. "I will do so." And we parted.

PART FIVE

JOHNS HOPKINS SCHOOL OF MEDICINE

1968
JOHNS HOPKINS SCHOOL OF MEDICINE
BALTIMORE, MARYLAND

At Smith, I never got around to having a boyfriend. I worked hard at chemistry, and I enjoyed it, but it didn't leave me with much free time. Just before I left Bermuda for my senior year at Smith, Mother sat me down. "Fiona. The time has come when you need to be open to meeting new people. You have a life to lead. You need to find a boy you like."

She didn't say what I knew she was thinking, which was that I needed to forget John Fitzwilliam. The problem was that I didn't want to forget John.

I promised Mother I would try to find a boyfriend, and I did make an effort. I went out with two or three boys, but nothing was serious. I even let one boy sleep with me, but that was a mistake. He had slept with other girls before me, but he hadn't learned anything from his other girls. When we were in bed together, and I suggested to him how to go about pleasing a girl – specifically, *me* – he was offended.

I knew exactly how it should be done; John had taught me.

So not having a boyfriend was my fault; I just wasn't interested.

I was in the spring of my second year at Johns Hopkins medical school when an intense, young pediatrician on the faculty lectured to my class on childhood vaccines. He was thin and wore tortoiseshell eyeglasses. I went up to the front after the lecture to ask him some question – I can't recall what it was – and we talked for two or three minutes.

I thanked him and was leaving the lecture hall when he called me back: "Doctor?" he said. This was a purely courtesy title; I was two years away from my M.D.

I turned back to him. "Yes, Doctor?"

"Do you have a chemistry background?"

"I majored in chemistry in college." Maybe whatever question I had asked reflected some knowledge of chemistry.

"I need a lab assistant. To assay an antibody. It's part of a research grant I have, but I haven't had time to do it myself. There's a stipend. But not much. Do you want the position?"

That was easy. The medical students who got the few lab assistant positions were stars who had been marked by the faculty for Great Things. But I had gotten this offer by merely asking a question after a lecture.

The antibody turned out to be for chickenpox. My first afternoon in his lab, I asked him, "How do I get a sample of the antibody?"

"Did you have chickenpox?"

"Yes, when I was five or six."

"Stick a needle in your arm. You'll find plenty of the antibody. Your immune system never forgets chickenpox."

A month later, I was working at my bench in his lab, and he stopped as he passed by. I expected him to ask how my work was progressing, but he didn't.

Instead, he said simply, "Will you go out with me this Saturday night?"

I said yes.

That August, just after my summer rotation, and just before my fall rotation at Hopkins began, the lease on the flat in Charles Village that I shared with three other women medical students was about to expire, and so he and I spent a Saturday morning packing up my belongings to move me to his flat.

He said I might as well move in since I spent most nights there anyway.

While we were packing, he found the photograph of me just after I had won Wimbledon, in its cheap plastic frame. I had never mentioned this part of my life to him. As far as I knew, he'd never held a tennis racket.

"What's this?"

"It's a tennis match I won. A long time ago."

"You look awful."

"Thanks."

He and I worked together, sitting side by side at the lab bench. His bench skills were far better than mine, and he took the time to show me how to conduct delicate assays without contaminating the samples.

Then he taught me how to prepare a scientific paper on my findings. I sat at my typewriter drafting the paper, revising it, revising it again, and again. Late at night, over our usual dinner of take out Chinese food, I reworked the text and tables of data until, at last, I submitted it for publication.

In early 1968, my paper finally appeared in *The New England Journal of Medicine*: 'Humoral immune response to ∞ herpesvirus 3. Hodgkin FA. From the Johns Hopkins School of Medicine.'

For a medical student, life doesn't get any better than that.

A week or so after our paper came out, I was walking down the main hallway of the hospital when the imperious Dean of the medical school passed me going in the other direction. I had never spoken to him, and I assumed he had no idea who I was. The Dean generally did not acknowledge the existence of individual medical students.

But he stopped. "Miss Hodgkin?"

"Yes, Doctor?"

"An interesting piece of work."

He didn't need to tell me that he meant the paper that had just been in *The New England Journal*. "Thank you, Doctor."

"I asked my secretary to check on your marks. She tells me you're near the top of the third year class."

"Yes." I didn't know what else to say.

"Your plans?" This was medical school code for what specialty I planned to go into.

"My father is a pediatrician, and I hope to be a pediatrician as well."

By pure luck, the Dean was a pediatrician himself. But how could he possibly treat children without frightening them? He certainly frightened *me*.

"Good. An interesting piece of work. Keep it up – " He paused for an instant and then said, "Doctor Hodgkin."

Purely a courtesy title. He turned and continued walking down the hall.

One evening during my pediatrics rotation, I came into my boyfriend's lab. I had spent the day being trained in how to care for ill children, and now I had hours of lab work in front of me.

I sat down beside him at our bench. He had made lemonade for himself, and he poured some for me into a glass beaker. We routinely ignored all the signs that warned against taking food or drink into the biomedical laboratories; we barely had time to eat as it was. He no longer saw patients but supported himself (and me, for that matter) entirely with research grants.

"Don't you miss treating children?" I asked.

He shrugged. "My clinical skills aren't strong."

I was included in his circle of research friends at Hopkins. Probably most of them had never heard of Wimbledon; that wasn't part of their lives. I never mentioned it. Our friends and colleagues assumed that my boyfriend and I would eventually marry and spend our careers at Hopkins. This was a compliment to me, because it implied that I had what it took for a career of research at Hopkins.

My boyfriend would be at Johns Hopkins permanently; he was a research star.

Late in the spring of my third year, my boyfriend took me out to a fancy dinner at a new restaurant in Baltimore, Tio Pepe. This was out of character for him, and I should have known something was up. In the middle of dinner, he asked me to marry him. He had even bought an expensive engagement ring for me. I told him that I was only 25 and wasn't ready to get married yet, or to make any commitment, which I intended as a gentle way of saying, "No."

I thought to myself guiltily that I had been plenty ready to be married when I had been only 19, and that the difference between then and now wasn't my age, but that I had been in love with John. I wasn't in love now. My boyfriend was disappointed and hurt, and so after dinner, even though I was tired, I took him by the hand, led him back to the flat, took off my clothes, and did my best to make it up to him.

Nearly two decades later, I was making dinner for my daughters, and I happened to turn on the television to catch the evening news. I was startled to see on the news a lecture room at Hopkins that I knew well from my medical student days. He was standing in the front of the room, just as he had the day he lectured to my class on vaccines. But now the lecture room was full of reporters, not medical students. He was still thin, but his hair was gray. He was just as intense as ever. He wore stained khaki trousers and a ragged sweater.

Earlier that day, the Karolinska Institute had awarded him the Nobel Prize in Physiology or Medicine for his work on childhood vaccines.

I hadn't seen him since I had taken my M.D. in 1969. We hadn't spoken since the late Saturday afternoon in July 1968 when I had talked with him by telephone from Claire's kitchen in Belgravia. When I returned to Baltimore, he already had left for 10 days to give a seminar at the Cold Spring Harbor Laboratory on Long Island. We had planned to make that trip together. I let myself into the flat and packed my medical textbooks, Rachel's old sweater, the framed photo of me after my final with Claire, and my other things.

As I was leaving, I locked the door and pushed my keys to the flat and to our lab through his mail slot.

I was going to chuck my career at Hopkins to become a pediatrician on Point Finger Road in Bermuda.

A reporter asked, "How did you start this research?"

He blinked his eyes for a moment. "I began this work with a colleague, Fiona Hodgkin, who was a medical student here at Johns Hopkins at the time." He stopped to think. "We used her blood as a starting point. She had chickenpox as a child. She published a paper about the antibody in her blood. In '68, I think. In retrospect, an important paper. Doctor Hodgkin deserves part of the credit for this prize they've given me."

Later, I read in the newspaper that he had never married.

July 1968
London, England

After I finished my third year at Hopkins, Father helped arrange a general surgery rotation for me over the summer in London at his hospital, Guy's. Claire picked me up at Heathrow. Her parents had retired to the country, and Claire, Richard, and their children had taken over the house in Belgravia. I was going to stay with them.

Claire had reluctantly given up her Alfa Romeo roadster for a Jaguar sedan that could hold her children. When I opened the passenger door, I had to brush the Animal Cracker crumbs off the seat before I could sit down.

Claire looked at the crumbs ruefully. "I dole out Animal Crackers to young Fiona to keep her occupied when we drive to the country. Richard says we have to leave off calling her 'young Fiona,' or else the double name will stick, and she'll be burdened with it for the rest of her life."

I laughed. I was young Fiona's Godmother.

"So," Claire asked, "how's your love life?" She had met my boyfriend on a trip to the States and made no secret to me that she didn't care for him.

"He's asked me to marry him."

"Oh, no! What did you say?"

"I told him I wasn't ready to make any commitment."

"Good! Fiona, he's not right for you. Has he ever been to Bermuda?"

"No," I admitted. Not only that, I thought, he'd never expressed the slightest interest in visiting Bermuda.

"And I don't think you should spend your time holed up in a laboratory."

This wasn't the first time Claire had said all this to me. Even though I knew the answer, I asked anyway: "Why shouldn't I do research? It's important."

"You need to be around people more. I want you to promise that this summer you'll be open to meeting new people. It's time. I'll find you someone else who's better for you." She left unsaid an important part of what she meant, which was that she would find someone *English* for me – not American. Claire and my Mother hadn't spoken to one another about me, at least as far as I knew, but they both said exactly the same things.

"I promise I'll be open to meeting people."

"Fiona," Claire said when we pulled up in front of the house in Belgravia. "You have a choice. We have a guest room on the third floor, or John's flat on the ground level is empty. The two boys are on the third floor, and they've been known to make a great deal of noise. You're welcome to stay in the flat if you like."

I thought for a moment. "I'd prefer the guest room, Claire. The boys won't bother me."

My first day at Guy's, I scrubbed and walked into an operating room to observe one of the senior consultants operate.

The consultant looked up when I came in. He wore gold-rimmed eyeglasses with a strip of white adhesive tape holding them to the bridge of his nose. "Well, a new face," he said.

The members of the surgical team chuckled. This was a small joke; with my surgical mask and cap, my eyes were the only part of my face visible.

The consultant asked, "Who are you?"

"Fiona Hodgkin."

The consultant went about his work on the patient and after a moment said, "There was a girl with that name some years ago who won the singles at Wimbledon."

"That's me."

"You've had quite a change in vocation, haven't you?"

"Yes, I have."

"Where are you training?"

"Hopkins. I start my fourth year in September."

At the name 'Hopkins,' he looked up at me. "You're English. Why train in the States?" He looked back down at his patient.

He thought I was English because I speak with an English accent. "I'm actually Bermudian. Both my grandmother and mother trained at Hopkins."

"A family of medical women, I see." He said this not entirely with approval. "So why are you here at Guy's?"

"My father did his internship here just before the war. He arranged for me to take my surgery rotation here."

"What's your father's name?"

"Thomas Hodgkin."

This got him to look up again from the patient. "Quite a famous medical name."

"My father is descended from the younger brother of the famous Thomas Hodgkin."

"Is your family Quaker, then?" The famous Hodgkin had been a Quaker.

"No, my parents are Church of England."

"Well, Miss Hodgkin, where did the famous Thomas Hodgkin train?"

"At St. Thomas's and Guy's medical school."

"Correct. And what is the second thing for which Hodgkin is famous?" The consultant was making another small joke. Hodgkin is best known for characterizing Hodgkin's disease, a lymphoma, in 1832.

"In 1822, he advocated the use of the stethoscope here at Guy's."

"Correct. For some reason we were reluctant to take up that handy device. Can't imagine why." Then he stepped away from the patient and asked, "Miss Hodgkin, are you scrubbed?"

"Yes, Doctor."

The consultant glanced almost imperceptibly at the senior anaesthetist, who checked the patient's vital signs and nodded to the consultant. The patient was stable as a rock, and a few extra minutes on the operating table for the training of a medical student would make no difference.

The consultant said to me, "Miss Hodgkin, have the heirs of William Stewart Halsted at Hopkins taught you to suture?"

"Yes, Doctor."

"Then come over here, and we'll see if you can suture as well as you can hit a tennis ball."

Then I knew that, even though I was a woman, I had been accepted.

Mark Thakeham was a Senior House Officer at a different hospital, but he heard I was in London through the medical grapevine. His schedule as an SHO was hectic and exhausting. Wimbledon was on, and Mark called the Club and got two seats in the players' box one afternoon during the first week. It was the first 'open' Wimbledon – that is, it was open to professional players. He rang me at Guy's and asked me to come with him.

I hesitated. I hadn't spoken to Mark in years, and I hadn't been back to Wimbledon since 1962. I was on the verge of saying 'no.' I would give the excuse of work.

But Mark said, "Fiona. Centre Court."

He was right; I couldn't pass up an afternoon on Centre Court.

We took our seats between matches, and there was a ripple of applause around Centre Court, which Mark joined.

"Why are they applauding?" I asked Mark.

"For you."

After the last match of the day on Centre Court, Mark and I went out to dinner at an Indian restaurant in SoHo. In the six years since I'd last seen him, he'd adopted the calm, unflappable, seen-it-all-twice demeanor many physicians have – I recognized it because I was in the early stages of trying to adopt the same demeanor myself.

When we walked back to the Tube after dinner, he asked me to have dinner with him again that weekend, and I accepted. I met him Saturday evening in Ken High, we had dinner in a pub, and then went on a long walk in Kensington.

One night the next week, he made dinner for me in his flat. He had become quite the chef. I was standing in the tiny kitchen of his flat, drinking a cup of tea and watching him make dinner, when I mentioned that I planned to spend a week in Bermuda with my parents at the end of my surgery rotation.

Mark said, "I need to go to Bermuda myself, but I haven't found the time. I haven't been there since we met. But I liked Bermuda. Mostly because of meeting you." He smiled at me. Mark could be charming when he felt like it; there's never been any question about that.

"Why do you need to go to Bermuda?"

"Do you remember Tempest? Where we met the first time?"

"Certainly, yes."

"My aunt passed away last year, and I inherited Tempest. It's standing empty, and I want to check on it."

"Oh, Mark, I'm sorry she's gone. I hadn't known. How did she die?"

"I was her physician. I could say she died of CHF." He meant congestive heart failure. "That's what I put on the death certificate. But probably it's just as accurate to say she died of old age."

I thought that Tempest perhaps wasn't the grandest house in Bermuda, but it was certainly in the running. The land tax alone on Tempest was probably more than the National Health Service paid Mark as a medical resident. But then it occurred to me. The upkeep on Tempest was no doubt looked after by some clerk at the Thakehams' firm of solicitors in the City. Mark probably hadn't the slightest idea of what it cost to maintain his house in Bermuda.

That week I found some reason or other to ring Mark just about every day, and we took to eating hurried lunches together in hospital canteens, and talking about our patients. I noticed, a little guiltily, that I never mentioned that I had a boyfriend in Baltimore. But Mark never did anything that would have forced me to make that choice. One day at lunch I was telling Mark about a surgical site infection in one of my patients that, personally, I thought could have been avoided. While listening to me, he reached across the table and took my hand. I took my other hand, put it on top of his and went on talking.

On the second Thursday of the fortnight, the Club Secretary rang me at Guy's and invited me and my guest to the ladies' final that Saturday. I accepted and telephoned Mark twice at his hospital to see if he could arrange to be off Saturday afternoon to come with me, but I couldn't reach him either time. He was busy with patients; he had been on duty since Wednesday morning, working flat out the entire time. I finally got off from Guy's around nine that evening and decided to stop at Mark's hospital on my way back to Claire's house.

I took the lift to Mark's ward and asked a nurse where I could find him. She said he was asleep in the House Officers' lounge, and she pointed me down a hallway toward a closed door. 'Lounge' was an overly grand name for this room. It was the size of a closet, and the only furnishing was a plain Army cot. There was a door to a tiny loo on the side of the room across from the cot.

A row of hooks was on a wall, with a doctor's lab coat hanging on one hook and a pair of trousers hanging on another. I was relieved when I saw a mop of strawberry blond hair spilling out from under a sheet on the cot; at least I had found Mark and not some other sleeping SHO.

I closed the door, went over to the cot and sat down, uncomfortably, on the side rail of the cot. I put my fingers into the mop of hair, and Mark slowly came around. He looked at me and smiled. "Hello," he said.

"Hello yourself."

He reached up, put his hand on the back of my neck, and pulled me down to his face. I stopped him and said, "Mark, I'll kiss you, but only after you clean your teeth. What in heaven did you have with your tea?"

He laughed. "I think it was lunch, actually. Didn't get to have tea. Let me up, then."

I stood, and he peeled back the sheet, got off the cot and stumbled into the loo. He was wearing only his boxer shorts. I took off my short medical student's lab coat and hung it on a hook beside Mark's long lab coat. His coat had in script on the left breast 'Mark Thakeham, M.D., Cambridge Medicine.' Mine had, 'Fiona Hodgkin, Johns Hopkins School of Medicine.' Each coat had a stethoscope hanging out of the side pocket. I stood there looking at the two coats hanging side by side.

Mark came out of the loo. He put his arms around my waist, I put my arms around his neck, and he kissed me. "To what do I owe the honor of this night time visit?"

"I wanted to ask you something, but now I can't recall what it was."

"I'm sure you'll think of it." He kissed me again and put his hand on my breast. I put my hand over his and pressed his hand to me. He took this as an invitation – and maybe that's what it was. He reached behind me and fumbled with the zipper on the back of my dress.

"There's a small hook at the top of the zipper," I said,

trying to be helpful, but he couldn't manage the hook and zipper.

After a moment, I said, "Maybe you should let me do this. Get back on your cot." He did.

I unzipped my dress, stepped out of it and hung it on one of the hooks. I went over to the cot and sat down again on the side rail. He pulled me down to him, kissed me, then reached behind me to the hooks on my bra. He stopped, looked at me, and said, "Is this all right?"

I laughed. "Yes. Can you manage it by yourself?"

He undid the hooks on the bra, pulled it away from me and dropped it on the floor.

He said, "See? I got your bra off without any help."

"I'm sure you've had lots of practice with bras."

I stretched out beside him, half convinced the cot would collapse, but it didn't. I said, "How exactly are we going to do this on a cot? It's too narrow."

He pulled the sheet over us and said, "Perhaps I should be on top of you. That might work."

It worked exceptionally well.

Afterwards, we were on our sides, with my back snuggled against him. He was holding one of my breasts in his hand.

He said, "I've wanted you for so many years. You have no idea how much I've wanted you."

"So how was it, at long last?" I was trying to mock him, but I didn't quite bring it off.

"Perfect."

I felt his hand gently caressing my breast. I said, "I'm small on top."

"You're perfect on top. Just what I want."

"Now I remember what it was I wanted to ask you."

"If talking about your breasts reminded you of what it is, I can't wait to hear."

"Don't be silly. No, I've been invited to the ladies' final on Saturday. I wanted to know if you can get out of hospital and come with me."

"I think so. That would be great. I can check and make certain in the morning that I can get that afternoon off."

"I thought we might take our tennis whites to the final. The outer courts are closed for play after the fortnight, but if we're discrete we can probably get away with playing a set or two after the final. No one is likely to be around to stop us."

Although Mark had been a member of the All England Club probably since the day he was born, and I was an honorary member because of my championship, even members were not allowed to play on the outer courts after the fortnight until Richard Hawkins and his crew had repaired the courts, which took weeks.

Mark didn't reply. He rolled me over onto my back and took me again, and while he was touching me I cried out so loudly that he cupped his other hand gently over my mouth and whispered, "Let's not wake the patients on the ward."

I spent the night on that wretched Army cot, and in the morning I took the Tube home to Hyde Park Corner and walked to Claire's. When I arrived, Richard had left for the City, and Claire was chasing her boys around, trying to get them ready for the swimming camp they attended on Hampstead Heath. Young Fiona was in her booster seat at the kitchen table, eating a bowl of porridge.

Claire was taking the boys out the front door to wait with them for the van that picked them up when she called back, "Fiona, will you see if young Fiona wants banana with her porridge?"

I sat down across from young Fiona and said, "Do you want me to slice some banana for you?"

She nodded solemnly, and I sliced half a banana into her dish.

I asked, "Is the porridge good?"

She nodded again. "Mummy made it for me. Will you read to me?"

Claire and Richard kept a pile of old children's books on the kitchen table. "I will read to you but finish your breakfast first. Then pick out the book you want to read."

Claire returned and looked at young Fiona with an appraising eye. "Do you need to visit the loo?"

Young Fiona nodded solemnly.

"I'll take her." I lifted young Fiona out of the seat and carried her down the hall to a small powder room.

When we returned, I put her in her seat, and she went back to eating her porridge.

Claire looked at me. "In whose bed did you spend the night?"

I was a bit disheveled. "Is it that obvious?"

"Obvious? You might as well have 'Just Had Sex' written in red lipstick on your cheek. So who was it?"

"Mark Thakeham."

"Now there's a name out of the past. How was he?"

"He certainly knows what he's doing. I'll say that for him."

"He treated you well?"

"Yes. Quite well."

"Did he make you come before he did?"

"Claire, you really are awful."

"Just curious. What's the answer?"

Young Fiona held up an old Raggedy Ann book and said, "This one." The book had belonged to Claire and John when they were children; it was held together with Scotch tape; either Claire or John, or maybe both, had scribbled in it with crayons.

"Can you get down from your seat?" I said to young Fiona. "Come get in my lap, and I'll read to you."

"So?" Claire said.

"Yes, he took care of me before he came." I smiled. "Both times."

Young Fiona said, "Raggedy Ann has red yarn for hair."

Claire cleared young Fiona's dish. "Interesting that Mark Thakeham appears on the scene after all these years. Is he in love with you?"

"I have no idea."

Young Fiona said, "Uncle Clem is Raggedy Ann's friend."

Claire said, "You could answer 'yes,' or you might say 'certainly not,' but if you say, 'I have no idea,' that means you think he's in love with you."

She was right, but I didn't answer her. Four centuries before, Claire definitely would have been hanged as a witch. I did think that Mark was in love with me.

Young Fiona settled herself in my lap and opened the Raggedy Ann book. I began to read: "*One day Daddy took Raggedy Ann down to his office and propped her up against some books upon his desk . . .* " I used my finger to point to each word as I read to young Fiona. I leaned over and kissed the top of her head.

Claire said, "So if he's in love with you, are you in love with him?"

I stopped reading. "I'm not in love with anyone."

Young Fiona asked, "Is Raggedy Ann just a doll, or is she real?"

Claire answered, "She is just a doll, but she's a real doll."

I read: "*Daddy wished to catch a whole lot of Raggedy Ann's cheeriness and happiness . . .* "

Claire said, "You're not in love with anyone because you don't want to let go of John. That's why you have this laboratory fellow in Baltimore, because you're not in love with him, so you can still hold on to John."

I was stricken. This was the worst thing anyone could say to me. My lower lip started trembling, but I managed to whisper, "That's not true."

Young Fiona asked, "Is Uncle Clem a real doll?"

Claire said, "I think it's completely true. I think when you're in bed alone, you imagine making love to John. Then you cry to yourself. You want to do that for the rest of your life, don't you? But you can't if you fall in love with someone else."

I started sobbing.

"That's exactly what you do, isn't it?"

She paused. "At night, when I go upstairs to make sure the boys are under their covers, I hear you crying."

I had tears running down my face. I nodded.

Claire came over to me, reached down, picked up young Fiona and stood her on the kitchen floor. Then Claire pulled me up and put her arms around me. "Fiona. Listen to me. You can tell John goodbye, and it won't be as hard as you expect."

Young Fiona looked up at me with a frown. "I want you to keep reading Raggedy Ann to me."

It didn't take Billie Jean King too long to defeat Judy Tegart, and then Mark and I went to the dressing rooms to change. We agreed to slip out separately and meet on Court 13. The outer courts were deserted and eerily quiet. When I walked out on the court, it dawned on me that this was the old Court 14, where I had played my first match at Wimbledon six years before. (In 1964, it had been renumbered 'Court 13,' but it was the same court.) In my mind, I could see the crowds and Claire yelling and jumping up and down. It had been beside this court that John told me he was in love with me. I felt it had all happened in another lifetime.

Mark arrived, and we played a set. The day was perfect, and while the court was badly bruised from two weeks of play, it was still an old-style Wimbledon grass court – fast, unpredictable, and fun. We were changing ends when Mark said to me, "It's just like old times." And I agreed.

We were both thirsty after our set, but there was no water on the court. A stray ballboy, apparently off on a frolic of his own, happened to walk past, and I asked him if he might find us some water. A bit later, he reappeared with not only one large thermos of water but also another thermos of hot tea with lemon.

Mark and I sat down on a bench and poured each other cups of water, and then tea. Mark leaned over and kissed me, and I kissed him back.

He pulled away and said, "You don't remember where we kissed the first time, do you?"

"Yes, I do. I had made a picnic lunch."

"We were at that lighthouse. What's it called?"

"Gibbs Hill Lighthouse."

Then he kissed me again, and I put my arms around him. He stopped kissing me. "Fiona, will you marry me?"

I took my arms away in surprise. "Are you serious?"

"Quite serious. I want to spend my life with you."

"Are you in love with me?"

"Very much so." He paused. "Always have been, actually."

"Mark, I can't marry you. I'm Bermudian, and I'm going to spend my life in Bermuda. You're English; you're staying here, in England. I don't want to call England my home." I was surprised to hear myself say so emphatically that I was going to return home to Bermuda, but once I had said it, it suddenly seemed obvious to me.

"I've thought about that," Mark said. It must have seemed obvious to him as well. "When I finish my term as SHO, I won't take a Registrar's position. I'll come to Bermuda and practice medicine there. We'll have our family in Bermuda."

I thought for a moment. "Well, there's another problem. I have a boyfriend in Baltimore. I live with him. He's asked me to marry him."

Mark was plainly put off by the news that I had a

boyfriend. I could tell he hadn't considered this possibility.

"Am I that unlikeable?" I asked. "I can tell from your face that you didn't expect me to have a boyfriend."

"You're likeable," he said. He reached over and put his hand on my cheek. "I've liked you since I first met you."

"To be honest, I've always liked you as well."

"What did you tell him? Are you engaged to him? I hope not, since you and I slept together."

"I told him I wasn't ready to make any commitment."

"Are you in love with him?"

"No. I'm not."

Neither of us said anything for a few moments. Finally, Mark said, "You asked me about being in love with you, so I'm entitled to ask you in return. Do you love me?"

I simply said goodbye to John. Claire had been right – it wasn't as hard as I expected. John didn't disappear; he merely took one step further back in my memory. Now in my mind, he was covered by a fine mist, as though I were looking at him from across the Serpentine in Hyde Park early on a damp morning.

I thought for a long moment, and then I shook my head and gave a short, rueful laugh.

Mark said, "Is there something humorous here that I've missed?"

"Oh, Mark, I'm sorry. I didn't mean to laugh. But I was just thinking about the flat in Baltimore that I share with my boyfriend. I suppose that both you and he would insist that I move out."

"I don't understand."

"It's all right. I could find a place of my own for my last year at Hopkins. Or maybe I could move in with one of the women in my class."

"What are you saying, Fiona?"

"Well, we couldn't get married now, could we? We would have to wait until I have my M.D. And I've taken my medical boards in the States. You agree? That would mean next summer, at the earliest.

"Yes, of course."

"So, you wouldn't want me living with my boyfriend this year? I mean, my former boyfriend?"

"Certainly not," he replied in a shocked tone.

"Well, then." I sat back against the bench. I was pleased to see that I had completely befuddled him.

"Mark, we're going to be away from one another for most of the next year. I'll be at Hopkins, and you'll be in London. I don't want you to so much as look at another girl. I'm not going to sit in Baltimore and worry about what you're doing."

"Fiona, I'm committed to you. I'm not going to look at any other girl."

"Good."

"Fiona, I'm in love with you. I want you to marry me. Are you saying you will?"

"I might work out my internship so that I could be in London. I like Guy's; maybe they'll take me in even though I've trained at Hopkins."

"Fiona, please give me a straight answer. What are you going to do?"

I sighed. "I guess I'm going to go back to Claire's and place an international call to Baltimore. I don't know if I'll be able to reach my boyfriend on a Saturday. If he's in our lab, I can get him, but maybe he'll be out and about." I looked at my watch. It was past five in London, so it was early afternoon in Baltimore.

"What are you going to tell him?" Mark asked.

"I'll probably begin by saying that I'd rather eat a lizard than tell him what I'm about to tell him."

"Which is what?"

"That a long time ago in Bermuda, I met someone, and this summer in London I've met him again, and I've fallen in love with him. And that I'm going to marry this person."

He leaned over and kissed me. "Let me come with you to Claire's."

I smiled. "No. I'll be upset after talking with my boyfriend. Claire would put you out on the street before she'd let you see me upset."

I thought for a second. "I don't mean to keep calling him my boyfriend. He's not any longer. So don't take that the wrong way. But I do have to tell him myself, and that'll be a sad telephone call. I can't help that. You're all right with my making that call? This just has to be all unwound, and it's unfair to him for me to wait even a day to tell him."

Mark said, "But you will marry me? You won't change your mind?"

"No, I'm not going to change my mind. I'm in love with you, and I'm going to marry you."

"Tonight you could stay over at my flat."

"No, give me an evening by myself. I need to move from one part of my life to the next. Claire will want to talk to me. And I have to write to my parents. Are you in hospital tomorrow?"

"Yes. I'm due to be off at seven Sunday evening, but you know how that works."

"I'll go to market tomorrow and buy something for us

for dinner tomorrow night. Do you hide a spare key to your flat?"

"Yes," Mark said. "It's under an empty milk bottle in the hallway."

"That's not an original place to hide a key."

"If I put it in an original hiding place, I wouldn't be able to remember where I put it."

"I'll let myself into your flat and make dinner for us tomorrow. I have to warn you that I'm not much of a cook."

"Will you spend the night?"

"Yes, I'll stay over. I'll bring some of my things. I have to be scrubbed at Guy's by seven Monday morning."

"We could make love again."

"Maybe. We'll see." I smiled at him. "I like keeping you in suspense. We'll be making love to one another for a long time once we're married."

"I look forward to that. I promise to make love to you when you're a grandmother." He's kept this particular promise.

He leaned over to kiss me again, but just then, someone called out loudly, "Hallo! You there!" I looked up to see Richard Hawkins, the groundskeeper, standing on St. Mary's Walk across Court 13 from us. "This court is closed."

Then Richard recognized me. "It's good to see you again, Fiona," he said. "And I'm sorry. But you know the outer courts are all closed. I have to begin working on them."

"Richard, we're not playing tennis," I said. "We've just become engaged to be married."

That stopped Richard in his tracks. "Oh. Well, then. Fiona, my congratulations." And he walked off.

SUMMER 1969
MY WEDDING
BERMUDA

The afternoon before my wedding, we had a family picnic on
Warwick Long Bay. Mark was holding me against his chest as
we sat on the beach, when he suddenly pointed down the beach.

I looked. Fifty meters or so away, Myrtle Hanson had
rolled up her skirt and was standing in the Atlantic surf,
holding young Fiona's hand. When the surf rolled out, Myrtle
found a fragment of a pink shell for young Fiona, and the
two of them bent over to marvel at the bit of shell.

Claire's head popped up. She had been sitting in a beach
chair talking intently with Rachel. From the way Claire had
been twirling her index finger, I could tell they were talking
about how a tennis ball spins in flight. As though there was
anything more to be said on that topic. Now it was almost
dusk, and Claire wanted to locate her children.

Her boys were climbing some rocks at the far end of the
bay.

Myrtle carried young Fiona back to our beach
encampment. She had fallen fast asleep on Myrtle's shoulder.
She put her down on a beach towel and then covered her
with another towel.

The only way to tell there was a little girl curled up under the towel was the blond hair spilling out from under one end of the towel, and the tiny left foot sticking out the other. Claire reached down and pulled the towel to cover her daughter's foot.

I can't recall which of us asked the question. Maybe it was me, but looking back – it might have been Myrtle.

"Will she be a Wimbledon champion?"

Rachel replied, "Yes."

And so, the next morning I married Mark in the garden of Midpoint. I wore Mother's wedding dress. She had altered it to fit me, just as my grandmothers had altered it to fit Mother, and she had gotten most of the mildew off it.

Father gave me away, and Claire and Rachel stood beside me. Myrtle Hanson was holding young Fiona. They had taken a liking to one another.

The sky that morning was the blue that you see only in Bermuda, and during the short service, I turned my head to hear the soft clop, clop of an old farmer's horse-drawn cart far below on Harbour Road.

KOOYONG, 1987

Late afternoon. A sunny day in Melbourne but cool for January. Claire, Richard, Myrtle, Mark, and I were having a late lunch on the balcony just outside the members' bar of the Kooyong clubhouse. The Australian Open was on, and there were huge crowds milling about on the lawns below us. I was amazed at how well the Aussies were able to stage a global tournament at such a small, private grass court club. But this year would be it. In 1988, the Australian Open would leave Kooyong forever and move to the composition courts at Flinders Park in Melbourne.

Young Fiona and Rachel were in the media tent for the (mandatory) post-match press conference. Earlier that afternoon, young Fiona had won her quarterfinal match at Kooyong against a top seed in three sets. She was in the semifinals of the Australian Open.

Just after young Fiona won, Claire had said to Rachel, "Will you go with her to the press conference? Keep her from saying anything shocking on television."

"Any suggestions on how to do that?" Rachel asked.

Claire thought for a moment. "Nothing comes to mind. But you're her coach, you'll think of something. Clap your hand over her mouth perhaps?"

Rachel snorted.

For lunch, Claire and I both ordered chicken salad sandwiches, and when the waiter set the plates in front of us, Claire, without a word, reached over with her knife and fork, cut my sandwich in two, deftly transferred the larger part to her own plate, and began eating.

I didn't bother objecting. Claire would eat everything in sight, even if the food in question happened to be on my plate. She would never change.

My twin daughters appeared on the balcony.

"Mom," one of them whispered. "You have to come see something."

"I'm having lunch."

The other twin clutched at my sleeve. "Now, Mom. You have to see this."

Myrtle looked at the twins with her head cocked to one side. Usually, one look from Myrtle was enough to cause the twins to back down from whatever mischief they were up to, but this time they persisted.

I sighed. "I'll be right back."

The twins practically dragged me inside the members' bar.

One of them thrust out her teenage hip and pointed at the wall in an exaggerated way. "Who is *that*?"

"That's the Club's portrait of Harry Hopman."

The twins rolled their eyes.

"Not the portrait, Mom. The *photo* next to it."

The old black and white photograph hanging on the wall showed a shy young girl clutching her racket to her chest.

"Oh. That's your tennis coach." The twins had grown up playing with Rachel on the grass court at Tempest, our home in Bermuda.

The twins looked at one another with their usual where-did-we-find-this-mother expression.

"Mom," one of them said. "It's not Rachel."

"It looks like her, though," the other said.

"But it couldn't be. The girl in the photo is a teenager."

"Yeah, it's not possible."

I laughed. "I have news for you two. It's a photo of Rachel after she won the championship here at Kooyong. May I return to lunch?"

The next day the twins played one another in the Australian junior girls' final. Claire and young Fiona knocked up with the twins before the match. Claire almost never hit tennis balls in public, and I could hear the excited whispers running through the crowd: "Claire Kershaw is practicing on court 8." Minutes later, the sides of the grass court were thronged with spectators.

It was even cooler that day in Melbourne, and young Fiona was wearing Rachel's ragged Kooyong sweater. I had given it to her the year before when she had been invited to play at Roehampton, where she had qualified for the Wimbledon draw.

It can be chilly in London in June, and I felt better knowing young Fiona had something warm to wear.

A steward arrived to take the twins into the old Kooyong stadium. The twins had Mark's strawberry blond hair and good looks. They were beautiful, really. I had sewn small Bermuda flags on their tennis dresses.

Young Fiona gave them each a hug. The twins adored young Fiona; to them, she was their older sister. Rachel said to the twins, simply, "Good luck."

Once we took our seats, Mark said to me, "I can't watch," and he put his head in his hands.

The chair umpire switched on her microphone and turned to her left.

"Lady Rachel Thakeham, are you ready?"

"Ready!"

The umpire turned to her right.

"Lady Claire Thakeham, are you ready?"

"Ready!"

"Lady Rachel to serve. Play."

Young Rachel tossed the tennis ball high and out, cocked her racket deep behind her shoulder, went up on her toes, whipped the racket forward, slammed the ball and ran toward the net.

Acknowledgements

On Saturday, 7 July 1962, the ladies' singles final at Wimbledon – in reality – was between Vera Sukova of the former Czechoslovakia and Karen Hantze Susman of the United States. Mrs Susman won 6-4, 6-4.

In 1961, the singles final was between two of the greatest British players, Angela Mortimer and Christine Truman. They played a classic three set match that Miss Mortimer won 4-6, 6-4, 7-5. Miss Mortimer (now Mrs Barrett) gave a thrilling description of this match in her book *My Waiting Game* (Frederick Muller, London 1962).

Anyone interested in the history of tennis should visit the Wimbledon Lawn Tennis Museum at the All England Lawn Tennis Club, where Mrs Barrett's racket – and her trademark tennis shorts designed by Teddy Tinling – are displayed, along with many other engaging items from the history of Wimbledon.

The tennis columnist and historian Bud Collins called the great and graceful tennis player Maria Bueno of Brazil the "São Paulo Swallow." She won Wimbledon in 1959, 1960, and 1964. In 1962 she lost in the semifinal to Mrs Sukova 6-4, 6-3.

In 1939, at Kooyong, Emily Hood Westacott defeated Nell Hall Hopman in the Australian championship final 6-1,

6-2. (Both Mrs Westacott and Mrs Hopman were Australian.) At Wimbledon, Alice Marble of the United States defeated Kay Stammers (later Mrs Menzies) of Great Britain 6-2, 6-0. Eleanor ('Teach') Tennant was there as Miss Marble's coach.

In October 1962, the Committee of Management "laid it down quite firmly that players must wear white throughout," as Lieutenant-Colonel Duncan Macaulay said. He described the Committee as "long-suffering" on the issue of ladies' undergarments. *Behind the Scenes at Wimbledon* by Duncan Macaulay with Sir John ('Jackie') Smyth (St. Martin's, New York 1965).

Alan Little, the Honorary Librarian of the Wimbledon Lawn Tennis Museum, has written fascinating books on the history of Wimbledon that have been invaluable to me. Mr Little's *Wimbledon 1922-2009: The Changing Face of Church Road* (Wimbledon Lawn Tennis Museum, London 2009) was especially useful. Also, Mr Little's *Suzanne Lenglen: Tennis Idol of the Twenties* (Wimbledon Lawn Tennis Museum, London 1988) is an important and quite enjoyable book on one of the greatest tennis players.

Audrey Snell, the Assistant Librarian of the Kenneth Richie Wimbledon Library (which is part of the Wimbledon Lawn Tennis Museum), has been extremely kind in arranging for me to do research in the Library.

I have relied on Christine Truman's *Tennis Today* (Arthur Barker , London 1961); Maureen Connolly's *Forehand Drive* (MacGibbon & Kee, London 1957); Teddy Tinling's *White Ladies* (Stanley Paul, London 1963); Susan Noel's *Tennis in Our Time* (W.H Allen, London 1954); *We Have Come a Long Way: The Story of Women's Tennis* by Billie Jean King with Cynthia Starr (McGraw-Hill, New York 1988), and *Court on*

Court: A Life in Tennis (Dodd, Mead, New York 1975) by Margaret Smith Court with George McGann. *The Bud Collins History of Tennis* has been indispensable.

Kathryn Drury was my first, and superb, editor. Terri Gaskill – a great tennis player and coach – gave me invaluable suggestions. My close friends Mark Eaton, Beverly Hodgson, and Linell Smith read the manuscript. Their detailed and helpful comments improved my writing so much more than I like to admit. Richard & Christine Jones of The Tennis Gallery Wimbledon, www.thetennisgallery.co.uk, found old tennis books and Wimbledon programs for me and gave me great encouragement.

This novel is fiction, but I have tried to recreate the atmosphere of amateur tennis at Wimbledon in the early 1960s. The many mistakes that I'm confident I've made are all my own responsibility.

Fiona Hodgkin
'Tempest'
Bermuda
March 2012

RUSS COFFEY

DENNIS NILSEN

CONVERSATIONS WITH BRITAIN'S MOST EVIL SERIAL KILLER

JOHN BLAKE

Published by John Blake Publishing Ltd,
3 Bramber Court, 2 Bramber Road,
London W14 9PB, England

www.johnblakepublishing.co.uk

www.facebook.com/Johnblakepub **facebook**
twitter.com/johnblakepub **twitter**

First published in paperback in 2013

ISBN: 978-1-78219-459-0

British Library Cataloguing-in-Publication Data:

A catalogue record for this book is available from the British Library.

Design by www.envydesign.co.uk

Printed in Great Britain by CPI Group (UK) Ltd

1 3 5 7 9 10 8 6 4 2

© Text copyright Russ Coffey 2013

Papers used by John Blake Publishing are natural, recyclable products
made from wood grown in sustainable forests. The manufacturing processes
conform to the environmental regulations of the country of origin.

Every attempt has been made to contact the relevant copyright-holders,
but some were unobtainable. We would be grateful if the
appropriate people could contact us.

CONTENTS

INTRODUCTION

*'History of a Drowning Boy unfolds as a tale of another
flawed man who committed 12 homicides. It is certainly no
whitewash of my life. I have written my past candidly.'*
DENNIS NILSEN

The above lines were written to me in 2003 from HMP Full
Sutton, Yorkshire, by Dennis Nilsen, one of Britain's
most notorious serial killers. I had found myself exchanging
letters with Nilsen while researching a magazine article about
a half-written autobiography he wanted to have published.
During our lengthy correspondence, prisoner B62006 would
try to persuade me of new insights he had into his former
behaviour. He wrote fluently and logically, interspersing his
answers with personable comments. Sometimes, in fact, he
presented himself so reasonably I had to remind myself what
he had done.

Between 1978 and 1983, Dennis Andrew Nilsen murdered
up to 15 young men. He met them in West End bars and then
invited them back to his suburban London flat for further

drinking and, possibly, sex. As they slept, he strangled them. The next morning, he would talk to the bodies. Once out of the flat, however, he would revert to his 'ordinary' self – quiet, neat and devoted to his pet dog.

It was this ability to act perfectly normally between the killings that enabled Nilsen to carry on killing for so long. During just over four years of murder, his colleagues at the Job Centre never noticed anything particularly alarming. They simply considered him to be shy and dull. There were some occasions, however, when his demeanour became a little unsettling. He could lose his temper quickly or become overbearing if the conversation turned to politics. On those occasions, even those who had tried to befriend him were struck by his intensity.

Nilsen was arrested on 9 February 1983, when fragments of human flesh blocking the drains of number 23 Cranley Gardens, Muswell Hill, were traced back to his flat. Inside, the police found the remains of three young men. The small, attic flat stank of death and neglect. The windows were flung open to disperse the smell. One detective had to hang back by the door to avoid being sick.

Nilsen's manner was as surreal as the state of his flat. Quite nonchalantly, he confessed to being Britain's most prolific serial killer. He spoke calmly and continuously, explaining that many of his victims had been runaways whom he now wanted to help identify. The police interrogations were as bizarre as they were disturbing.

When the press reported the contents of Nilsen's confessions, these revelations sent a communal shiver up the nation's spine. But for some of the psychiatrists who worked on the case,

INTRODUCTION

Nilsen's behaviour in interviews made words like 'mad' and 'bad' seem utterly inadequate. They believed that his actions stemmed from extremely complex personality problems.

Many years later, academics and other writers would also attempt explanations of what had gone on. In March 2012, one psychologist who knows Nilsen well, Matthew Malekos, published a controversial 300-page thesis that invited readers to consider whether, in prison, the killer may have actually psychologically 'recovered'.

But, even if that were so, recovered from what? He hadn't been deemed to be insane, so what was he? What were his drives and motives? Did he really have an emotional disorder or was he simply a psychopath? The title of one successful book on the case, *Killing for Company*, suggested Nilsen seemed, in part, to want companionship from his victims. Newer theories appear in TV documentaries every couple of years.

Part of this interest is just macabre fascination. But there is also the fact that so many of the details derive from the killer himself. Even before his trial, Nilsen wrote hundreds of essays in which he attempted to comprehend his psychology. During 30 subsequent years in prison, Nilsen has continued to attempt a dialogue with the outside world.

Part of his motivation is undoubtedly self-publicity. But might there also be more to it? Nilsen's autobiography, after all, *seems* to show some real desire to understand his killing urges. It is now several thousand pages long and has been seen by only four people, including me. For years, Nilsen dreamed of having it published.

His ambitions were quashed in the late nineties when the

prison authorities realised what he was up to. The working draft, *History of a Drowning Boy,* was confiscated. In the years that followed, Nilsen used legal aid to take the prison service to court to get his book back so that he could finish it. In 2011, the *Daily Record* estimated that his trips to the courts had probably cost the tax payer £65,000.

I first contacted Nilsen after reading a newspaper article about his manuscript. Like many journalists who have written to him, I was on a routine search for stories. He responded quickly and, soon, his letters became a regular fixture in my life. I had, initially, expected to find corresponding with him disturbing in an immediate way. But Nilsen's written persona was, on the surface, amusing and charming.

He wanted me to inform the nation that he was ready to tell all. Through a friend of his, he gave me full access to his writing. As a result of what I was shown, in 2003 the *Sunday Times* magazine commissioned a cover feature called *Memoirs of a Serial Killer.* While writing it, I discovered to my surprise that, while most people found the idea of the autobiography revolting, there were some who believed he was worth listening to. The authorities, however, were consistent in their line that his manuscript was pornographic and outrageous.

Still, Nilsen remained adamant he had worthwhile things to say. Just before one court hearing, he wrote to me: 'I am not contained, mute and immobile in a glass jar as some kind of eternal official specimen of popular "evil". As I am alive, I must live as a man.'

'Living as a man', for Nilsen, meant being able to read and write. Being able to fulfil himself was a lot more than his victims could ever do. And therein lies the crux of the moral problem presented by Nilsen's writing. Clearly, to be in the public interest, Nilsen's book would need to be more than just amateur self-analysis. At the very least, it would need to provide a very rare insight into the workings of a killer's mind. It would need to explain convincingly why he did what he did.

After his trial, Nilsen confessed to his biographer, Brian Masters, that he simply enjoyed killing. Now he wants to retract that and offer a more psychologically complete answer. He wrote to me: 'I was under constant pressure from almost everyone I spoke to, to admit that I had enjoyed killing. After my trial, in order to give Brian Masters a "happy" ending to his book on me, I wrote to him saying I probably did enjoy it. I was grasping for an explanation, a certainty, instead of leaving the whole sorry conundrum hanging diffused in the air.'

When I read those lines they simply struck me as evasive. Yet, when I read his full manuscript it seemed *History of a Drowning Boy* offered something of greater interest; at least for those with the stomach to read it. It was not just *what* he said that seemed revealing, but also the way in which he said it.

Nilsen's overall story is predictable – a self-pitying tale of growing up like 'a dog that had never been patted', and then turning into a dysfunctional 'lone wolf'. The details, however, are more telling. In the passages where he explores his sexual imagination, the prose is thick with fantasy and detail. Still, these words need very careful interpretation. Nilsen focuses just on what interests him and often changes his story. Without points of comparison, his writing is often frighteningly misleading.

The book you are reading explains both what Nilsen has to say, and also tries to put it in context. To do so, I have drawn on many years of research. These include interviews with victims, police and others who knew him.

The archives of Nilsen's writing run into several boxes' worth. When I was first loaned *History of a Drowning Boy* back in 2003 – at the time of the *Sunday Times* magazine project – it comprised four volumes: 'Orientation in Me'; 'After the Feast'; 'A Long Way Down and Rising' (about his time in Wakefield and Albany Prisons); and 'Whitemoor: A Volume of Extremes'. Since these, Nilsen has written more volumes, copious essays, and has continued to write letters to me on the clear understanding that I might one day use these, and his unpublished manuscript, to write more about his work. Such professional interest in his autobiography has formed the basis of our correspondence. In the following chapters, material from these letters, and the manuscript, has been interwoven with my own words and with information from other sources to give a sense of what I believe Nilsen's finished autobiography would look like. Naturally, emphasis has been put on the most psychologically significant aspects.

There can surely never be any definitive answers as to why Dennis Nilsen did what he did. So why write another book about the man and the case? Many may feel that people like Nilsen are best forgotten about; they are evil-doers whose stories are macabre and possibly corrupting. A more liberal and rationalist approach, however, might be to say that Nilsen and others like him represent a problem that society has to confront. He himself says, 'I lived with and among you all.' That much is true. And if his evil-doing stemmed from psychological disorders that went unnoticed, we surely need to know as much as we can about their origin and nature. Despite all the interest in serial killers over the past 30 years, little is understood about how their internal world drives their exterior behaviour. We need to know more.

In addition to looking at Nilsen's explanations for his crimes, this book is also concerned with the way in which he has tried to tell his story. How has he managed to get people to listen? What does this say about us? And what exactly is it that people find so interesting about the case? Finally, it is essential that Nilsen's story be seen constantly in conjunction with the perspective of his victims. Where possible, I have spoken to those who have been directly affected by his horrific crimes.

Ultimately, it is up to the reader to make up his or her own mind about Nilsen's writing. To that end, I have been careful to present the material clearly – both Nilsen's own accounts and also the testimony of those who have known him. In particular, it would have been impossible to present a clear and balanced account without the help of DCI Peter Jay, victim Carl Stottor, victim's son Shane Levene, Scotland Yard's Crime Museum, and authors Brian Masters and Gordon Honeycombe.

Russ Coffey, May 2013

1

9 FEBRUARY 1983

'I accept moral responsibility and guilt and punishment which the law and justice demands. It has been thus since the moment of invited arrest in that top flat at 23 Cranley Gardens in that snow-driven evening in February 1983.'
DENNIS NILSEN, IN A LETTER TO THE AUTHOR

Over the years, the story of how Dennis Nilsen was arrested has been told and retold until it has acquired a ring of modern folklore. It goes like this:

On Thursday, 3 February 1983, residents of 23 Cranley Gardens, in the north London suburb of Muswell Hill, found their drains were blocked. They called a drainage engineer from Dyno-Rod. His second visit was on Wednesday, 9 February, a particularly freezing cold day. After careful thought, he concluded that pieces of flesh and bones were causing the blockage. Unsure if they were animal or human, he decided to call the police.

Three officers arrived in a squad car. After peering down the manhole, all agreed something wasn't right. They fished the pieces of grey matter out from beneath the manhole cover and took them to the lab. An hour later, the pathologist confirmed them as human. In the mortuary, the detectives knew they were dealing with something hugely significant … and particularly grim.

They returned to Cranley Gardens. An inspection of the outside of the building seemed to indicate that the flesh had come from a pipe that led to the top flat. The neighbours told them that the man who lived there was peculiar and that he should be back from work in about an hour. DCI Peter Jay said they would wait. Rubbing their hands to keep warm, the three men discussed what they knew about Nilsen – his name, age, and that he worried his neighbours. Still, they had little idea of what he might be like. How might a man who had possibly been chopping up bodies and flushing them down the toilet react to arrest?

Nilsen was also waiting. He had spent the afternoon at work mentally preparing himself for his arrest. Since leaving for work that morning, he been quite convinced the game was up. He knew the body parts he'd been flushing down the toilet were still blocking the plumbing.

When Nilsen finally returned to his flat, the police had moved into the warmth of the lobby. Nilsen opened the door to find DCI Jay staring at him. He knowingly returned his gaze. Jay began by asking about the plumbing.

In his calm Scottish voice, Nilsen replied, 'Since when were the police interested in people's drains?'

The policemen suggested they take the conversation upstairs. In the flat, Jay explained about the human remains.

'How awful!' exclaimed Nilsen.

Jay nervously snapped, 'Stop messing around ... where's the rest of the body?'

Then, in a matter-of-fact way, Nilsen took them to the damp, cold front room and opened one of the wardrobes where he had stored bodies. He said he had much more to tell and wanted to do it at the station.

In the car back to Hornsey Police Station, the detectives asked their prisoner what it was he wanted to tell them. Had he killed two men?

'Fifteen or sixteen over four years,' was Nilsen's reply. That made him the most prolific multiple killer yet discovered in the UK. And just like in the movies, he was quiet, intelligent and personable. His writing still often is.

In his version of those events above, however, Nilsen changes the emphasis so that it is he at the centre, looking for 'help'. He says the police were unsure of themselves. It was he, he says, who finally tired of concealing his 'problem' and who led the police each step of the way with his sudden, immediate and full co-operation.

Either way, the stark truth was that three young men had been senselessly murdered in that particular flat. At least nine had been killed in another. As Cranley Gardens was a top-floor flat and Nilsen didn't have a car, it had become inevitable that he would soon be caught. Nilsen even says that he deliberately 'invited' arrest by his activities. There is no evidence for that.

What the police did find plenty of evidence for was that Nilsen suffered from a severe and dangerous personality disorder. The pot on the stove had been used to boil a human head, and the odour of death hung thick throughout the flat.

In the wardrobe were bin bags filled with the remains of a Scottish youth called Steven Sinclair. Nilsen had killed him two weeks earlier, and now he wanted to explain everything.

The way he did so was distinctive. He talked almost as if he had been in love with Sinclair. In one notebook, Nilsen wrote, 'I stood in great grief and a wave of utter sadness as if someone very dear to me had just died.'

The line was written next to an ink drawing of the corpse called 'The Last Time I Saw Stephen Sinclair'. The juxtaposition seemed quite mad. The affection he claimed to have felt for the young man was matched with a vile disregard for his body. The torso had been cut down the middle and was separated into two halves. The lower part of the body had been removed with a clean cut from just above the waist. The eyes had been boiled in their sockets. When the pieces were re-assembled on the mortuary slab, they had turned different colours.

Stephen Sinclair was typical of those Nilsen would bring home. He was the sort whose story interests no one, and the kind of young man that Nilsen felt he could take under his wing. Sinclair was 20 years old and only 5ft-5in tall. He had come down from Scotland, travelling without a ticket on the InterCity Express from Edinburgh to London's King's Cross. Like many of the runaways who arrived at that station, he had come with little more than a vague feeling that the big city had something for everyone, even him.

Sinclair met his killer on Wednesday, 26 January. Nilsen isn't sure exactly where. In one version, it was in a pub called the Royal George in Goslett Yard near Denmark Street where he had once worked. One witness, however, thought he saw Sinclair hanging around with someone fitting Nilsen's description some days before. So, despite what he says, Nilsen, did, quite possibly, mark Sinclair out as a potential victim beforehand.

Another, more likely, account has them meeting by the slot machines off Piccadilly Circus. This was then a well-known gay 'cruising' area where older men would try to pick up rent boys or runaways looking for money. Dressed in a leather jacket, tight black jeans and with tattoos on his hands and arms, Sinclair would have hardly stood out. As a well-spoken man in his late thirties, neither would Nilsen.

Nilsen was 6ft 1in, slim, dark-haired and good-looking despite his oversized glasses and functional suit. We know from victims who escaped, that his manner when picking people up was usually friendly but dominating. The conversation between him and Sinclair was therefore probably one-sided, with their shared knowledge of eastern Scotland helping it along. As they chatted, Nilsen would have appeared sympathetic and kind, and would have spoken with complete confidence as if he knew everything about everything. He found Sinclair attractive, especially approving of the fact that he was small and fair – two of his physical preferences. Nilsen cared less for the fact that he was a delinquent and a drug addict.

Sinclair would have seemed like a safe bet. Not only was he a runaway but he had also just been in trouble. He had been being caught stealing at a St Mungo's hostel and bailed to appear before magistrates on Monday, 12 February. It was hardly the first time Sinclair had got himself into bother. In fact, he'd rarely been out of trouble since he was born Stephen Guild in 1962.

He was illegitimate and was soon taken into the custody of the local authorities. After 14 months he was put up for foster care, and came into the home of Neil and Elizabeth Sinclair who adopted him to be a brother to their three daughters. Stephen Sinclair, however, wet his bed and constantly bunked off school. Things became so bad that a doctor's advice was sought. It transpired that he had psycho-motor epilepsy.

He was then institutionalised until he was 12. By his mid-teens, he was also diagnosed as educationally sub-normal and spent time in Borstal. He soon graduated to prison. When he got out, things became worse. On one occasion, he slashed his wrists and, on another, he attacked his sisters. There was also an occasion when he tried to burn the house down.

Eventually, Sinclair was re-fostered into a new family. But the same old problems rose to the surface. As he turned 18, he was a drug addict, a glue sniffer and a recognised, opportunist criminal. At this time, though, there is no particular indication he was homosexual.

Wherever they met, we know that, very soon afterwards, Nilsen invited the young man on a tour of the West End pubs. He bought him anything he cared to drink and insisted on being called 'Des', explaining he hated the name Dennis. At closing time – 11.30pm – Nilsen suggested they go back to his flat for more alcohol.

In *History of a Drowning Boy*, he describes their journey home. They took the Northern Line up to Highgate. Sinclair had started feeling sleepy. As they got off, Nilsen noticed his companion was becoming woozier. During the mile or so walk back to his flat, Nilsen says he doubted he 'understood a word he said in his half-drugged Scots brogue'.

Muswell Hill was a pleasant, leafy area where urban London dissolved into greenery and space. Most of the large, semi-detached houses remained intact as family homes for genteel and affluent city workers. 23 Cranley Gardens, a tall Edwardian house with Mock Tudor beams, was different. Later, when it appeared under the headline 'HOUSE OF HORRORS', it looked every bit the part. The house had been split into small bed-sits. There were tiles missing and the paint was flaking off. The landlady lived in India and the agents were in Golders Green. Tenants came and went without getting to know each other. In particular, the strange man living in the attic kept himself to himself.

In the dark, cold and full of drink, Stephen Sinclair was unlikely to have paid particular attention to the outside of the building. Once inside, they went up two flights of stairs and, when Nilsen opened the door, Bleep – his small, black-and-white cross-breed dog – jumped up and licked their hands. The flat was smelly, small and damp. As Sinclair walked in, he would have seen a grimy gas stove in small galley kitchen to his left. It adjoined the hall. The bathroom was opposite. The cooker, cooking pot and bath have now been preserved in Scotland Yard's 'Black Museum' as a permanent reminder of the state of mind of the man who owned them.

Ahead of the kitchen was a door leading to the front room. This led to the other main room, the bedroom, in which was a double bed, a comfortable armchair, a stereo, the TV, posters, plants and a scented candle. The room at the front was not used. It contained a large wardrobe and some tea chests. It had been reported that, no matter what the weather, the windows were flung wide open.

There are a number of accounts of what happened next. Even before writing *History of a Drowning Boy*, Nilsen gave two versions. The first was his confession to the police. He told DCI Jay that when they came in and put on the television, he was pleased to see the working-class drama *Boys from the Blackstuff* being broadcast. The programme appealed to his socialist ideals. Sinclair sat on the floor and Nilsen in the armchair. They watched the programme while drinking the alcohol they had picked up on the way.

Towards the end, Nilsen noticed that Sinclair had disappeared to the corner of the room to inject himself with drugs. That disappointed Nilsen. He put The Who's *Tommy* on his stereo. With his headphones tightly clasped to his ears, he says that he listened to all 75 minutes before dozing off. In a police statement later, he claimed, 'I can't remember anything else until I woke up the next morning. He was still in the armchair and he was dead. On the floor was a piece of string with a tie attached to it ... I know I must have killed him ... I must have made up the piece of string that night. I don't know.'

Months later, after the trial, Nilsen wrote an account for author Brian Masters, which is reproduced in his book, *Killing for Company* (extracts of which are reproduced in this book by special permission). Here, he let his memories flow as if reliving the moment:

I am sitting cross-legged on the carpet, drinking and listening to music ... I drain my glass and take the 'phones off. Behind me sits Stephen Sinclair on the lazy chair. He was crashed out with drink and drugs. I sit and look at him. I stand up and approach him. My heart is pounding. I kneel down in front of him. I touch his leg and say, 'Are you awake?' There is no response. 'Oh, Stephen,' I think, 'here I go again.' I get up and go slowly and casually through to the kitchen. I take some thick string from the drawer and put it on the stainless-steel draining board. 'Not long enough,' I think. I go to the cupboard in the front room and search inside.

On the floor therein I find an old tie. I cut a bit off and throw the rest away. I go back into the kitchen and make up the ligature. I look into the back room and Stephen has not stirred. Bleep comes in and I speak to her and scratch her head. 'Leave me just now, Bleep. Get your head down, everything's all right.'

I was relaxed. I never contemplated morality. This was something which I had to do. I knotted the string because I heard somewhere that this was what the thuggi did in India for a quicker kill. I walked back into the room. I draped the ligature over one of his knees and poured myself another drink. My heart was pounding very fast. I sat on the edge of the bed and looked at Stephen. I thought to myself, 'All that potential, all that beauty, and all that pain that is his life. I have to stop him. It will soon be over.'

I did not feel bad. I did not feel evil. I walked over to him. I removed the scarf. I picked up one of his wrists and let go. His limp arm flopped back on to his lap. I opened one of his eyes and there was no reflex. He was deeply unconscious. I took the ligature and put it around his neck. I knelt by the side of the chair and faced the wall. I took each loose end of the ligature and pulled it tight ...

I held him there for a couple of minutes. He was limp and stayed that way. I released my hold and removed the string and tie. He had stopped breathing. I spoke to him. 'Stephen, that didn't hurt at all. Nothing can touch you now.' I ran my fingers through his bleached blond hair. His face looked peaceful. He was dead. The front of his jeans was wet with urine ... I got up and had a drink and a cigarette. He had made no noise; I had to wash his soiled body. I ran a bath ... I returned and began to undress him. I took off his leather jacket, jersey and T-shirt. Then his running shoes and socks. I had difficulty with his tight, wet jeans. He still sat there, now naked, in the armchair ... his body was pale and hairless. He had crêpe bandages on both forearms. I removed these to reveal deep, still open, recent razor cuts. He had very recently tried to commit suicide ...

I picked up his limp body into my arms and carried it into the bathroom. I put it into the half-filled bath. I washed the body ... I sat him on the white-and-blue dining chair. I sat down, took a cigarette and a drink and looked at him ... His eyes were not quite closed. 'Stephen,' I thought, 'you're another problem for me. What am I going to do with you? I've run out of room.'

The next morning ... I lay beside him and placed the large mirror at the end of the bed. I stripped ... and lay there staring at both our naked bodies in the mirror. He looked paler than I did ... I put talcum powder on myself

*and lay down again. We looked similar now. I spoke to him
as if he were still alive ... I thought how beautiful he looked
and how beautiful I looked ... He just looked fabulous. I
just stared at us both in the mirror. Soon I felt tired. I got
in between the sheets ...*

*'Goodnight, Stephen,' I said, switched off the bedside light
and went to sleep. I was up a few hours later. It was an
ordinary day of work for me ahead.*

That 'ordinary day' at work was as an executive officer at the
nearby Kentish Town Job Centre. Nilsen had been in the job
for less than a year. For the previous seven years, he had
worked in a junior role at the Denmark Street Job Centre.
Prior to that he had been a security guard, a policeman (for
eight months) and a cook in the Army. But although he had
joined the Army aged 15, he still seemed highly educated.
This is what had struck many of his colleagues when they
first met him. He was quiet and bookish until the
conversation turned to one of his pet subjects, like left-wing
politics. Then he would quickly become verbose and,
sometimes, domineering.

Nilsen's extensive knowledge could also make him
interesting. But his inability to know when to stop talking
meant that, more often than not, he was a bit of a bore. Still,
Nilsen often made his workmates laugh. He had a sharp, dry
wit and never missed a copy of the satirical magazine, *Private
Eye*. He still subscribes to it in prison.

For the fortnight between murdering Stephen Sinclair and
his arrest, Nilsen continued normally at work. He interviewed
applicants and complained about Margaret Thatcher. But

although for the first week he was his usual businesslike self, after that he started to become fractious.

Nilsen's most vivid recollections of the last week before his arrest are not to be found in *History of a Drowning Boy* but in essays he wrote for author Brian Masters, and which were later quoted in *Killing for Company* – the result of an extraordinary relationship of trust between subject and writer. The project began when Masters wrote to Nilsen while he was awaiting trial asking for co-operation in studying his case. He was one of two writers who did so. The other, ex-ITN newscaster Gordon Honeycombe, had recently written about some of the Met Police's most famous cases in *Murders of the Black Museum*. That, clearly, made him well qualified on the subject. Masters, however, had a CV ranging from biographies on Sartre to Georgiana, Duchess of Devonshire, and Nilsen apparently felt that a man of such sensibilities would be better suited to understand him.

Over the next year, Nilsen filled 55 prison-issue exercise books with thoughts and feelings for Masters. He wrote in incredible detail, and with apparent candour. He began by speaking about was what had happened at his first flat – how he had burnt bones on bonfires and put flesh out by the fence for the rats. He then proceeded to explain how the problems of getting rid of the bodies at the second flat led to his arrest.

From all available sources, this is what happened in the last seven days leading up to Dennis Nilsen's arrest: Jim Allcock, a builder, lived on the ground floor of 23 Cranley Gardens with his girlfriend, a local barmaid. Two other girls lived on the same floor and the middle storey of the building was unoccupied. On Thursday, 3 February, Allcock noticed that his toilet didn't work. He tried removing the blockage but it wouldn't clear. The next day, he decided to call the management agents.

Early on the morning of 4 February, Allcock noticed his other toilet didn't work either. When he spoke to the agents, he requested to be put directly in touch with a plumber. But now he also wondered if it was just his flat. So when his girlfriend, Fiona Bridges, bumped into Nilsen, she asked if he was also having a problem with his toilet. He replied he wasn't. Bridges also noticed that he had been drinking. That wasn't unusual.

Nilsen had actually gone to the pub to prepare himself for the process of getting rid of the 'problem' he had in his flat. He says this was a practice he found distressing and his solution was to get drunk and force himself to do what was necessary. First, Sinclair's body was removed from one of the wardrobes. Then he made sheets from bin liners and put them down on the narrow kitchen floor. Finally, while still drinking Bacardi and Coke, Nilsen set about cutting up the body with a set of sharp chef's knives.

On the hob sat a huge, steel cooking pot, similar to those he'd used in the Army Catering Corps. Its purpose was to soften the tissue sufficiently to enable it to be flushed down the loo. The water took a full half-hour to come to the boil, by which time Nilsen had got the head off and started to remove the innards. The organs smelt terrible, but the body, thankfully, wasn't particularly messy. Nilsen says he couldn't stand the sight of blood, and was always relieved how little there was after a body had settled for a few days. By midnight, he was too drunk to finish.

When he went to bed, he still hadn't made any connection between him and the drainage problems his neighbours were complaining about.

The following Saturday morning – 5 February – suffering from a bad hangover, Nilsen decided to lie in. Meanwhile, the plumber had started inspecting the toilets and drains outside. He concluded that the blockage was a job for specialists. A call was put through to Dyno-Rod, but they informed him that they couldn't send an engineer around until the following Monday. When Bridges and Allcock saw Nilsen leaving the house in the early afternoon, they told him it might be better if he didn't use the toilet in his flat.

Now Nilsen started to worry that his activities were causing the blockage. He decided to do something about the mess and bought cleaning products and air fresheners before returning home.

That afternoon, by chance, Nilsen's sometime friend, Martyn Hunter-Craig, popped round. He says Nilsen looked more agitated than ever before. When Nilsen opened his door a fraction, Hunter-Craig could see his friend's face was a ghostly white.

'You can't come in, Skip,' Nilsen said, 'I'm tied up with someone.'

Hunter-Craig describes smelling what he calls an unusual 'lavatorial' smell which he thought might be vomit. He assumed Nilsen was drunk and probably in a complex sexual situation. As a former male prostitute, Hunter-Craig was used to seeing all kinds of things, and discreetly ignoring them.

Nilsen devoted the whole of Sunday to cleaning up. He finished cutting up the body, and put the parts in bin liners.

Then these and the partially boiled head were covered with newspapers and stick deodorants.

On Monday, 7 February, Nilsen went to work feeling on edge. He was irritable and curt with his colleagues. He was resigned to the distinct possibility that when he came home the police would be waiting for him. But Dyno-Rod had failed to turn up and matters hadn't escalated. Nilsen went to bed that night wondering if he might yet be able to escape detection.

The following morning, Nilsen again went to work in a tense mood. When he returned, it was sleeting. Mike Cattran, a 30- year-old engineer from Dyno-Rod had just arrived. Nilsen went straight up to his flat. Cattran went down to a manhole cover at the side of the building along with Jim Allcock. Cattran looked down, looked back up at Jim Allcock, and said, 'I haven't been in this job for long but I know this isn't shit.' He suspected the matter was from a rotting animal, but couldn't be sure what, or how it had come to be there in such quantities. At 7.00pm he phoned his manager, Gary Wheeler.

His manager's first reaction, as reported, sounded like it may have come from a 1970s TV show. He asked if there were Pakistanis in the building. Cattran replied that there weren't but that he had concerns that someone was doing something untoward. They agreed to leave it until the next day.

By now Nilsen had come down to see what was going on. Along with the occupants of the ground floor – Allcock, Bridges and two more – they listened to the engineers discuss what they had seen. Allcock said he wanted to know exactly what was causing the blockage. Cattran replied that he needed to look in daylight, and not to worry – there was probably a perfectly innocent explanation. He turned to Nilsen and asked him, 'Do you flush dog food down the pan?' Nilsen replied that he didn't.

Nilsen went back to his flat and wrote a letter to the agents complaining about the state of the building, including the drains. He asked that 'routine upkeep and maintenance' of the house be attended to, to keep 'living standards at a tolerable level'. He moaned about the lights in the communal areas before arriving at the important issue: 'When I flush my toilet, the lavatory pans in the lower flats overflow (since Friday, 4 February). Obviously the drains are blocked and unpleasant odours permeate the building.'

This wasn't the first time that he had written such a letter. Complaining was part of his nature. His real intention here, however, isn't clear. Maybe by complaining he could deflect attention. Or maybe, as he told me, he really was 'inviting the end' of his career as a murderer.

After writing his letter, Nilsen came down to find that Cattran was still there. Before he left, the three men at the house all took a look down the manhole together. Seeing how much the matter looked like flesh, Cattran remarked, 'Looks like one for the Old Bill'.

'It looks more to me like someone has been flushing down their Kentucky Fried Chicken,' Nilsen replied. Again, he returned to his flat to consider his options.

When Nilsen later told the police about his thoughts that night, his words were carefully chosen. He said he had first wondered if he should run. But where could he go? As a former policeman he knew that he wouldn't get very far. Besides, he claims to have thought it cowardly. Then, he says he contemplated suicide, but this scared him. He paused for a moment. Then he continued to say that he was concerned that if he wrote a suicide note, no one would believe what he would have to say. Besides, he wanted to face the music because he 'owed it' to 'all the others' to let their families know what had happened.

Nilsen was also worried about his little, one-eyed mongrel. Although he says he possesses a lifelong 'genius' for being isolated from others, it was different with animals. He told the police he didn't want to let her down. Sadly for Nilsen, Bleep was eventually put down after contracting an illness while waiting to be re-homed by Battersea Dogs Home.

Whatever Nilsen was thinking, his thoughts would have been seriously affected by the rum and Coke he was knocking back. Around midnight, Dennis Nilsen decided to deal with the drain problem at its source. He went down to the manhole cover and cleared some of the 'particles of white flesh', disposing of them over the hedge in the back garden. Then he remembered what he'd said to Cattran about the chicken pieces. In the morning, he would go to Kentucky Fried Chicken and replace what he had removed with thighs and wings. Surely, he thought, everyone would lose interest?

When Wednesday, 8 February came, Nilsen never did buy that chicken. He had been spotted that night going outside by Jim Allcock, who questioned him. Nilsen said he'd been outside for a pee. Allcock didn't believe him. He and Bridges had listened to their neighbour bang and clatter with the manhole cover for ten minutes. All the time, Allcock held a large spanner in his hand. Later, they heard Nilsen repeatedly trying to flush the toilet on the landing.

In the morning, they heard him leave at approximately 7.30am. Cattran arrived with his boss Wheeler about an hour later. The only tenant left in the building now was Fiona Bridges. Cattran took his boss over to the manhole, lifted the cover and shone a torch down. The flesh had gone.

Cattran was bewildered. He told Wheeler that he was in no doubt about what he had seen the night before. The men walked over to the front of the house where Bridges was standing in the doorway in her dressing gown. When they told her about the mysterious disappearance, she explained what she and Allcock had seen the night before. All three of them went back to the drain and Cattran reached in. He pulled out what looked like a human knuckle, and then three more pieces of flesh and bone. Then they called the police.

Nilsen was now sure this was going to be his last day at work. He placed a note in his desk. It said that if he were to be reported to have committed suicide, it should not be believed – someone would have killed him. Despite having been a police constable, Nilsen was paranoid about authority. Then he suddenly became quite cheerful. He would tell Masters that it felt like a burden had been lifted; he was 'tired and prepared for what lay ahead,' and also 'sickened by the past, the present, and a doubtful future'. As he left the office, he put on his new, bright-blue-and-white scarf. Some colleagues commented on it. It, in fact, had belonged to Stephen Sinclair.

A brief summary of the events preceding the arrest appears in *History of a Drowning Boy*. In the main, however, Nilsen seems satisfied with how the events of those five drama-filled days have already been told. It's hardly surprising, as much of the commonly-told story actually derives from his own confessions. Now, Nilsen doesn't seem particularly interested in adding more to his thoughts and feelings. Significantly, he doesn't complain, as he does so frequently, that he has been misrepresented.

The reason soon becomes clear. Nilsen's priority in writing his book seems not to re-write the well-known stories about him, but to 'correct' what he believes to be the misconceptions about the overview of his life. In letters he told me how he wanted to demonstrate the 'human' aspect of his past and to show how a potentially 'viable human being' developed a desire to kill.

He says he needs to do so because he believes that, despite the quantity of material that has been written on the case, no one has actually understood his psychological make-up. Most of the analysis he has read in the press he dismisses as sensationalist nonsense. Of greater concern to him is his belief that the one 'serious' study on his case, Brian Masters' *Killing for Company*, published in 1995, missed 'so many insightful clues'.

If Masters had indeed missed certain 'clues' it was not for a lack of possible material. During the project, he had got to know his subject personally in the way that a documentary maker or anthropologist might have done. For a further eight years after publication Masters continued to visit Nilsen out of both a sense of obligation and professional interest. During this period, Nilsen gave him the impression he had welcomed his insights. But towards the end of this period, Nilsen began to feel Masters was exploiting his life story.

In the early 1990s, Nilsen turned against both the author

and his book. '*Killing for Company* is so pretentious,' he later wrote to me, 'that it disappears into the contradictions of its own confused academic fog. With *History of a Drowning Boy* comes the rain.'

Nilsen began to compose his first draft in Albany Prison in 1992. He had been prompted to write by a letter from an American psychiatrist. He had also found that under the influence of a (claimed) easy supply of marijuana, he found he could look back on his life with greater clarity.

Initially, over a period of several weeks, Nilsen wrote late into the night while his budgie, Hamish, flapped around his cell. The first thing he wrote about was his earliest memories growing up in the far north-east of Scotland. What was particularly striking was the emphasis Nilsen placed on the poor relationship he had with perhaps the most influential person throughout his formative years – his mother.

2

GROWING UP

'My mother suffocated me like a boa constrictor.'
DENNIS NILSEN, IN A LETTER TO MATTHEW MALEKOS

In December 2010, Nilsen's mother, Betty Scott, died. She was 89. Some months later, I asked Nilsen if he knew about her death. His reply was typical. He wrote, 'I can tell you exactly when my mother died – it was 23 November 1945.' Similarly, the feeling that she'd been dead to him from the moment he was born runs throughout the first 50 pages of his autobiography.

To the outside world, however, Nilsen's mother seemed a warm, caring lady. Many journalists who travelled up to the village of Strichen, near Fraserburgh, on Scotland's far northeast tip to interview Scott, considered her a rather dear old sort; religious and quite unable to understand how the gentle boy she had raised could be associated with such awful things. Although these reporters only saw her public face, those who knew her better, such as Nilsen's biographer Brian Masters, agreed.

In her public statements, Betty Scott maintained it was for others to judge her son and that she would stick by him. Nilsen, however, never believed a word. It was all lies, he would say, designed to hide the truth of what a rotten mother she had been. In 1985, he ended their relationship with a letter.

Nilsen's and his mother's accounts of his childhood broadly agree on the facts. It was what was going on *behind* Dennis's eyes that he feels his mother never understood. Nilsen says he felt different, unlovable, and needing to hide what he thought and felt.

Betty Scott did notice her son was a little introverted but did not have the time to worry about it. There were five other children to look after. Besides, she thought Dennis would eventually find a niche to suit his artistic, sensitive temperament or maybe his love of animals. In the last 27 years of her life, however, Scott would spend her days trying to work out what had gone wrong. She drew nothing but blanks.

Dennis Nilsen spent many hours pondering the same question. Now he feels he has answers. He is not inherently evil, he says, but rather 'an ordinary man driven to extra-ordinary conclusions'. He is on a mission to make the world understand it was extreme psychological circumstances rather than the essential 'him' that had created a perfect storm in his head. Two out of the three psychiatrists at his trial also partly agreed. They argued he suffered from a variety of 'personality disorders'; a term for abnormalities of mind that fall short of being full psychotic illnesses.

Nilsen dismisses such psychiatric concepts as 'psychobabble'. He believes his crimes will only be fully understood by reading an account of his life story, told *his* way. This is what he claims *History of a Drowning Boy* to be: a serious enquiry, and not a 'whitewash' of his life.

There is one man who seems to agree with many of Nilsen's claims – Matthew Malekos, a 31-year-old psychologist living in Cyprus. They started corresponding in 2000, when Malekos was 18. Twelve years later, Malekos published a thesis on Nilsen called 'The Birth of Psychopathy: the Psychology of a Serial Killer' (2012). In the closing chapter, Malekos suggests that Nilsen's 'therapeutic' writing may have helped him conquer the factors that once made him a psychopath.

Nilsen doesn't explicitly go that far, but he still claims his book is a thorough 'investigation' into the 'recesses' of his mind, and he starts with his infancy. *History of a Drowning Boy* opens with: 'As the unique amalgam, in a new genetic configuration of contributions from a man and a woman, one is born into the world. Therefore at birth I was as different from other people in much the same way as my fingerprints were different from other people's.'

Although Nilsen accepts he was born 'different' from others, he will not concede his nature should have *necessarily* caused his later problems. 'It was not these differences which spawned destructive behaviour later on in life,' he wrote to me in 2003, 'but an utter repudiation of them by my parents, peers and a conventional repressive society.'

The first chapter of Nilsen's manuscript elaborates on this sense of rejection. Olav Nilsen, his father, had been virtually absent since his birth. Yet, although Nilsen clearly resents his lack of a father figure, it is his feelings towards his mother which dominate his thoughts. On the first page of his book, he even complains bitterly about how she treated him when he was just a tiny baby.

In 1946, life was hard for everyone in the small Scottish fishing town of Fraserburgh, which had been hit hard by the war. For the residents of the top flat in 47 Academy Road, things were particularly austere. The living space was terribly cramped. Nilsen's grandparents lived in one bedroom and Nilsen, his mother and brother in another. Nilsen says it was a cold, uncaring, dour and religious environment.

As a baby, Nilsen thinks he was especially sensitive to the unemotional atmosphere that surrounded him. He says he has reason to believe his mother and grandmother would pass him around like an 'unpleasant object'. There were no loving hands, he laments, but rather, he says, he was 'acted upon' in 'rituals' of 'carrying, stripping, bathing, powdering, dressing and laying out', by 'strong and towering powers'.

Nilsen says because his world consisted of harsh, domineering women, his first emotional connections were weak. More importantly, he says the way his body was bathed and changed in a 'ritualistic' way profoundly affected his basic emotional and sexual needs. Then he makes an explosive assertion which sets up his entire story. He speculates whether the rituals he later performed on the dead bodies of his victims – the compulsion to dress, undress and wash the victim's corpses – were, in fact, all re-enactments of scenes from his infancy. Somehow, he feels, the emotional deprivation of early childhood had imprinted itself on to his sexual subconscious.

This concept needs further explanation. It's not only absurd to think imperfect mothering, alone, could have had such a catastrophic effect, but it also sounds as if he may be trying to fix the blame at such a distant past point in time that no one can argue. On the first point, Nilsen agrees that his earliest experiences weren't, in themselves, *sufficient* to corrupt his subconscious needs. The rest of his first chapter attempts to explain those other formative childhood events that he feels set his emotions down such a dark and disturbed track.

In order to understand Nilsen's developing psychology, it's crucial to appreciate how he feels about his birth town. Fraserburgh – also known as 'the Broch' – is a mid-sized fishing town 35 miles north of Aberdeen, in the district of Buchan. The town centre is Victorian and grey. Most of these buildings are built of granite slabs which, in winter, can look like prison walls. Close by are dour housing estates. The harbour may be more colourful but it is decidedly functional.

Many residents feel trapped by the remoteness and sense of insularity (in recent years it has also been dubbed Scotland's heroin capital). Mother Nature doesn't help the sense of bleakness. The persistent winds whip up salt spray, the gulls are constantly screeching and, in winter, it seems dark all day long. But there is also a more uplifting side, especially when the sun shines. The surrounding land is of the kind that is perfect for golf links, and the beaches of Fraserburgh Bay are long and sandy. The natural surroundings can be quite spectacular. And that is the only positive thing Nilsen ever has to say about his birthplace.

Nilsen describes the Broch as a rain-lashed, cultural backwater full of bigots – some religious, others just rough. In one essay, he describes the freezing climate as 'magnified by the cold commanding calculation of other people'. He says he felt totally insignificant, and describes the emotions he felt as a child: 'Big people wore clothes in black and grey and they were forever issuing orders. I was one of the little people to be controlled and ordered about.' Then, in his essay called 'Feelings' (quoted by Matthew Malekos in his thesis), Nilsen gives a metaphor of reaching out to the world only to find his 'hand dirled by the sharp crack of somebody's thin hard stick'.

The stylised prose continues throughout. Nilsen says he was treated like a street dog, with an emotional life that was 'a world of cold maximum power and minimal warmth of close tactile love. I took my place in the line for processing. I was a few points above the status of street urchin.'

Despite the obvious exaggeration, the fact that similar accounts convinced psychiatrists at his trial indicate that Nilsen's words probably do reflect genuine feelings. The worst aspect of Aberdeenshire life, for him, was the sense of hardness and brutality. He observes it was a necessary character of the fishing trade which, when Nilsen grew up, generally thrived. The life of the fishermen was, he says, 'a harsh, uncompromising life constantly tacking close to the cold lips of sudden death'. But that didn't make it any easier for him to warm to them or they to him. As his own brother said of Dennis, 'Fraserburgh isn't a very good place for a poofter.'

After Nilsen's arrest, most locals – both from Fraserburgh and his second home town of Strichen – concluded that Dennis had been born with something 'wrong' in his brain. That belief persists today. Even apart from what he had done, it was not hard to believe that there might have been something wrong with him. And it was also the case that mental instability was not unknown within Nilsen's own family – a great-aunt of his had spent most of her life in a mental asylum. It's also true that generations of inter-marrying meant that mental problems were, in fact, not uncommon in the area.

Dennis Nilsen, however, wasn't a simple product of the local gene pool. His father Olav Nilsen, was a Norwegian resistance soldier who had come over during the Second World War. He had done so as a part of the British-organised 'Shetland Bus'. The Nazis had occupied Norway since 1940, and in 1941 the British Secret Service set up an operation to bring key personnel over to the Shetland Islands or northern Scotland using Scottish fishing vessels. Olav Nilsen was one of those who made their way to northern Aberdeenshire. Fraserburgh, with its RAF bases, was a centre of military activity at the time. In fact, it was even nicknamed 'Little London' because of all the air-raids it had received. Other than how he arrived in Scotland, very little is known about Olav Nilsen.

Nilsen's maternal line came from the Whyte family. His grandparents were Andrew and Lily. They were born in the 1890s into what he calls 'poverty, hard work and danger'. They married young and they first set up home at Inverallochy, a small port near Fraserburgh. Later, they moved to Broadsea, a little way inland. Finally, they settled in Academy Road in Fraserburgh, where Dennis Nilsen was born and where he, his mother and siblings would live until 1954.

Academy Road, like much of Fraserburgh, was comprised

of geometrically square, granite council houses terraced into four reasonably-sized flats. In 'Feelings', Nilsen describes them as 'blockhouse-prim, solid and grim with a black smoke of hell spouting from the red clay chimney pots standing in neat rows over the grey slate roofs.' Number 47 was at the end of one small terrace. The Whytes occupied the top flat.

It was an uninspiring place to live but the couple never aspired to more. Besides, they never had any money. Despite working all his life as a fisherman, Andrew Whyte failed to own his own boat. This meant he was dependent on other fisherman for his livelihood and, when times were lean in the town, he would be unemployed. He found claiming welfare shameful. When his wife had to supplement their social security money with cleaning work, that humiliated him even more.

Andrew would try to compensate by telling elaborate stories. Down at the harbour, he had quite a reputation. Back at home, though, he was careful not to let his story-telling get in the way of the family's spiritual life. God and the Bible were woven into their daily routine and it came as a great comfort to them when their daughter Betty, as a teenager, also became interested in the 'Faith Mission'. In her later years, Betty Scott would talk a lot about her faith. Dennis, however, remembers his mother's evangelicalism with scepticism. He thought, at heart, she was sensual rather than religious. In one letter to me, he moans, witheringly, that the only character trait they ever shared was a 'fondness for cock'.

Whether or not Betty Nilsen had a particularly flirtatious nature when Dennis was growing up, there is no doubt in her early twenties she turned many of the heads of the servicemen looking for relief from the war. As Fraserburgh became increasingly important as an RAF base, many local halls were commandeered as makeshift places of rest and recreation. On Fridays and Saturdays, romance happened quickly. Betty Whyte was petite with a delicate, pale face framed by brown hair, and would use all her youthful guile to sneak past her parents to get to social events. If it proved too hard to make it to the evening dos, she would try in the cafés during the afternoons.

This was how Betty Whyte met Sgt Olav Nilsen of the Norwegian Resistance. Olav was 6ft-2in tall, fair and rugged. He came over and rescued her from the unwanted attention of some RAF boys who had invited themselves to the table where she and her friend were sitting. Betty was won over by his gallant act and, afterwards, they walked off down the street together, hand in hand. It was March 1942 and she was 21.

They got married a couple of months later on 2 May. Things almost immediately started to go wrong. Olav soon left in search of more excitement and, no doubt, other women. And whatever military value he might have had – no one seems to know – quickly expired. He ended up in a tobacco factory. This was entered as his profession on Dennis's birth certificate. He was also known for drinking heavily in the town's pubs. Betty stayed in her grandparents' flat. But despite the unconventional marriage, Olav still managed to father three children by Betty. The oldest was Olav junior; the youngest was Sylvia. In the middle was Dennis, born on 23 November 1945.

Olav senior took some interest in the eldest child but, otherwise, he didn't take any of his responsibilities seriously.

Later, Dennis would discover 'Nilsen' wasn't even his real name. It was a pseudonym Olav had adopted for his Scottish adventure. Nilsen says this contributed to his poor sense of identity as a child.

During his first decade in prison, Nilsen would look back over these early years like a detective in search of clues. In letters, he told me how he suspected his mother had been hiding things from him. Eventually, he became convinced that Olav wasn't even his real dad. He thought that explained why he and his sister were treated differently, and how it was that, when Sylvia was born in 1948, Olav petitioned for divorce on the grounds of adultery. He believed that they had had a different father.

As Nilsen stewed over his origins, his bitterness about his relationship with his mother festered. Increasingly, he felt that all his life she had been hiding important information from him. 'Why will she not face me on any visit?' he demanded rhetorically in one letter to me. In another fit of pique, he wrote, 'Mrs Betty Scott is protecting herself from any hard and embarrassing questions in the future.' Later in the letter, Nilsen remembers his mother losing her cool and shouting, 'You wouldn't know your father if you met him in the street.' Why not, he wondered? There were plenty of photographs of him, after all.

The more Nilsen reflected on his relationship with his mother, the more theories he developed. One was that his very existence reminded her of an affair, or worse … maybe a rape. That, he thought, would, at least, explain his mother's reluctance to touch him and why she was so keen to dump him on the 'cold practicality' of Granny. Such thoughts helped Nilsen believe that his family really was partly to blame for his later problems. In a letter, he complained to me there was 'only one villain' in Brian Masters' *Killing for Company*. His mother, he felt, should have been a close second, with his father not far behind. But of all the traumas Nilsen has given as reasons for his psychological warping, the one mentioned most often did not directly concern either.

For many years, Dennis Nilsen considered the death of his grandfather to be the defining event of his early life. The incident happened when he was almost six. At the time, the family was still living in the grandparents' flat. Nilsen remembers there being an unhappy atmosphere and continual arguments between mother and grandmother about how to look after the children. Even when things were quiet there was tension.

Grandad, however, exuded a kind of calm, masculine serenity. It drew Dennis to him. Everyone noticed how unusually close they were. In her last television interview, Nilsen's mother even held back a tear as she reminisced about how Dennis and Grandad would be seen walking around the town and looking at the boats in the harbour. She said at weekends they would fly kites down by the beach. Her heart was warmed by the sight of them together – it helped compensate for the lack of a real father.

In October of 1951, Whyte, uncharacteristically, started complaining of extreme tiredness. He quit choir and missed church, but still he carried on working. One day, we hear, he went out to sea looking particularly seasick. The next morning, he failed to appear up on the deck. His crewmates went to his bunk to wake him; they found him dead. It was 31 October and he was 62.

Nilsen first described this day soon after his arrest. It wasn't just the death, he said, but also the cold, emotionless way the news was broken to him that caused his emotional scars. One day he remembered running around amid the normal bustle of everyday life and the next his mother was telling him to go and see Grandad 'laid out' in his coffin.

Grandad's body was displayed in the front room. Apparently, no explanation was given as to what had happened nor to what it meant. Grandad just lay there in a cheap, plain, wooden box. In his book, Nilsen tells us the undertaker had dressed him in white long-johns and his weather-beaten face looked like it needed a shave. When little Dennis asked why he looked so strange, the response received was that it was because Grandad had 'gone to a better place'. Nilsen says this shocked and confused him. He felt he was being asked to accept things he couldn't comprehend. Would he see his grandad again 'when he was better' he wondered? If not, then why did Grandad leave? What does it mean to be dead?

Nilsen's initial account led Brian Masters to conclude that seeing his dead grandfather started the boy's personality problems. He believes that while Grandad was laid out, death and love became fused in his mind. To make matters worse, simultaneously, his inner world became totally separated from his outward personality.

Nilsen encouraged this theory: 'My troubles started there,' he told Masters, 'it blighted my personality permanently. I have spent all my emotional life searching for my grandfather and, in my formative years, no one was there to take his place.' But now he says he previously overstated the importance of the event. Whereas it was once the defining event, now he is more inclined to consider it to be merely part of a jigsaw – the other elements were his poor mothering, the rejection of his difference by his contemporaries, misdirected sexuality and a sense of utter worthlessness.

There is also more to Nilsen's re-evalution of his grandad's passing than just readjusting its importance within a general scheme. His whole attitude towards the man has changed. Anyone familiar with the hazy memories of Grandad reproduced in *Killing for Company* would immediately notice a radical change in tone in his autobiography. His fond memories have all but disappeared. There's no 'being borne aloft on the tall, strong shoulders of my great hero and protector, my grandfather', or being rescued by Grandad's 'Magic Sponge'.

The reason for this change in attitude is that Nilsen now thinks there may have been more to his grandfather's apparent kindness than he realised as a little boy. After careful reflection, he believes his grandad may actually have been a 'hesitant' sexual abuser. This is reflected in the new accounts he gives in *History of a Drowning Boy*. For instance, he says, 'He would take me out on long walks over the sand dunes and golf links … On the dunes at the far end of the bay, near the stream flowing into the sea … he would take me out into the dark, slit-windowed pill box and take down my short pants and hold my penis and told me to urinate … Tired by the long journey, I would, invariably, fall asleep and be carried home … My conscious memory is of his strength and a feeling of comfort and security. These were my only real, one-to-one, personable physical contacts with someone who took a beneficial interest in me. He may have been a tepid paedophile, but I do not remember him as threatening or oppressive.'

In a later chapter, Nilsen elaborates on his grandfather's 'special' interest in him. He wonders if, during the long walks he remembers so well, his grandfather may have drugged his tea, and possibly inserted his finger in his anus. He feels this might explain why, as a young boy, he was fixated with defecation. More recently, Nilsen has discussed his new memories in letters exchanged with psychologist Matthew Malekos. The conclusions have been that, as a young boy, and irrespective of any actual sexual abuse, Dennis had conflicting feelings of love and fear towards Grandad. Sometimes the old man could be fond but, on other occasions, he was tyrannical.

As such, young Dennis's feelings towards him may have been a mixture of love and hate. If so, Grandad's death would have prompted both grief and guilt. Malekos suggests that unresolved childhood feelings of 'control and domination' may even have been present in Nilsen's mind when he murdered. It's an intriguing idea, but without any corroboration as to another side to Andrew Whyte's character, it is pure speculation.

Once Grandad had died, it was Dennis's mum and granny who were left to bring up the three children. Nilsen's feelings towards his grandmother at this time are almost as ambivalent as those towards Grandad. In 1983, he wrote in *Killing for Company*:

...the wireless played 'Workers' Playtime', 'Have a Go' and 'Music While You Work', and while Mother went about her seemingly endless washing and housework she sang along with all the popular tunes. The open coal fire burned in the grate with a folding metal guard over it, with always something drying on it ... It was a crowded but happy room. Mum being on her own was a dab hand at interior decorating. She had become self-reliant in her daily struggles to make ends meet. There was always lots of washing hanging ... [after church] we would return to Academy Road for Sunday dinner. Granny would prepare all the food the day before as she was loath to do anything on the 'Lord's Day'. I still have not known anyone to make a Scotch broth as good as Granny.

In *History of a Drowning Boy*, this wistfulness has all but gone. Granny now takes her place alongside his mother as one of the 'shrill', 'domineering' women who helped make the small flat in Academy Road such a cold and uninviting place.

Lily Whyte – Granny – died in 1990. At this time, Nilsen had been in the habit of writing autobiographical notes in a diary. In *History of a Drowning Boy*, he expands some of these thoughts to explore his confused feelings towards his grandmother. He talks about 'the drab, grey life of dear departed Granny'. Then he wonders what kept her going until she was 96. His visual image is of a hard-bitten fish-wife who never stopped to think, in case thinking made her realise the tragedy of her life. He concludes that for all her good intentions, she suffered from emotional paralysis that knocked any gentleness out of her.

Betty, Olav, Dennis and Sylvia finally moved out of Granny's house in 1954. They travelled a mere couple of streets away to a flat above what is now a florist's shop in 73 Mid Street. The move marked the end of a period when Nilsen claims he would spend lonely afternoons wandering the mile-and-a-half down to the beach to be alone with nature. Common sense, however, suggests that such stories were exaggerated.

Whether or not Nilsen was really allowed to wander all around town as a young boy, life certainly changed when a local builder called Adam Scott started to court Nilsen's mother. His presence brought increased structure to the household. Betty Scott would later say it made another depressing council house feel like home. They were married six months later. Life with three children had readjusted Betty Nilsen's priorities for a partner. Reliability was now prioritised over glamour. Adam Scott was thick-set and of average height with receding hair. He worked as handyman for the council and if he didn't have much money to bring in, at least he was honest and determined to treat his stepchildren as if they were his own.

Nilsen's book swiftly deals with his mother's remarriage. He doesn't want to attach much psychological significance to the upheaval it caused. Still, he does admit to being upset by the lack of affection he received, and that was a reason to resent Adam Scott. In particular, he talks about disgust at hearing his mother and Scott making love, which they did with 'rapt abandon' producing four babies 'practically one after the other'. Soon, however, Nilsen says he stopped blaming Scott. He decided that if his mother didn't show him love, then that was entirely her fault. And once he realised this, he says in

History of a Drowning Boy, he started to pity Adam Scott in the face of his mother's domineering character:

> *My stepfather was a semi-literate, shy, County Council labourer who was completely dominated by my mother. He had a quiet personality and violence and malice were completely against his nature. She wore the pants in the house. She would often goad him into 'doing his duty' (as the man in the house) with oblique taunts questioning his potency in being reluctant to beat we kids for misdemeanours.*

Nilsen omits any mention of his mother's claim that now he went from withdrawn to disobedient. And that wasn't just at home – he also received cuffs around the ear from the local constable. Instead, Nilsen just tells us how cold his house-proud mother was. And, during this period, it seems Betty Scott did fail to show Dennis proper maternal love. She herself admitted so, saying that during 1954 she found it almost impossible to hug him. No amount of self-admonishment seemed to change this. There was just something about his difficult, unresponsive nature that prevented her from wanting to touch him.

When things became uncomfortable at home, in his piece called 'The Psychograph', Nilsen says he liked to imagine himself as a 'Saturday matinée hero'. Although having his head in the clouds was typical, the accompanying details are, again, less convincing. He says, for the 'first and last time' in his life, he joined a childhood gang who took part in the 'full range of schoolboy antics and adventures'. His friends, we hear, were 'inquisitive, daring, and mischievous'. He would have us believe that they sailed boats, built rafts and scaled rocks. But the water in which this was supposed to have happened was the very water of which even hardened fishermen were wary. Eventually, however, Nilsen says he tired of these children and their 'dull aspirations'.

Now, Nilsen says, he started to look increasingly to his imagination and animals for company. There were two boys he did still get on with – Farquar Mackenzie and Malcolm Rennie. Together, they would go to abandoned air-raid shelters to find fledglings. The three of them would make nests for them in fish boxes and shoe boxes. Nilsen's favourites were called Tufty and Jocky. One day, when the boys went to play at the shelter, they discovered some local tearaways had killed the pigeons. With a display of emotion absent from later life, Nilsen says he sobbed his eyes out. A similar occurrence happened when his rabbit died of cold in its hutch some months later. The animal's pen had been outside in the back yard.

In *History of a Drowning Boy*, Nilsen complains bitterly that the reason such things happened was because his mother wouldn't allow animals inside the house. In interviews, she would say it wasn't practical to keep them. But Dennis was always convinced the real reason was because she didn't share his love of nature.

Nilsen's relationship with animals recurs throughout his writing. He calls himself a 'critter person' and said to Matthew Malekos: 'I like them, and they like me.' Even as he wrote those lines, he was being kept company by budgies in his cell. But the dynamic between Nilsen and animals is more complicated than simple affection on his part. From his manuscript, we now learn that that, when younger, there were occasions when he wanted to be cruel to animals.

The act of deriving sexual pleasure from hurting creatures – known as 'zoosadism' – has been observed in a number of serial killers. It's often seen as a precursor to violent sex attacks. Nilsen's new confessions about these moments of cruelty, however, don't sound as though he's trying to copy something he's read. He writes with the same detached confusion as with his murders, as if he simply can't explain his actions. What his behaviour shows, though, is that as early as the age of nine, Nilsen's ability to empathise with any other creature was badly malfunctioning.

In *History of a Drowning Boy*, he says: 'In 1955, I did something which thoroughly ashamed [sic] me, then as now. I slipped a wire around a friendly cat's neck [in a disused toilet]. I pulled up the cat by the wire attached to the cistern pipe. It struggled briefly under the wire. After it was dead, I prodded it and turned away disgusted by my own cruel behaviour. I wanted to see the reality and process of killing and death. I was not excited by the act.'

Shortly after the cat incident, Nilsen finally escaped the harsh atmosphere of Fraserburgh. The family moved into a larger council flat in the village of Strichen, a small village about eight miles inland from Fraserburgh. There is a short main street with a few streets running parallel to it. The focal points are a couple of pubs and a village store and, like Fraserbugh, most of the buildings are in the granite style.

The family's new address was 16 Baird Road, and it was where Nilsen spent what many would assume to be the most formative years of his childhood. Nestling at the foot of Mormond Hill, Baird Road is one of Strichen's nicest streets. Its houses stand out by being faced with red stone and are generously sized. Although Nilsen never says so, one imagines it would have been a comfortable place to grow up. And, most importantly, although the village was dull, it was not hard like Fraserburgh.

Nilsen, however, gives the impression of disliking both the village and his school. The teachers weren't much better than those 'schoolmarm spinsters' in Fraserburgh who would bully him with mental arithmetic or make him feel like a 'scruffy urchin'. He resented the way his mother spoke to them. Nilsen claims she would kowtow to any figure in authority. Others simply remember Betty Scott just conscientiously trying to make everyone understand their financial circumstances. One teacher, Melita Lee, said that when there was a school trip to Belmont Camp in Perthshire, Nilsen's mother offered all she could afford – 10 shillings – and even though it fell short, the school accepted it.

Melita Lee was one of the locals who remembered Nilsen best at the time of the arrest. She considered him hard-working, able, very good at art, but with no interest in sport of any kind. Academically, she thought he was probably B stream. Nilsen's mother thought he was mainly in the C class – the lowest. Still, she was proud of his artistic talents, especially the day he managed to get higher marks than Bruce Rankin, who went on to teach art in a local school.

Other than art, Nilsen enjoyed English and history the best. But, looking back on his schooldays, he talks more about receiving six strokes on the palm of the hand than about those who introduced him to ideas. Judging by the testimony of others the punishments he talks about probably reflect feelings more than actual events. And these feelings were increasingly hidden. While the schoolteachers thought him simply solitary and introverted, the young boy thought he was alien. 'Nature', he would tell Brian Masters, had 'mismatched' him from 'the flock'.

Nilsen's memoirs now show that, within a year, he was processing reality in an abnormal and dangerous fashion. Increasingly, he talks in terms of experiencing life as an internal 'film', a term he uses for his constant fantasising. This was considerably more than a bad case of Walter Mitty-style daydreaming; it was a pathological way of interpreting reality. Maybe it would have been more benign if the ingredients to hand had been different. But Nilsen believes he was still dogged by his memories of Fraserburgh – the unhappy home life, the raging North Sea and a series of stories of fishermen dying by drowning that the adults would tell.

During these early years in Strichen, these memories combined to produce a fixation with death and water. As puberty approached, such thoughts became increasingly confused with sex. Or, at least, as an adult, looking back on his childhood, Nilsen was unable to distinguish between his erotic imagination and things that had happened during walks on the beach.

A psychiatric report, written before the trial, discusses a story that, at the time, he claimed was literally true. Nilsen had said that when he was about 11 or 12 while visiting Fraserburgh Bay, he decided to walk into the North Sea –

fully clothed. As he was wading, knee-deep, he lost his footing and started to drown. The next thing he remembered was being in the sand dunes by the beach. His clothes had been removed and lay in a neatly folded pile next to him. On his stomach was some sticky fluid. He thinks he saw a 16-year-old boy staring at him. Nilsen concluded that the boy had fished him out of the water and then masturbated on his torso.

The psychiatrist, James Mackeith, who quoted the story, considered it bizarre. Nilsen now concedes in *History of a Drowning Boy* that what he had said was fantasy. But when trying to recall the actual events behind it, the results again sound just like his sex dreams: 'On the crowded holiday beach one day in summer I saw the lifeguards rescue a young man swimmer. I was fascinated to see this seemingly strong young man being carried from the sea, limp and almost naked, and given artificial respiration. My eyes opened in wonder as he later 'came alive'. My fascination increased as my eyes travelled over his nakedness and became fixed on the bulge under his swimming briefs.'

The other drowning stories in the manuscript, the non-sexual ones, are more likely to be literally true. One involves Mr Ironside, a senile old man, who had gone wandering off. A group of volunteers searched for him all day long. As the summer evening drew on, Dennis joined in. He says he saw a 'bundle' down by the river, and pointed it out. The rescue Land Rover was summoned with its ropes and ladders. Nilsen describes seeing them haul up the body of the old man dressed in a cap, pyjamas and Wellington boots. It reminded him of what had happened to his grandfather.

The final 'water' story involved a friend of his brother's called Billy Skinner. This one, however, also demonstrates a disturbing hostility that Nilsen was quietly harbouring towards some of his contemporaries. Nilsen seems to have been jealous of Skinner and the 'insider' types. Whereas he felt he was on life's sidelines, Skinner was playing in the same 'tough-kid' gang as his brother Olav. On the day he drowned, Skinner had been showing off on the rocks near the lighthouse museum. He'd knocked his head and fallen into the water. Despite efforts to rescue him, he couldn't be revived. 'The sea doesn't care how tough you think you are,' Nilsen remarks. He then wonders what Skinner, in life, would have made of the indignity of an old nurse washing his dead, naked body.

Nilsen felt similar resentment towards his brother Olav, the 'normal' son who seemed to get all the attention. Nilsen's older brother was gregarious and manly. He enjoyed football, billiards, snooker, cards, horse racing and, when old enough, chasing girls. Despite Dennis's bitterness towards him, he was also fascinated by him. When he was 10 or 11, and his brother 13 or 14, Nilsen says he would grope his brother's penis in their shared bed. To Dennis, this was part of natural development. He also feels sure Olav derived some pleasure from the experience. But shortly after, he remembers Olav calling him 'hen' in public, a local Buchan dialect term for woman. Others just thought it a funny name – he seemed to prefer being with the girls after all – but Dennis says he knew his brother was trying to humiliate him, and why.

As part of his further sexual experimentation, he thinks he might also have groped his sister, Sylvia, the sibling he liked the most. He thinks he touched her mainly because he was curious about developing bodies. But he also wonders if it was his fondness for Sylvia that caused him later to be attracted to boys who looked like her. That, in turn, prompts him to classify the incident as an example of his potential bisexuality.

The prose in *History of a Drowning Boy* becomes more urgent when he recalls the 'embryonic' sex games he remembers in the 'parks' – little more than small play areas – of Strichen. He calls these 'sightings'. They were occasions where boys would pin down girls and feel under their clothes. One summer afternoon in the park, the young Dennis saw his brother pin down a girl and put his hand up her skirt. Nilsen says he was upset to see that his brother was such a bully. But sometimes older boys would pin down younger boys, and Nilsen found this exciting. Once, he says, he was pinned down and fondled. He didn't find it unpleasant but he was annoyed that the boy was bigger and stronger. And in his autobiography, he cites other occasions when he did the same to another boy:

> *There was no violence as such, just wrestling him to the ground and putting my hand up his short pants to feel him. I only did this on two occasions and it seemed to be a passing phase. It was a need to feel a surge of power over another person. It was an embryonic sex act ... perhaps a rehearsal. On another occasion I had a wrestling match with a beautiful, almost delicate boy who lived next door.*
>
> *He was about a year younger than me and his build and features had a feminine quality about them. Like me, he was no 'football type'. I soon overpowered him and was*

astride him, pinning him down by his arms held down on the grass. I held him there looking down at his close, handsome face ... I held him there and we gazed into each other's faces. We did not speak ... only the language of our eye contact.

Nilsen writes this passage as though he feels some romantic understanding existed between him and the boy. The reader, however, is again left wondering whether this was just Nilsen's imagination. Some of his fancies were even odder. For a while, he had a crush on a drawing of a boy who was on the cover of his French text book. He also remembers being attracted to two 'special' effeminate boys at school. Apparently, they made him feel like a girl who would faint if they spoke to him. Nilsen says he would watch others and imagine things he would like to do. He was aroused when he saw another boy masturbate for the first time behind some sheds near the park.

Although the knowledge that he was attracted to boys made Nilsen feel ashamed, he was proud of the creativity he thinks is tied up with his sexuality. One evening in particular sticks in Nilsen's memory. It exemplified the gap between his burgeoning identity as a 'creative homosexual' and the lack of imagination around him. He describes the family sitting down to watch television. Around him, he saw 'kitschness' in the decorations, low aspirations in the literature and repression in the religion. On the small black-and-white TV a modern ballet was being shown. When he saw the male dancers in their tights, Nilsen said he was excited. The feeling was cultural as well as sexual. His mother just shouted, 'Get this filth off!' Hostility welled up in him. Why couldn't she understand his world?

Nilsen cites the low cultural ambitions of 16 Baird Road as another example of how he felt his differences were rejected. He thinks it was damaging for him not to have had any of his talents and sensibilities nurtured. Later, he and Matthew Malekos discussed whether such low cultural aspirations in the house may have denied him 'the building blocks of human need'. In his thesis, Malekos conjectures whether Nilsen's claims of emotional impoverishment match existing theories of how psychopaths are created. He finds some evidence to suggest that they are.

Whether or not the atmosphere in 16 Baird Road really damaged Nilsen psychologically, he certainly resented it. It encouraged him to retreat further into his private world of the imagination. He says that he liked to feed this with movies, and this seems to have made him try to format his fantasies to make them more like films he had seen. Strichen was much too small to have a movie theatre, however every so often a projector would be set up in the town hall. Nilsen would go as often as he could.

Retreating to the world of make-believe, he found he could replace the world-as-it-was with the world-he-wanted-it-to-be. Up on the silver screen, he saw father figures in actors like James Stewart and Gary Cooper. With James Stewart, Nilsen felt a sexual as well as parental attraction. 'Life looked better through the oblong frame of the movie screen,' he writes. When on his own, he imagined he was in a movie, which he considered a great improvement on 'the drab dullness of real life'. Only one person in his family seemed to understand the power of the imagination like he did, and that was his Uncle Robert.

Aunt Lily's husband, Robert Ritchie, was a design engineer by trade, but also a man of ideas and culture. His pride and joy was an expensive hi-fi system on which he would play Dennis the great symphonies. While the music was playing, he would regale the boy with tales of the left-wing struggle. These stories may have opened up the welcome possibility that Uncle Robert and his kind could be right and most of the world wrong. They may have been the primary reason that socialism later became so attractive to him.

Then, at the age of 14, despite the influence of Uncle Robert, Dennis did something that took everyone by surprise: he joined the Army Cadet Force. We hear that, despite being physically weak and disliking authority, he found firing guns and, more particularly, the other boys, thrilling. That last point is made at great length. Nilsen spends paragraph after paragraph detailing how thrilling he found seeing them in their PT kit.

But although much of what he says is merely sexual, Nilsen also seems to want readers of his book to join in his youthful enthusiasm for the Army. Nilsen knew that, as much as he would have liked to have been able to develop his artistic side, in the general area of the Broch there were limited prospects to do so. Given his realistic options, the idea of adventure and male camaraderie certainly seemed more interesting than joining Uncle Robert in the Consolidated Pneumatic Tool Company. Above all, Nilsen had had enough of Aberdeenshire. He knew that in the Army there were all sorts of roles he could try. His favourite idea was to try to be a cook. After a very brief spell in a fish canning factory, he went down to Aberdeen to the Army Recruiting Office and took the exams. He passed them with ease. He then signed up for a period of nine years.

One July morning in 1960, Adam Scott took Dennis Nilsen to the station to catch a steam train to London. The lad had high hopes of his new life. He would be able to see the world and have great adventures, far from the small-town attitudes of Strichen. He had, however, misjudged his ability to fit in with young, 'normal', heterosexual men. It would take a further 22 years and the lives of at least 12 young men before Nilsen could really start to accept his sexuality and background. Being frank with himself began with his nine months awaiting trial on remand.

3

PRISON LIFE – BRIXTON

*I seek only to reach out to engage with the human
dimension which is anathema to rigid
officials of the retribution machine.'*
DENNIS NILSEN, IN A LETTER TO THE AUTHOR

The nine months Nilsen spent on remand were filled with conflict and confrontation. His crimes and odd personality caused him to be shunned by fellow inmates. Worse were the constant arguments he got into with warders. On occasion, these led to his being detained in solitary confinement. But by the end of his time on remand, Nilsen had begun to stabilise. He was helped both by the lack of destructive stimuli – sex and alcohol – and by the fact that, for the first time in years, he was no longer isolated.

Not only were there people surrounding him, but there were also others interested in him. Nilsen no longer felt invisible and it encouraged him to record his thoughts. Once he had started to write, a pen rarely left his hand. Every scrap of paper in his cell became covered in his dense, spidery handwriting. He was on a search for anything in his past –

such as the death of his grandfather – that might provide him with a reason why he had become a killer.

In *History of a Drowning Boy*, however, rather than recall his intense introspection, Nilsen chooses to concentrate on what he considered to be the awful regime of Brixton Prison and the injustices he felt were heaped upon him. The chapter he writes about the period before the trial is fascinating, frustrating and frequently unpleasant. Nothing in what he says is straightforward. Nilsen constantly seeks to cast himself in a better light by putting others down. Petty grumbles are given as much space as his reflections on how he had become 'addicted to murder'.

Nilsen's description of the day of his arrest is a case in point. Immediately after the arrest, the police had driven Nilsen over to Hornsey, a smallish police station two miles east of where he had himself been a probationary police officer. Nilsen says that Peter Jay, Geoff Chambers, Steve McCusker and Jeff Butler didn't know what to expect from him. Jay, for his part, says Nilsen seemed 'extremely odd' and he knew he would need to be played carefully.

In particular, Jay suspected that, as a union man, Nilsen would be noticing whether the regulations were being followed. He was right. It shows in Nilsen's description of Chambers as 'having forgotten a lot of the basic principles of police evidence gathering despite his exalted rank,' and his statement that he was pleased his treatment was 'correct and amiable.' Indeed Jay's friendly, light-hearted and efficient manner created an environment in which Nilsen felt comfortable enough to talk freely.

When Nilsen set about unburdening himself, his manner

seemed relaxed and his words informative. Internally, however, Nilsen says he felt very differently. He says that 'playing the part of a villain was new to me' and being 'absolutely isolated and friendless I entered into a spirit of bonhomie with my captors'. His conscience, he adds, was 'in desperate need for relief'.

Jay remembers Nilsen as being quietly spoken but with a strange swagger. During the interviews, he drank endless cups of coffee, chain-smoked cigarettes and his words were peppered with his black humour. It resulted in many infamous remarks, such as: 'I don't know how many bodies I had under the floorboards at any one time. I didn't do a stock check.'

Nilsen's book makes no apology, however, for his black humour. He does claim, though, that that he talked more freely than he felt he should have. 'Previous commentators,' he says, 'have grossly underplayed this ... element of fear.' Despite being photographed daily to minimise any threat of being beaten, Nilsen says he was worried 'the police might hang [him] up in a cell and call it suicide'. But given his first-hand knowledge of police practice this is hardly convincing. Similarly, when he says that, on his second day in custody, he turned away a solicitor because he didn't want to be told to remain silent, it as if he really wanted to appear in as good a light as possible to *himself*.

Soon, the detectives started to worry that, despite such behaviour, their prisoner might stop co-operating. Jay effectively led the investigation. He is 6ft 3in with a tough 'old school' manner. His boss, DCS Geoff Chambers, was nicknamed 'Fag Ash and Confusion'. Jay told me how aware they were of the time pressure they were working under. Without an extension they only had 48 hours to charge Nilsen and, even though he was talking constantly, there was still the task of corroborating what he said.

With the body of Stephen Sinclair reassembled on the mortuary slab, they decided to concentrate on his murder. Once Nilsen was detained on one charge, they would be able to question him about others at their leisure. But before this, Chambers and Jay had the press to deal with. The newspapers had first learnt about the goings on in Cranley Gardens after Mike Cattran had contacted a local reporter from Muswell Hill who then tipped off Fleet Street. Because of this, Jay and Chambers had to quickly call a press conference. The reporters were all looking for a quote for their front page. 'How long,' one journalist asked, 'has Nilsen had this unusual habit?'

Chambers and Jay were conscious that if the papers reported too much it might hinder their investigation. They needed to act quickly. So at 5.00pm on Friday, 11 February 1983, Dennis Andrew Nilsen was charged with the murder of Stephen Sinclair. The case was now placed *sub judice*, with reporting forbidden until the trial.

Meanwhile, Nilsen was now starting to prove a difficult client for his solicitor, a cheerful man called Ronald Moss. At his first court hearing at Highbury Magistrates' Court on the Saturday, 12 February, Nilsen forewent the customary blanket over the head and walked out in the full glare of the press. Images of him in his large spectacles and neat side-parted hair made the front pages of the tabloids, pictures which are still often shown today.

Nilsen's behaviour may or may not have been a case of him trying to stage-manage his image. It was also down to the fact that once he got it into his head to do something a certain way, that was how it had to be. After unburdening himself of his crimes, he wanted to believe he had rejoined the world of decent, morally upstanding people. He says in his book that that morning he didn't want to hide away like a common criminal. In a letter to me some years later, he wrote: 'On my arrest, I regained the moral high ground. My commitment was clear. To assist in every possible way to bring lawful justice to the past, present and future … I am still firmly wedded to the moral code with the added degree of maturity which comes from the enlightenment of experience.'

On 18 February 1983, with most of the interrogation now concluded, Nilsen was taken to Brixton Prison. He was held on remand there from February until his trial in October. Going to Brixton was more than just a journey a few miles south. Hornsey had looked like the police station he had himself worked in, and Chambers and Jay gave him endless snacks and cigarettes. Brixton felt like what it was – prison.

It also epitomised everything bad about the Prison Service in the 1980s. The corridors stank of unpleasant food and male bodies; noise clattered around the bare walls and in winter it was constantly freezing. The physical discomfort was only part of it. The reality of what Nilsen had done was also starting to sink in. If killing was an addiction, here was the cold turkey.

Nilsen knew his eventual prospects were bleak. The best case scenario lay in a sentence mitigated by 'diminished responsibility'. This could lead to a reduced sentence or, just as likely, being sent to an asylum until considered 'cured'. That possibility terrified Nilsen. One psychiatrist who visited, reported: 'He is preoccupied with avoiding a mad label.'

Nilsen wasn't just afraid, he was also angry. He was particularly furious about the idea that men who hadn't yet gone to court were still treated like criminals. He says he no longer felt dangerous and wanted bail arrangement where he could be 'held in prison custody away from the crude violence of the Brixton Prison Authorities'. Later, he also says he was surprised that DCS Chambers should imply 'that if [he] were to be released from custody [he] would go around killing people and cutting them up'. Despite his open confessions, Nilsen deemed himself to now be 'harmless'. Why couldn't other people see it, he thought?

After returning from his bail hearing – it had been swiftly refused – Nilsen was taken off to a private room to talk to Paul Bowden, a senior Home Office psychiatrist. It was meant to be a pre-trial evaluation about his competence to stand trial. Bowden was sure Nilsen was not schizophrenic nor otherwise incompetent. But after an hour together, Bowden began to feel there was something about his excitability that was concerning. He recommended an eye be kept on him for his own safety. Nilsen was thus sent to the hospital wing and stayed there, as a potential suicide risk, month after month, throughout his period of remand.

Being kept in the hospital wing – what Nilsen considered to be 'solitary confinement' – angered him even more than before. Rather than being more relaxed, as one might expect, the authorities exercised additional powers over inmates in the medical unit. These included patient isolation for up to 23½ hours in a solitary cell. Nilsen alleges he was held like this for most of the time.

Although he didn't have many friends, in his first couple of weeks in Brixton, Nilsen says he did still receive a couple of visitors. One was Cathy Hughes, who had taken over as Denmark Street Branch Secretary at the CSPA Union. His boss Janet Leaman also wrote but didn't visit. In her letter she said she wouldn't believe the accusations until they were proved. Her words were warm and reminded Nilsen how his cynical humour had 'always hit the spot'. But between such, short-lived, signs of support, and Brian Masters getting in touch, Nilsen mainly relied on stilted conversations conducted between cells for companionship.

Some descriptions of those he met at this time are given in *History of a Drowning Boy* to highlight what a terrible place Brixton was. If they are to be believed then, for once, Nilsen might have had a point. Two cells down the corridor was an inmate called David – not his real name. His was a particularly sad case. He'd had been charged with the murder of his baby daughter. He claimed that the murder had been committed under the influence of drugs and he had no memory of it. Nilsen says he thought that David needed immediate treatment for his drug problems.

After telling the reader how awful this situation was, he gives a flavour of how he would interact with David. He remembers one afternoon in particular. It was just after the prison library trolley had done its rounds. Nilsen asked David if he could swap his book of poems for David's copy of the *Complete Works of Shakespeare*. They started to discuss David's case. Soon, the conversation turned to the unfairness of wearing prison uniform. How can they make you dress as a prisoner, they agreed, when you haven't yet been convicted of anything?

From the injustices of prison life, Nilsen moves on to the plight of some of the more wretched prisoners he saw. For the most part, he says inmates were just 'ordinary human beings' in adverse circumstances. Nilsen says that 'in crimes of emotional/sexual psychology, it is a case of "there but by the grace of God goes anyone"'. But what to do with such prisoners? Nilsen says he thought prisons were there to help rehabilitate, not to further brutalise those to whom life had already been cruel. He concluded the prison authorities didn't really want to manage their inmates back into society, but 'warehouse' them like 'animals in a zoo'.

If he doubted for a moment that prison warders were thugs, then meeting another inmate – we'll call him Carlton – settled the issue. Here was another very tragic situation. Carlton was standing accused of throwing a child out of a window during a burglary. The child had died as a result. Nilsen and Carlton spoke to each other during cell-to-cell conversations and exercise periods. It soon struck Nilsen that Carlton had mental problems. In fact, he thought he had no place being there at all. On top of that, he seemed to be the victim of racial abuse. Carlton was a heavily-built black man, who, Nilsen claims, was repeatedly beaten by the prison guards.

On one occasion, it was apparently just because he was listening to Bob Marley. Nilsen vividly describes the guards' language: 'Don't you play that fucking jungle music in here, you black cunt.' When the prison doctor came to do his rounds on the medical wing, he allegedly ignored Carlton's injuries. Carlton was eventually committed to Broadmoor. Before he left, he thanked Nilsen for not blanking him. It was written on a Mother's Day card and Nilsen included it in the papers he gave Masters.

Nilsen enjoyed acting protectively – and, probably, domineeringly – towards weaker inmates like Carlton. Some were very grateful for his support and assistance. Peter Jay told me that, when he and Geoff Chambers travelled over to complete their final interviews, they were surprised to see other prisoners come up behind Nilsen and slap him on the back. It appears that, in particular, Nilsen helped others write letters to their girlfriends or lawyers.

Mostly, however, Nilsen was a nuisance to all around him. The governor, A J Pearson, told him one day that after all he had done, he had a cheek going on about prisoners' rights. But Nilsen could only see the hypocrisy on the other side. To him, the authorities were punishing people by breaking the law themselves. His chapter on his spell on remand is replete with accusations of beatings, the forced administration of drugs such as chloropromazine (an anti-psychotic), and placing prisoners naked in what he referred to as 'strip cells' in the 'punishment block'.

As a prisoner on remand, Nilsen was given an allowance of 88p a week. He was allowed to supplement this with his own money, but since he had resigned from the Civil Service (to spare them any embarrassment, apparently), he had no salary. Nilsen's main outgoing was tobacco. As a lifelong chain-smoker, he'd been so concerned about running out in prison; the day he arrived he'd switched to roll-ups. Cigarettes and writing materials were Nilsen's necessities. When he could access money, it would be spent on newspapers and batteries for his small radio.

Dennis Nilsen may have had some friends among weaker prisoners, but a significant number objected to his very presence there; some because of what he had allegedly done, but others just disliked his aloof personality. One of Nilsen's lowest moments in the pre-trial period came when the prison governor banned him from attending chapel. Despite his atheist beliefs, Nilsen had been a regular visitor to break up the interminable hours spent locked up in his prison hospital cell.

The governor was worried that Nilsen's presence might cause a disturbance and present a threat to 'good order and discipline'. That wasn't how Dennis Nilsen saw it. In *History of a Drowning Boy*, he describes this incident as his 'expulsion' from 'religious activity'. He felt the chaplains should have stood up to the governor and describes them as 'Christian hypocrites', and 'worse than cockroaches'. They were forever 'crossing to the other side of the road', like in the parable of the Good Samaritan. The reader is left feeling that what really got to Nilsen was that the Church was meant to be there for all humanity. If it rejected him, what, then, was he?

If the world saw him as a monster, Nilsen's 'inner film' was still working out ways to be the hero of his story. He found it, temporarily, when he fell in love. In between writing his self-admonishing essays, Nilsen had become infatuated with a young psychopath, who was also on remand, called David Martin. They met for short periods in the exercise yard. He was small, effeminate and bisexual. It is possible their relationship may have developed if circumstances had been different. But, as it stood, it was largely one-sided. While Martin seemed initially to enjoy Nilsen's attention, he was also smitten with an ex-model called Sue Stephens. Eventually, Martin sent a note to Nilsen to stop pestering him. Still, the 'couple' was gossiped about in the prison. One warder described them as the 'copper who liked killing queers with the queer who liked killing coppers', referring to Nilsen having been a policeman and Martin having shot one of them.

It was easy to see why Nilsen might have been attracted to David Martin. His story read like the plot of a gangster movie. He was a career criminal who had been in and out of prison all his life. Martin had resumed offending in 1981 after an eight-year sentence for fraud. His spree started with a series of burglaries on video stores to get equipment to start an adult movie business. A month later, he raided a gun store in Covent Garden. Finally, in August 1982, he broke into a film-processing laboratory, shooting a policeman in the leg before escaping.

Martin then fled to Spain. While he was away, detectives located his flat. Just as he returned, the flat was being put under surveillance. The only person they saw going in and out, however, was a slim, blonde girl. Then information reached them that Martin himself enjoyed dressing up in women's clothes – they had been watching him all along.

On 15 September, Special Branch waited outside the flat for the 'blonde with the Adam's apple' to return. As armed officers approached him, Martin pulled a gun out of the top of his stockings and pointed it at them. They responded by shooting him in his neck.

Some months later, after he had recovered, Martin escaped from Marylebone Magistrates' Court, using clips and pins hidden in his long hair to pick the lock. With his fur-coat collar up and a stack of papers in his arms, he then walked out of the building. News of the escape spread over the front pages, and a manhunt was launched.

When Nilsen chatted to Martin in the exercise yard, he discovered just how close he'd been to Martin's subsequent, dramatic arrest. That their stories might be connected appealed to Nilsen's sense of romance. In a ten-page sequence, his manuscript describes the last week of January in 1983.

Nilsen had killed Stephen Sinclair on Wednesday, 26 January 1983. The next morning, he says he woke with a hangover, but still felt ok to do a normal day's work. When he got back, he spent some time admiring Sinclair's naked body and then he decided to go for an evening's drinking at the fashionable, gay-friendly, King William IV pub in Hampstead.

Half an hour before Nilsen had arrived at the 'King Willy', Martin had been arrested in Hampstead Tube station. One of the regulars at the bar was talking about how the police had shut the Tube station down. But Nilsen says at the time he was more interested in where he might find some action. He decided to move to the Sir Richard Steele pub near Belsize Park Tube just down the road. The police were there, too. Nilsen asked what was going on; the constable replied they had arrested a dangerous criminal.

Later, Nilsen got a cab back. He describes getting home and letting the dog out into the garden downstairs. Then he went up to his room, lifted Sinclair's dead body up and placed him in the chair in the next room. Filling his glass, and turning on the tape player, he turned to the dead man. Without any apparent shame or embarrassment, Nilsen recalls saying to him, 'You're a lot better off than the poor bastard they've got down the Tube station.'

Although Dennis Nilsen and David Martin served remand time together in the summer of 1983, they became separated that autumn when Martin was moved from Brixton to Parkhurst. Suddenly, Nilsen felt isolated. Impulsively, he wrote to Martin's solicitor, Ralph Haeems, to see if he might represent them both. Any contact, he decided, was better than none.

Retaining Haeems as solicitor was not simply a romantic gesture by Nilsen – it was also a shrewd choice. Haeems had no qualms about representing notorious clients, frequently with favourable results. He was himself a colourful, unconventional character. Although brought up in Bombay, Haeems later relocated to London's East End, and he was Jewish. During his career he acted for the Krays, defended clients in the Brink's-Mat robbery and helped acquit a convicted paedophile, Russell Bishop, of the 'Babes in the Wood' killings. If ever there was a man to find a way to mitigate what Nilsen had already admitted to, it was surely Ralph Haeems.

By the time he appointed his new legal adviser, Nilsen had dismissed and re-appointed the previous solicitor, Ronald Moss, three times. In between these periods of appointment, he even tried to represent himself. Nilsen's dismissals of Moss always sprang from the same complaint – he felt that his lawyer simply wouldn't help him stand up to a prison regime, which he felt repressed and bullied him. He wanted Moss to give him legal help to put an end to what he saw as the intolerable conditions of the hospital wing, and the 'solitary confinement' that inevitably resulted from his own efforts to square up to the strictures of life inside.

Above all, Nilsen objected to the 'monster' tag that everybody seemed to apply to him. Did no one appreciate the psychological complexities of a case like his, he would ask himself. One afternoon, he became so frustrated, he started tearing up his case papers. The act of tearing up the papers landed Nilsen another spell in an isolation unit for behaving 'irrationally' or, as the doctors on the unit might have considered, to safeguard his own safety.

After appointing Haeems, things initially went well. Nilsen eventually, however, became disenchanted. By the end of their relationship, he would describe Haeems as the sort of man who had a 'tax-deductible heart'. Some months earlier, he became convinced Haeems briefed friends in Fleet Street about current cases. This was doubly intolerable. Nilsen felt that if his solicitor kept such company, the least he could do was lean on them to tell the world how badly Dennis Nilsen was being treated. He felt he was doing a better job of that himself.

There had been two incidents over the summer of 1983 when Nilsen got a story in the papers, and he considered both a success. In May, Nilsen wrote to the *Guardian* newspaper, complaining that he had been misrepresented when Alan Rusbridger's column had claimed he'd been a member of the Social Democratic Party. Nilsen pointed out that he was a socialist rather than a liberal, and that he'd never joined any party in his life. In fact, when asked to tick a box on his union forms, it had always been 'independent radical'.

And then there was the 'Chamberpot Incident'. At the end of the summer, Nilsen decided to show those around him that he would not stand for the inhuman conditions under which he was being kept. It had all started when Nilsen's objections to the conditions of remand had resurfaced. He had threatened to protest against the way he, a man who had not yet stood trial, had to wear the clothes of a prisoner, by walking around naked. The response from the warders had been to tell Nilsen to remain in his cell. This, in turn, then had prevented him from being able to 'slop out'. The faeces and urine built up in his pot to the point where the pot was overflowing with effluent. Determined to win the stand-off, on the evening of 1 August, Nilsen shouted 'stand clear' and threw the contents through the bars and out of the cell on to the landing. Several guards were hit and they retaliated robustly. In the ensuing scuffle, Nilsen lost a tooth, picked up a black eye, and earned himself 56 days in solitary confinement.

During Nilsen's nine months on remand, his only regular visitor was author Brian Masters. The resulting study, *Killing for Company*, would go on to win the 1985 Gold Dagger crime writing award. Such a close relationship between author and criminal reminded some critics of Truman Capote's *In Cold Blood*, his celebrated study on the perpetrators of the Clutter family murders in Kansas. Masters' observational dynamic was, indeed, so unusual, it later became the subject of a BBC documentary, *Monochrome Man*.

Brian Masters grew up in a prefabricated house on

London's Old Kent Road, where his sickly, hunchbacked mother and ineffectual father had been housed after the war. Prospects for children like him, he says in his autobiography *Getting Personal* were limited. However, he was determined to better himself. One episode at school changed the course of his life. Looking to win a prize for best school project, Masters wrote to the acerbic TV personality Gilbert Harding, asking to interview him. Harding agreed to the request and afterwards invited his young interviewer to tea. Later, he made it his business to educate the ambitious lad. Masters is very clear that his motives were entirely genuine.

Harding's mentoring helped Masters earn a place at Cardiff University, where he ended up with first-class honours in French Literature. He built on this by writing studies on Sartre and Camus. In his thirties, he moved on to biographies about British royalty. One on Georgiana, Duchess of Devonshire, was particularly well received.

In his early forties, Masters was interested in understanding the extreme possibilities of human behaviour. He read about the Nilsen case over breakfast one morning in his west London home. As he got to the end of the third page of revelations about the murders, he read a line about Nilsen enjoying reading Shakespeare. He wondered if this might be the opportunity he was looking for to study someone at the farthest end of the human spectrum. Towards the end of March, and ignorant of the protocol about writing to prisoners, Masters wrote a letter addressed to Nilsen c/o Brixton Prison. In it, he asked if he might want to co-operate with a book project. He also included a copy one of his previous biographies.

Although he knew he'd given the introduction his best shot, the author was only half expecting a reply. What he received on 30 March was truly chilling. The first line read, 'Dear Mr Masters, I pass the burden of my past actions on to your shoulders.'

Authors in England are not, in fact, allowed to contact prisoners on remand unless express permission is given. Masters' initial letter had slipped past the prison censor. When the correct procedure had been explained, Masters then contacted Nilsen's solicitor at the time, Ronnie Moss, a cheerful man whom he describes as looking more like a publican than a solicitor. Moss helped him make the correct application to the authorities concerning the writing project.

Meanwhile, he was given a one-off visiting order to meet Nilsen as a friend. On 20 April, they met in Brixton's noisy visitors' room. From what he had read, Masters was expecting a nervy, introspective man only comfortable expressing himself on paper. He was surprised to find in Dennis Nilsen a tall, imposing figure, 'bristling with confidence'.

Shortly after the meeting, the Home Office gave Masters the green light to carry on with his visits. This worried DCI Jay and DCS Chambers. Their investigation was still ongoing and they were concerned Masters' influence might affect Nilsen's attitude and co-operation. They also doubted Masters had the stomach for what he was about to undertake.

He was therefore summoned to the station where they showed photographs of what they had found in the flat. The portfolio included gruesome pictures of Sinclair. In his own memoirs, Masters describes 'the lips boiled away, the eyes soft and gluey, and the hair drifting to one side', as examples of the sort of images he would never be able to forget. But these pictures also confirmed to him that here was a unique opportunity to explore the reality of evil.

Masters was not used to handling criminals. His recent subjects had been members of the aristocracy. But, whether by design or default, his approach turned out to be the key to open Nilsen. Masters just went ahead as normal and the prisoner responded with lengthy answers.

Nilsen would later tell me that the reason he had been so candid was because Masters was 'all there was', implying that if he had had any alternative outlet, he might have taken it instead. In truth, Masters was both a skilful interviewer and a sincere man. Nilsen also appears to have hoped that his sensitivity would also enable him to understand one crucial aspect to his character: his sexuality.

Increasingly, Nilsen let his guard down. It wasn't just the crimes he spoke about. He issued a stream of thoughts on his entire existence. One letter to Masters listed all the roles he had played in his life: schoolboy, soldier, chef, projectionist, policeman, clerical officer, executive officer, drunk, sexualist (male and female), murderer, animal lover, independent trades union officer, debater, champion of social causes, do-gooder, dissector of murder victims, grand vizier, and probably 'lifer'. He went on to speculate that if there were a God, what a strange set of 'priorities' he must have had for him.

The more Nilsen opened up, the more friends and even the Crown's trial psychiatrist, Paul Bowden, warned Masters that Nilsen might be manipulating him. Bookish and dapper, Brian Masters didn't look much like a match for someone like

Dennis Nilsen. Masters, however, felt equal to all of Nilsen's games. He was, though, very aware he would need to play detective to find out the truth.

It wasn't just a case of judging what to believe but also finding the words to describe the drama of a man struggling to process a spree of 15 murders. His thoughts are given in a chapter called 'Remand'. Here, Nilsen's moods are described as a 'kaleidoscope ... shifting from elation to gloom, from resignation to despair, from regret about the past to hope for the future'.

During the remaining months before the trial, Masters visited twice a week. Throughout this period, Nilsen wrote his thoughts and biographical reminiscences daily in prison exercise books (he would also carry on writing after the trial). Under the agreement Masters had with the prison and Home Office, he was allowed to use anything Nilsen had written but nothing from the face-to-face meetings. He even had to sign a formal undertaking to that effect.

Soon, Brian Masters started to experience what appeared to be Nilsen's fierce loyalty. At first, it seemed like one of his impulsive friendships. Eventually, however, he decided it was mainly an obsession with principles. During the summer, some prisoners suggested to Nilsen that Masters was a 'plant' for one of the tabloid newspapers. It made him extremely angry. He felt Masters was now his friend and an attack on the author was an attack on him. As the rumours grew, he responded by sulking and refusing to talk to his solicitor. This protest seemed childish.

Nilsen seemed confused by his own emotions. In one notebook, he described them as 'the most toxic substances known to man'. His words match, remarkably, a profile of 'covert schizoid personality' described by the psychiatrist Dr Salman Akhtar. Such people are characterised as being, amongst other things: cynical, grandiose, sensitive, creative, voyeuristic, amoral, autistic, hungry for love and envious of others' spontaneity. Nilsen wrote it must be a 'wonderful gift' to 'throw your arms around someone and just weep'. At that moment, he seemed to accept that, for much of his life, normal emotions had been beyond him.

More usually Nilsen presented the impression that he was convinced he had now returned to 'normal'. Of course, it was odd that he felt so little sadness for his victims, but he didn't feel there was essentially anything wrong with him. Yet whenever he put pen to paper, the results inevitably showed him to be disconnected from his crimes. Most strikingly, there were a series of drawings of his last victim, Sinclair. These 'Sad Sketches' were accurately drawn renditions of how his remains appeared after they had been dismembered. They were accompanied by notes recounting how he had cut up the corpse. Masters described them as being drawn with 'energy and pride', and 'an odd kind of perverse affection'.

As 24 October 1983 – the date set for the trial – drew closer, Nilsen's mood swings seemed more extreme than ever. One moment he could be cheery and, minutes later, he seemed tortured. 'I go through a personal hell each day,' he says in *Killing for Company.*

The divisions within him in the run up to the trial were, however, still consistent with a personality that was under pressure but basically working. That impulsive infatuation with Martin, the sudden friendships in the exercise yard, the erratic defence strategy and the compulsive writing may simply have been him coming to terms with being a murderer. His behaviour even reminded Masters occasionally of Raskolnikov, Dostoyevsky's motiveless killer whose reflections are the subject of the classic novel, *Crime and Punishment*.

Nilsen even said that he hoped if he accepted all blame, maybe he could look the parents of victim Ken Ockendon in the eye. Of all his victims, Ockendon was the most inexplicable. Nilsen had met the 23-year-old Canadian tourist in a pub one lunchtime. The young man had a loving family and probably wasn't homosexual. The two of them had enjoyed an entire day together. Nilsen had seemed genuinely confused as to why he had killed him. In order to atone for what he had done, he told Masters he wanted to accept any punishment the law prescribed and some more besides.

Eventually, however, he seems to have changed his mind. Nilsen pleaded not guilty on the grounds of diminished responsibility. On 3 November, the 12 men and women of the jury were initially unable to agree whether there might be something sufficiently wrong with Nilsen's brain to mitigate his actions. The next day, however, a majority verdict was accepted, and Dennis Nilsen was a guilty and an evil man.

During the trial, which is the main focus of Chapter 10, Nilsen had tried to convince the outside world of the context of the crimes. Once that failed, he felt had only his own writing to fall back on. In his letter to me, he stated, 'I explain but *do not* excuse. We are not talking about studious "evil" but human inadequacy. Men will admit to potent criminality or controlling powerful "villainy" but never "inadequacy". My crimes flowed from personal inadequacy developed over a lengthy period. It was a desperate possessive "aggression", almost spiritually passive in the motive and heat of expression.'

The evening following his life sentencing – with a minimum of 25 years to serve –Dennis Nilsen was in the hospital wing of Wormwood Scrubs Prison, and appeared utterly despondent. One of the orderlies let him watch TV. Nilsen says in *History of a Drowning Boy* that he sat blankly in front of it, considering his position: 'The world that I looked at on the TV was not the world that I had known before… Everything had changed drastically and I now felt like a ghost looking at an alien world of flesh and blood people. With an endless sentence ahead of me, I felt that I had been expelled from society for ever more.'

4
OLD KIT BAG

*'The Army gave me an education, a trade, and the key
to travel to other worlds. The north-east of Scotland
was no place for a young, gay man.'*
DENNIS NILSEN, IN A LETTER TO THE AUTHOR

Nilsen's memoirs focus hard on his childhood and life in London for answers to his behaviour. But neither begin to explain how he could have set out one night in 1978 for the pub, and then woke up the next morning a murderer. Thousands have worse childhoods than Nilsen, and almost as many young men deal with alienation through casual pick-ups and excessive drinking. But, if Nilsen's raking over his first 30 years raises as many questions as answers, it does show *when* his mental abnormalities developed most uniquely. That was in the 11 years he spent in the Army. Nilsen's accounts of his inner life during this period make for chilling reading. Ironically, it was a time when he was never short of company, structure or normality.

In the Army, Nilsen travelled the world, learnt a trade and had responsibility. But he also became used to death, felt sexually ashamed and became accustomed to knocking his consciousness into submission through drink. Most disturbingly, he developed sexual fantasies that started with partners who were totally passive, then those who were unconscious, and finally involved the dead.

There was nothing particularly sinister in his make-up, however, when he alighted on Aldershot station platform in September 1961. He was not yet 16, quite tall, physically weak, enthusiastic and immature. As a boy soldier, Nilsen was posted to 'V' squad, along with 20 others of the same age. Aldershot was then a large garrison town on the Surrey–Hampshire border, surrounded by woodland and close to the stockbroker belt. Virtually the entire town was given over to the Army, and squaddies filled the local bars and canteens. This was still the pre-Beatles era and Elvis played on the jukebox for the whole of that year. In the nearby genteel market towns of Farnham and Guildford, wealthy commuters tutted when they saw young soldiers visiting their towns but, back in Aldershot, Nilsen and his companions saw a role model on every street corner. And being in such a densely military environment encouraged the youngsters. Together, they learnt discipline and drill, and all the other things the Army does to turn young lads into men.

Nilsen, in particular, says he became friendly with three of the boys: Brian Bacher, Chris Innerd and Eric 'Tabs' Talbot. Some of Nilsen's happiest memories were of the three of them and their adventures. In 1962, they travelled to Cornwall and Devon together for the 'Ten Tors' competitive hike on Exmoor as part of their physical training. But Nilsen was unable to finish due to his weak legs, and he vowed he would never let this happen again. Soon, he started to show an aptitude for cross-country running. But no amount of 'manning up' seemed to be able to rid him of his homosexual thoughts. The tightly scheduled days might have kept them at bay for a while, but there was nothing he could do about the nights.

Nor was there anything he wanted to do. Nilsen's dreams became a comfort to him; he seems to have gone as far as trying to plan them in advance. There is one he still remembers vividly today. It was benign and involved him and a friend lying warm and naked under a fur blanket in a cabin while a blizzard blew outside. In contrast to most of Nilsen's later sexual experiences which rarely got beyond the physical, in this fantasy he cherished a sense of togetherness. Still, it wasn't an equal relationship; Nilsen enjoyed the thought of a submissive partner he could protect. It was the two of them against the world. He wrote in *History of a Drowning Boy*: 'We would stay there in warm comfort together forever. We never talked in the dreams. We would get up occasionally to eat food silently before a blazing fire. We would listen to the outside world on the radio. It was bliss, naked under these furs, in each other's arms and the soft smoothness of his skin against mine. Strangely, we never fucked in these dreams. Very odd.'

The boys in this fantasy always had to conform to a certain androgynous physical type. Other than that, they could be of any race. Nilsen loathed racism in all forms and was determined never to discriminate. Here, in the parade squares of Aldershot, Nilsen says that around him in the 500-strong regiment he was disconcerted that he could only see 'one

Indian and no blacks'. He comments that it upset him whenever he heard 'nigger' jokes. Nilsen found black men attractive but oriental men were his favourite: 'I did, however, develop certain sexual, physical preferences in my males. I liked smooth men. Hairy men were a complete sexual turn off for me. I liked Chinese, Japanese and Filipinos; in fact, any type as long as they were smooth-skinned. Fat and well-muscled males, again, were a complete sexual turn off. I suspect that my attraction to Orientals has a lot to do with the fact that a lot of them display the characteristics of boys.'

Photographs from this period show an excited young man in round glasses and a smart green jumper getting on with the various activities of barrack life. He was healthy and well-disciplined and as happy 'packing' beds and scrubbing floors as any 16-year-old might be expected to be. After a year-and-a-half, Nilsen was made a junior corporal, and put in charge of a dorm of younger boys. There was one half-Dutch boy that he took a particular shine to. One day, Nilsen found him in his bed space crying. Nilsen claims that he wanted to put his arms around him and talk to him like 'Mum', but that wasn't 'what big, tough corporals did'.

Nilsen, however, was hardly considered a big, tough corporal – although his colleague, Eric Talbot, in a television interview remembered him occasionally trying to impress by trying to throw his weight around.

Nilsen was, in fact, extremely insecure. He remembers his biggest fear on arriving at Aldershot being the prospect of the communal showers. He thought that his genitals might be smaller than everyone else's and, more importantly, he might start to get an erection at the sight of other naked bodies.

There was a rumour that when this had happened before, other boys had responded by 'shoving a broomstick up his arse'. In the end, the showers proved nothing to worry about.

There was still, however, plenty in his behaviour that some found odd. Some would laugh about his stupid grin or the fact he seemed prudish about girlie magazines. Yet to others he was just normal and quiet. Dusty Payne, a platoon sergeant, couldn't believe it when he saw the news in 1983. Could this really be the Dennis Nilsen he'd known in the 1960s? Later, after reading articles in the papers, there was no mistaking it. He wrote first to the governor at Albany and later to Nilsen. Payne told the governor he remembered Dennis as a reserved lad who performed his job conscientiously and whom he recommended for Junior Sergeant. He also, somewhat surprisingly, thought he remembered Nilsen's mother visiting, and her being a 'quiet, warm lady'.

Payne thought something drastic must have subsequently happened to Nilsen for his mind to have become so dark. In a letter he wrote to Nilsen's prison governor, he speculates as to whether it could have been his time serving in Aden. Something, however, was already wrong in Aldershot. On the outside Nilsen may have seemed a 'loner who did the job to the best of his ability', but behind his exterior appearance, his 'inner film' had now developed into a serious condition. It was threatening to undermine his ability to differentiate between the world as it was and existence as he liked to imagine it. 'I had two separate lives,' Nilsen writes in his autobiography, 'the real life and the fantasy life. When I was with people I was in the "real" world and in my own private life I snapped easily into my fantasy life. I could oscillate from one to the other with instant ease.'

As had been so when he had reached puberty, Nilsen felt as if he were a film director controlling his own imagination. When, after three years, he passed the 'senior education test', he was disappointed that he 'had no one to cheer [him] on except the heroes in [his] mind'. One imagines internally, though, he was imagining a triumphal scene climaxing in the year of 1964 with everyone throwing their berets in the air.

The military exams Nilsen had taken were generally considered to be an equivalent to school O-levels. He ended up with a solid but unremarkable five passes: Maths, English, Map-reading, Current Affairs and Catering Science. Most importantly for his future army career, he also passed the B2 catering exam. And even though Nilsen was to be a cook rather than a soldier, he had still developed well enough physically, completing full training on foot, arms and weapons drills. When, at 18, he took part in the passing-out parade in the summer of 1964, he says he felt ready for 'the man's army'.

That summer he went home to Strichen for a brief period of leave. On the second weekend he hired a scooter to go to Fraserburgh to see Granny. He skidded on some mud and hit his head quite badly, but no serious damage was apparent. Nilsen was upbeat, proud to show what he was doing with his life. He eagerly spoke of the excitement of his first posting. This was to be in Osnabruck in north-western Germany. Family members were pleased, if surprised, that the quiet boy writing poetry upstairs had not merely survived life as a cadet but wanted more.

Nilsen, of course, knew his time in Germany was going to be a more rugged adventure than anything he had experienced in the south of England. But he thought it would just be more exciting. So far, the experience of leaving the backwater of Fraserburgh for Aldershot had proved the right thing to do. He had no reason to think that the adult Army would do anything other than further expand his horizons.

Some months before his nineteenth birthday, Nilsen was driven over to Germany in a coach full of young men. The NATO barracks were a large, concrete complex surrounded by fields and woodland just outside Osnabruck's medieval market town centre. The British Army presence was part of the wider NATO mobilisation in Europe during the Cold War.

Nilsen was attached to the Catering Corps within the Royal Fusiliers. He continued to train as a soldier and practice field manoeuvres, but his working life was focused around cooking in the mess. The team was headed up by the squadron quartermaster sergeant 'Badger' Maitland who was quick-witted and hearty. Nilsen admired him, and the fact he liked a drink made him approachable. Likewise, the cooks he worked with were an amiable, 'hard-working, boozy lot'. Nilsen was soon very taken with the drinking culture. Within the barracks complex there were various bars, with some catering to individual squadrons, while others, like the NAAFI bar, were for everyone. It was much more exciting, however, to go out to the city centre at weekends.

As Nilsen casts his mind back, rather than recalling his work or the intricacies of life in the barracks, he mainly mulls on his socialising. He remembers being someone who drank to ease his shyness but who was still one of the lads. It's unlikely, however, that others saw him the same way. The testimony of various colleagues indicates he was seen as the squaddie who couldn't hold his drink, and whose low tolerance, in turn, made him irritating to those around him – especially when Nilsen started to get drunk and spoiled others' chances with girls.

Dennis Nilsen's homosexuality was well hidden. Being gay was still far from being tolerated in the Army. Nilsen would therefore follow others to various rough and ready watering holes and pretend to be equally excited about the hunt for girls. One Saturday night, in one of the pubs far from the city centre, Nilsen's entire squadron were questioned about a shooting in a bar. They had been in the area when a man shot a local taxi driver after an argument. The murderer was Leslie Grantham who would later find fame in the 1980s as 'Dirty Den' in the BBC soap opera *EastEnders*.

Nilsen spent just over two years in northern Germany. As a private, he slept in a 'bed space' in a medium-sized dorm. Towards the end of his two years in Germany, dorm inspections were sufficiently relaxed that Nilsen even managed to keep a dog called Rexie. He named it after his first cuddly toy, which he says his mother threw away in a bid to tidy up.

It is while describing his posting to Osnabruck that Nilsen's memoirs start to change tone. The exuberance and lightness of youth is increasingly replaced by descriptions of his dark, fantasy life. Often the lines between reality and desires seem blurred. This was particularly so one Sunday morning, when

Nilsen says he woke up to find himself passed out on top of a mattress with a fat, young German called Hans. They were in a flat on the outskirts of town. Nilsen assumes that they had just passed out in the same room after a night's drinking. He spent the next day, however, imagining that the man had interfered with him.

It pleased him to think that he might have been abused while totally passed out: 'My mind thrilled at the thought of this fat German undressing and fondling me,' he says. The fact the other man was fat and ugly accentuated Nilsen's desire to feel androgynous. He desperately wanted some sexual activity to have happened. While he was working, he would daydream about scenarios where a sex-starved young squaddie might try to relieve some sexual tension with him. And how much more likely would that have been to occur than if he was out cold and passive? This, in turn, led to him pretending when he was out drinking to pass out in the hope that someone would carry him home and take pleasure in his body.

Nilsen's strange behaviour when drunk eventually also got him into fist fights. He is careful to avoid discussion of these in his memoirs. They are, however, recorded in his army record, including one particular all-day drinking session which ended up with him getting into a fight which later required medical attention. Nilsen does, however, describe one incident he was ashamed of. It involved his dog Rexie, and was like a watered-down version of his earlier story about killing the cat. One afternoon, he says, he placed the dog on top of his locker and terrified her by growling, just to see her cower. He describes seeing her fear which 'excited a frisson of power' within him. Eventually, she fell off the locker and cut herself on his bed. At that point, the cruel mood broke and he says he remembers starting to cry with guilt.

In January 1967, Nilsen was informed of a new posting. It was in Aden in the Gulf of Arabia, now part of the state of Yemen. This British Protectorate had found itself in a state of emergency after a series of terrorist attacks from Islamic extremists. A decade or so since the Suez crisis, Britain was now considering whether the time had come to leave the port of Aden. If the time had almost come to leave, however, Harold Wilson's Government didn't want the action of anti-colonial terrorists to be the trigger.

Fuelled by increasingly radical Islamic fervour, the rebels became more and more obsessive. Just as in modern-day Afghanistan, troops operated in near-impossible heat and difficult terrain against a fanatical opposition. Nilsen describes being flown over in a VC10 airliner. When he arrived in Arabia, it was like 'walking into the blast of a baker's oven'. He thought the terrorists seemed in complete disarray with 'everyone intent on killing everyone else' and 'the only point of agreement being killing the English'.

Nilsen's kitchen served the Military Provost Staff Corps. They were in charge of detainees at the Al Mansoura Prison. The prison was a walled fort, with a disused gallows guarded by gun towers. The town of Al Mansoura is now a suburb of Aden City. At that time it was a warren of low-rise, breeze-block buildings with a single road running through them. It was situated five miles from the city and port of Aden. The military complex was basic and functional. Unlike the tented townships that made up other military bases, however, the barracks here were buildings built out of red clay. Their colour merged in with the surrounding desert.

On active service, even the cooks were required to take full part in the patrolling. As Nilsen walked the dusty roads, he says he would see dead bodies casually discarded by the roadside. He says he didn't find anything exciting in the 'shot-up mechanics of death' while also pointing out he didn't like to think of attractive male bodies spoiled. The way he talks suggests those bodies didn't excite him, but they certainly helped desensitise him to the reality of death. He started to become very blasé about his own safety, volunteering for dangerous patrols and, when off duty, drinking copiously before wandering off on his own. It was an impulse he didn't understand.

One afternoon, while off duty at the Steamer Point army base, near the old city, Nilsen decided to hitch-hike his way the few miles to Al Mansoura. He was picked up by a lorry, which then drove straight through terrorist-ridden areas. Nilsen says that although he was wearing his 'civvies', there could be no mistaking what he was. He thinks the only reason he survived may have been because the rebels assumed that he was part of a set-up.

Yet he says he was excited by the experience. Again, he offers no explanation as to why the line between life and death was so thrilling. It is likely, however, that being in a conflict zone had reawakened his childhood fascination with death and sex. It is also likely that Nilsen can't fully remember what did and didn't happen. The whole experience of being in Aden was so different from anything a young British soldier might have experienced; it would surely have had a dreamlike quality. Nilsen's imagination would have amplified that. Even the geography would have appeared fantastical. The city of Aden nestled in a volcanic crater connected to the mainland by an isthmus. Zealots who looked like they had come straight out of a film lived in a harsh desert, further inland.

Nilsen liked to re-imagine one incident over and over again. It was even cited at his trial as an example of his difficulty in separating fact and fantasy. The event occurred one Friday evening when Nilsen had gone with others to cool down in the Oasis bar in Aden city. After a night's drinking, and unsteady on his feet, he decided to hail a cab back. He says he did so casually, as if 'in the West End of London', not 'somewhere where any Westerner was likely to be killed'. In the back, full of rum and beer, he passed out on the leatherette seat.

Suddenly, he felt a violent blow to the back of his neck. Nilsen passed out. When he came to, he was naked in the boot with his clothes in a pile beside him. The cool metal was pressing into his body. Outside, someone was turning the lock. Nilsen felt a sense of detachment. As soon as the boot was opened, he says he hit the ugly, old taxi driver with a jack. The man slumped to the ground, motionless. He took the man's clothes and ran for it.

Whatever happened, it certainly wasn't as described. The reasons for Nilsen's confusion between reality and imagination in this particular story, however, become clear in his autobiography. This incident was part of the same developing fantasy theme as the 'Fat Hans' scenario. Some kind of altercation probably did happen in that taxi, but Nilsen wanted it to have been much more unpleasant than it was. He wanted to imagine he had been stripped by an old man and interfered with. He wanted sex, and for it to be close to an experience of death.

Another far-fetched story does, however, contain a greater ring of authenticity. Again, it involved the line between life and death. Nilsen occasionally drank with one particular private who was full of stories and enjoyed impressing his colleagues. One afternoon, during a quiet period, the private told Nilsen he had something interesting to show him. He led him through a set of doors, which gave out into a large courtyard; in the middle stood a fully operational gallows. The private's job was to perform routine maintenance. Although unused, it was kept in working order.

Fascinated, Nilsen climbed the scaffold. His friend shouted up that if you supported your body weight with your arms on the rope, you could probably put the noose around your neck and drop down the trap-door. He was half joking, but that, though, was exactly what Nilsen did. He pulled the noose over his neck and then took the weight and dangled over the open hole. 'I was buzzing with fear and excitement ... my eyes drawn to the gaping hole of eternity,' he says. His friend rushed up the steps, frightened that Nilsen's arms weren't strong enough. But as he reached him, Nilsen had swung back onto the platform and was grinning.

By June 1967, Nilsen was posted further round the Gulf to what is now known as the United Arab Emirates. Then, they were called the Trucial States, an area where the British had signed a truce with the local sheikhs. Nilsen was to be the head of kitchen at the Trucial Oman Scouts officers' mess at

Sharjah. Oil had just been struck in nearby Dubai and money was starting to flow into the area. The TOS was a British paramilitary outfit intended to keep order in various protectorates and Sheikdoms across the Gulf. Life in Sharjah couldn't have been more different from the posting in Aden. It was like going from hell to a holiday. Around him, Nilsen saw people wearing distinctive patterned Arab head-dresses. They reminded him of scenes from *Lawrence of Arabia*, one of his favourite films.

Dennis Nilsen was finally able to relax. Agreeable evenings were spent drinking with servicemen and ex-pats. This was also where Nilsen experienced his first significant sexual experience. It was with one of the teenage Arab boys assigned to clean the officers' rooms. These 'bearers' had the responsibility of tidying the rooms, washing and cleaning kit. Nilsen alleges that some had got into the habit of providing sexual favours in return for money to take back to their impoverished families. If it stretches the imagination to suppose such practice was rife, it's not totally implausible they occasionally happened.

Now that Nilsen was an NCO Corporal, he had his own room. One evening, after bringing in some laundry, a boy of about 14 lingered. Nilsen says his nerves and inexperience almost resulted in him walking out. But just as the boy was turning around, the corporal realized what was going on and urged him to stay. With sentimental hyperbole, Nilsen describes their sexual liaison in *History of a Drowning Boy*. He said he felt 'wedded to him' and thinks the boy didn't really want money because he felt the same way, too: 'He enquired, "You like nice boy?" My brain was playing the "Hallelujah

Chorus". I stretched out my hand. "Come over here," I intoned, and patted the bed. He did as I had bidden and I took one of his hands in mine. I placed his hand on the hard, straining, 7in baton clearly shaped through my jeans ... he lay on his back and looked up at me with those deep-brown, doe-like eyes.'

Nilsen claims to have had sex with the boy (although elsewhere he claims he didn't actually have full sex until the age of 27) and that he was the active partner. Whether or not this was an exaggeration, Nilsen probably did have his first homosexual experience in Arabia with a teenage boy prostitute.

The way he talks about the months that followed indicate a change. He had suddenly become enlivened to the possibility he might yet be a sexual being. Now, when Nilsen went to the Carlton Hotel in Dubai, he did so feeling homosexually experienced and grown up. This bolstered his ego, which, in turn, helped him to believe that the oil executives sipping on their Martinis were eying him up as a rent boy. He thought this was a bloody cheek and switched to the Royal Flying Kunjah Club, where he fell in with a group of heavy drinkers. Nilsen describes them as 'kindred rebel spirits'. He was particularly fond of a young man nicknamed 'Smithy'. When the Combined Services Entertainment flew in Harry Secombe, Mike Yarwood and Dickie Henderson, Nilsen remembers sitting next to him. They enjoyed the impersonations of Mike Yarwood, and found Harry Secombe's gooning around hilarious, but Nilsen became upset when Henderson came on and started singing the song 'Love and Marriage' with the words *John and Mary, John and Mary ... she's a lesbian and he's a fairy ...*'

The following week, Smithy fell off his Land Rover and died. The incident added to an array of psychologically volatile factors. That this was all happening against a backdrop that only seemed half real may well have made things worse. In front of him, life was quickly and easily turning to death. Many of those lives were of young men with whom Nilsen wanted a forbidden intimacy. He was driven to ever deeper secrets and, the more private his fantasies, the more they skewed off at tangents.

If one single event could be said to have led to Nilsen's later desire to possess dead bodies, it almost certainly happened one afternoon in Sharjah. This is the first indication we get in Nilsen's manuscript that his internal life had moved from disturbing gay fantasies to abnormal, paraphilic, sexual fixations.

Nilsen's room had a lock and he had got into the habit of using it to ensure total privacy while he spent afternoons masturbating in the nude. Sometimes, he would admire himself in the mirror while doing so. One day, he realized, using the free-standing mirror, he could create an effect whereby he could visually 'split' his personality such that it felt he was enjoying a sexual act with another man. This was narcissism in a very specific sense, Nilsen writes: 'It was a very large mirror and I came to over-admiring myself in it ... I would become aroused by my relaxed body ... I imagined someone (the mirror's view) looking at me and lusting after my body. In fact, I was lusting over my own body.'

The next step in the ritual was lying on the bed while positioning himself so that his head was no longer visible. He, the watcher, was one person, the passive reflection another. As the watcher, he would play one role: 'The man dominating the body had no face but he was always a dirty, grey-haired, old man.' The boy in the mirror was a smooth, passive 'victim'. This, too, would be Nilsen. As he developed this fantasy, he would take turns in playing both roles. The fantasies again derived from experiences like the Fat Hans/Arab taxi driver incidents. All future fantasies would also follow the same pattern of an older, powerful, brutal individual dominating a young, smooth, lifeless body.

Over the course of the summer, the fantasies escalated. Nilsen remembers one, in particular, frightening him. It was a scene imagined to be in the Second World War and again involved an old Arab. The other body now was not merely passive – it was an attractive, blond, young Nazi soldier who'd been recently killed. In his imagination, before the Arab finally has sex with the dead boy's body, he washes and carries it, just as Nilsen would later do with the men he killed. The fantasy ended with the old man having full sex with the dead body. Nilsen says he 'loosened his hold on the boy's back and legs and his naked form flopped askew in limp rest, still impaled on the man, spread-eagled in pure lust'.

The worse Nilsen's private sex fantasies became, the more psychologically isolated he also found himself. His internal world was so far removed from anything that he could possibly ever talk about, he had no problem walking out of his room with an innocent expression. As such, none of Nilsen's colleagues had any reason to suspect that when Corporal Nilsen came out of his room he had been doing anything other than taking an afternoon nap.

In January 1968, Nilsen returned to the UK and was posted to the 1st Argyll and Sutherland Highlanders at Seaton Barracks, Plymouth. Being back in familiar surroundings quelled his wilder fantasies. Besides, with no locks on the doors, he couldn't carry on masturbating in front of mirrors. Instead, he just spent more time watching TV. But despite home soil helping to normalise Nilsen's sexual mindset, two incidents from that time are revealing. The second was, in fact, in all probability, another crucial step on the path towards becoming a killer.

The first happened in the barracks in Plymouth one Saturday night. Nilsen was watching late-night TV. In a dormitory down the corridor, some young privates had smuggled in a local barmaid. As Nilsen walked down to use the toilet, he heard a whimpering sound. With a mixture of curiosity and concern, he popped his head round the door. He was appalled to see his comrades were taking it in turns to have sex with the girl. Cowardice, however, stopped him intervening. Instead, he just went to bed, saying nothing. The next day, he considered he had failed the girl. But although he says he was ashamed, he also clearly took some pride in the fact that he could consider himself a good, compassionate man, unlike those others who had been involved in the attack.

This story may also have been included to prepare the reader for the next new confession. Nilsen's first sex attack was callous and opportunistic. It shows that by the age of 22, he had lost any compunction about serious sexual assault. This incident he describes may not have quite matched the 'fantasy ritual' that later would characterise the killings, but the fact that the victim was unconscious is significant. Nilsen's behaviour before and after also showed he'd now managed to compartmentalise sexual matters completely from the rest of his life. Where sex was concerned, there were no limits.

It started when a chance conversation at his barracks revealed that he and a young private, Frank, were to be sharing a long train journey to Bristol (the details have been changed for obvious reasons). They decided to travel together and, once the train pulled away, started drinking in the buffet car. When their money ran out, they moved on to their supply of beer cans and whisky. As the train drew level with Coventry, the young man passed out. Nilsen realised that he had an advantageous position. He carried the half-conscious man to the toilet and propped him so the man's head was lolling around the toilet seat. This gave him an idea for how to knock him out. He started to let the man's head smash against the toilet bowl. Then he undressed and orally abused him while inserting his finger into his anus. All the time, Nilsen had an erection and contemplated whether he might rape him. People, however, were banging on the door. 'Fear took over and I hurriedly washed him and washed the stain on his jacket,' he says. After it was over, Nilsen was able to carry on as if nothing had happened.

Later, during this period of leave, Nilsen decided to go up to Scotland to visit his family. Once occupied with family business, the sexual assault hardly seemed to exist for him. He was pleased to hear his sister Sylvia had married the son of one of the local dairy farmers. Still, he was a little concerned that, at 16, she was a little young to have got hitched. But at least she had got out of the Broch – they had emigrated to Toronto, Canada. His brother Olav, meanwhile, had married a Geordie girl. Nilsen was glad to see that his older brother had only got as far as working in a nearby factory.

Betty Scott would later tell reporters how she remembered Dennis being keen to impress with his cooking and seeming in good spirits. In the evenings, he would be quieter, retiring to his room, as was his custom, to write poetry. No doubt, at other times he would have talked excitedly about how he would be returning to Germany. There was a short stint in Cyprus to see out and then he was off to West Berlin.

One thing Nilsen didn't say was that he had heard the city had begun to re-establish its pre-war reputation for decadence and hoped this might include homosexual possibilities. When Nilsen arrived a month later, he was stationed at the Montgomery barracks, set in woodland in the Spandau district near the border. The 24-year-old corporal's predictions seemed to be partly correct. There was both more drink going around, and more sex. It was not, however, the sort he was seeking. 'The lads' encouraged Nilsen to visit a prostitute one night.

The brothel was in a central location, probably of the sort where two or three girls were set up in a small flat. Nilsen was afraid of what his friends would think if he refused, so he went along with what everyone else was doing. The girl would have seen him as no different from many other drunken customers. She aroused him with her mouth, before getting on top. Nilsen was then, more or less, a passive participant. He was pleased that he managed to ejaculate. It proved that to him that he could, at least, be bisexual. But still, he says, he had no particular inclination to repeat the experience, especially when sober.

The homosexual opportunities he had hoped for did not materialise in Berlin. This posting did, however, give him the opportunity to take up a hobby that had long fascinated him. On his NCO's pay packet, he had found that, almost without trying, he was saving money. Then, one afternoon, presumably in the Friedrichstrasse near Checkpoint Charlie, he saw an 8mm movie camera for sale. On an impulse, he bought it. He subsequently started to film everything he saw. He even took his new toy to an anti-Vietnam demonstration, where he filmed the authorities tear-gassing the protestors.

When he told his colleagues about what he had been doing, they laughed at him. It would have been an odd thing for any British soldier to be doing but, in his case, it was just another sign of his peculiarity. In Nilsen's mind, however, he was a colourful 'outsider' figure. He imagined how he might be portrayed in a movie, getting up to all kinds of crazy schemes. The next week he wrote to the Ministry of Defence asking to film Rudolph Hess in Spandau. But although their reply implied they thought him a little mad, nothing more was made of it.

Briefly, Nilsen sounds as if he might have been quite happy. For a while, he put his deepest sexual preoccupations out of his mind and just enjoyed the opportunities afforded by travelling with the Army. In January 1970, at the age of 24, he was sent to Bodenmais ski resort in Bavaria. Here, the Argyll and Sutherland Highlanders were taught alpine skills as part of their complete combat training. The ski school was based up around an old mountain farmhouse overlooking the Zeller Valley and Nilsen's job required him to cater for 30 officers and NCOs in a large and spotlessly clean kitchen.

Nilsen felt that the locals liked him, but he was disturbed because there was still simmering Nazi sympathy there.

There were also frequent opportunities to socialise. All the time Nilsen was mixing with the locals, he never betrayed his innermost sexual feelings. He describes one evening as an example. There was a beer festival taking place, and one night he went to a party at a Biergarten belonging to a local character called Hans. Hans loaned Nilsen a pair of Lederhosen to wear for the evening. One of the local girls flirted with Nilsen that night. He thought she looked a bit like Natalie Wood and was delighted when she kissed him on the verandah. It provided perfect cover for his real thoughts which were fixed on a young private. He was pleased to have fooled everyone. 'I'm a better actor than Rock Hudson ever was,' he boasts.

After Bavaria, Nilsen was soon transferred to Fort George in Inverness-shire, only 70 miles from his birthplace. The barracks practically adjoined the battlefield of Culloden Moor where the Jacobite rebellion was quashed in 1746, something that Nilsen would most probably have been aware of, and might have been frequently inclined to lecture others about. But while this may have wound up his colleagues, no one could complain about the quality of Nilsen's work. He had become an efficient and reliable cook, reaching Grade B. In August 1970, Nilsen was then transferred across the Cairngorms to Ballater where the Queen's Royal Guard (Balmoral) was based. Despite his proximity to Strichen, however, Nilsen never took the opportunity to visit his family.

Nilsen's last posting in the Army should have been the most convivial and relaxing of his career, as it was for most of those posted to the NATO Ace High signals station at Maybury on the Shetland Isles. The military base was located at the southerly tip of the largest island. The dramatic beauty spots of Sumburgh and Fitful Head were nearby. In this small community, the locals and the servicemen – mainly signals engineers – mixed freely and everyone knew everyone else's business. Eligible women outnumbered the bachelors, and there was a lively dating scene. Nilsen's disastrous crush on a young Welsh soldier, however, started a chain of events that would lead him to be cast into bedsit life in London, romantically frustrated, and without any supportive influences.

Corporal Nilsen spent almost two years at Maybury. During this period, he saw himself as a romantic, artistic figure. He talks as if he was now comfortable in his sexuality but frustrated by the lack of opportunity. Without any outlet for his sexual desires, he says he divided his spare time between filming the areas of natural beauty on the island, like Fitful Head, and joining the drinking crowd at the Maybury Club.

Others remember things differently. One such contemporary, now in his sixties – we'll call him Rob Ferrier – was a 26-year-old NCO when he met Nilsen. He first emailed me in 2005 after seeing my *Sunday Times* magazine piece online. Knowing I had read Nilsen's book made him curious to know what Nilsen had said about Maybury. He also wondered just how much of Nilsen's material I believed.

Some days later, we spoke for the first time on the phone.

'Having been stationed with the bloke, and having seen documentaries, I have often been struck how much journalists assume what he says is actually true,' he told me, adding, 'I would advise anyone writing about him to take his autobiographical claims with a large pinch of salt.'

Ferrier is a jolly, slightly grizzled character with the build of a former rugby player. He has a good memory, and his recollections are consistent with many details found in *History of a Drowning Boy*. However, when I wrote to Nilsen to ask him what he remembered of Ferrier, his reply was, 'Who ... and exactly *what* ... is he?' Could he really not remember, or did he not want anyone else to challenge his version of events?

Ferrier recalls Nilsen's overriding characteristic at 25 years of age being immaturity. He remembers him constantly trying to impress and says he had a 'very low tolerance to alcohol which he would still consume at every possible opportunity'. Nilsen also had one particularly irritating habit – he would jump out from behind bushes and wave his movie camera at courting couples behind the Maybury Club. Yet, although people considered him a bit awkward socially, nobody guessed he might be homosexual. Ferrier even asked me whether it might be possible that Nilsen resorted to gay sex because he was such a failure with women. It seemed strange to many that he was such a flop with the girls – he wasn't bad looking, after all. Most concluded that he drove them away though a combination of poor personal hygiene, clumsy manners, and a habit of becoming intoxicated after half a pint.

Nilsen's own recollections of his drinking and socialising during this period are again confused with his sex dreams. He describes one incident that took place in the spring of 1971, where he says he was given a 'Micky Finn' or spiked drink from a local who then interfered with him while he slept. It reads like a carbon copy of the incident involving 'Fat Hans' and what he hoped he'd do to him. Ferrier was bemused when I asked him about this. He says there could have only been one possible candidate and he could never have been audacious enough.

When Nilsen's mind wasn't on sex or work, it was on his home movies. Whether or not he spent as much time filming nature and or creating dramatisations involving friends as he claims, he definitely did become a projectionist at the Cine Club. His enthusiasm resulted in his being sent on the short Services Kinema Corporation (SKC) course at Beaconsfield. After a fortnight, he returned, qualified to set up the 16mm cinema equipment. But now that he knew a little, he started to tell others what to do. His manner and interference exasperated everyone.

The story was the same in the workshop where soldiers were encouraged to practice hobbies. One afternoon, he tried to work a large piece of mahogany on a lathe without first centring it. When it came off, he almost knocked out the instructor. Worse was to come with his pets. A shop in the island's capital stocked exotic animals. Nilsen's first purchase was a Mynah bird, which he let fly freely around the room he shared with a colleague. A senior officer, the next day, told him to return it. Some months later, he replaced it with a mud turtle he named Napoleon XIV (after the band that had had a hit with the novelty song 'They're Coming to Take Me Away, Ha-Ha'). Initially, he kept it under his bed in a piece of polystyrene packing covered by mud and water. Ferrier told me: 'The smell was atrocious! At this stage, the RSM gave up. He was approaching retirement. Nilsen's roommate was less than amused. Nilsen used to feed the beast lumps of raw meat. He would wait until the Cook Sergeant was out doing the daily shop and sneak it into the kitchen, where he would feed it on the food prep table.

'His sense of humour was such that he'd challenge people to try to take the meat from the turtle. It would sit there with its foot/flipper pinning down the chunk of meat. Nilsen would make comments like, "I bet he'd prefer some fresh flesh, like from you!" He'd make such comments to visiting women.'

Corporal Nilsen would also try to make himself seem more intelligent than others by ostentatiously referring to the books he had recently read. On one occasion, this was a collection of the Marquis de Sade's writings. He delighted in trying to shock others with it. But when Ferrier quoted it back to him a month later, he says Nilsen struggled to place what was being said. Most of the 'boys' thought him a pseudo-intellectual.

Nilsen did, however, earn some respect for his natural artistic flair. Photographs he had taken hung in the clubhouse for years after he left. He remained, however, much more interested in moving pictures. After a short stint back in Scotland catering for the Signals engineers, he returned to the Shetlands in the spring of 1972 and spent much of his spare time with his movie camera. He shot the annual Viking festival and the seas and skies by the cliffs of Fitful Head. Then, in May, he met someone with whom he felt he could share his artistic passions.

Terry (his name has been changed) was actually just a homesick, naïve 18-year-old, easily dominated by older and more forceful personalities. He was small, with blond hair and was youthfully handsome. Nilsen liked to teach him to use the projector and to take him to the local beauty spots to act out little scenes. In his autobiography, Nilsen remembers, 'We worked, played and walked the sheer scenic beauty of the high, rugged cliffs and the golden stretch of Quendale Bay. I filmed him running, jumping, and in the full range of usual situations.'

Some of these scenarios apparently involved Terry playing dead, and Nilsen talks about how he would review the footage in the evenings. 'I was certainly excited by a passive image of him. There was no gore or anything like that involved. Afterwards, when he was not around, I would watch all the footage of him and afterwards needed to go to the bathroom and masturbate.'

Cross-country running gave Nilsen another excuse to spend time with Terry. At 26, despite the smoking and drinking, Dennis was in good physical shape. He would challenge Terry to long cross-country races. After a sprint finish to one run, they both collapsed on the grass. Lying and panting, Nilsen patted Terry on the chest. For him, it was a sign of intimacy and unspoken understanding. But just as Terry was beginning to find Nilsen annoying, the latter was beginning to become obsessed.

After drunken nights at the clubhouse, Nilsen would sidle up to Terry and pretend to have passed out. His hope was that Terry would touch him to revive him. One night, when Terry was drunk, homesick and apparently on the verge of tears, he took the opportunity to hold the young Welshman's hand. The fact that Terry didn't immediately remove it confirmed to him that there was an understanding between the two. He asked him into the Laundry Room, and says in his autobiography, 'As we were coming to the Laundry Store, I suddenly said to him, even taking myself by surprise, "We can go into the Laundry, as I've got the only key. We won t be disturbed." He replied, "I don't know what's happening." He pulled himself away and darted out of the outside door. "God," I thought, "You've really done it this time … you've lost him for good."'

Nilsen says he had a cigarette and then went to look for him. He was sitting, dejected, on the grass outside. The morning, he says, brought a 'drifting apart' which continued until their relationship 'exploded briefly'.

It started when Nilsen became convinced a Signals Sergeant was a closet homosexual trying to steal Terry away. Nilsen's anger and jealousy grew. He calls it 'a fissure in my life' and says that 'tremors were beginning to register on the obvious seismograph of my temperament'. He decided to confront the sergeant outside the hotel. Full of drink, he directly accused him of being homosexual and in love with Terry. Rob Ferrier told me he also remembers this night. Nilsen had turned up at the hotel drunk, and started ranting incoherently.

The next day, Nilsen then went to Fitful Head to contemplate a suicide bid by throwing himself off it. He came down and went to bed. Two days later, he decided to challenge Terry to a fight. He says, 'I wanted him to see that I was hurt and angry. After I taunted him, he came at me with flying fists. He wrestled me to the ground. With blazing eyes and no words, he put his hands around my neck. I stared mutely at his wild expression and saw the red fever in his eyes … It was all finished. It was not the only thing that was over. I had already decided that I would let my current time in the Army expire without enlisting for a further three years … I could see no workable future for a homosexual in the British Army. There comes a time when we outgrow living out of a military kit bag and moving around like a gypsy.'

Nilsen also gives two others reasons for leaving the Army. The first was homophobia; second, he says he was ashamed of the conduct of the British Army in the Bloody Sunday Massacre, where 13 civilians had been shot dead in Londonderry in January 1972. Rob Ferrier remembers another incident which he says was the real reason Nilsen didn't re-enlist. It involved his mud turtle, Napoleon XIV. In an email to me, he says:

Eventually, Napoleon XIV was his downfall. His roommate became more and more angry and frustrated over the smell and filth in his room. This escalated into a full-scale row one night. The offended person had gone out drinking and had returned spoiling for a fight. I was awakened by the altercation and slamming of doors.

When I went into the corridor, Nilsen was charging down the corridor from the kitchens brandishing two large boning knives (his tools). I ordered him to put down the weapons. He refused, waving them in my face. I repeated the order, qualifying it with the threat that, if I had to take them off him, I'd break his damned arms and then put him under arrest. That gave him pause and he dropped the knives and ran away. Meanwhile, his drunken roommate had clambered out his room window and disappeared.

I thought, 'Bloody great, another bloody hero!' That was when I heard the sounds of a fight from the vicinity of the common room. The roommate had actually nipped around the outside of our quarters to tackle him from the rear. Having had enough, I decided to root the RSM out of his quarters and leave him to sort it all out.

At the time, Nilsen was applying for extension of service beyond 12 years. His poor personal hygiene and the attendant disciplinary problems affected that application. I was personally consulted as to what disciplinary action should be taken against him. I suggested – and his Cook Sgt concurred – that the application for extension of service could be refused with no need for further action. He was gone within the month.

Before Nilsen left the Islands, he says he had one last drinking session which ended in his burning all his films. He couldn't, however, bring himself to burn the footage he had taken of Terry, and just before he left he gave Terry his personal projector and all the footage of him. Rob Ferrier is dubious that the fire could have been of any size or he would have remembered it.

As for Nilsen's 'exemplary' record, Ferrier suggests it was the Army's custom to send people out with a generous reference wherever possible. In truth, Nilsen's career had been blighted with more than just never making it past the rank of Corporal. Nilsen had frequently got into trouble, just never so seriously as to be formally disciplined. Still, Nilsen had got through, and now had a General Service Medal and life membership of the Army Catering Corps regimental association to show for the 11 years and three months he'd served. Those institutional skills were never more useful to him than in his first years in prison.

5

PRISON LIFE – THE FIRST DECADE

'We are dead men locked in a tomb;
the living dead, privileged by selective animation.
We are required to be neither seen nor heard.'
DENNIS NILSEN, IN A LETTER TO THE AUTHOR

Dennis Nilsen likes to tell people that, including the time he spent in the Army, and the police force as well as his prison sentence, he has spent most of his life in the service of Her Majesty. He is now fully institutionalised, having been in prison for over 30 years, with no prospect of release. Prisoner B62006 (Nilsen's original prisoner number – his current number is A6191AC) started his life sentence started on 4 November 1983 in Wormwood Scrubs.

After the trial, Nilsen was first taken to the reception area in the medical unit. When he got up the next morning, he would have seen that the Scrubs looked like a bigger version of Brixton. It was almost as cold and just as noisy. After a couple of days, Nilsen was taken from the hospital and brought to C-Wing. When he arrived in the exercise yard, he says the 'throng parted like the Red Sea'.

Settling into the new regime was, again, something he found particularly difficult. On remand, Nilsen had spoken of the need for his crimes to be punished. He even seemed to welcome jail as a way of cleansing his conscience. Now, the reality hit home. In Nilsen's literal and logical world, he had been prescribed a simple denial of liberty, not a hard, meaningless, negative life. When it came to it, he didn't welcome his punishment one bit.

Many inmates considered him a 'nonce' – slang for sex criminal – and felt free to give him as hard a time as they liked. He didn't fare much better among the others. Stories leaked to newspapers suggest Nilsen's intellectual pretensions made him seem arrogant. One of the first was 'JAIL MEN HATE NILSEN THE BRAGGER'. Nilsen cut it out and put it in a folder. Subsequently, he would keep scrapbooks of every mention of him in the press along with comments about inaccuracies and the outrageous 'monsterisation' of him.

Nilsen was immediately designated a Category A prisoner – the highest security level, and one from which he has never been downgraded. His single cell measured approximately 6ft by 8ft. Inside the cold walls were an iron-framed bed and a desk. In 1983, Victorian prisons such as the Scrubs had not yet been converted to have in-cell toilets and sinks. Prisoners used buckets and bowls. Nilsen's prison uniform was plain grey, like the bare painted walls. He was permitted a small amount of cell association – the time a prisoner is allowed to socialise in other inmate's cells. Mainly, however, he chose to mix in the evenings in the TV room. There was also socialising at meals, exercise periods and work time. To begin with, however, Nilsen didn't speak to many others.

If new friends were hard to come by, Nilsen was equally disappointed by people he used to know. Janet Leaman – the manager at the Kentish Town job centre who once offered support – had stopped writing after one letter. Then there was Martyn Hunter-Craig, the man who had almost walked in when Nilsen was dismembering Stephen Sinclair. After the trial, Nilsen had been puzzled that Hunter-Craig had paid him a visit in the cells. Now, he believed the reason was that he had been looking for stories to sell. It annoyed him intensely.

Nilsen and Hunter-Craig had first met in 1978 in the Crystal Room amusement arcade in Leicester Square. Hunter-Craig had been about 18 and Nilsen 32. The young drifter with a handlebar moustache hardly looked younger than the man who stood behind him. 'You won't win much on that,' Nilsen had said with friendly cynicism. They got chatting, went for a drink and a pizza and eventually Nilsen invited Hunter-Craig back to his flat in Melrose Avenue. The evening went well. Over the next few years, Hunter-Craig became a frequent visitor.

When in March 1983 the police tracked Hunter-Craig down they asked him if he remembered anything suspicious in Nilsen's behaviour during the time they had been friends. Hunter-Craig immediately remembered an incident which clearly suggested his friend had once tried to kill him. It was one morning in 195 Melrose Avenue when he had woken up to find the room filled with smoke. Nilsen had told him he'd been trying to dry a towel. Now, however, he admits, in fact, he had been trying to knock his friend out before strangling him. This was one story Nilsen didn't mind him selling. Other stories, like the *Sunday People*'s 'HITLER FANTASY OF THE BEAST OF CRANLEY GARDENS', he deemed outrageous.

If such inaccuracies infuriated Nilsen, at least he could take comfort from the fact that people were talking about him. Although he relentlessly complains about their treatment (one section of his memoirs is subtitled 'The Monsterisation of a Multiple Killer: the Media Treatment of My Case'), the pages he devotes to analysing what was said about him are a sure indication that, without the infamy the papers gave him, he would have found it hard to be simply prisoner B62006.

During the day Nilsen liked to divert himself productively. In Wormwood Scrubs, all prisoners other than those on 'full-time education' were required to work. For a full week, Nilsen could earn a little over £20. He found life in the workshop cathartic. Five days before Christmas 1983, he recalls going in one morning to pack video games into boxes. The Flying Pickets' 'Only You' was playing on the radio in the background. Nilsen had previously only seen video games before in the Piccadilly arcades. He was impressed that people could now have them at home.

Nilsen left work that lunchtime in a good mood, feeling satisfied with himself. He was also looking forward to receiving a visitor that day. In the afternoon, Brian Masters – still writing *Killing for Company* – drove over to see him. He was still Nilsen's only visitor. Sitting opposite each other, surrounded by wives and kids, a small boy approached Nilsen with a half-eaten Mars Bar. 'Do you want a bit, mister?' he enquired.

With Masters in front of him, Nilsen couldn't resist the

performance opportunity. Masters remembers him saying, 'No thank you. My mother taught me never to take sweets from strange kids.'

That afternoon was cold and turning windy. As the sun was going down, Nilsen remembers someone in the exercise yard whispering, 'You'd better watch your back, mate.' He went to sleep that night feeling uneasy, and trying to put the comment out of his mind. It occurred to him that people probably said that kind of thing a lot in prison.

The following afternoon, at the same time, Nilsen took his customary walk. Again the weather was foul. As Nilsen was sheltering by a wall rolling a cigarette, a figure came over to join him. He looked up. Suddenly there was a soft blow to his left cheek. A metal object clattered to the ground. With blood dripping on to his shirt and his cigarette in his mouth, Nilsen realised that he'd been slashed across the cheek with a razor.

Later that day, and after giving the matter quite some thought, Nilsen identified the assailant as Albert Moffat, a small-time gangster, typical of the 'little men' who thought prison life could make them into big shots. But, despite his disdain, Nilsen had refused to let a prison warder take a Polaroid picture of his injuries. He says he didn't want to be seen cosying up to the police or prison service, or getting their help. He wanted everyone to know that, ultimately, he was still in charge.

The next day he read a story in the *Daily Mirror*, whose headline was 'RAZOR ATTACK ON KILLER NILSEN'. That afternoon he was summoned to the governor's office, to discuss segregating him off for his own safety. Nilsen resisted the idea, and eventually won. Showing potential aggressors that he would not be cowed was only part of his rationale. Nilsen had another reason for his 'strong man' behaviour. He explains he was still trying to impress David Martin from afar and didn't want rumours reaching the object of his former infatuation that Dennis Nilsen was a grass.

Martin had other things on his mind. The thought of returning to prison had plunged him into a deep depression. He soon started to feel suicidal. On 15 March, after receiving a 25-year sentence, he hanged himself in his cell in Parkhurst. Nilsen wrote to Brian Masters to say he felt he needed to do something. As he wasn't allowed to attend the funeral, he asked if Masters would go on his behalf.

Masters contemplated what he should do. By committing himself to such a serious project, he concluded he had entered into a series of obligations to the people involved – so he agreed. He delivered the single white and red roses Nilsen had ordered, along with the message that read 'In fondest love, Des'. In his media scrapbook, Nilsen noted that the *Sun* wrote a piece the next day headlined 'MONSTER'S TWO RED ROSES FOR HOUDINI'. They'd called him a monster and got the colour of the flowers wrong.

Some months later, when Moffat was brought to trial for the razor attack, Nilsen was still determined to carry on acting tough, despite no longer having Martin to impress. On 18 June 1984, he was ordered to testify. Dressed in his suit and with his newly-grown moustache he again looked every inch the civil servant he'd once been. He hardly needed to give evidence; Moffat openly admitted to the attack.

His defence was that Nilsen had made homosexual advances and the incident had been prompted by a knife threat on him. After several hours' deliberation, the jury decided that there was insufficient evidence for a conviction. As he left the court, Moffat bragged Nilsen would be attacked again for being so arrogant.

In the autumn of 1984, Nilsen was transferred to Wakefield Prison in Yorkshire, a mixture of Victorian and new buildings; it now specialises in sex offenders. In 1984, it was a hard place full of hard men. Nilsen expected life to become increasingly bleak. He feared more attacks and resigned himself to longer periods spent in solitary confinement. Instead, in Christmas 1984, Nilsen started the most enduring romantic relationship of his life.

The 'romance' was with an armed robber called Jimmy Butler. He was from Yorkshire with a broad accent and gauche manners. Of medium height and build, he also looked remarkably like Keith Richards from the Rolling Stones. The armed robbery had initially landed him a life sentence but it was reduced to nine years on appeal.

Nilsen's manuscript describes being attracted both to Butler's left-wing leanings, and his naïveté. Despite his crimes, Nilsen saw in him a wounded, almost child-like 28-year-old. They soon started to refer to each other as 'brother', and would describe the regime and the government as 'the bastards'.

Butler also had abundant energy. He encouraged Nilsen to practise his chef's skills again, and the two of them ran a small curry business during recreation periods in the common room kitchenette. The facilities were intended for the preparation of food bought from the prison shop. In reality, the small electric oven was used more for food smuggled out of the kitchens.

Nilsen revels in his description of the black-market economy in prison. He also seems surprised to find that things really did seem to fit the stereotype of the prison movies he'd seen. The unofficial 'currency' was 'tobacco, cannabis and any saleable commodity from the prison canteen'. Allegedly, there was a 'bookie on every wing', eager to relieve inmates of whatever was being used for money and, in turn, that 'money' could be spent on anything from pastries to having one's laundry done. Nilsen also says that Butler deliberately courted the attention of men who were attracted to him. There was one in particular who had formed an especial attachment, a paunchy Scotsman whom we'll call Graeme.

Nilsen and Butler's romance started like teenagers hanging around in the dorms, and Graeme would invariably be found frequenting Butler's cell. Butler would send notes to Nilsen asking him over. The three of them would sit there looking awkward and not knowing what to do. Triumphantly, Nilsen says that Jimmy eventually publically 'dumped' Graeme and started 'going out' with Des.

Nilsen's descriptions of their early liaisons, significantly show what seems, for him, to be an unusual interest in someone's character and not just their body. When they first met, Nilsen had just bought a new budgie, Hamish, which had fallen seriously ill. Butler wandered in and warmed the bird in his mouth, bringing it back to life. Nilsen saw this as an inner sensitivity, which, he says, he found appealing. What follows next, however, is a fairly graphic description of a homosexual affair. Like many such passages in the book, it is hard to decipher Nilsen's primary aim: to prove a functioning sexuality – at the time of the trial he indicated that outside of his imagination he was asexual – or just to enjoy thinking about sex. Still, letters exchanged between Nilsen and Butler do show this was a genuine, two-way affair.

A little over four years later, in 1989, Butler would also corroborate their relationship in an interview with the *Sunday Mirror*: 'To everyone else he is a monster, but I know the man. I am proud to have known him,' he said. 'No one else has been more special … he is the most caring person I have ever known.'

Butler and Nilsen offer different accounts of the end of their relationship. Butler says that Nilsen's constant questioning about his unhappy childhood led to frequent arguments and eventually caused him to punch Des in the face. Such events were eventually too much for the governor, who had Butler transferred. Nilsen's descriptions of their arguments – over Butler's dislike of Nilsen's cannabis and classical music, and Nilsen's low tolerance of Butler's Bob Marley *Legend* album – sound more like an infatuation coming to an end.

By the end of 1984, with Butler gone and more time on his hands, Nilsen again started to brood about what he had done with his life. He decided – possibly quite sincerely – that he should atone for his past actions by living his prison life as constructively as possible, starting by developing his existing talents. Ideally he says he would have liked to have swapped his job in the workshop for the option of 'full-time education'. But this was over-subscribed, so he asked instead to apply to join an Open University course. The education department informed him that he could be eligible as long as he avoided psychology. He plumped for social sciences.

In the end, Nilsen's OU efforts came to an end after only three months. If, as seems likely, it was down to his own limited ability to stick at something, he won't admit so. Instead, he complains it was all down to the lousy way Wakefield Prison ran its education department. For example, he complains that they only provided one old black-and-white TV to watch the educational programmes. And if he wanted a tape player to listen to other lessons, he was told he would have to give up his record player. And there was no way, he says, he was going to let that happen.

Having failed with the OU, Nilsen decided to educate himself by listening to Radio 4, a habit that would become a permanent part of his prison life. But in Nilsen's scheme of personal rehabilitation, self-education wasn't sufficient. He also wanted to become politically active again. He felt there could be almost no end to the issues he might champion in prison. Nilsen the 'union man' was reborn. Prisoner B62006 started by dispensing practical advice to other inmates. Some, later, even wrote to him from their new prisons to thank him for his help. Such feedback was extremely important in helping Nilsen to believe that there was more to him than the murders. But, now, more than anything else, Nilsen wanted to know what Brian Masters had made of him.

In January 1985, Nilsen received an advance copy of *Killing for Company*. He devotes 10 pages of *History of a Drowning Boy* to his analysis. The first thing he disliked about it was the title. He'd wanted *The Case of Dennis Nilsen*, which, of course, would have given him star billing. His opinions on the contents were more ambiguous, but still generally just as negative. On the one hand, he says the book was 'the only serious study on my aberrant actions'; on the other, he calls it 'another Monster book, cloaked in learned technique'.

By using a straightforward biographical style, Masters had made his starting point not a criminal phenomenon, but rather a human being who had done evil things. That his biographer didn't simply assume he was subhuman had initially pleased Nilsen. But by the time he had got to the end of the book, he became extremely indignant that Masters seemed to conclude that Nilsen was not really fit to sit alongside other human beings.

In particular, Nilsen picked up on the little details; one was Masters' speculation that he would happily butter his morning toast while there was a head boiling on the stove. In his typically literal way, Nilsen is quick to point out that the actual truth was that he lived on takeaways.

Another line that Nilsen particularly objected to was one that appeared in Masters' conclusion: 'It is Nilsen's invulnerability to the squalor of human remains that makes him finally unrecognizable.' Nilsen argues that because he would sometimes be sick when cutting up bodies he could not have been immune to the presence of rotting flesh. But he also partially contradicts this by questioning why people are so concerned by what he did to the dead bodies. The wicked thing, he says, was to kill. A corpse, on the other hand, can't feel.

There are also passages in *History of a Drowning Boy* that indicate prisoner B62006 may also, partly, have been positively emotionally affected by someone having taken an interest in him. One sentence stands out as a fleeting sign of warmth: 'I like Brian very much, with all his faults and weaknesses and I hope he feels the same towards me.'

By late 1985, neither Nilsen nor Masters could quite seem to work out their attitudes to the other. Masters was still visiting Nilsen and had also become a friend to his mother. He told me he could have just 'dropped' Nilsen after the book, but what would that have said about him? The situation he now found himself in, he reasoned, surely carried responsibilities. But after publication of the book, Masters' public pronouncements on Nilsen appeared to become stronger, as if he felt he needed to emphasise the full horror of what he had done. That, at least, was how it seemed to Nilsen. When Prisoner B62006 heard Masters on the radio or saw newspaper articles he had written, he became more and more resentful. He later expressed it to me with one of his soundbites: 'I'm afraid to pick up the phone,' he wrote, 'in case I get the answerphone saying, "Please speak after the high moral tone."'

Most of the reviews of *Killing for Company* applauded the skill with which Masters had handled the difficult balance to be struck. There was one dissenting voice – author Gordon Burn, writing for *Time Out*, felt that the many lengthy extracts from Nilsen's writings were tantamount to giving Nilsen a mouthpiece. He described Nilsen and Masters as being 'in business'; Nilsen had provided the story, he felt, and Masters had retired to the library to write it up without much further research. Such comments may have under-appreciated the skill and experience with which Masters rendered the material. But there was still, however, a danger that readers would simply read the extracts of Nilsen's writing and ignore the commentary. This was especially true because in the written word, and then through subsequent editing, Nilsen was more persuasive and articulate than he ever had been face to face.

Burn went on to write a highly acclaimed book on the Yorkshire Ripper case called *Somebody's Husband, Somebody's Son*. Brian Masters later found a point of comparison to his study of Nilsen with that of the American serial killer Jeffrey Dahmer (arrested in 1991). They were both gay men of a similar age, who lured back other gay men. A letter Nilsen wrote to Masters on the case, and the psychology behind such gay sex crimes, ended up in a piece the latter wrote for *Vanity Fair*.

By 1986, Nilsen was becoming militant about his sexuality. Now that AIDS had hit the public agenda, he wanted to campaign for gay rights in prison. He had even taken to walking around with a pink triangle sewn on to his uniform. It was a form of protest to allow condoms to be made freely available. When this went largely unnoticed, Nilsen wrote to the authorities. They replied that gay acts were contrary to 'good order and discipline'. Nilsen passed his observations over to the magazine *Gay Times*, including a comment from the authorities that the idea that prisoners could buy condoms with their own money was both ridiculous and offensive. Despite the source, the magazine felt that the issue of AIDS in prison deserved a mention.

And although Nilsen's crimes were against the gay community, letters written to him show that some gay men were interested in the idea that his murders might have been born of psychological isolation. During his first decade in prison Nilsen's mail bag became well-filled. Many letters were from loners who appeared to get some feeling of potency from proximity to a killer. Some were fixated; one teenage girl wrote almost daily. Her letters became increasingly disturbed, with suicide being discussed. Nilsen never replied.

Extraordinarily, one of Nilsen's previous victims also wrote. His name was Carl Stottor. He was 5ft 11in with long blond hair. When he composed his first letter he was 25, and four years had passed since Nilsen had tried to kill him. During this time, Stottor had suffered from depression and other post-traumatic conditions. Initially, he had thought the trial would bring closure, but it just threw up more questions. The lack of clarity over what exactly had happened, and why, continued to build up, causing ever-increasing emotional pressure.

On 16 February 1986, Stottor decided to ask prisoner B62006, directly, why he had tried to killed him. They exchanged letters over a period of months. I had heard about the correspondence from newspaper cuttings, and decided to track Stottor down. I met him one July afternoon in his flat on the south coast. The man who opened the door was frail, but welcoming. He was glad I had made it down to see him, as so many journalists had written about him without bothering to make the effort to visit. For several hours, and over several pots of tea, Stottor described what he now believes happened.

One Wednesday night, in the summer of 1983, Stottor found himself in the Black Cap in Camden, a gay pub that specialised in drag acts. Stottor was feeling depressed; he had recently run away from a violent boyfriend and still had carpet burns on his face from the last attack. While he drank his lager and lime, and contemplated his life, Stottor's gaze was drawn to Nilsen, who was chatting to a local at the bar.

After Nilsen's companion left, he came over and asked Stottor about his face. Stottor immediately noticed his eyes were big and brown. He seemed kind. Nilsen smiled and assured Stottor he was still pretty. Conversation flowed naturally. They soon discovered that both felt alienated from their families. It made Stottor feel Nilsen was someone he could confide in. At closing time, Nilsen suggested that they return to his flat. In the cab back, they held hands.

Although the evening went well, there were still two things that happened before the attack that made Stottor feel uneasy. First, on the way back, Nilsen became furious with the taxi driver about the route, and paid him in the smallest change he had. The second occurred later in the flat. Stottor had been sitting cross-legged on the floor listening to Laurie Anderson's haunting 'O Superman'. He said it was his favourite song and Nilsen replied, 'You haven't even heard it til you've listened to it through these headphones.' As he listened, he became aware that Nilsen was standing behind him staring at his head.

These, however, were just uncomfortable moments in an otherwise pleasant evening. Stottor hardly cared about the state of the flat, and it didn't really seem that bad – 'shabby', but certainly not the worst he'd been in. The smell was a mixture of wet dog, stale dog food, cigarette smoke, damp and air fresheners. Stottor was much more interested in his new friend. They drank Bacardi and got drunk and, despite having told Nilsen that he was not up for any kind of sexual activity, they started to kiss and cuddle.

Stottor remembers the petting as normal, and tactile. Then the Bacardi started to take effect, and he was sick. They decided to go to bed, where they cuddled and fondled a little more. Instead of a blanket, Nilsen had an open sleeping bag. Nilsen drew Stottor's attention to the zip, which had come away from the padding, hanging loose like jagged rope. Nilsen warned him about getting caught in it.

An hour later, Stottor suddenly felt a sharp pain around his neck. Nilsen was strangling him with the zip he had been careful to tell him about. It later became apparent that Nilsen was using sufficient force to cause blood vessels in Stottor's eyes to pop. For several minutes, the young man instinctively fought against death, flailing around ineffectively. Nilsen then took him to the bathroom to finish him off. He ran the bath and then forced Stottor's head underwater. With his head held hard under the surface, Stottor could no longer resist the urge to breathe and started to inhale the water.

At this point, Stottor says he felt he was giving in to death. For Nilsen, this was the moment he began to feel his sex ritual going wrong. In his manuscript, he says he stopped the attack because Stottor had now been 'rendered passive'. The goal of the fantasy had been achieved and there was no need to go further. This seems highly implausible, if for no other reason than Stottor had already been extremely passive through alcohol and sleep before the strangulation had started.

Whatever the reason, once the 'moment' passed, everything changed. Nilsen says he then comforted Stottor, telling him about the zip and that he'd had to splash water on to him to bring him to. They cuddled some more, and in the morning he saw Stottor off.

Stottor told me that, after the initial 'drowning', he passed out and then regained consciousness underwater. He then passed out again. A while later, he says he experienced what might have been an out-of-body experience. He felt like he was floating in the room, looking down on a young, blond man laid out on the floor by an armchair. The man looked dead. Then a dog started licking his face. Another man was in the room. He was tall and dark. Realising the man by the chair was still alive, he approached him.

Stottor now believes he was finally revived the *following* morning, after he had been in the flat for 35 hours. Nilsen then walked him to the Tube. From here Stottor made his way to the Royal Free Hospital, where he told the doctor he had got caught up in a zip. The doctor shook his head and told him, 'You've been strangled. Somebody may have tried to kill you.' His state of shock deepened.

When I asked Stottor about the letters that he and Nilsen had exchanged, he seemed partly embarrassed and partly disgusted. He said he was still confused about what had happened. There had been times, he confessed, using one of his favourite lines, when he didn't know if Nilsen was his 'murderer or his saviour'. As there had only been two people in that room, he'd decided to ask the other one for an explanation.

Nilsen's manuscript also talks about the correspondence. He says he was happy to write to Stottor, but mindful that too much contact might not necessarily be helpful. It seemed to him that Stottor might be attributing everything that made him unhappy about his life to that single attack. Nilsen says in *History of a Drowning Boy*: 'I bore the man Carl Stottor no feelings of personal malice ... my fateful and traumatic encounter with Stottor has to be viewed in proportion with this true light which places me as just being one of a succession of competing forces in his greatly troubled life.'

In 1987, the letters between Nilsen and Stottor stopped. Stottor says the closest he ever got to an explanation as to why Nilsen had spared him was an unconvincing feeling that a 'thin strand of humanity passed between us'. He now believes the real reason he was spared was down to something infinitely more practical – Nilsen had decided he didn't have any more room for another dead body.

1989 was Nilsen's last full year in Wakefield. In *History of a Drowning Boy*, Nilsen tells his would-be readers he still had enough prison enemies to keep him in the newspapers, and sufficient friends to supply him with 'pot'. When contemplating his life in a marijuana haze, Nilsen felt he could see the whole of eternity stretched out in front of him. He describes the phenomenon in philosophical language. Life, he says, seemed short and insignificant. The experience was given a grandiose name: 'Nilsen's Second'.

Soft drugs were now an important and integral part of his life. He found they helped both his emotions and his ability to think. Instead of making him paranoid, as they frequently can, he says they would enable him to be tranquil and meditative. When he got high, he could think back and 'see' his victims in an almost peaceful state.

But, when off them, an opposite state of mind would, apparently, often bother him. He says his crimes might 'intrude' on to him with 'periodic reminders'. If someone's face put in mind a victim, for instance, he might become physically sick. Nilsen talks as though he liked to put his offending past into a mental box marked 'emotional breakdown' and doing so was easier when he was 'out of it'.

It wasn't just the drugs that helped Nilsen cope with his past. The whole atmosphere of prison helped. There were people everywhere to whom Nilsen could compare himself and not come off so badly. On his wing was Archibald Hall, a serial killer butler who, in old age, had become an avuncular figure. And, for a while, Nilsen found himself locked up with the 'country's most violent prisoner', the man who had changed his name to that of the actor Charles Bronson, whose violent assaults on staff had turned an 11-year sentence into seemingly indeterminate incarceration. Nilsen marvelled at his physique and spirit.

Much more terrible than Hall or Bronson was Ted Paisnel. For 11 years, Paisnel had roamed the island of Jersey at night, dressed in rubber and chains, raping women and children. Now he seemed just an ordinary bloke. In fact, the most incredible thing about him – that his wife had stood by him all this time – seemed almost reasonable.

Towards the end of the year, Nilsen experienced the last 'romantic' relationship he would have, or at least talk about, in prison. It was a sex-offender whom we'll call Peter Chapple. He was 34 and good looking, although emotionally stunted. Chapple was serving a sentence for having sex with teenage boys. Before talking about their relationship, Nilsen makes some remarks about Chapple's character that are revealing both about his ability to judge others and also how he saw himself at the time. Nilsen says that Chapple would prefer to divert himself in activities like maths and computers than take part in the 'risky world of adult emotions'. Nilsen, with his own preference for books, saw himself as emotionally superior.

Even though Chapple was emotionally immature, he was still one of the most powerful personalities on his landing. Initially, Nilsen's attraction to someone with such a strong character might seem odd. The way he had chosen his victims had indicated, after all, that, typically, he would seek out those with weaker wills for company. In this instance, one reason for the attraction, other than looks, soon becomes apparent. Nilsen was drawn to the fact that Chapple was an instinctive musician. This was a skill Nilsen greatly coveted. For his 43rd birthday, Brian Masters had bought Nilsen the cheap Casio electronic keyboard he'd asked for. Now he wanted to learn to play it.

After hearing Chapple demonstrate how it worked, Nilsen immediately decided they should write a musical together. He would be the wordsmith and Chapple the composer. Nilsen had taken charge of the relationship, and also shown his potential partner what a creative force he was. The plans stalled a week later. After two sessions trying to come up with musical ideas, it became apparent that Chapple couldn't compose. Nilsen emphasises that he was still desperate to do *something* creative. He proposed putting on a comedy revue. No one, however, wanted to be in it.

Undeterred, Nilsen started submitting poetry for prison magazines, and composing on his keyboard. He tells us that he had his eyes on the prestigious Koestler Awards for artistic achievement in prison. But whereas Nilsen's plays and art were of a good amateur standard, the quality of his music couldn't match his desire to produce it.

In 1990, Nilsen was transferred to Full Sutton Prison, a relatively new maximum-security facility in Yorkshire. Many prisoners objected to his presence. Nilsen says in *History of a Drowning Boy* that, when he arrived, he was made to feel about as welcome as a 'dead pig in a synagogue'. He describes violence, too. One night, two hooded men burst into his cell with a bowl of boiling water into which sugar had been dissolved to make it boil hotter. He picked up the only object to hand, a battery for his keyboard, and threw it in their direction. Being unco-ordinated, it hit the wall above them. Still, it made them drop the water.

The next day, he was transferred to the segregation unit. He spent virtually the whole summer there. Afterwards, he was told he was going to be part of the trial for the Vulnerable Prisoner Unit scheme. VPUs were being set up in various prisons across the country to protect prisoners who might become a target from others, such as terrorists and policemen. In practice, the VPUs were mainly used for sex-offenders; in Nilsen's words, 'ghettos for nonces'. He didn't enjoy the company he was now keeping. The prisoners on the VPU were a concentration of the facility's least popular inmates. As such, it isn't hard to believe some of his allegations. Despite being segregated, Nilsen says at mealtimes he saw human faeces in the custard, and razors in the pies.

The following year (1991), he was moved to the VPU in Albany on the Isle of Wight. It was a 1960s-built prison that later specialised almost entirely in 'vulnerable prisoners'.

The regime was austere – there was no cell association, and evening association in the common room was by rota. Nilsen was sent to work in a wood mill, a far cry from the education, drama and art he enjoyed. This was labour and damn hard. If Nilsen had once expressed a desire to suffer to atone for his crimes, he didn't like the reality of the wood mill one bit. Constant arguments with the guards and instructors earned him spells in the segregation unit. As in Brixton, he would refer to it as 'the punishment block'.

While Nilsen was settling into life in the VPU, the prison reformer Lord Longford asked if he might start visiting. Longford sought to bring redemption. He was a devout Roman Catholic who fearlessly sought out the most unpleasant cases to whom he chose to bring his message. In particular, Longford had become famous for visiting the Moors murderer Myra Hindley. It was his belief that she should be granted parole on the grounds of her religious conversion.

As much as Longford preached forgiveness, his religious beliefs also made him highly intolerant of homosexual practices. But despite this, Nilsen's accounts of Longford are warm. He is so pleased to have been the recipient of so much attention he initially sets Longford's religious beliefs aside. Eventually, though, Nilsen found those beliefs to be incompatible with his own, and he says he amicably asked him not to come any more. The peer is characterised as 'saintly', but with a body and face which looked like they'd 'been pickled in alcohol'. For his part, Lord Longford's diaries describe Nilsen as aloof and strange, but admirable in how he busied himself with positive and constructive hobbies. Longford was also struck by Nilsen's odd sense of humour, remembering one comment by Nilsen to him one day: 'You might have met the queen, but I know lots of queens.'

Nilsen's view on Longford was, no doubt, positively affected by the latter's defence of Nilsen's intrinsic 'humanity' in a newspaper interview with Brian Masters. The way Nilsen tells the story, Masters had again been speaking about him in those terms he liked the least – as some kind of demon – and Longford had replied by saying that he believed that everyone had a human soul.

Although Masters was still visiting Nilsen, privately Nilsen was feeling increasingly resentful towards him. The bitter tone of the manuscript suddenly changes, however, when Nilsen describes hearing of a street attack on Masters. Nilsen wants the reader to feel, despite everything, he still perceives Masters as a fundamentally kind man. He is appalled, he says, that the horrible attack might be connected with anything he could have said or done. It wasn't – in fact, it was a simple mugging.

But Nilsen now was no longer reliant on Masters as the sole constant in his life. He had just 'met' the best friend he was ever to have, Jonny Marling, details of whose identity have here been changed. He was of medium height, dark-haired and lived a normal, suburban life. Marling had obtained Nilsen's address from the Prison Service, having first become fascinated by the story he read in *Killing for Company*. In response to Marling's open and enquiring letters of introduction, Nilsen decided to try to make their friendship work. The serial killer and the suburban family man exchanged a flurry of letters, often running to both sides of seven or eight pieces of paper.

The subject of one of the first was what to make of the

American psychiatrist, Walter Powlowski, who, in May 1992, asked Nilsen to write a 'sexual history' to assist him in a study on serial killers. This project soon fizzled out. However, in July, a British sociologist asked for a similar essay. Nilsen started … and kept writing. That summer, he remembers in *History of a Drowning Boy* that he was also approached by a producer from Central TV who wanted to interview him. They asked him if he had written anything. He had. The first draft of his 'writings' was typed with such force that the keys almost went through the paper. It opens with: 'This is a narrative compilation including what I believe to be the salient features of my sexual history.'

His sex life, proper, began as he drifted through his late twenties in London.

6
ADRIFT IN LONDON

'The psychological struggles and
rages had festered for years.'
DENNIS NILSEN, IN A LETTER TO THE AUTHOR

One scene dominates the many 'real-crime 'documentaries that have been made about Dennis Nilsen: Nilsen and another man are pictured enjoying last drinks in a smoky bar in London's West End. It's the late 1970s. The street outside is wet and Piccadilly's neon lights reflect in the puddles. Inside, we see a close-up shot of Nilsen's rum and Coke. The imagery serves to illustrate how Dennis Nilsen's twenties and early thirties were dominated by alcohol and casual liaisons.

A similar picture emerges in one chapter of Brian Master's book, *Killing for Company*. It is called 'Police and Civil Service'. Here, however, the depiction is partly created by use of Nilsen's own accounts. His contributions emphasise his sensitivity to the superficiality of the gay scene. These are described as his 'lonely years' where 'everything was transitory. His words had a bizarre effect on some who read these passages.

After publication of *Killing for Company*, the number of

men and women who wrote to Nilsen steadily rose. These letters now exist in a private crime archive where I was invited to view them. Most were from highly emotional, young women. One correspondent opened with the words 'I am not a crank ...' and another reassured Nilsen with the words 'it's not very nice feeling lonely and different'. There were also a few who seemed to be so taken with the idea that a sensitive young gay man could find himself so totally estranged from society they appeared to overlook what he had actually done. A fair few young men even attached photographs of themselves.

Many of these people were, probably, themselves emotionally disturbed. Yet that, in itself, doesn't explain why Nilsen's life story touched such a chord. It seems it was the manner in which he had *described* his loneliness that had the effect. The elegant way he wrote – or possibly plagiarised other's words – made people feel his sentiments were authentic. 'Anonymous sex,' he said in *Killing for Company*, 'only deepens one's sense of loneliness and solves nothing. It's like compulsive gambling. Sex in a natural place is like the signature at the end of a letter. Written on its own, it's less than nothing. Signatures are easy to sign, good letters far more difficult.'

It wasn't just sad, lonely individuals who were fascinated with Nilsen's story. In 1988, ITV's *South Bank Show* aired a film of a 'modern ballet' called *Dead Dreams of Monochrome Men*. The press release said the dance was loosely based on Nilsen's life and explored 'interwoven notions of loneliness desire and trust', and that 'society's homophobia often results in tragic consequences'. Almost a decade later, a 'cult' gay author, P-P Hartnett, would publish a book entitled *Call Me*, in which he explored the loneliness of those who exploit contact adverts in search of transitory affection. Hartnett corresponded with Nilsen while he wrote it, inviting the killer to comment on the emotional content.

Later, Hartnett even helped with the first edit of *History of a Drowning Boy*. In long hand-written letters, Nilsen would give detailed explanations of how he felt the work should be completed. That handwriting is instantly recognisable. It is tight, slanted and the pen is pushed so hard it almost goes through the paper. His handwriting closely matches characteristics the Israeli graphologist Anna Koren has observed in 'schizoid murderers': angularity, pressure, tension and a tendency to cover the entire page. Schizoid personalities are usually considered to be emotionally cut off, often very sensitive and sometimes exhibit a rich, vivid imagination. Much the same could be said of the better prose Nilsen used to describe life in the late 1970s.

On 7 November 1972, Dennis Nilsen, then 27, caught the train from Aberdeen to Edinburgh and changed on to the London express. He was full of optimism as he looked out of the window from the smoking car.

As he travelled south, Nilsen reflected on the two-month break he had just spent in Strichen. There had been an unpleasant incident at his brother Olav's house. The film *Victim*, which had themes of homosexuality and blackmail, was being shown on the TV. Olav had taken every opportunity to direct barbed comments about 'poofs' and 'queers' towards his younger brother who sat there red-faced and fuming. As he looked out of the train window, he still felt enraged.

Then, during the rest of that long trip he took stock of how things had gone for him. It pleased him that many of those he had known seemed to have reached their plateau, whereas he felt he was moving on. But, for the most part, the Broch just made him feel sad. He remembered walking around his childhood haunts, starting with the bleak, bare Mormond Hill. Then he went to the river where old Mr Ironside had died. Later, he walked to the grave of Brian Strachen, who had been killed in a motorbike accident. The grave of his grandfather Andrew Whyte was just across the way. As he looked around him, he must have been struck by the ephemeral nature of human life. He felt it was exactly the right time for him to go to where he might have a future.

Nilsen's first task on arriving at King's Cross was to install himself in temporary accommodation. He found a room in a hostel and the next morning contacted the army career advice service. At its south London offices, the careers officer suggested he might be suited to a role as a prison officer or policeman. The idea of being a prison officer was an instant turn off.

He then contacted the police careers service in Victoria Street. By the end of the week, he was walking through the door at the recruiting office at Harrow Road. While his drinking may well have exerted its toll on his mental health, physically he was in good shape. He walked through the medical, and the Met Police said they were happy to take his army certificates in lieu of O-levels. Everything in his written test and interview indicated he was suitable.

ADRIFT IN LONDON

By December 1972, Dennis Nilsen was living in a single room in the Metropolitan Police training school at Hendon Police College, near Colindale, a north London suburb that sits at the foot of the M1. The once attractive Georgian-style building was beginning to show its age and would soon be knocked down and replaced by a purpose-built block. Still, if the old buildings were decaying, some felt they had collegiate charm.

Life as a probationary police officer started with a 16-week induction course. For almost four months, Nilsen was taught the basics of being a constable. On theoretical side, there was government, law, powers of arrest, traffic regulations, police regulations and court procedure. Even more important was the practical instruction: how to investigate; the basics of first aid; how to subdue criminals; and, of course, how to be courteous with the public.

Nilsen wrote to his mother telling her all about his exciting new life. Betty Scott was not only proud but immensely relieved. She had been worried about how unsettled Dennis had seemed during his visit. Olav told her what had happened at his house and Betty had heard how one night Dennis had got into an argument with some local boys in the Station Hotel. It had ended with him being pushed over and humiliated. She had been concerned Dennis might have been on the slide. But now he was going to be a policeman, so surely that would see him back on track.

It may well have done, if there had been other positive influences. But in the end, joining the police did nothing to help wean Nilsen off his increasing dependence on bizarre masturbation fantasies. The force just supplied a new set of people from whom he felt alienated, which, in turn, left him able to drift further into his secret life. Partly, the problem came from the fact the environment was still too macho. But it was also because Nilsen's sexual thoughts were, again, directed at colleagues. This manifested itself physically in swimming lessons that started in the first week at Hendon.

Being able to swim was a requirement of the job. But Nilsen was utterly afraid of water. In order not to draw attention to himself, he claimed to be a 'weak swimmer'. Like others in his position, he was put down for lessons until he was ready for the life-saving classes. Later, these would involve towing a colleague, who would pretend to be unconscious, to the side of the pool. The fact the bodies were so inert played straight into Nilsen's specific sexual fixation. He would invariably become physically aroused, and often needed to find excuses to stay in the water until he had calmed down.

Such episodes were an early sign he was going to have as much difficulty settling in here as in the Army. This time, however, he was less bothered. Now there was a whole city of people out there for him to meet. All he had to do was find the right ones, and soon he found out where to start looking.

Nilsen's induction into gay London life began, ironically, in a 'girlie' bar. One evening, in the Section House, Nilsen found himself falling in with a group of young probationers who had decided to go off on an adventure in Soho. In Windmill Street, one young police cadet decided to show off by using his warrant card to get them all into a strip club. Nilsen, uninterested in the girls inside, soon made an excuse to leave. In the street outside, he was convinced he saw Sir John Gielgud talking to a young guardsman. Nilsen mentioned it to his colleagues, along with the fact that he was convinced that many guardsmen were gay.

Nilsen records in *History of a Drowning Boy* that the next day, no doubt in response, the Training Officer giving the following address: 'You can spot a queer a mile off because they all wear white polo-necked sweaters, red corduroy trousers and Hush Puppies, and they hang about in Earls Court.' That evening, Nilsen says he took a Tube train 'and checked the [Earls Court] High Street, for an "interesting" pub'. He describes a smoky, dark establishment with frosted windows:

In one bar there were lots of men in leather pants, jackets and caps and they were of all ages ranging from young men to proto geriatrics with white, short hair. A lot of them seemed to opt for the straight 'Kojak'.

I transferred myself to the bigger bar which was crowded out. I knew instantly that it was a gay bar because everyone looked you up and down and passed on the appropriate comments to one another. 'Oh, look at her, nice dish (arse) ... Do you think she's butch or bitch?' etc.

It was a bit unsettling the first time and I didn't know what to expect or what to do. I was not in on the special language of the thriving gay subculture. What I didn't know was body language and, after I fortified myself with a couple of stiff drinks, I was chatting to a slim, young man who was eyeing me up.'

By 10.00 in the evening, Nilsen found himself being invited by the young man back for a coffee at his, only a few blocks away. The flat was up a long flight of stairs and, at the top, he was surprised to find a wife and baby in the kitchen. The man put his finger to his mouth and hushed Nilsen, motioning that they should tip-toe to the spare room. But the short, sturdy woman had seen them and chased them out. Undeterred, Nilsen hailed a cab and told the man he was going to come back to *his* place. The 16-week course at the Police Training College was almost over, and he was sure that he could get away with having a 'drunken friend' crash over in his small room. He propped a chair up against the door to make sure no one could get in and, in the morning, he got up extra early to sneak the man out.

Instead of feeling more comfortable about sex, however, such encounters seemed to make Nilsen more aware of how society only just tolerated homosexuality. In his essay 'The Psychograph', Nilsen describes the attitudes he'd become used to: 'In the military, as in the country as a whole, homosexuality was considered to be a serious criminal offence [it was legalised in 1967]. In the Judeo-Christian Western world, the idea of "unnatural sexual practices" remained an unspeakable vice performed between moral degenerates. Genuine expressive love between two consenting males was dismissed with curt terms such as "buggery", "sodomy" or "indecency".'

The cumulative effect of such attitudes – from Fraserburgh, the Army and the police – had left him with a very significant residue of guilt. The result was that when he did start meeting other gay men, rather than looking for a long-term partner, he was invariably attracted to other people whose primary objective was simple, physical gratification. It was lonely, but at least easy to keep separate from his work life.

In the spring of 1973, Nilsen passed the initial set of police exams with a 'high' mark. He was then posted as a probationary officer to Willesden Green near Wembley. As a probationary constable, Nilsen was required to learn on the job. He would go out on the 'beat', both in a pair and, later, alone. Like many of Nilsen's stomping grounds in North London, his 'patch' of Willesden Green was a shabby suburb. The tree-lined avenues contained substantial Edwardian and Victorian houses, which, on closer inspection, turned out to have been split into flats for the poor, often Irish immigrant, community.

Nilsen was given a mentor called Peter Wellstead, who believed young probationers would benefit from experiencing the uglier aspects of policing right from the outset. He started with the morgue. Before proceeding into the actual mortuary, the probationers were given a briefing in the corridor. They were then let in three at a time.

Nilsen wasn't bothered. He was confident he had seen enough exploded bodies in Aden to be able to detach himself. Inside the room, things were every bit as grisly as they had been warned. There were metal trolleys with dead bodies cut open from the neck to the navel. The back of the heads were sawn open, exposing grey folds of brain matter. The other trainee needed to be sick; Nilsen was unaffected.

Something else happened in that room, however, to make Nilsen realise quite how disturbed his sexuality had become.

On one slab was a 12-year-old girl. Smooth, slim and blonde, Nilsen thought how she looked like a little boy. As she was being wheeled around, her dead hand flopped out next to the assistant's, an old man with a slight hunchback. Nilsen became aroused, and looked away. But he couldn't stop imagining the old assistant abusing the unblemished 'passive' body.

That night, he went out again to the gay pubs of Earls Court, a west-central London area also known for its Australian population. He was beginning to appreciate the freedom he now enjoyed. The following night, he again went to the pub; and then the night after that. Frequenting gay bars, such as the Coleherne, became his main method of looking for pick-ups. He found the idea of cruising public toilets and cinemas seedy and disgusting. Although extreme, his actual sex life was, by the standards of many on the gay scene, reserved. As we've already seen, according to one of his accounts, he claims not to have experienced penetrative sex until the age of 27.

When it finally happened, it was not from one of his trips to the gay bars – it was an opportunistic rape. The victim was a teenage boy whom Nilsen had met during a social visit to a gay drop-in centre run by a Church of England curate. On certain evenings, a small hall would become a place for advice and warm drinks for youngsters, many of whom were runaways. Nilsen invited one Scottish boy out to the pub. As they got more and more drunk, Nilsen realised he had nowhere to go, so he asked him if he'd like to spend the night in a cheap hotel. En route, he bought some rum.

Back in the hotel, the youth passed out on one of the two

single beds. For the second time, Nilsen saw the opportunity for having a sexual encounter with an unconscious male body. 'I lifted him up into my arms and just stood there for a moment savouring the power of the situation. I looked down at his helpless, vulnerable nudity dangling in my arms,' he says. He then pulled the boy's trousers down and started to bugger him in his sleep. In the morning, everything was normal. The boy went on his way, and Nilsen remembered it as a thrilling encounter.

Nilsen presents this story as part of his explanation of how he developed a deep 'psycho-sexual' need. To understand his logic, one must first accept his understanding of the effect of a series of traumas in his life: his dysfunctional childhood had left him feeling inadequate; this turned his sexuality in on itself, forcing him to become reliant on fantasies. And experiences in the London gay scene, being anonymous and depersonalised, easily became extensions of this destructive, internal world.

Although Nilsen talks about psycho-sexual fantasy 'needs', in fact, they read like something more psychologically straightforward: a catalogue of perversions whose pull was irresistible. And despite anything he might say about having problems controlling his thoughts, Nilsen cannot give any persuasive reasons for acting on them. Nilsen's development of normal empathy clearly seems to have stalled in early childhood. He bridles at any such suggestions. His letters are full of indignant mentions of the word. Nilsen seems fascinated by the idea of empathy but never able to grasp the real meaning.

Commenting on a report compiled for a probation

hearing, for instance, he says, 'I have always had deep empathy with my victims. I know both the pain of their lives and the degree of loss caused by those who loved them.' Empathy didn't feature as a natural part of the actual attacks, he says, because in those instances he was acting out of a compulsion, not out of free will. He does admit he had to desensitise himself when he came to destroy the bodies. Nilsen denies, however, that he ever desensitised himself any more than, for instance, people who work for the ambulance service or in morgues.

We have seen, by now, abundant evidence of Nilsen's tendency to desensitise, compartmentalise and separate aspects of his world on an almost permanent basis. From the story of the rape, for example, he moves easily on to other subjects. He recalls a series of films he had enjoyed watching, and says that he particularly admired Stanley Kubrick. From films he moves on to art and his favourite painting – Gericault's *The Raft of Medusa*. And then he goes straight back to sex and death. He tells us the painting features an image of an old man with a dead, naked boy on his lap. He would use that scene in his fantasies.

By mid-1973, death had now become a fixed theme in Nilsen's sex fantasies. Although he didn't have a mirror, he would play new variations on old themes in his head before going to sleep. In one, the ugly old man was replaced by a handsome, powerful, well-muscled black man. The passive character was now an emaciated, teenage junkie, dead from an overdose.

Nilsen attempts several explanations of what he calls the

'psychological conundrums' of his fantasy life. 'In sexual intercourse,' he tells us in 'The Psychograph', 'the magic number is two.' Being a loner, he felt this was beyond him. So his subconscious responded by splitting itself into two sexual elements. These two 'types' in his sexual imagination would always correspond to the old man and the youth, with the man active and the boy totally passive. 'This passivity,' Nilsen says, 'ranged from being drunk, drugged, asleep, comatose or dead.'

Nilsen's mind was the 'curator' of both parts. The sexual thrill – or in his terms 'frissive excitement' – came from the combination of extreme passivity and absolute power. He would typically imagine himself in one role or the other, but feels at a deeper level he was always both. 'The goal,' Nilsen says, 'was never to dwell in unreality but to coax the need out of its closet into the real functioning world.' But this never happened. Instead, he says, his fantasies or 'Fortress Fantasy Psychograph', only brought him short term 'medicinal' value because his long-term 'entrenchment' resulted in 'augmenting his isolation'. The more he did it, the more he 'came to depend on it for nourishment'. In simpler words, the fantasies only ever made things worse.

The more Nilsen withdrew into his world, the less impression he made on his colleagues. There were suspicions about his sexuality, but otherwise he was seen as a competent loner. Still, there was something about him that seems to have given at least one other colleague an uneasy feeling.

Journalist John Lisners in his book *House of Horrors* tells a story that when news got out about a multiple murderer being found in North London, before Nilsen's name had been released, a former colleague was heard saying, 'If it's true he's an ex-copper, my money's on it being Dennis Nilsen.'

Nilsen was evidently becoming increasingly estranged from his colleagues. It seems he was now beginning to see himself as an outsider figure, siding with anti-establishment heroes he would read about. 'The more I got to know my colleagues,' he writes, 'The more I thought I might be in the wrong line of work. Police and villains looked much the same.' He shirked patrolling for men engaged in 'indecent acts'. If he saw two young men parked up in a quiet road, he crossed over. What were they doing, other than trying to connect with other human beings, he thought. As for himself, he was becoming increasingly convinced of the emotional limitations of promiscuity.

Nilsen's manuscript is, however, less bleak on this period of his life than he was later in his confessions to Brian Masters. Ten years on, in 1983, Nilsen observed in *Killing for Company*, 'I was left with an endless search through the soul-destroying pub scene and its resulting one-night stands … passing faces and bodies, the unfulfilled tokens of an empty life. A house is not a home and sex is not a relationship. We would only lend each other our bodies in a vain search for inner peace.'

But now, he describes the summer of 1973 in brighter terms. That June, Nilsen met a young man in the William IV in Hampstead, one of London's greenest and most sophisticated areas. Unlike the Coleherne, the 'Willy' was not an exclusively gay pub. But with its proximity to the cruising ground of Hampstead Heath, it took on that quality at many times during the week. The man in question – whom we'll call Derek – had a mane of androgynous, long blond hair and looked like a glam-rocker.

They went back together to Nilsen's room at the Police Section House which, in all the drunken excitement, Derek had assumed was a hostel. Again, with a chair pressed up against the door for privacy, the pair engaged in sexual activity that Nilsen rated as one of the most enjoyable sex experiences of his life. When Derek awoke, Nilsen was putting on his uniform. 'Is this the police station?' asked Derek.

Nilsen replied with a flirtatious joke about 'taking down his particulars'.

As he walked out of the Section House, the sergeant stared across at him. Derek's appearance suggested to Nilsen's senior officer that he was not the sort of man who should have been 'passing through' at that time of the morning. Nilsen explained his presence by saying that he had just sold the young man a fish tank. He then walked Derek down to the Tube and, just to show what rebellious spirits they were, they kissed full on the mouth just before the doors closed. Nilsen still had his policeman's hat on. He describes the incident triumphantly.

Derek proved to be just another young man looking for sexual adventure. Nilsen, however, was now looking for someone to be close to. The two met on a number of further occasions, but it soon became clear to Nilsen that Derek was really interested in sleeping around to make him feel better about himself. The last time Nilsen saw him was in 1975. On that occasion, Derek asked if he could 'borrow' money. The encounter left Nilsen with more than a bad taste in his mouth – he discovered he'd contracted gonorrhea.

At the end of 1973, at the age of 27, Nilsen decided to go no further with the police. A rumour exists that he was informally asked not to continue after a colleague reported him for masturbating in the morgue, but there isn't much evidence to support the claim. Nilsen says he just felt he was in the wrong business. He wanted to have fun, but had found the police force to have been full of bigots. He now just wanted to be a normal citizen.

During the winter of 1973-74, the UK was in the midst of a depression. The pop group Slade might have been celebrating their huge hit, 'Merry Xmas Everybody', but elsewhere an oil crisis had just ended and the three-day week was about to start.

Nilsen, however, was feeling optimistic. Just before Christmas, he moved into 9 Manstone Road, a sub-let bedsit in a Victorian house just off Cricklewood Broadway (another mixed suburb with a large Irish immigrant community). Despite Nilsen's initial sense of hopefulness, the festive period soon became lonely. His only company came from occasional trysts in bars. He wrote to his mother as he did periodically throughout the year, but had no other contact with his family. There were no friends to give him support, or to give him an injection of normality or common sense.

In the first week of January, the Labour Exchange found Nilsen a job as a security guard for the Department of the Environment. Compared to the police, it was straightforward. Mainly, it just involved patrolling various government buildings in different parts of town. In one office in the Shell building, next to Waterloo, he found a book on toxicology. Two photographs brought home to Nilsen his increasing sexual interest in dead bodies. One was an image of a boy who had died of drowning; the other was a colour photo of a boy with rigor mortis. By a trick of the light, his flesh tones suggested that he was still alive. That photograph made Nilsen realise that he could be 'frantically aroused' by the idea of someone being at the 'dividing line between life and death'. He contemplated stealing the book. As he writes about this, his prose becomes even more direct and confessional.

Another story from this period also rings true, even though it is utterly bizarre. It finds Nilsen trying to act out his 'old man fantasy' with a dead gorilla. It was in the warehouse of the Natural History Museum, and the gorilla was stuffed. Nilsen was again working as a security guard. He was patrolling one night when he came across the animal, which, with its false eyes, looked alive to him. More importantly to Nilsen, the dead primate looked 'powerful'.

Nilsen had recently dyed his hair blonde, and thought he looked young, Aryan and pretty. The contrast between himself and the gorilla provided just the frisson he enjoyed. Looking at the gorilla, Nilsen says his heart beat harder and harder until he could no longer resist the urge to strip off. He placed the gorilla's hand on his naked flesh. Having no mirror, he imagined he was looking down on the scene, and the gorilla was about to carry him off. But when he looked down, he found that the gorilla only had a 'pathetic little stump' for a penis. His arousal subsided, and he put his clothes back on.

With his new blond haircut, Nilsen says he now particularly enjoyed admiring himself when masturbating. When old men in bars eyed him up, however, it made him furiously angry. Nilsen's new look also drew the attention of his neighbours. Eventually, other tenants complained about him bringing men back. Entertaining was forbidden and Nilsen was given a warning. He took this as a sign he was at another crossroads in his life. Night was a time for being gay, he felt, and not for masturbating with gorillas. He would find a new flat and a new job and live his life in London to the full.

The next few months were no happier though. Nilsen resigned from his security guard job, and then with £8 he got by selling his General Service medal he set himself up in another bedsit, this time in a detached Edwardian house in nearby 80 Teignmouth Road. 'Like Dickens' Mr Micawber', he said, he felt that some job or other was bound to turn up. He went down to the Labour Exchange (later the Job Centre) in Denmark Street in the heart of the West End. 'They didn't couldn't find me a job, or give me money … but they did give me a job. Working for them,' Nilsen writes.

Despite nestling among guitar shops, the employment centre dealt with the low-paid jobs for the restaurants in nearby Soho. Nilsen's experience in catering made him a good fit. Initially, he was frustrated not to be put on front-line duty interviewing clients – instead, he was relegated to answering phones – but he still found the work environment better than anything he had previously experienced. It was a much more accepting atmosphere than the police or Army. One colleague called him Des, and from that day the name stuck. 'Des' became convinced some other colleagues were closet homosexuals. He also liked the way that some of the women in the office guessed he might be gay. If asked, he would confirm it quietly with a smile.

With a regular job and a decent roof over his head, life

didn't seem so bad. In Nilsen's internal 'film' he saw himself as the leading man in a picaresque, sexual adventure. One night he woke up in the bed of an aristocrat's butler; on another, it was a small-time Australian soap actor. But by the summer of 1975, however, another 'incident' occurred. One afternoon, Nilsen says in his autobiography that he met a 17-year-old called David Painter at the Job Centre where he had been looking for work. Later, Nilsen, bumped into him in the street. Nilsen was probably aware by this stage that Painter had mental problems of some sort, and knew that there'd be the risk of trouble if they went back to his flat. But Nilsen refuses to admit he did anything wrong that night, other than try to seduce someone who was particularly vulnerable:

> *Risk became hard fact when I picked up a 17-year-old 'disturbed' teenager named David Painter ... I don't think he had an experienced alcohol intake. We watched TV at my room at 80 Teignmouth Road, watched a reel of test film I had shot of London and had a few Martinis. He knew he was sleeping with me in the single bed and he entered it as naked as did I ... (I) just put my arm around his body. To my utter amazement he threw a screaming fit ... running around the house ... 'Oh God,' I said to myself, 'a nutter!' ... later, I did my best to calm him down but he barged into a glass partition, in front of other tenant witnesses in the house.*

Nilsen felt he had no option but call the police himself. Painter was taken to hospital where he claimed that Nilsen had tried to assault him sexually. And so the civil servant was brought in … to his old police station, Willesden Green. He was questioned and then put in the cells for the night. In the morning, Painter and his parents decided not to press charges and Nilsen was released. The incident was logged. These were the days of manual typewriters and index cards and there was no easy way of recording incidents that could then be easily linked to those of a similar nature.

On the Monday morning, Nilsen didn't mention the incident. No one in the office ever did or ever would have any reason to guess that their colleague's home life was anything other than humdrum and lonely. His work was administerial, and, for the most part, he got on with it quietly. Sometimes, in conversation, however, he would vehemently put forward his opinion on every aspect of events in the news. He says he was now 'ensconced in the noisy, empty, jungle/desert of the Metropolis'. Elsewhere, he described the empty world of the bedsitter as 'devoid of any supportive community of neighbours', a 'lifestyle of underground trains and clerical work'.

Nilsen disliked his superiors. He felt they disapproved both of his sexuality and trade union activities. But, among his co-workers, there were still plenty who shared Nilsen's socialist ideals. Occasionally, they would ask Nilsen for a drink after work. He may have been eccentric and opinionated, some thought, but maybe he just needed some encouragement? Nilsen would, as often as not, join them, but invariably he would soon become unsettled and leave early, in favour of the gay bars. Of those bars, he says they 'left me with a kind of forlorn sadness which came from a long, frustrated run of "one-night stands" with the strangers bent on promiscuity

nnis Nilsen being driven from the Old Bailey in a police van, without
customary blanket over his head, after being sentenced to life
prisonment on 4 November 1983. He had insisted on being uncovered
all his hearings.

Photo ©Mirrorpix

Nilsen in police uniform: he trained as a policeman at Hendon
Police College. *Photo ©Mirror*

The house at 23 Cranley Gardens, Muswell Hill, North London, where t
remains of three of Nilsen's victims were discovered in the drainage.
Photo ©Mirror

The necktie used by Nilsen to strangle Stephen Sinclair. *Photo ©Mirror*

Nilsen in the army at Maybury: his movie camera was instrumental in
confusing reality with fantasy. *Photo courtesy Brian Mas*

rs Betty Scott, mother of Dennis Nilsen, in June 1988.   *Photo ©Mirrorpix*

e dunes by Fraserburgh Bay where Nilsen believes his grandfather may
ve abused him.   *Photo ©Russ Coffey*

n oil painting-cum-collage, called 'Bacardi Sunrise', which Nilsen
eated whilst in Whitmoor Prison.   *Photo ©Mirrorpix*

A letter in Nilsen's own handwriting to author Russ Coffey.

Photo ©Russ Cof

Nilsen's pet dog, Bleep, pictured at Battersea Dogs Home where she passed away three weeks after the arrest of her master. *Photo ©Mirror*

Police plastic covers in the garden of 195 Melrose Avenue, Cricklewood, North London, where Nilsen started his killing spree, hiding the bodies under the floorboards of his flat. *Photo ©Mirror*

my Butler, with whom Nilsen had a 'romance' whilst in Wakefield Prison.
Photo ©Mirrorpix

ompilation tape which Nilsen made of his own music. He also
igned the artwork. *Photo ©Russ Coffey*

house at 16 Baird Road, Strichen, near Fraserburgh, where Nilsen
nt his most formative childhood years. *Photo ©Russ Coffey*

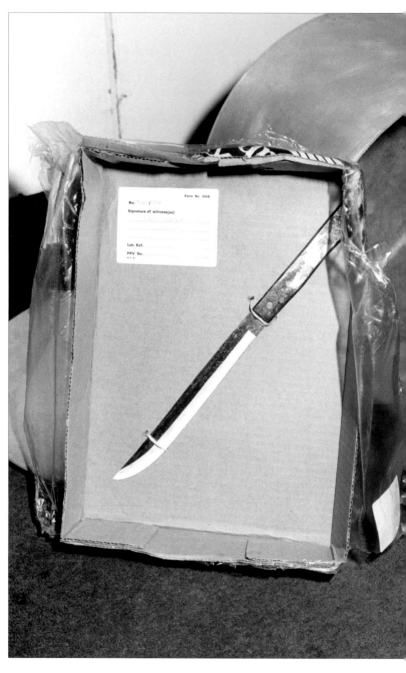

The carving knife used by Nilsen to dismember the bodies of his victim

Photo ©Mirro

rl Stottor, who survived an attack by Nilsen, pictured in August 2005.

Survivor Martyn Hunter-Craig pictured outside 23 Cranley Gardens. He often stayed with Nilsen over a period of three years without realising that he was murdering people during that time. *Photo ©Mirror*

rather than the permanent relationship of my aspiration. I became trapped in a treadmill of work, drink and isolation.'

In the summer of 1975, at the age of 29, Nilsen finally found himself in an approximation of a domestic relationship. It began with a letter telling him his father had died. Olav Nilsen had ended his days as the manager of a fish canning factory in Ghana. He was on his fourth wife and had died of a heart-attack. The letter informed him that Olav's surname wasn't actually Nilsen, but Moksheim. Apparently, Dennis also had half-brothers and sisters he'd never heard of.

Olav Moksheim left Dennis £1,400. It was very welcome and accelerated his desire for a domestic life. Now that he had some money behind him, Nilsen decided he wouldn't just let life happen. That weekend, Nilsen got chatting to David Gallichan in the Champion pub in Bayswater. Gallichan was 18, approximately 5ft 9in, skinny and blond with a friendly, round face. Dennis impressed the youngster by telling him he used to be a soldier. Gallichan had come up from Weston-super-Mare in search of the bright lights and was easily impressed. Small and exceptionally effeminate, with what Nilsen called 'the mentality of a 15-year-old', Gallichan easily succumbed to the older man's suggestion that they set up home together.

After just one night in 80 Teignmouth Road, the pair went flat-hunting. The result was finding 195 Melrose Avenue, a substantial Victorian-conversion garden flat on the other side of Cricklewood and about a hundred yards from Gladstone Park. It was a good-sized, if poorly presented, semi-detached property, extended at the back.

Upstairs were two small flats and, downstairs, two larger ones. Nilsen and Gallichan's flat was the rearmost of the ground-floor apartments. They had two rooms, a bathroom and a small kitchen. The living room (in which they also sometimes slept) had French windows to the rear and the kitchen was next to it. The bedroom had a bunk bed that Nilsen eventually converted to be just a top platform.

Nilsen decided to splash some of his inheritance money on home comforts, but first he wanted to make a project of the garden. The two of them spent an entire week doing it up. Gallichan would take the day shift while Nilsen was at work. In the evenings and weekends, Nilsen took over.

After all this work, he felt it only fair that they were granted sole access. He wrote a letter to the agent, Leon Roberts of Ellis and Co, explaining how only their French windows had direct access and only they seemed to care. He told him all about the stone paving he had put down, and the plum trees he had planted. It seemed reasonable, and Roberts signed the letter without coming down to inspect. Months later, Roberts dropped in to see the garden he had heard so much about. It struck him as the most bizarre outside space he had ever seen, with a series of mini fenced-off sections, and strange features.

Nilsen had also been careful to make sure animals were allowed. He brought his budgie, Hamish, over from Teignmouth Road, and bought a fish pond from a pet shop in Willesden. From another pet shop the two of them picked out a black-and-white mongrel puppy. Nilsen says he named her Bleep because she made a bleeping noise when they first brought her home. Later, the couple picked up a stray kitten named Deedee, standing for Des and David.

Next, they started to decorate. Gallichan painted the walls and Nilsen bought paintings and armchairs. This should have been a happy time – it was far from it. Some of Nilsen's Super 8 film footage of them still exists and it makes for extremely disturbing viewing. Nilsen is relentlessly angry. Sometimes there's a reason, such as when some roof plaster fell down, but more often than not it seems driven by an inner rage. Invariably, Gallichan bears the brunt of all this anger. We see 'Twinkle' – Nilsen's nickname for him – being told he isn't holding the camera right or that he's looking like 'a right poof'. Gallichan simply smiles back.

At least Nilsen was able to provide for him. But despite luxuries like a quality stereo and a decent television, the differences in their characters meant they rarely shared them. Gallichan didn't like classical music or progressive rock; classic films bored him, too. Sexually, too, Gallichan became more interested in other men he would meet in town. He told a reporter that Nilsen wasn't very good at or interested in sex.

Nilsen complained that Gallichan was too hairy, bony and too thin. He may well have added 'too real'. After years of reflection, Nilsen also seems to have been aware of this:
'I viewed my surroundings through an oblong, movie format. That's probably why I was never able to get very close to people because my attraction was for ideal, theoretical people who presented a simplistic relationship free from the problems and complexities of real people. Despite living in close proximity to David Gallichan for 18 months, I didn't really know him at all.'

Nilsen couldn't stop 'Twink' sloping off to the bars of Soho. Still, if they were no longer lovers, they were still a household.

On one occasion when Nilsen's half-brother Andrew was in town, Des was pleased to be able to invite him over to 'their' house. At the Job Centre Christmas party in 1975, Des showed Twinkle off as his 'companion', thereby eliminating any doubts over his sexuality. But, at home, they avoided each other as much as possible.

Even in January, when IRA bombs were going off in Soho, Nilsen preferred to frequent the gay bars there rather than go home. By March, he and Gallichan were hardly speaking. One night, Twinkle brought home a 15-year-old boy. Nilsen claims he seduced the youth for the night and dumped him back on Gallichan in the morning. When Gallichan woke up for his dishwashing job, he didn't know what to do about the boy. He decided just to leave. That evening, Nilsen returned to find the electricity meter smashed and the money stolen. He was furious.

He was also beginning to feel ill from gallstones. Initially, he put his dull pains down to a diet of beer, rum and cheap takeaways. By April, the doctor had told him otherwise, but an operation couldn't be scheduled for another couple of months. Depressed, he started hanging around the gay drop-in centre again.

By the time Nilsen had had his operation, England was enjoying a record heatwave. Once he was fit again, he was keen to spend the rest of the hot evenings in an alcoholic haze and looking for sex. He describes a number of people he met that summer. The functional encounters suggest a series of anonymous individuals, mainly oriental. And they left him with scabies and crabs.

By day, Nilsen was always the same old colourless

'monochrome man', to use the title of his own essay written in Cranley Gardens, but in the evenings his emotions were momentarily released by triggers that would cause them to overwhelm him with startling intensity. Music and alcohol were the main catalysts. Alcohol, he says, was also the 'social lubricant' that enabled him to turn sexual possibility into reality. It would give him 'amazing strength', both literally and figuratively. He stresses, however, that he was never an alcoholic in the sense that he *needed* to drink *all* the time. His drinking was 'episodic' with long gaps between 'binges', and this was true throughout his adult life. During drinking sprees, Nilsen would sometimes have black-outs; they worried him.

The more Nilsen got drunk, the more Twinkle probably wanted to leave. The beginning of the end came in the spring of 1977. Nilsen says it involved his first exposure to 'death and disturbing bereavement'; an odd statement after his experiences with his grandfather, Aden and the police morgue. This story actually involved Bleep's puppies, after she'd become pregnant by one of the neighbour's dogs. One night, Nilsen went down to the off-licence to buy some rum and asked Twinkle to look after them. When he returned, two of the pups had drowned in the garden pond.

Nilsen was livid. He started to think about ways of getting rid of his, now unwanted, flatmate. Two weeks later however, Gallichan, unprompted, met an antiques dealer and moved with him to the West Country. Nilsen doesn't make a great deal of the passing of Twinkle out of his life.

DCI Peter Jay, and defence psychiatrist Patrick Gallwey, however, considered the abrupt end to Nilsen's dreams of domesticity to be a catalytic event. For Jay, Nilsen couldn't bear the rejection of Gallichan leaving, and decided he now wanted companionship that he could control. For Dr Gallwey, a breakdown of that relationship triggered another phase of his personality disorder.

The accounts in *History of a Drowning Boy* of the next year-and-a-half years are increasingly desperate. In 1983, Nilsen told the police that he responded to Gallichan's departure by picking up a Swiss au pair girl in a bar in the West End, and reminding himself he could be bisexual. He no longer mentions this. Instead, Nilsen presents a catalogue of all the short flings and friendships he made over the summer of 1977 – Barry Pett, Stephen Barrier and Steve Martin all stayed for a while at Melrose Avenue. Steve Martin stayed the longest (about four months); Pett and Barrier stayed for a number of days. Nilsen wants the reader to believe he was perfectly able to partake normally in gay culture, but that it was lonely and fragmented. Instead, the reader is left feeling uneasy about what was clearly happening within him and fearful of what he might do next.

In 1978, Nilsen met Martyn Hunter-Craig, a young man who had recently moved to London and changed his name from Martin Tucker to mark this new chapter in his life. Now, in a big city, he wanted to start again.

Home had previously been Exeter in Devon, where he says his parents had a tumultuous relationship, often arguing, separating and reuniting. As he reached puberty, Hunter-Craig was diagnosed as having emotional problems and was sent to a special school. He always seemed lost in a dream world and there were also suspicions over his sexuality. He told me: 'I wasn't camp or outrageous as a teenager. I was quite withdrawn. I didn't like it; I didn't want to be that way. I was made to feel quite dirty about it. I've had that hang-up ever since … I think I feel wretched and dirty about it. I don't like it but that's the way it is. I can do nothing about it, can I?'

Hunter-Craig had been in London for some months before meeting Nilsen, but he's not quite sure how many. He found odd bits of casual work and, when it was hard to come by, he would supplement it, where necessary, by sleeping with men for money. Hunter-Craig thinks he met Nilsen around Easter time in 1978; he was nearly 18. Nilsen approached him in an amusement arcade in Leicester Square and struck up a friendly, light-hearted conversation. He looked smart in his beige suit and, without his glasses, his 'sincere' brown eyes were clearly visible.

Hunter-Craig told me: 'We went back to Melrose Avenue and, between then and the time I saw him just before the arrest, I would go there every couple of months or so … definitely a few times a year. I would stay for a couple of days when I needed somewhere to stay. It was very awkward in those days if you were on Social Security. You couldn't book in anywhere, unless it was a hostel, because of the delay getting the cheque from the DHSS. My work was casual. If I wasn't working, I would see who I knew might be able to put me up. From the beginning, he said, "If you need somewhere to stay, please come back".'

Journalists have been unable to agree on Hunter-Craig's testimony. He has appeared on several documentaries but, after the trial, some writers were cautious of him. Ex-*News of the World* journalist John Lisners wrote: 'Men [like Hunter-Craig] are social misfits ... strange, emotionally-battered young people ... Why was Nilsen attracted to people like this? Why did the apparently respectable, well-groomed civil servant with a flair for politics invite a self-confessed prostitute who lived in a fantasy world back to his flat?'

Other journalists just seemed to dislike him. Douglas Bence, from the *Daily Mirror*, wrote: 'Nilsen had said to him, "Come to bed." Cash changed hands next morning and the impoverished prostitute found he had a free season ticket to a gay bedsitter.'

When I asked Nilsen directly about his relationship with Hunter-Craig, he answered that he had known him but only casually. And yet Hunter-Craig's DHSS card was one of the items that police found in Nilsen's flat. He also shows detailed knowledge of both flats that Nilsen had lived in. Ultimately, Hunter-Craig's credibility rests on personal judgement.

I traced Hunter-Craig in the summer of 2010. He was living in a council flat in North London. I put a note through his letter box and he replied by ringing the number I'd left. After that, we met twice in nearby pubs. From the old newspaper cuttings I had seen, I was expecting a rangy, wild-looking fellow. When I first I met him in a beer garden near the Heath, he was now stocky and nervous. His voice was soft and he complained of suffering from panic attacks. When I asked him what he'd like to drink, he explained he was trying not to drink at that moment. Although he hadn't been a drinker during the time he'd known Nilsen, he'd made up for it later, apparently. As he rolled his cigarettes, I could see that his fingers were yellow with nicotine stains.

They also shook as he spoke. Although clearly a damaged person, Hunter-Craig also seemed to me to be essentially quite gentle. I sensed he was working hard to keep himself together. He told me he was being treated for his anxiety in a local medical centre and had also been taken on with some paid work there. Most of what Hunter-Craig told me rang true. Sometimes, and often quite obviously, he would exaggerate his knowledge of something or someone. But on the important facts, he was consistent and I found myself generally satisfied that the details he provided of Nilsen during the murder years were largely accurate.

He told me that they had had a brief physical relationship and described what it had been like. 'He was very stiff. I remember saying at the time – although now it seems awful – I said it's like having a relationship with a dead body. He laughed. Well, it wasn't that funny. I said, "I wish you could be a bit more like that when you're doing something." He was passive. Many times you would just lay there. I would say, "Well, this isn't much fun, is it? Are you going to move your legs a little bit?"'

On another couple of occasions, sexual contact was light. 'It was just a bit of fumbling. He'd get naked and then fall asleep. Des wasn't really gay in the sense of relationships. He couldn't really be physically intimate, if for no other reason that he was usually so out of it.'

But Hunter-Craig feels that, as far as he was concerned, Nilsen mainly wanted companionship, and not a sexual relationship. He says Nilsen even suggested he move in. The memories Hunter-Craig relayed to me were a mixed collection of impressions and episodes. While talking, he would frequently look down with a pained expression.

Nilsen's constant playing of classical and sophisticated pop music – material which 'really turned Des on' – particularly struck Hunter-Craig being, as it was, so different from the music most of his friends listened to. Nilsen's favourites were Rick Wakeman, Mike Oldfield, Elgar, Mahler and Aaron Copeland. If there was a Western on TV, he says that Nilsen would insist they watch it, even though he knew they bored his friend. When commenting on people in the news, he remembered that Des admired strong people, even though he wanted to be with weaker types.

In general, however, Hunter-Craig found Nilsen to be a moderately kind and interesting person. Otherwise, he says, he wouldn't have wanted them to be friends. He does, however, remember Nilsen often provoking arguments for fun; sometimes he was just rude. Hunter-Craig says he didn't mind when Nilsen referred to him as 'Skip', short for Skipper, meaning someone who hung around the docks, but hated it when he refer to him as 'she'. In these spats, Hunter-Craig says he would always give as good as he got. He thinks Nilsen liked that.

Despite Nilsen's interest in film, they would rarely actually go to the cinema, which Hunter-Craig thinks was partly because you couldn't drink in them, and Des always wanted to get drunk. So for entertainment they would either watch TV or go out to north London or Soho pubs. When in company, Hunter-Craig remembers Nilsen being shy and feeling self-consciously like a bore until the moment that, quite suddenly, the alcohol started to work. Then confidence flooded in. After this point, if Nilsen sensed that people were muttering about him, he would become furiously angry. In the taxi or Tube back home, he would explode into a rage. 'It was never to their faces,' Hunter Craig recalls, 'always behind their backs. He would usually say that he was too intellectual for them.'

Back at the flat, Nilsen was fascinated to hear about Hunter-Craig's mother. How did *she* accept his homosexuality, he would ask? The question would be asked so he could make the point that he didn't dare tell *his* mother. He knew how she would react. That was why he was so reluctant to go home for Christmas. That seemed odd to Hunter-Craig; from Nilsen's description and her letters, he didn't think she sounded too bad.

And surely, he thought, a trip home would be nice opportunity to get away from the shabby flat? But although Hunter-Craig remembers the flats as being rough, he says they were certainly not out of place for a bachelor in the late 1970s. 'Everyone was poor then, and people less house-proud.' Since leaving the Army, however, Nilsen had become very particular about his own personal hygiene, but he was unbothered about his living space. Hunter-Craig describes the smells of the flats as being 'an extreme mustiness'. He remembers remarking to Nilsen in Cranley Gardens, 'Des, what is it about that smell? It seems to follow you around.'

7

WHITEMOOR

'The bodies have gone, everything is gone, there's nothing left, but I still feel in a spiritual communion with these people.'
DENNIS NILSEN, IN A CHANNEL 4 INTERVIEW

On Wednesday, 21 January 1993 at 8.00pm, six million viewers tuned in to Channel 4's *Viewpoint 1993: Murder in Mind* to see Dennis Nilsen, the country's most infamous serial killer, speak. Anyone looking for a ghoulish encounter would not have been disappointed. Dressed in a well-fitting prison-issue shirt, the 47-year-old Nilsen leant back in what looked like a supremely relaxed pose. Only the ashtray in front of him betrayed his nerves.

If members of the public thought it odd that Nilsen had been allowed such TV exposure, officials at the Home Office went into virtual meltdown. During the week leading up to transmission, government lawyers petitioned the High Court for an injunction to stop the documentary going out. Whatever permission had been given to the film-makers, they said, was based on misunderstandings. On the day before the broadcast was due, however, their lawyers stood on the steps of the Royal Courts of Justice and admitted defeat. There was nothing now that could be done to stop the documentary going ahead.

The footage of Nilsen was actually just a small part of an hour-long film on criminal profiling. It was just a clip of about four minutes, used as an example of how understanding killers might help to catch them. Forensic psychologist Paul Britton asked a number of questions off-camera. A close-up of Nilsen behind a table filled the screen. The first thing Britton asked him was how he disposed of the bodies. In a leisurely, schoolmasterly Scottish accent, Nilsen replied:

> *'The summer brought a smell problem. I asked myself what would cause this, and came to the conclusion it was the innards. I would pull up floorboards. I'd find it totally unpleasant. I'd get blinding drunk, and start dissection on the kitchen floor.'*

'But if you are going to dismember a body on the kitchen floor, what about the mess?'

> *'What mess? No, no, no … If I were to stab you now, there would be lots of blood. The heart is pumping away, there would be blood splattering all over the place. But funnily enough, in a dead body there's no blood spurts or anything like that. It congeals inside and forms part of the flesh. It's like anything in a butcher's shop. There's little or no blood.'*

The film then cut away from the prison to Brian Masters, who was filmed walking through university cloisters. The narrator explained about Masters' book and how, for years, he had continued to visited Nilsen. Then, facing the camera, Masters explained his theory of how the death of Nilsen's grandfather had caused Nilsen to associate love with death. He said that when Nilsen wore talcum powder in his mirror fantasies, he did so because he wanted to look dead. The video image then cut back to Nilsen:

'Making myself up to be dead has nothing to do with being dead. It's making myself up to be as different as possible to look like someone else. This first occasion you have this young man. You have bathed him. He is now me. He is now my body in the fantasies.'

'And so what would you do to him?'

'Carry him in – make him appear even better. I would have some Y-fronts in cellophane. In put that on him because it enhanced his appearance.'

'And then what?'

'I would undress him.'

'What would you do with the body? Would you leave it there on the floor wrapped up, or would you do other things with it?'

'The most exciting part of the little conundrum was when I lifted the body. When I carried it, it was an expression of my

*power to lift and carry and have control. And the dangling
element of limp limbs was an expression of his passivity. The
more passive he could be, the more powerful I was.'*

Whatever producer Mike Morley had had in mind when he
approached Brian Masters to help introduce him to Mr
Nilsen, he could hardly have hoped for a better performance.
Not only was Nilsen confident, relaxed and intelligent, he
also sounded superior. If Channel 4 had wanted to capture
footage of a real-life Hannibal Lecter, then that is exactly
what they got.

Their short, edited soundbites made Nilsen seem potent.
The man who later described the incident to me in letters,
however, simply appeared angry and petulant. He certainly
wasn't prepared to give Central TV, the production company
responsible for making the film, any sneaking regard for their
skill in achieving such a tricky interview. In a letter to me
about the interview, Nilsen recalls:

*The interview, recorded by two cameras, took one whole
day. I asked for no payment nor did I wish to know the
questions in advance. In the room were two men
introduced to me as cameramen, Paul Britton (who asked
the questions) and Mike Morley overseeing the whole
production. I had also loaned Britton Parts I and II (of the
autobiography) to help him with my background (I had a
job getting these back. He returned these eight months
later only when I wrote to Home Office HQ in
complaint). So the interview was 'in the can' and I
awaited the finished product.*

In January '93, the shit hit the proverbial fan. The then Home Secretary, Kenneth Clark, had found out about the project and, politically embarrassed, sought a High Court injunction to stop Central TV using any of the footage. The Home Office's case (all news to me) held that the taped interview had been conceived and made by and for the purposes of police training by ACPO (Association of Chief Police Officers) and approved as such by the Home Office. It was never meant for public broadcast, as was wrongly claimed.

So it seems that Morley acted as a front man in a deal with the immediate organisers, and in return he was promised use of some of the footage. As all my letters are censored, it is clear that all in authority at Albany knew full well what was being organised. It also transpired that these two 'cameramen' were, in fact, a Chief Superintendent and a Chief Inspector. The deception had been thorough.

In 2012, I asked Michael Morley in an email to tell me what he thought of a précis I had give him of Nilsen's recollections. He said he thought they were 'not completely accurate, not completely inaccurate either'. The film had initially been cleared, he told me, but authorisation had been removed at the last moment by the Home Office who failed to inform ACPO and the prison. As such, filming went ahead.

Nilsen still seethes over the incident. His indignation, however, is less directed at Morley – to whom he was grateful for the gift of a typewriter – than towards Britton, who had held on to the manuscript for so long. In his writings, he points out that Britton – generally thought of as the inspiration behind ITV's *Cracker* – was later widely criticised for his involvement in the arrest and then subsequent collapse of the case against Colin Stagg for the murder of Rachel Nickell on Wimbledon Common in 1992.

By the time *Murder in Mind* was aired, Nilsen had been moved from Albany Prison on the Isle of Wight to Whitemoor Prison near Peterborough. This brand-new facility had been constructed on the site of some old railway marshalling yards a couple of miles outside the town of March. It was a return to the old Victorian-style wing accommodation. Out, says Nilsen, were the 'hard-to-police' corridors, and in were open galleries.

Nilsen's VPU was housed within a Special Secure Unit situated at the one end of the compound. Nilsen describes the SSU as a 'prison within a prison', with wings A and B for 'vulnerable prisoners', and C and D for 'normal' prisoners. He says that there was a thriving underground economy – illegal alcohol, knives and cannabis were, apparently, commonplace, and everything from drugs to exotic love birds were available for sale. Those who had money were 'taxed' by minor gangsters. Life was noisy, too, with people shouting from their windows late into the night.

Nilsen says in his autobiography that he just wanted to get on with doing his time quietly: 'Most prisoners just wanted to do their bird and get the hell out of prison. But they were bullied by the gangsters whose philosophy was that of the loser who, in all his self-deluded insecurity, continues to believe he is a winner. The recidivist blames everyone for his failure in life other than himself. If we are to make any positive progress, we must address our own offending behaviour.'

As before, Nilsen's way of 'addressing his offending behaviour' was by throwing himself into the things he believed he was best at, including writing. In the spring of 1993, he turned his creative energies towards both his archive of personal autobiographical pieces, and to the number of regular correspondents he had. Some of these were 'fans', thrilled to be in dialogue with such a notorious criminal. But others, including criminologists, psychiatrists and sociologists, had sincere and legitimate, professional reasons to want to try to understand him.

In response to their questions, Nilsen would often try to contextualise his crimes. It was illogical, he would say, to demonise a criminal suffering from a psycho-sexual disorder any more than, for example, a terrorist. If anything, he felt, sex offenders were less culpable than other criminals, as their free will was compromised by a compulsive disorder. Nilsen thought the 'evil' actions of many of his neighbours were simply 'men succumbing to the pressures of their psychological predicament'. His reaction to the murder of a child killer a couple of cells down from him was that it was just 'another pointless killing to satisfy … the lust for revenge'.

In July 1993, Nilsen received a letter that particularly flattered his ego. It was from an aspiring author called Peter-Paul Hartnett. Hartnett had just begun writing *Call Me,* later to become a cult hit in certain gay circles. At the time, however, Hartnett was working as a special-needs teacher-cum-photographer. One subject that particularly interested him was that of isolation in gay urban culture. The early drafts of what would later become *Call Me* went by the title *A Nasty Piece of Work*. The book told the story of one man's trawl through the world of classified sex adverts. Hartnett's anti-hero, Liam, claims to be a serial killer and, in the final book, frequently makes references to Nilsen.

Hartnett first wrote to Nilsen after reading one of his letters reproduced in the *Evening Standard*. Nilsen had been asked by journalist Tim Barlass to comment on a gay serial killer operating around Earls Court. He would later be identified as Colin Ireland, but at the time he was known as the 'Gay Slayer'. It was believed his crimes might have been connected with Coleherne pub in Earls Court.

Nilsen had also been familiar with that pub. The words of his letter seemed to reveal him as being a bit of an expert on a certain twilight world. Hartnett wondered if this extreme personality might possibly become a sounding-board for his project. In the letter, he explained he was mainly interested in Nilsen's thoughts on isolation and Hartnett's writing, not on Nilsen's crimes. After a few letters, the two men decided that their conversations might be better conducted face to face.

The governor's office initially granted a one-off discretionary hour together. Nilsen describes the meeting in his book. He says he was thrilled to meet someone he considered so glamorous. Hartnett, aged 35, was tall, about Nilsen's height, with similar dark hair and a boyishly handsome face. Nilsen says, 'He looked really cool, and we hit it off as if we had been acquainted all our lives.' Later, after conducting a full background check, the prison authorities found unspecified reasons to decline further visiting rights. Still, Hartnett and Nilsen kept up a correspondence that would last for years.

The recognition Nilsen received from Hartnett and Barlass made Nilsen feel like an amateur psychologist. Now that he felt he was coming up with valuable answers, he was increasingly keen to tell anyone who cared to ask that he had received very little analysis of his own condition. In 1993, however, the prisoner was persuaded to take part in the country's new Sex Offender Treatment Programme – one of the world's first. Pilot projects had been judged a success and now the SOTP was being rolled out across the country. The scheme was underpinned by the principles of Cognitive Behavioural Therapy (CBT).

CBT is a process of intensive therapy designed to alter how people think and behave. Today, it is widely used to treat everything from depression to paedophilia. It is a 'talking therapy' but, unlike psychotherapy, CBT concentrates on practical techniques to modify attitudes and behaviour. Typically, sex offender patients on such courses will be required to work their way through folder upon folder of worksheets. They will question their sexual preoccupations, impulsiveness and emotional control. Afterwards, a series of exercises will be prescribed to change the way the subject thinks and acts. Where possible, these might then be tested with lie detectors or other measuring tools.

The therapy, however, is heavily reliant on motivation and co-operation. Patients really have to want to change and work hard for it. Nilsen soon decided that the programme was not telling him anything he hadn't already worked out for himself. He hardly mentions the course in his autobiography. Elsewhere, in essays and letters, what he has to say is disparaging. In his essay entitled 'Anatomy of an Official Conclusion', he says: 'I learned nothing new from this SOTP which I had not learned from myself years before.'

Part of this attitude was down to Nilsen's natural antipathy towards psychology and authority. But it was also because, after several years of self-analysis, the serial killer believed he now possessed the ability to unravel his own psychology. Underpinning his examination was a theoretical framework he had come up with and which he called the 'Psychograph'. This was a term that had been used previously by phrenologists and handwriting experts to describe a graphical representation of mental attributes. For Nilsen, however, the psychograph is simply the mental map that early experiences leave as their legacy for the adult.

Nilsen didn't just apply the concept of the psychograph to himself. He started to use his theories as a way of describing the workings of other killers. One was Jeffrey Dahmer, about whom Brian Masters was in the process of finishing a book. On the surface, Dahmer's crimes, around Milwaukee in the USA, were carbon copies of Nilsen's. He was another gay loner, who brought men back and killed them in perversely 'affectionate' ways. Nilsen, however, doesn't like the comparisons that many have made. His analysis of Dahmer is full of quibbles that any similarities between them are superficial. He wants it known he didn't keep trophies, or regularly take photographs, or have desire to eat any human flesh.

Nilsen also pours scorn on Masters' book, *The Shrine of Jeffrey Dahmer*. He writes in *History of a Drowning Boy*: 'I certainly got no clearer recognition of Dahmer the man from reading it. Dahmer's aberrations were sculpted in society's response to his malforming "psychograph", which trapped him in an impersonal fantasy life. His genetic uniqueness had succumbed to the battering of a lack of psychological nourishment. In early years, he had become so removed from tactile and emotional contact with his fellow creatures that his condition became ingrained by volition of combined circumstances acting throughout his life.'

An incident from Master's promotion of his book on Jeffrey Dahmer proved the catalyst to end the ongoing contact between killer and author. In May 1994, Nicky Campbell from BBC Radio 1 interviewed Masters about his unusual relationship with serial killers. Towards the end of the interview, the conversation moved from Dahmer to Nilsen.

Nilsen doesn't say *exactly* what it was that he objected to so much – now, however, that was almost beside the point. More than anything, Nilsen was incensed at the way Masters had taken 'possession' of his life story. He mentions feeling a surge of annoyance about being what he calls 'Masters' commodity'. Now, he felt, was the time to terminate their strange relationship. He did it with a phone call.

Despite being a Category A prisoner, Nilsen was allowed to use a phonecard. Whereas now prisoners may only call people on approved lists through an operator, in those days, Nilsen says, prisoners allowed to use the phone could call straight out. Nilsen's first telephone call in 11 years was to the Garrick Club in London where Brian Masters was a member. When he was put through to a bar steward he asked him to find the author and say 'Des' was on the phone. Masters was chatting with actors Keith Waterhouse and Rodney Bewes. When the steward told him who was calling, Masters nearly spilled his drink, fearful that Nilsen might have escaped. Nilsen appears to have enjoyed making Masters uncomfortable and informed him that he wanted to end their ongoing relationship. Masters told me that this 'came as a relief'.

In 1994, Nilsen had been a convicted prisoner for just over 10 years. He may have no longer had any contact with his family nor Brian Masters, but he did have Jonny Marling and other correspondents. Moreover, despite frequent disagreements with the authorities, he knew if he behaved himself, theoretically, after another 15 years he would have been eligible to apply for parole.

In the back of Nilsen's mind was always the thought that one day he might be able to taste freedom. Any such flickers of optimism, however, were extinguished in the summer of 1994 when rumours spread about a change in the law that was going to allow the Home Secretary to set 'whole-life tariffs'. Previously, all sentence-setting was the preserve of judges. But in December 1994, Michael Howard, the Conservative Party's Home Secretary, drew up his list of those who would be subject to the principle of 'life meaning life'.

The passage in *History of a Drowning Boy* that deals with this is full of bravado. Nilsen proudly informs readers that his reaction to seeing his name there was stoic. He apparently doesn't want people to think his emotions could be so easily affected by acts of others. More revealing about his psychology, however, may be how he describes reactions to the only woman on the list, the Moors Murderer, Myra Hindley. Nilsen comments on the public perception of her, and the feelings of her victims. His words show a disturbing perspective: 'It also seems that some relatives of the cruelly murdered children have themselves been contaminated by perpetual active hatred of the hated object. Hate is not a very healthy foundation on which to build anyone's life. It's a sad indictment of the progress of the human spirit when the relative of a victim can announce, "Hate is all I have".'

Even though Nilsen's words are grotesquely offensive, it is likely he isn't really thinking about Hindley's victims at all. By condemning the 'hate' he sees directed at Hindley, Nilsen implies that he feels any hatred similarly directed at him is also unfair. Throughout his writing, Nilsen frequently talks about other killers in terms that sound like a projection of feelings about his own case that he has difficulty approaching directly. Many years later, for instance, he observes that the Soham murderer, Ian Huntley, may have been far more ashamed that he could be aroused by two small girls than he was about killing them. And Nilsen says that Huntley, Brady and Hindley – in fact, most multiple murderers – could only kill because they were totally devoid of empathy for their victims. Interestingly, Nilsen may not have been forming this opinion without some first-hand evidence – in 1999, the *Daily Star* reported that Nilsen had had some correspondence with Ian Brady.

After discussing Hindley and the other killers on the 'whole-life tariff' list, Nilsen ends with a declaration of how in tune with morality he feels he has again become. He seems suddenly uncomfortable about how his previous words might be perceived: 'Personally, I will not be pleading for release in my own case because the pain my actions have caused will only terminate with the deaths of the sufferers. When the pain of life touches me, I force myself to think of the pain of my victims (including relatives) and that brings me back to learning how insignificant my suffering is.'

Although Nilsen has never appealed his sentence, in 1992 and 1993 he started thinking about it. Among working drafts for *History of a Drowning Boy* are some scribbled notes entitled 'Appeal Papers'. There were no thought-through plans of action, but he did devote a number of sheets of A4 to discussing – seemingly just to himself – how he exaggerated his confessions at the time of his arrest under what he says was pressure from Jay and Chambers at Hornsey Police Station. He then speculates as to whether, by bringing this to the attention of a court, he might persuade them to reduce his sentence to manslaughter.

Such musings, however, were short-lived. Ironically, just at the time he was thinking about whether an appeal might ever be possible, his descriptions of life sound like the words of a man who was becoming comfortably institutionalised. Indeed, throughout 1994, Nilsen's life sounds more like a man at college than a Category A prisoner. He describes an almost never-ending series of hobbies and extra-curricular activities. Nilsen says he contributed a column to a magazine for inmates called *The Insider*, under the humorous moniker 'Nilsen, The Pink Panther' (as distinct from Donald Nielson, The Black Panther).

There were also regular contributions to a small circulation adult comic called *Bozo*, described as the 'the mad uncle of *Viz*'. Elsewhere, he acted in a play, John Godber's *Up 'n' Under*. Nilsen's aspirations as a visual artist were satisfied when his friend Jonny Marling sent in a large canvas. The result was a large oil painting-cum-collage called 'Bacardi Sunrise' which included a cut-out photograph of a naked youth.

Marling had now been a regular visitor for some years. When a visit wasn't possible, they would sometimes exchange tape recordings. Nilsen would send recordings that showed progress with his new favourite hobby – writing music on his electronic keyboard. His rudimentary musical doodles were given grand names like 'Symphonic Suite', and 'Nilsen's Prelude'.

The relaxed atmosphere abruptly changed on 9 September 1994. Life at Whitemoor was turned upside down in the prison when six IRA prisoners from the Special Secure Unit escaped. When they were apprehended, a pistol was retrieved; it had been used to shoot a dog handler. Semtex was discovered in their property.

The authorities reacted to the breach with a massive clampdown. Special searches were conducted on every prisoner. In Nilsen's room, the guards found copies of two soft-core gay magazines, *Vulcan* and *Him*, that Nilsen enjoyed. He was livid. 'The establishment reeked of active homophobia,' he moaned, adding, 'Their attitude had not changed since Wakefield in the mid-80s.'

Some years later, stories about Nilsen's belief that gay pornography in prison was an equalities issue would become national news. In April 1995, however, the *Daily Mirror* felt they had better stories to run. They printed a three-part series. First was a story about Nilsen's grief over a dead budgie; then they showed photographs taken by warders in Nilsen's cell on a disposable camera sent in by Marling; finally, they published a long piece about a pilot scheme in Albany that had included Nilsen in its testing procedures. It involved the deployment of a Penile Plesythmograph (PPG) machine which was used as part of the Sex Offender Treatment Programme. The *Mirror*'s story was headed '250 JAIL PHOTOGRAPHS TURNED ME ON TO GIRLS'.

The PPG technology was not originally intended to be used on sex offenders. It was pioneered by the Czechoslovakian military in the 1950s to ascertain whether conscripts who claimed to be homosexual to avoid national service really were what they claimed to be. The device works by attaching two bands on the body: a strain-gauge on the penis to measure engorgement, and a cuff on the finger to measure sweat. A series of images are then shown to the patient to determine the trigger of sexual arousal. The images include controls – images of 'appropriate' sexuality – and scenes depicting 'deviant' interest. Along with polygraphs, or lie detectors, the PPG is considered an extremely important tool for offender rehabilitation.

The *Daily Mirror* reported that while the tests were being set up, Nilsen had quipped, 'I suppose I'll have to pay you for this.' Once completed, he complained, 'You should be paying me for this – it's rubbish.' When the results came back, Nilsen mocks them by saying that they were so off target they indicated he was primarily attracted to middle-aged women. As for the pictures intended to arouse paedophiles, he said they were 'so boring I couldn't concentrate'.

Nilsen simply wasn't prepared to enter into the spirit of the programme. But still, in *History of a Drowning Boy*, where Nilsen talks about the PPG machine, his observation are humorous and, probably, perceptive. His says that while the images were presented to him, his mind was wandering off. If his fingers were sweating, he tells his would-be readers, it was probably because he needed a cigarette. He wondered if other subjects simply became turned on by having a female psychiatrist ordering them to drop their trousers before placing a cuff on their penis.

Nilsen had considered the PPG machine to be the stuff of fiction, and not even particularly good material. Still, such experiences and, no doubt, also stories he would hear from fellow cons, contributed to an idea that he might try to write fiction himself. Around this time, he had heard that his pen-pal P-P Hartnett had given up his day-job teaching to become a full-time writer. How hard, he wondered, could it be?

What Nilsen started to write was, quite incredibly, the premise for a serial-killer movie. It involved a fashion photographer called Sed Neslin. He owned an old Securicor van, into which he had fitted a lever from the cab which could divert exhaust gases to the back. In spring and summer, he would go and cruise up and down motorways looking for hitch-hikers, both male and female teenagers, whom he could lure with promises of taking modelling pictures. He would bundle old junk on to the passenger seat, so he could have an excuse that it was essential to travel in the back. The cargo area of the van was sound-proofed against screams, and whatever sounds might have still penetrated were blocked out by tapes he would play of 'The Laughing Policeman' and 'My Old Man's a Dustman'. At his home, Neslin has a studio in his basement with a preparation table in the middle, with vices to hold bodies and cosmetics to apply to them. He photographs the bodies in all kinds of poses before packing them into his freezer.

'Cynics,' Nilsen writes, in apparent ignorance of how utterly appalling his story is, 'will say he [Nilsen] is planning his next crime.' Nilsen was now, however, thinking of himself as much as a writer as a murderer, and he was encouraged to do so by others. He would soon even see his name appear alongside Edgar Allan Poe, P D James, Truman Capote and Norman Mailer when Ruth Rendell published an excerpt of his essay, 'The Psychograph', in an anthology she had edited. It was on the subject of why people murder and was called *The Reason Why: An Anthology of the Murderous Mind* (1996).

In the summer of 1996, the former television newscaster Gordon Honeycombe rekindled an earlier interest in writing a study on Nilsen's crimes. Honeycombe had been a familiar figure to British audiences first from 1965–77 as an ITN newscaster. From 1984–89, the 6ft-4in Cornishman presented the news bulletins on ITV's new breakfast show, *TV-am*. On screen, with his prominent receding hairline, he looked authoritative, if slightly stern. Off camera, he was a hearty character with a successful sideline as an author. One of his most successful books had been about Scotland Yard's Crime Museum, being published just before Nilsen's arrest. In April 1983, Honeycombe wrote to Nilsen suggesting that he might consider supplying him with information to help him write a study on the case. Nilsen asked his solicitor Ronald Moss to reply that he would rather have Masters write about the case.

After leaving *TV-am* in 1989, Honeycombe retired to Australia, and would occasionally return to the UK to visit friends. In September 1995, a chance conversation in a London pub led to him discovering that one of Nilsen's surviving victims, a Scotsman called Douglas Stewart, was living nearby. Now he saw another opportunity to deal with the subject. Apparently, Stewart wanted to talk. Honeycombe had also read about Carl Stottor's letters to Nilsen from an article in the *Observer* newspaper. The author wondered if there might be enough material available to tell the Nilsen story from the victim's perspective.

When Honeycombe met Stewart, however, he found him odd. The young Scotsman told a far-fetched story about Nilsen having an accomplice. Even though it seemed outlandish, Honeycombe decided to follow this up on his next trip. He also wondered if Nilsen himself might co-operate in his project. Back in Australia, Honeycombe wrote to Nilsen reminding him how, in 1983, he had written to him with a proposal to write about the case. Then he told of his meeting with Stewart and explained the rationale behind his 'victims' book. In the letter, Honeycombe also made a suggestion that Nilsen might consider contributing his own thoughts and memories.

Nilsen replied with a long letter. He said he would be happy to contribute, but warned that Honeycombe might find Stewart untrustworthy. It seemed very odd to the author that someone might want to volunteer such judgements about someone they'd tried to kill. In the end, however, Stewart did indeed prove unreliable – or, at least, unavailable. When Honeycombe tried to reach him again, he had disappeared.

Now that Honeycombe was in touch with Nilsen himself, and he seemed prepared to talk, he started to wonder if he might actually use the killer's confessions as the starting point for a project that would look at the case from all sides. If Nilsen would co-operate, Honeycombe thought, he could start by looking at how Nilsen remembered events and then fill in the other parts of the story with later research. He wrote to Nilsen with a series of questions.

The prisoner responded to each point in turn. Above all, he said he wanted to make it clear he didn't think Masters' book was satisfactory, and he wanted to put the record straight. There was no need, however, for him and Honeycombe to embark on a lengthy autobiographical correspondence about his life as he was, in fact, already writing a book.

This presented a potential problem. If Nilsen was writing a book, Honeycombe was sure he would be doing things in his own, inevitably unreliable, way. But he remained undeterred. He was sure if he could persuade Nilsen to let him use his memoirs to form the backbone of a book, then he would be able to balance his words with the testimony of others.

Another letter was dispatched to Nilsen saying he could be able to help with a publisher but *only* if Nilsen relinquished any idea of editorial control. Honeycombe pressed on him the need for this to be a serious, credible study, not a volume of a serial killer's propaganda. Honeycombe emphasised how it was imperative to include statements from people who had opposing perspectives.

Nilsen seemed to agree with these suggestions. He even volunteered a suggestion for what he might like to do with his royalties – he wanted them offered to a victim's charity. The manner in which Nilsen expressed it, however, betrayed signs of his pathological ego: 'I would never exploit revelations in my own life for personal financial gain. Now that would be immoral,' he said. He then speculated whether, with film rights, his royalties might amount to half a million pounds.

Within months, Nilsen completed two more volumes of memoirs. But by the spring of 1996, Honeycombe's publisher had now decided the project was too controversial for them. He told Nilsen not to worry, as he still had others in mind, and to make sure the serial killer didn't go cold on him, he kept writing from Australia. Soon, however, he started noticing a difference in Nilsen's letters. Direct replies to questions were avoided and increasingly replaced by Nilsen deriding the prison system or emphasising his achievements.

Honeycombe decided he might get further by talking to Nilsen directly. On his next trip back, in July 1996, he asked for a visiting order to be submitted. In response, he was granted a two-hour session. Honeycombe later told me that the first thing that struck him on arriving at Whitemoor was how incredibly tight the security was. Even tea and coffee could only be bought with plastic tokens.

Honeycombe said he bought a cup of tea and sat down. The visitors' room was like a school hall. Despite the post-IRA escape atmosphere, the warders he spoke to recognised him from his TV work and were chatty and friendly. They also appeared to be slightly proud of their high-profile prisoner. When Nilsen finally arrived, he seemed taller than he had imagined. His manner was confident, and educated. But with the thick glasses, grey hair, bad teeth and pale skin his general appearance was 'somewhat like a seedy academic'.

Nilsen spoke in a jovial, slightly bombastic manner. But at several points in the conversation, Honeycombe told me he couldn't help looking down at Nilsen's thin, white and peculiarly shaven hands that had robbed his victims of their lives. 'How can I trust this man enough to work with him?' he wondered. He was also curious about this friend, Jonny Marling, to whom Nilsen constantly referred.

Nilsen had now apparently developed a total and unquestioning faith in Marling. Just as Nilsen had wanted to offer up everything to Masters during the high point in their relationship, so Nilsen now sought to entrust everything to this new friend. All of his writing was sent straight to Marling's lock-up in Bath. And so, after seeing Nilsen in prison, Honeycombe immediately scheduled a meeting at Marling's home.

When Marling opened the door of his suburban home, Honeycombe was immediately struck by the normality of his married life. Marling was 29, with a pleasant, well-spoken manner. He had two daughters and ran a successful business.

And yet he also had a garage full of Nilsen's writing and correspondence. After the pleasantries were over, Marling went through the boxes on the kitchen table.

Looking through all the letters sent to Nilsen, Honeycombe noticed many of these 'admirers' included photographs of themselves. Many of these, Honeycombe noticed, looked just like Nilsen himself. After about an hour going through the letters, Honeycombe asked if he could see the manuscript itself. But now there was a problem; Des, it seemed, had actually placed it in the hands of a solicitor for safe keeping. And it wouldn't be easy to get access.

Marling explained why. After sending the manuscript to the solicitor's – Blakemore's of Stratford-upon-Avon – one of the firm's partners had become nervous about the extent to which they could legally act as an intermediary. They had decided to go to a QC for clarification. This resulted in a bill of £3,000. Honeycombe didn't want to pay it, and so, Parts II, III and IV of Nilsen's memoirs stayed in the solicitor's safe until 1998 when Marling came up with the money. Honeycombe returned to Australia.

One section of the book, however – 'Orientation in Me', Nilsen's so-called 'sexual history' – was waiting for him when he got back. This volume had been written separately from the rest of the book and Nilsen had managed to have it sent out independently. Honeycombe decided to start on this and deal with the gaps in Nilsen's life separately. But before he started investing any more of his own time in the project, he wanted to clarify in writing that Nilsen was unambiguously in agreement with what they were doing. Despite Nilsen's reasonable manner, he didn't trust him one bit. He told me he felt that he was being manipulated, and that Nilsen sought to destabilise him by not answering his questions.

Honeycombe's fears that Nilsen was playing some kind of 'power game' were soon confirmed. Nilsen now denied ever having been aware of any plans for the book to include other people's opinions. This was – unequivocally – to be '*his autobiography*' he said. Honeycombe says, 'As with others before, like Brian Masters, and most of his correspondents, Nilsen lost interest and dumped me.'

Nilsen, however, was undeterred by the setback. He wrote to P-P Hartnett – now an established author – and asked if he might help edit the book. Hartnett agreed. But when Nilsen started to try to formalise this arrangement, he discovered that the prison authorities, who had previously seemed uninterested in what he was doing, were now well aware of the nature of the manuscript and wanted to prevent him progressing with it. Nilsen recalled in a letter to me, '[The Home Office imposed] a ban on all discussion of the project between me and P-P. Letters were stopped and sent back to him (contracts etc). I was also informed that no draft of the MS would be allowed into prison and that I would never be allowed to see or read the published book.'

There was still nothing, however, to stop the existing drafts being published. Furthermore, Nilsen felt he and Hartnett could make some progress through coded letters and by reading out extracts on audio cassettes. He told Hartnett he was happy for him to try to start generating interest. This led, in 1998, to a piece appearing in the *Daily Mirror* with the headline 'EX-TEACHER WHO WANTS £30,000 FOR KILLER NILSEN'S SICK MEMOIRS'. This sum was the amount they claimed Hartnett wanted for the serialisation rights. There was also talk of a film. Hartnett was quoted as saying, 'It is sensational. It is not the rantings of a madman. It is well written. Your readers will be astounded.'

Nilsen, however, felt that even if someone was prepared to publish the book as it was, the book was still far from satisfactory. And he had also now lost faith in Harnett's ability to complete the project. He complained to me that, based on what he had been able to see, Hartnett's 'voice and style intrude too much'. On top of that, the attention the news stories had brought on him had again resulted in copy of the gay pornography magazine *Vulcan* to be confiscated along with a 'sexy art book' by Pierre and Gilles. This had made him furious.

It was the *Daily Mirror* article about Hartnett and the '£30,000' autobiography that prompted my first letter to Nilsen. Having recently completed a journalism diploma, I was in the habit of scouring the news for stories to investigate. I had previously read *Killing for Company*. Between that and what I had read in the newspaper, I found the idea of him writing an autobiography intriguing. How could he or any publisher justify it? It wasn't just the offence it would cause, it was equally the prospect of him being deceptive. But for the purposes of a newspaper story, Nilsen's possible motives just made it all the more interesting. I decided to add him to my list of speculative letters that week.

Before writing, I thought hard about how to approach him. Gitta Sereny's book on Mary Bell had just been released – Bell had killed children when still a child herself – and rather come straight out and interrogate him about *his* book, I decided to ask him what he thought of that one. A week later, I received a 16-page dissertation handwritten in thick, black Biro. The subject of Mary Bell had clearly struck a chord: 'The Mary Bell controversy,' he told me, 'is generated by a fear, on foundations of hypocrisy, by society which becomes deeply agitated when the spotlight of close examination falls upon itself and our own hallowed myths. History had dismissed the traumas of Mary Bell from its consciousness merely by placing her outside the realms of human experience, with the expedient use of the label "monster", and shelving her inside a penal institution. This method spared society from having to acknowledge their association with her name and saved them the bother of having to think too much of her actions as a human in a community. Justice was done and she was gone – out of sight and out of mind. Her voice is always the voice of others.'

Nilsen sounded like he was writing more about himself than Mary Bell. He seemed insistent that *his* voice was that of others. The subtext was that he wanted people to know he still existed and to hear it from him. Most importantly for me, at the time, was that he seemed prepared to give me a privileged insight into what he had to say. I started to ask around for a publication interested in a piece on Nilsen. Several were keen, but I needed more material. I wrote back to Whitemoor Prison. Over the next seven months, Nilsen wrote me nearly 30,000 words of autobiography, politics, poetry and chat.

At the outset, dealing with Nilsen felt less unnerving than I had feared. In the main, he seemed quite charming and eccentric. Despite his constant complaining, he was also interesting. It wasn't just his crimes and prison life he spoke about – he had well-considered cynical opinions on current affairs. He was also funny. 'Functioning under prison management isn't only punishing,' he once told me, 'it's embarrassing.'

Reading Nilsen's letters could also, quite literally, be educational. He was so keen to show off his learning, sometimes it seemed like he was copying things out of an encyclopaedia. He would quote people like Edward Gibbons and Henri Amiel. Sometimes, I wondered if this might also be because he was slightly autistic. If he spoke about a typewriter or cassette player, there would always be the exact make and model number. And he would also become a little vexed if I forgot to acknowledge the exact date of his last letter, as if you had broken a rule of protocol that was very important to him.

Nilsen's adherence to his etiquette meant he would always reply by return of post. And he never sent unsolicited letters; he thought that inappropriate. Sometimes, there seemed something almost quaint about exchanging letters in this way. I could often forget this was a man who had repeatedly killed. Despite his intensity, he seemed like many other fastidious, nerdy oddballs I'd known. He was fixated with details, and creating arguments that defended his world view. When I later saw his cartoons, drawings and tape recordings, it struck me that, if this had been the only side to his character, he might have made a reasonable schoolteacher.

When Nilsen spoke of his crimes, his lack of perspective was quite terrifying. He could talk about squeezing the life out of someone in one sentence and the confiscation of his spider plant in the next. His proclamations of remorse always felt like he was saying what he thought were the 'right things'.

He told me, 'Just because I do not make demonstrative expressions of remorse does not rule out that I can and do feel great personal remorse for the damage my actions have caused. Weeping and pain is a very personal circumstance not open to exhibition at official interviews. Remorse is not just saying it, it is doing it.'

Despite his protestations that he was living the most positive, constructive life he could through his hobbies, I remained unconvinced that Nilsen was actually doing anything that he didn't like. Soon, I started to notice that for all he said, he never actually seemed 'sad'. He neither seemed to want to shed tears nor listen to others. He wrote as if he felt he was a guru dispensing wisdom. This superior demeanour made me feel reluctant to challenge him. Later, I wondered if I was being manipulated or just being hesitant? I thought maybe I was frightened of whether he might be able do something unpleasant if I upset him. Maybe he had some nasty friends on the outside.

At the end of the year, I had a pile of letters but no real story. I started to wonder why exactly I was writing all these letters, and decided to stop.

It was several years before another newspaper article prompted me to write to Nilsen again. During that time, I would sometimes wonder who else wrote to Nilsen, and how he spoke to them. Later, when I saw examples, I discovered my correspondence was not atypical. He dispensed the same empty-sounding words to everyone, and had written Matthew Malekos an almost identical letter to one he had written me: 'If I had been really strong morally I should have called the police that morning I killed Stephen

Holmes. I did not and many others died as I clung selfishly to self-preservation and remained subservient to a selfish power of the ritual. So I am fully culpable for my results and that is that: I guess I will have to resist complaining about length of sentence.'

8
FROM FANTASY TO MURDER

*'In 1978, I entered a personal pit of imbalances which scored
10 out of 10, and this became unbearable to the point of acute
desperation. In the past, I had had always a couple of points in
my favour. Now I had nothing: I drank and became a
murderer to begin the cycle. More drinking at the despair
I was a murderer and more murders. It was a downward spiral. There was no one I had trust in to turn
to but a small dog who could offer no solutions.'*
DENNIS NILSEN, IN A LETTER TO THE AUTHOR

Dennis Nilsen's calm recollections of how he strangled up
to 15 men are horrific. Moreover, despite being true, they
are so stylised they barely seem real. The most graphic accounts
were written in 1983. Later confessions are, thankfully, more
about reasons than acts – in *History of a Drowning Boy* he
mainly directs the reader to things he has said previously for the
details. Still, those earlier words show how little he saw his
victims as real people. Fifteen young men were described
simply in terms of their appearance. Their deaths were written
about almost like fantasies. Among all the minutiae and florid
prose there is no believable sense of the physicality of killing,
nor mention of the terror in the victim's eyes.

Nilsen's first murder was the day before New Year's Eve 1978. He was now 33 and had spent Christmas alone with his dog. He told Masters that his loneliness had become 'a long, unbearable pain'. His manuscript underscores that disconnection to the world around him. It was the bitterly cold 'Winter of Discontent'; misery engulfed London. Sex fantasies, drinking and isolation had got the better of Dennis Nilsen. By the time New Years' Eve was looming, his self-pitying desolation was coming to a head. He sat at home drinking and listening to music. In a letter to me, he said: 'Man knows not what alienation is until he has experienced the severity of absolute detachment I was feeling on the morning of 30 December '78.'

That evening, he felt he had to get out of the house. It was a quiet day in town. People were either relaxing after Christmas or gearing up for the New Year celebrations. Only one pub near Melrose Avenue was full. It was the Cricklewood Arms on Cricklewood Broadway, known for its rough Republican Irish crowd. It was not the sort of place that Nilsen usually frequented. The same was true of the young man he met by the bar, but at least he was Irish. Nilsen hoped he might also be homosexually inclined.

Nilsen told police: 'He was much shorter than I was. About 5ft 6in. He was southern Irish and had short, dark-brown, curly hair. His hands were rough. At closing time he indicated to me that he had too far to travel. We went back to Melrose Avenue and started drinking. We had a damn good old drink and, later on, I remember thinking, "He'll probably be going soon – another ship passing in the night".

'The next morning, I had a corpse on my hands. He was

dead … I wanted company over the New Year. There was desperation for company. My tie was around his neck.'

Nilsen talks as if his actions took him totally by surprise; the facts suggest otherwise. We now know from *History of a Drowning Boy* that he had long been used to taking advantage of unconscious bodies and masturbating to scenarios that involved death. Furthermore, can we really believe he spontaneously came up with the method of strangulation using a tie? Surely, if he had strangled the boy without having ever imagined the scenario, he would have done so with his bare hands? Instead, he used the far more efficent and certain method of wrapping a tie aroud his neck and pulling with all his might.

Nilsen will never, however, allow any suggestion that his crimes were premeditated. Instead, he simply tells us that depression, alcohol and a deviant sex drive came together that night. In his pseudo-psychological language, murder then became 'a cruel medicine to sedate encroaching insanity'. He says 'fantasy exploded into reality', and that, 'loosened by alcohol', he lost all control. The explanations he gives are, nearly all, very hazy.

Comparing what he has written at different times helps fill in the picture. The description he gave at Hornsey Police Station was brief. But another account of the same event, this time written much later for Brian Masters' *Killing for Company*, is much more elaborate. It also gives a much clearer sense of how fantasy and the opportunity came together.

Nilsen says he 'snuggled up to him and put my arm around him. He was still fast asleep … I pulled the blanket off us and halfway down our bodies. He was on his side turned away from me. I ran my hand over him, exploring him. I remember thinking that because it was morning he would wake and leave me. I became extremely aroused and I could feel my heart pounding and I began to sweat. He was still sound asleep. I looked down on the floor where our clothes lay and my eyes fixed on my tie. I remember thinking that I wanted him to stay with me over the New Year whether he wanted to or not. I reached out and got the neck tie. I raised myself and slipped it on under his neck.'

Still, he is vague about what was so arousing. Was this a scene that he had recently used in masturbation? Or was it that he had really become physically excited at the prospect of attacking his victim? In *History of a Drowning Boy*, however, Nilsen does, finally, attempt a psychological explanation of the emotional subtext. After he got the youth back to the flat, he says he started to have flashbacks to the boy in the cabin from his adolescent dreams. Simultaneously, he both wanted that moment not to end, and for the body of the young man to be part of his 'old man' mirror fantasy. Specifically, he wanted to become the old man, and for the boy's body to represent himself. He describes his murder rituals as a 'dualism' and a 'perverted sort of mating' with himself: 'The whole conundrum is alive with Narcissusia [*sic*] – this almost total attachment to self. When eventually the body is put out of sight and changes into decay, it reappears as something new: i.e. putrefying dead meat to be disposed of. The paradox about my fantasy view of these bodies is that the primary aim while they were in use was to make them look as pure and alive as possible.'

In other words, he believes that when he obtained a body,

it was really a way of having sex with himself. And, as soon as that body started to decay, he no longer saw it as connected to the living person it had once been. It was something 'other' – an object to be disposed of.

It took 23 years for the 'Irish youth' to be identified as 14-year-old Stephen Holmes. Holmes was not a runaway, nor was there any sign he had had gay tendencies. On the contrary, he was popular and liked loud music and football. The night he disappeared, he had just been to see a local rock band. Full of rebellious energy, he may have dropped into the pub in Cricklewood on his way home to see if he could get served and to keep warm before getting the bus home. Just as seeing a band had seemed a grown-up thing to do, being in a bar with an adult would have flattered him. Holmes would also probably have soon become too intoxicated to make sensible judgements about whom he was talking to.

The boy's mother, Kathleen, a waitress, reported her son missing soon after his disappearance, and continued to campaign to find him until her death in 2002. With few good photographs of Stephen, she failed to make headway. Holmes' remaining relatives have found it too painful to talk about his death.

After killing Holmes, Nilsen washed his body and lay him down on his bed. The sexual possibilities of having him there were offset by the immediate shock of the situation. Nilsen's confessions, however, sound more confused than horrified. He was sure the police would soon turn up. And yet, instead of hiding the evidence, he wrapped the body in a curtain and went to bed for the rest of the day to sleep off his hangover.

The next day was New Year's Day. Now, with a clearer

head, Nilsen started to panic and tried to put the body under the floorboards. But rigor mortis had set in and it wouldn't fit.

He waited another day. Now the body was less stiff, so he pulled the boards up again. The cat, Deedee, got in there, and it took several minutes to coax her out. Nilsen was pleased, however, to see how wide the spaces were between the beams supporting the floorboards. Once removed, there was plenty of room to put the body in.

He ripped up Holmes' clothing and put it with his shoes into the dustbin. A week later, he wondered if the body had started to decompose. He disinterred it, and then stripped himself naked before taking the body up to the bathroom, washing and inspecting it. The body was still intact. He admired Holmes' corpse for a while, then he contemplated buying an electric carving knife to cut it into smaller pieces. After some moments, he dismissed the idea as ludicrous. Finally, he placed the body back under the floorboards where it stayed for a little over seven months.

It wasn't until 11 August 1979 that Nilsen decided to get rid of the remains. Still wrapped in the curtain, he placed the body on a large bonfire. The fences around the garden were about 6ft high, but the scene was still clearly visible from neighbours' windows. Nilsen didn't, however, go to any great lengths to hide the pyre. In various declarations of loneliness, he says he no longer believed anyone really cared what went on in his flat.

The most obvious psychological effect becoming a murderer had on Nilsen was simply to increase his general sense of depression. After the arrest, Nilsen would tell DCI Jay that it 'amazed' him that he had no tears for the victims. His later writings make references to his extreme unhappiness, but he says it was a private matter and didn't change his behaviour at work. It didn't stop him paying his bills, or writing letters to his mother. He did, however, do one thing to try to try to stop it happening again.

In the period of a little more than seven months between killing and burning Holmes, Nilsen made a concerted effort to reduce and change the pattern of his drinking. To begin with, he says he thought he must have committed the murder because he had been blind drunk and lost control. There is no particular reason to doubt that he really believed this – especially as he now went to some effort to change his behaviour. He didn't give up drinking altogether – he would see occasional friends or sometimes go for a drink after work – but he avoided drinking heavily in gay bars and inviting young men back.

Although Nilsen made modest efforts to avoid committing another murder, he had no interest in handing himself in. For four years, he says his main instinct was for what he called 'self-preservation'. Thoughts of suicide even came before walking into a police station. He couldn't see what purpose turning himself in would serve anyway. Surely it would be better, he reasoned, just to make sure he started to live a more productive life?

Nilsen's solution for how to live with himself was to 'become a workaholic', throwing himself into his trade union work at the civil service union, the CSPA. By the end of 1979, he had now been the Denmark Street Branch Secretary for over a year and, in meetings, Nilsen felt energised by the socialist idealists.

On 12 August 1979, after disposing of Holmes' body, Nilsen felt back in control. He started going back to the West End bars, getting drunk and talking to strangers. One Saturday in October, he met Andrew Ho, a young Chinese student. They met outside an arcade in Leicester Square near where Nilsen first met Hunter-Craig. After a couple of drinks in a pub, they returned to Melrose Avenue. They drank some more and then the young man initiated a conversation about bondage.

Nilsen claims Ho soon made it clear he wanted money, but that he wasn't interested in paying for sex. Another idea began to form in his mind; he told Ho to sit still while he bound his feet together. With his feet immobile, Nilsen went to his cupboard and produced a tie. Ho started to scream, and struggle. He broke loose, picked up his clothes and ran out of the house. Later, he called the police.

When they arrived at Nilsen's flat, he knew how to convince them that this had just been part and parcel of a lively homosexual encounter. In his memoirs, though, the confession is very casual: 'He was quite right – I did try to strangle him – but I was too sober to give it unbounded immoral force and he escaped the effort. Naturally, he didn't want to make a written statement or attend court.'

Despite the matter-of-fact way he talks about it, Nilsen claims to have been very concerned by the incident. Still, the shock wasn't enough to go make him abstain from alcohol again.

Much more alarming to him, though, seems to have been what happened just before Christmas – the murder of a young, bright, middle-class, apparently heterosexual tourist, with whom Nilsen had spent a friendly afternoon.

FROM FANTASY TO MURDER

The killing of Kenneth Ockendon was an anomaly within Nilsen's overall pattern of victims. Other than the fact he would not have been immediately missed, everything else about the murder was an apparent departure from the normal modus operandi. Not only was Ockendon close to his family but, during the afternoon they had spent together, he made Nilsen feel good about himself by being interested in him. Whether it was this or, simply, because he feels it is expected of him, Nilsen makes more of a show of being upset by this murder than any other.

Kenneth Ockendon was a young Canadian on holiday. His parents, Ken senior, and wife Audrey, however, originally came from Croydon. Kenneth junior was born in February 1956, and was 14 when the family emigrated to the Toronto suburb Burlington in Canada. Ockendon's father soon found a job as a janitor; his son trained to be a welder.

By the autumn of 1979, he had been saving for months for a three-month adventure revisiting childhood haunts and catching up with friends and relatives. In September 1979, when he landed at Heathrow he was a young-looking, slight 23-year-old with shoulder-length dark hair that betrayed his love of heavy rock music. This was the wildest thing about him. He drank and smoked in moderation, and his other main hobby was photography. Socially, he was polite and well mannered.

Ockendon's trip started with a visit to the Lake District with an old friend. He had plenty of money and made regular phone calls home. When he got down to London, he methodically ticked off all the relatives on his list. He was also in almost constant contact with his mother's brother, Gordon

Gillies. Then on Monday, 3 December, Kenneth Ockendon disappeared, having spent the previous night in a small hotel in London's shabby King's Cross area.

Ockendon called Uncle Gordon at about 3.00pm that day. He said that he wanted to go back to Canada for Christmas, and could he come over on Wednesday, 5 December to pick up some cash being kept safely for him. During their conversation, Uncle Gordon could hear voices and music in the background, and asked where he was. He replied it was the Princess Louise, an ornate Victorian pub that apparently had live jazz. There wasn't, however, a band playing until the evening. Ockendon was standing at the bar when Nilsen came over and started asking about his camera.

Ockendon's failure to pick up the money from his uncle was so out of character, Gordon made a mental note to bring it up with Kenneth's mother the next time they spoke. As Christmas approached, still no one had heard from Ken. The police were then called in. Foul play was soon suspected. Having paid for another night at the hotel in advance, it was clear he had intended to stay longer. Moreover, his property was still there, including a pub guide and a diary from which they were able to trace his various movements up to the day he disappeared.

The following February, Ockendon's parents flew into London. At a press conference, they declared they were, 'staying here as long as it takes to find Ken'. The police warned them to be prepared for the worst, but they refused to give up hope. Posters were circulated around the capital and the disappearance was featured in an episode of *Police 5*, which Nilsen later told detectives he saw. He doesn't, however, describe any sense of anguish at seeing the parents' TV appeal.

Nine months on, Ken and Audrey were still placing more advertisements in newspapers carrying financial rewards for information. As late as December 1982, on the third anniversary of his disappearance, fresh posters had been put up on notice boards in police stations across the capital.

In February 1983, a cigarette in hand, Dennis Nilsen told police what had happened to Kenneth Ockendon. He described how he had met him in the pub which he said was also popular with gay men. It was a day off for him. A remark Nilsen made about Ockendon's camera started the conversation but, soon, they also chatted about music and where Nilsen's sister lived in Toronto. At about 3.00pm, Nilsen suggested that he take the young man on a tour of London landmarks where he could get some nice photographs. They went down to Trafalgar Square, The Mall and over to the Houses of Parliament.

As it began to get dark, Nilsen again mentioned his large record collection. He persuaded him to come back to his flat, where they listened to Rick Wakeman, The Who's *Tommy*, and the Royal Philharmonic's *Hooked on Classics*. While Ockendon had the headphones on, Nilsen knocked up a quick ham, egg and chips. After they ate, they went to the off licence to get some rum and beer.

Then they settled in for the evening. Nilsen was thrilled by the young man's company and how he seemed to find him interesting. Ockendon had an open nature and was no doubt enjoying meeting someone new. He had become used to making quick friendships from the hostels and small hotels he had been staying in, and 'Des' seemed like someone whose company he would fondly remember at the end of the trip.

If there was a moment when Nilsen decided Ockendon represented a second opportunity to make a sex fantasy real, he doesn't say. He just told police it was about 1.00am that he found himself tightening the headphone cord around Ockendon's narrow neck. He was shouting, 'Let me listen to the music as well.'

Ockendon didn't struggle. Nilsen then quietened down the dog – 'Shut up, Bleep … this is fuck all to do with you!' – and he put her out. The headphone flex was untied and a Bacardi was poured. Then he stripped and washed the body and placed it in his bed. He poured himself more to drink and listened to all the records again. Finally, he went to bed and kissed and caressed the body. When he woke in the morning, he says he 'noticed' the person next to him was cold.

Ockendon was now what Nilsen calls a 'prop' in his fantasy. To satisfy the requirements of the fantasy, Nilsen needed to remove any reminder of who the person had once been. He wrapped all his victims' possessions in bin bags and put them out for the dustman. The body was placed in a cupboard, and off he went to work. At lunchtime, he bought a cheap Polaroid camera.

When he returned, he removed the body from the cupboard, lay it out on the bed, and used up his 15 instant prints, creating a permanent record of his acts. Then he got in bed and placed the naked, dead body on top of him. He says he watched TV in this position. He talked to the body, and cried in appreciation of its beauty. His behaviour was, in plain language, insane.

After the 'ritual' was over, his behaviour became more rational. The next day, he collected all the albums they had listened to together, took them out to the garden and smashed them with a spade.

Some days later, Nilsen showed a similarly extreme reaction towards the same music tracks that he'd listened to that night with Ken Ockendon. Nilsen was on the organisation committee for his office Christmas party, and had been largely responsible for organising and cooking for about 80 people. He had found such responsibility a huge honour and prepared very carefully, including making tapes of any music he felt might be appropriate. But he forgot that the tapes he had prepared included many tracks he had enjoyed with Ockendon, including *Hooked on Classics*. When the music came out of the speaker, he was shocked. His face turned white, he poured his drink away and went outside for air.

Once back in his flat, reality and fantasy again became blurred. Nilsen removed the body, sat it on a chair and played the music that he'd brought back from the party, while drinking himself into a stupor.

Nilsen's third victim was Martyn Duffey, born on 6 July 1963 in Birkenhead near Liverpool. He was murdered sometime between 13 and 19 May 1980, and was not yet 17. Duffey's parents, Roy and Patricia, had divorced a few years earlier. At 15, he left school only to find there were few unskilled jobs left in the Merseyside ship industry. He began to get into trouble, being caught stealing and threatening other boys. One day he walked out of the house, hitch-hiked to London and slept rough for a week. When he eventually turned up at the Soho Project, a homeless charity, they paid for him to return home.

Prior to his final disappearance, Duffey had been seen by a number of psychiatrists and social workers. He kept up a correspondence with one in particular. Despite his drug taking and casual gay sex, she helped him to complete a catering course and get a girlfriend. 'Above all else,' she warned, 'stay away from London.'

Duffy ignored this advice. When he met Nilsen, he was sleeping rough around Euston station. When he spoke to police, Nilsen remembered it was the day he had returned from a union conference in Southport but couldn't remember the precise date. He would have seen a trip to the station as an opportunity to look for the young runaways that hung around that area. Having just been up in Merseyside, he would also have had plenty to talk to Duffey about. Nilsen can't remember much about their conversation back at his flat, other than the fact that Duffey was extremely exhausted. After only had a couple of cans of beer, Duffey said he had to go to bed.

In *Killing for Company*, Nilsen says Duffey was lying on the top-bunk platform: 'I remember sitting astride him (his arms must have been trapped by the quilt). I strangled him with great force in the almost pitch darkness with just one side-light on underneath. As I sat on him, I could feel my bottom becoming wet. His urine had come through the bedding and my jeans.'

Nilsen then carried the body down from where he had strangled him. Duffey was still just alive. He took him to the kitchen, filled the sink and drowned him. The body was then moved to the bathroom. He stripped both himself and the dead youth and then sat in the bath with him. Then the body was hoisted on his shoulders and carried back up to the bed. In *History of a Drowning Boy*, Nilsen comments that it was the youngest-looking body he had seen. That was a turn-on.

Afterwards, Nilsen put the body in a cupboard and, another two days later, the floorboards came up again. In a perfectly rational act of covering up his tracks, Nilsen threw Duffey's chef's knives away, having first let them rust so they wouldn't attract attention (sloppily, he also forgot to throw all of them out). He also found a left-luggage tag in Duffey's pocket and went down to Euston to retrieve and dispose of the property – an old suitcase.

By the middle of 1980, Nilsen was becoming less emotional about being a murderer. He would later tell psychiatrists that seeing a fresh body now panicked him no more than going on patrol in Aden. But he has never spoken about what made him give in to his urges once he had picked someone up.

At Hornsey Police Station, he spoke of the killings as if they had simply happened without input from his conscious mind. 'I've killed people,' he said, 'but I can't understand why those people. There's no common factor ... when I voluntarily go out to drink, I don't have the intention at that time to do these things ... they're not fore-planned ... I seek company first, and hope everything will be all right.'

After 30 years of reflection, he hasn't got much further with understanding the mechanics of what happened on any of those fateful nights. Either that, or he doesn't want to say. The closest we get are a number of statements that imply that, when he was feeling low, seizing an opportunity to satisfy his sex ritual temporarily relieved him of his feeling of inadequacy.

Nilsen's vague analyses contrast with an internal prison report written in 2000. This attempted a slightly more clinical analysis of the psychological factors that enabled Nilsen to kill. The authors listed them as: (1) development of deviant sexual fantasies leading to enactment; (2) poor behavioural controls further disinhibited by alcohol; (3) breakdown in an intimate relationship; (4) emotional detachment employed as a maladaptive coping strategy; (5) callousness and lack of empathy.

The report, written for a probation review, annoyed Nilsen so much that he produced a very lengthy 'rebuttal' report of his own called 'Anatomy of an Official Conclusion', in which he downplays the idea of deviant sexual fantasising, and rejects the idea that he's 'compartmentalising' in a way that is different from every other member of society:

It is not the deviant sexual fantasy which leads to enactment, but the addiction to the ritual. A fantasy is a set of ideas in the mind. The ritual is no fantasy – it is real … The fantasy images themselves were not images of enacted violence … What was outrageously abnormal was how the images were translated into reality on the ground. What was callousness and lack of empathy was then only true within the trance of the ritual …

… Most people compartmentalise different areas of their lives. One separates one set of interests and relationships from other sets. A man may belong to a

football supporters' peer group that is distinct and separate
from his workplace peer group and from his family unit.
It's ... how we all function in the community ... the
notion of compartmentalisation (as) somehow special and
unusually directly related to my past offending is spurious.
Emotional detachment ... is an acquired trait or coping
strategy development.

This statement is not very clear. Nilsen's evasive language threatens to obscure the meaning. What he seems to be saying in the first passage is that he sees a distinction between his sex fantasies which, in themselves, were relatively benign, and his compulsion to act these fantasies out by acquiring 'passive bodies'. He accepts that the ritual was callous but thinks that it happened in a kind of 'trance' over which he had little control.

As for the aftermath of the killings, Nilsen thinks the way he dealt with the bodies was within the range of what a normal person might do when faced with an extraordinary set of circumstances. It did not, he thinks, represent a pathological detachment nor indicate there was anything inherently wrong with him.

Throughout 1980, Nilsen continue to function normally at work and in union activities, but he was now increasingly likely to murder at night. In August, Billy Sutherland, whom Nilsen met in a gay pub in Soho, became his next victim. He was a 25-year-old father of one and, allegedly, an occasional male prostitute.

Sutherland had grown up in a slum estate in the north of

Edinburgh, surrounded by drug dens. Six years before he met Nilsen, he moved into a flat with a girlfriend, Donna, who soon gave birth to their daughter. When the girl was three, he decided to move to London. Donna joined Billy for a while but soon missed home. When she returned, Billy stopped calling. It struck her as very out of character.

When reports of Nilsen's activities hit the news in 1983, Donna immediately felt this was the reason why he hadn't been in touch. She called Billy's father, who contacted the police. In Hornsey, the detectives showed a photograph to Nilsen. He nodded his head to indicate he had killed Sutherland. He couldn't remember much more, however, than the fact he had strangled him from the front with his bare hands.

Between August 1980 and September 1981, Dennis Nilsen murdered between five and eight young men. He attempted to murder at least one more – Douglas Stewart, the man whom Gordon Honeycombe had met in Soho. Nilsen's memory of this period is poor, but there's no reason to disbelieve the general pattern of behaviour described to the police. This would involve drinking and listening to music with the victim, followed by sudden, impulsive murder. Over the following few days, Nilsen would admire, masturbate over and talk to the body.

Nilsen's manuscript makes some additional confessions. He says that he would shave any body hair from the bodies to make them conform to his physical ideal. He elaborates on the thrill of dressing them up. Sometimes, he wished he'd had lipstick. He did have talcum powder and this he used to make them smell nicer and, ironically, to make them look more alive. When he picked up the limp bodies, he would become extremely aroused and have to masturbate.

When he talks about what he did with the dead bodies, he wonders again if this excitement at holding the dead, limp bodies derived from being carried and washed by his mother and grandmother. Nilsen, however, has no definitive explanation as to how these 'infantile connections' worked their way into his sexual composition.

He is much clearer about what he isn't than what he is. He is not a 'lust murderer', like Paul Kürten, the 'Vampire of Düsseldorf' to whom he was compared in *Killing for Company*. He says he never derived a direct, sexual thrill from the actual act of murder. Time and time again, Nilsen repeats the purpose of the attacks – to acquire a lifeless body. To illustrate this, he says that to find the bodies attractive he would pretend he had stumbled upon the scenario, and ignore the fact that he had killed them. He even claims that if he had had access to a 'knock-out drug', he mightn't have killed them at all. But, of course, we know that most of his victims were already significantly incapacitated through alcohol.

Besides, common definitions of 'lust murder' do match Nilsen's activities. They include deriving satisfaction from playing with dead bodies, and a fascination with dead genitalia. Nilsen clearly enjoyed interacting physically with dead bodies. *History of a Drowning Boy* also reveals for the first time that Nilsen would have liked to have kept some of the body parts as trophies. He says he would have particularly liked to keep the genitals, if he'd had a suitable liquid in which to preserve them.

'Lust murder' is closely related to necrophilia. Nilsen again, specifically denies being a necrophiliac. Other than on one occasion where he confesses to have had sex between a corpse's buttocks, he denies ever having had penetrative intercourse with any of the bodies. He does, however, say he would occasionally sexually abuse men who had passed out drunk in his flat. Interfering with a limp, unconscious body, however, was not sufficient to fulfil the main fantasy. That still required a dead body.

Finally, Nilsen is adamant he never ate any of the bodies of those he did kill. He thought about feeding some chunks to the dog as they looked strikingly like beef, but he didn't trust that the bodies didn't carry disease. Indeed, one of the corpses in the flat was later found to be carrying the Hepatitis virus.

In Hornsey Police Station, Nilsen confessed he'd killed 12 men in Melrose Avenue; he now claims the real figure was nine. His says he felt pressured by Jay and Chambers, and exaggerated as a result. When I told Peter Jay that Nilsen was now denying three of his victims, Jay shrugged his shoulders and replied that he 'seemed pretty sure about them at the time'. He then retrieved the list of victims the police had compiled from Nilsen's interviews. The list of those murdered at Melrose Avenue was as follows:

1. *Irish youth* (between 17 and 19 years old). 5ft 6in. Met Nilsen 29 Dec 1978. (Now known to be Stephen Holmes.)
2. *Kenneth Ockendon* (23). 5ft 8in. Met Nilsen 3 Dec 1979.
3. *Martyn Duffey* (16). 6ft 1in. Met Nilsen 17 May 1980.

4. *Billy Sutherland* (26). 5ft 9in. Met Nilsen Aug 1980.

5. '*Irish labourer*' (between 27 and 30 years old). 5ft 9in. Met Nilsen October 1980 in the Cricklewood Arms. He was tall with rough hands, and wore an old suit. Now denied.

6. '*Mexican or Filipino*' (20s). 5ft 10in. Met Nilsen November 1980 in the Salisbury Arms in St Martin's Lane. Slim and looked like a gypsy. Possibly a rent boy.

7. '*Vagrant*' (20s). Met Nilsen late autumn 1980, at closing time at the top of Charing Cross Road. He was emaciated, with a pale complexion, and had many teeth missing. He wore a trench coat and outsize trousers. They took a taxi back to Melrose, where Nilsen strangled him in his sleep with a tie. He told police: 'I felt exhilarated on some kind of high. I put a tie around his neck and pulled it tight. His legs were like he was riding a bicycle. It was as easy as taking candy from a baby. I thought I was doing him a favour. I had the impression his life had been one of long suffering.'

8. '*Starving Hippy*' (late 20s). 5ft 11in. Met Nilsen October or November 1980 in the West End around closing time. He wore bleached jeans and was strangled with a rope. Interestingly, Nilsen later wrote the following to Brian Masters: 'Long-haired hippy, why did I bring you back? I tremble at your death and permanent presence. I brush the hair from your eyes. I try to shake you alive. I want to say that I'm sorry and see you walk away. I try to

inflate your lungs, hopelessly, but nothing of you is working at all.' Now denied.

9. '*18-year-old, blue-eyed Scot*' (18). Met Nilsen January 1981 in the Golden Lion in Soho. He wore a green tracksuit top and trainers. Nilsen told police he'd challenged him to an end-of-night drinking contest. He commented, 'End of night … end of drinking … end of person.'

10. '*Belfast boy*' (early 20s). 5ft 9in. Met Nilsen February 1981 somewhere in the West End. He was slim.

11. '*Skinhead*' (about 20). 5ft 5in. Met Nilsen April or May 1981 at a street food stall in Leicester Square. He was muscular, with tattoos on his arm and 'Cut Here' beside dotted lines on his neck. He wore a black leather jacket, a studded belt, boots and a T-shirt. Nilsen told police he hung his torso up for 24 hours. Now denied.

12. *Malcolm Barlow* (23). 5ft 7in. Met Nilsen 18 December 1981.

Malcolm Barlow was the last victim to die in Melrose Avenue. Like Sinclair, his troubled life epitomised the tragedy of many of the victims. Barlow was the kind of vulnerable youth whose problems caused him to slip through every net. He was born in 1957 in Rotherham near Sheffield, and from an early age he suffered from epilepsy. He was 11 when his mother died; afterwards, he was looked after by his sister Doreen. She soon found him unmanageable. He would lie, steal and, occasionally, sleep with men and then try to blackmail them. When he became too much for his sister to cope with, he started to move from squat to hostel, funding himself through benefits.

On Thursday, 17 September 1981, when Nilsen left the house on his way to work, he found Barlow slumped against a garden wall a few houses down from his own. He asked him what was up. Barlow said his epilepsy pills had made him feel faint. 'You should have someone professional look at you,' said Nilsen. He insisted Barlow come back to 195 Melrose to sit down. After some time, Barlow still looked ill, so Nilsen walked down the road to the phone box – his own phone was disconnected – and called an ambulance.

The following evening, when Nilsen returned from work, Barlow was sitting on his doorstep. Barlow said he'd been discharged and had nowhere to go. Nilsen thought this was a nuisance but still invited him in. He cooked some food, and plonked himself in front of the TV with a Bacardi and Coke. Barlow asked if he could have one, too. Nilsen says he questioned whether he should really be drinking whilst taking pills, but Barlow, apparently, insisted.

After a couple of drinks, Barlow fell unconscious. Nilsen was both annoyed to think he might have to go out to the phone box and get another ambulance, and concerned that the police might become involved. He thought about his options for about 20 minutes, and then killed him. He doesn't remember it well nor talks about it in his manuscript.

The murder of Barlow provided Nilsen with the last body to dispose of at Melrose Avenue. This was September 1981. Ever since the summer of 1980, Nilsen had been getting rid of the evidence in a series of unthinkably gruesome ceremonies.

Three rotting bodies under the floorboards had been causing flies to buzz all around the house. Even with deodorants under the boards and insecticide sprayed twice a day, it was like a scene from a horror film.

Initially, Nilsen was content to simply get the bodies out of the house. He wanted to re-inter them in the garden shed he had built for Bleep. To do this, he decided he should cut them up and then transport them piece by piece in old suitcases left by a previous tenant. It was a warm summer Sunday afternoon when he started. He placed the bodies on the small stone floor between the cooker and the fridge. The sight in front of him was so disgusting he wasn't clear what needed to be done next. The smell was atrocious; some heads had maggots crawling out of eye sockets and mouths. He says he began quickly to knock back some Bacardi and Coke. He is keen for the world to appreciate how unpleasant he found the act of dismemberment.

In truth, however, despite what he says, the drinking didn't quite come first. Before he could start, he needed to masturbate next to the victims. We know this from interviews with psychiatrists before his trial. He told them that masturbating was his way of saying 'goodbye'. After the symbolic gesture, he then poured his drink, put Bleep outside, and fetched his sharpest kitchen knives and some bin liners.

He then stripped off. Naked and drunk, with plastic sheets all over the floor, he hacked away at the corpses using the techniques he had learnt as a chef. He pulled flesh off the bones, snapped joints and severed spines. Even with a butcher's training, this was a difficult, physical process. Every so often, he says, he would be sick in the sink.

Occasionally, he would cut himself. The French windows in the living room provided a draught of fresh air but he didn't walk out to them to avoid treading any human remains around the living room.

Heads were put in the large cooking pot (the same that had been used at the Christmas party) and, when the job was done, the foul-smelling viscera were put in plastic bags in a space between the double fencing for what he would later call the 'wee beasties of the night'. Soon, they rotted away to nothing. The suitcases were put in the shed with a number of deodorants. Eventually, a low wall was built around it, and more bricks and debris piled on the cases.

Between August and November 1980, Nilsen killed three more men. With the other bodies now in the shed, he had room to place these under the floorboards. He did so in a very chaotic manner. In fact, apparently, on one occasion he forgot about a body in a cupboard and was only reminded when he opened the door.

In December, Nilsen decided to draw a line under his activities by lighting another massive bonfire. On a freezing Saturday, he set about building a 5ft-high pyre. Between the end of Nilsen's garden and the next street was a small patch of waste ground. He found some discarded furniture there and carried it over. Nilsen broke up the furniture and wood and then arranged the pieces into a 2ft-deep base. Then he made another 3ft ring out of other timber he'd collected. When he was sure that the bodies would fit in the middle, he went out to the pub.

The next morning, he got up at 6.30am. He went outside

to check there was no one around. As the garden was not particularly private, Nilsen had to rely on the neighbours keeping themselves to themselves. He prised the floorboards up and the bodies wrapped in carpets were taken outside. It took all his strength to lift them. Even though it was freezing cold, he was sweating. Next, he pulled the door off the shed and shone his torch in there. The cold had caused most of the flies to die; their bodies lay like a carpet on the cases. Elsewhere, there was a sticky fluid. The cases at the top were intact but those below had started to disintegrate.

By dawn, the bodies were within the makeshift wooden pyre which was now covered with tyres, and doused with paraffin. He lit it and then spent the day watching it burn. Throughout the day, he had the French windows open and played Mike Oldfield's *Tubular Bells*. From time to time, he would go out to inspect the bonfire. In a letter to Brian Masters, he said it was like a Viking ship going to Valhalla. He told the police: 'The fire burned extraordinarily fiercely. There were spurts, bangs, crackles and hisses. This I took to be the fat in the bodies burning.' Nilsen also says that children prodded the fire, but although there was a playground nearby, it's unlikely they could have got that close.

By burning all evidence, Nilsen claims to have felt able to start over. If there was no evidence, how could he even be sure that it had really happened? There was nothing but ash. In truth, however, he hadn't really eradicated all the signs. The other reminders – such as medallions, bracelets, watches and tobacco tins – just didn't bother him as much. He would happily wear or give away items from the dead, whom he considered, before their bodies were destroyed at least, to be 'part of the household'. Some items were found by police in 23 Cranley Gardens.

After the fire, Nilsen brought back a 'pick-up' from a pub in St Martin's Lane. They had some sexual contact, and later he left. This encounter made him feel he was capable of normal, spontaneous activity. Such moments may even have been partly what he had in mind when he told me in a letter: '[Masters] writes me as cold and seemingly indifferent as his own prose style. I had, in my life, days of sun, colour and laughter, but you will search long and hard without spotting them in a tome constructed to describe my monstrosity and never the humanity along the road of events.'

There were no other 'rays of sunlight' in 1981. Between January and April of that year, he killed an Irishman, a Scotsman and, probably, an English skinhead. And yet, even with this prolific murder rate, he only occasionally missed work. He had an extraordinarily hardy constitution. Hunter-Craig told me that around this period Nilsen would happily drink all night, and then get up to go to work without trouble.

When he reached the office, he simply got on with the task in hand. But now he did so increasingly begrudgingly. He was unhappy about an ongoing problem he had with the promotion panel. Nilsen had, around this time, been told in a letter from the panel that he was not eligible to work for the Overseas Workers Section at Denmark Street because his manner with colleagues was 'usually outspoken and often overbearing'. His superiors were concerned this might also manifest itself with the public.

He felt the letter constituted a smear on his name. But it was more a sign that the disturbance just beneath the surface was beginning to show. But it wasn't until the summer of 1981 that his emotional problems really started to take over. The drinking became increasingly reckless and, during stupors, he would invite opportunist thieves back. He says he was also 'gay-bashed' which, undoubtedly, would have further soured him against the world. This culminated one night in Nilsen walking back from the Cricklewood Arms and then being mugged. His best jacket, shoes and wallet were taken. The wallet contained £300, a month's wages to Nilsen. In other incidents, Nilsen lost his beloved movie camera and projector.

Finally, the stress came to a head and the civil servant collapsed at the end of Melrose Avenue. He thought he may be having a heart-attack and staggered to a phone box and called an ambulance which took him to Park Royal Hospital. He was kept under observation for a day. The doctors told him, however, that that there was nothing physically wrong with him. He was simply suffering from extreme stress and exhaustion.

In the end, however, it was simple disagreement with the landlord that caused Nilsen to leave Melrose Avenue. The landlord was fed up with the electricity meters being constantly forced – the acts of Nilsen's 'guests' – with no explanations given. The rent was often late, and there were complaints about the awful smells coming from his flat. Nilsen had already had an inkling that there was a plan to evict him. On two occasions, he says he came back to find foreign-looking men outside, who said they had instructions from the landlord to inspect the flat. Nilsen took this as intimidation, and said so in a letter to Leon Roberts of Ellis and Co.

One day in June, Nilsen returned from work to find that the entire flat had been vandalised. Almost everything he owned, including his music collection and his record player, was either smashed or covered in creosote. The same thing had happened in the flat upstairs. Bizarrely, Nilsen called in the police. The culprit was never found. Now left with only the suit he wore and with no one else to complain to, Nilsen told his colleagues about what had happened. They had had a whip round and, two weeks later, presented him with a cheque for £85. Nilsen was overwhelmed. He wrote a letter saying how a cynic such as he 'seems to know the price of everything and the value of nothing'. The letter ended with a quote: 'Sympathy is a supporting atmosphere, and in it we all unfold easily and well.'

In August, the heat had brought the smell and the flies back. Nilsen knew he needed to act soon – he decided on another bonfire. As before, he dismembered the bodies first. The process was even more revolting than before. There were more maggots and more effluent. The bags of viscera were put into the same gaps in the fence. He boiled the flesh off the skulls in the pot he'd used before. This time, he couldn't use the shed as a storage facility as he'd burnt the door hoping he'd never have to use it again. Instead, he packed the other body parts with soil and deodorants and placed them back under the floorboards, waiting for the right moment.

It was approximately a month later that Nilsen killed Malcolm Barlow. That created another problem of storage –

there was no longer any room under the floorboards. He stuffed the body in a space under the sink. Shortly afterwards, a letter from the landlord's agent arrived on the doormat saying that they needed to take possession of the flat. They could offer him a place in Cranley Gardens and £1,000 compensation.

Nilsen started to build his last fire two days before he was due to move. The next day, it burned brightly. In the morning, the removals van arrived. For the second time, he could try to start again as if none of this had ever happened.

9

CRANLEY GARDENS

*That awful, never-to-be-forgotten smell of decomposing
human flesh was obvious. I looked at Nilsen and said.
'Your drains were blocked with human remains,' and
with a deadpan face he said, 'Oh my God, how awful!'*

DCI Peter Jay

On a misty autumn day, Dennis Nilsen climbed into the
cab of a small removals van and, no doubt, with a few
overbearing words of advice about the route, travelled the
few short miles over to Muswell Hill. 'Driving away,' he told
Jay and Chambers, 'was a great relief.' The destination,
Cranley Gardens, mainly comprised respectable family
houses. It was situated on a steep slope with grand views at
the top. Number 23 was, however, for short-term renters
with low horizons. According to the neighbours, from time
to time there had even been virtual down-and-outs and
squatters on the middle floor.

This would be Nilsen's home for 16 months. During that
time, Nilsen murdered three young men, and attempted to
kill at least five others. When he arrived on 5 October 1981,

though, he appears to have hoped that a change of scenery could cure him of his 'addiction' to murder. It was not blind optimism. He was now living somewhere where the disposal of bodies would prove very difficult. Not only was there a shared garden, but even to get a body that far involved two flights of stairs. And, as Nilsen had never learnt to drive, there was no means of easily transporting the remains of victims away from the area.

The other tenants living in Number 23 found Nilsen eccentric but not out of keeping with the sort of people you might expect for that house. The occasional guests that Nilsen would receive, such as Hunter-Craig, noticed the new flat seemed a bit more Spartan than the last. But they also knew about the robbery at Melrose Avenue and that he was still replacing his possessions. And at least this new flat was bigger with a much better kitchen.

As with Melrose Avenue, the flat comprised two main rooms – a bedroom and a living room. Off these were a galley kitchen and a bathroom. Both were built into the eaves and had prominent, sloping ceilings. Initially, Nilsen decided to live in the bedroom and sleep in the front. Later, he would do most of his living and sleeping in the back room. He soon replaced the stereo that had been stolen with a cassette player and bought a black-and-white TV. Along with his record collection, some posters (oddly including a page-three pin-up) and a couple of house plants, it soon became somewhere not entirely out of keeping with how one might expect a bachelor on a limited income to live.

The new flat was also in a much more genteel part of town than Cricklewood. If the weather was nice, it was just a 10-

minute walk down to the Tube in Highgate. On cold winter days, or if Nilsen had had too much to drink, there was also a bus that could take him up the steep hill home. Without the depressing memories and smells of Melrose, he started to become more comfortable again about encouraging guests. Hunter-Craig remembers him saying, 'I like having you around Skip; it stops me doing naughty things.'

During the first few months at Cranley Gardens, Nilsen talks about experiencing varying levels of control over his urges. Without any actual killings, he still felt he was essentially winning the battle. But there were some near-misses.

In November, in Soho's Golden Lion, Nilsen approached an earnest young man called Paul Nobbs. He was a London University undergraduate reading Slavic studies, with thick, curly hair. At about 6.00pm, Nilsen had noticed Nobbs being aggressively chatted up at the bar, and intervened. Nobbs thought it a gracious thing to do. After a couple of drinks, they went back to Cranley Gardens to drink Bacardi, eat snacks and watch *Panorama*.

After watching the *Nine O'Clock News*, Nobbs phoned his mum from the payphone in the hall and said he'd be back later. An hour later, the Bacardi had started to take effect. Nobbs phoned again and said he'd now be back the next day. The pair went to bed. Nobbs says he tried to initiate sex, but Nilsen said he didn't 'do' penetration.

In the middle of the night, Nobbs awoke with a terrible pain in his neck and throat. In the bathroom, he saw his eyes were severely bloodshot. Nobbs was shocked and disorientated, but still had no idea he'd been attacked.

Nobbs went to the toilet, and then returned to the bed and quickly fell asleep. At 6.00am, he awoke again. In the bathroom mirror, he saw the bruising around his neck. He felt dazed.

Back in the bedroom, Nilsen was sitting upright. When Nobbs came in, he commented that the young man looked awful.

'Thanks very much,' replied Nobbs.

Nilsen asked what had happened. Nobbs shrugged his shoulders. Nilsen said he should go to see a doctor.

In hospital the worst was confirmed. Still, Nobbs didn't want to go to the police out of embarrassment. And he was confused. After all, Nilsen had seemed such a nice, reasonable man; why would he want to kill him? The injuries left him in bed for a few days.

Some weeks later, another incident occurred that gave Nilsen more comfort that he might be regaining control; he had found himself with a perfect opportunity to attack and yet didn't take it. At the end of a long night in a local pub, he had found a young man slumped against the bar. Nilsen took him home and let him sleep on his bed. He put the electric fire on and placed a blanket over him. He felt aroused and masturbated next to him but, still, didn't feel compelled to kill.

In *History of a Drowning Boy*, Nilsen speculates on the possible reasons. He thinks it might have been less to do with self-control, or even the amount he had had to drink – the usual reason why attacks went wrong – rather than a function of the precise details of his 'psychological addiction'. He explains that, that night, vital parts of his 'fantasy' were absent. Here, as with Carl Stottor, he says, there was no thrill to be got from 'rendering' the young man passive; he was already passed out. Whatever the real reason, the fact that the potential victim walked out of his flat probably came as some relief. There would be no more murders for four months.

Christmas 1981 was, still as lonely and self-pitying as ever; Nilsen doesn't talk much about this period. But a letter found in his flat at the time of the arrest – and now the copyright of Brian Masters – tells us something of his feelings during that period:

> *Dear Mum,*
> *Just my (annual) note to keep you, at last, informed that I am still alive and reasonably well. I've moved into a new flat (self-contained) on Friday. It's more expensive than my last one (with much better facilities).I still have the dog (now six years old) and still function as an employment officer and trade-union branch secretary.*
> *I hope everyone is keeping well. I am sure you will agree with me that it is easy to lose touch when we are living in two different worlds, 500 miles apart. Love, Des*

By 'reasonably well', Nilsen meant coping with his loneliness by seeking out others with equally chaotic lives. He found them in his usual haunts – the bars of Soho and the West End. This was how he met the man who, months later, would be the victim of his first murder in Cranley Gardens.

John Howlett, 28, was 5ft-10in tall with an impressive physique. He was the son of an electrical inspector from High

Wycombe who had left home as a teenager. To support himself, he would take on casual work, his favourite being helping out in travelling fairgrounds. But when they first met in a Soho pub, Howlett told him he had been a Grenadier Guardsman. He seemed an unlikely military man but, then again, so was Nilsen.

In March 1982, their paths crossed again. 'John the Guardsman' recognised Nilsen standing at the bar of the Salisbury pub on St Martin's Lane. He approached him, explaining he was down from High Wycombe for the day. After a few drinks, Nilsen suggested they move back to his flat via the off-licence. Nilsen cooked a meal and they watched television and drank until late. When the late film started, Howlett said that he was tired and asked if Nilsen minded him getting some rest. Nilsen did mind, but Howlett went to lie down anyway. Around midnight, when the film had finished, Nilsen went into the next room and found Howlett in his bed.

'I didn't know you were moving in,' he said with a scowl. He suggested calling a taxi, but Howlett just grunted. Nilsen went back next door, poured himself a drink and had a think. He didn't like Howlett, nor did he find him attractive.

Nilsen's police confessions state he killed Howlett simply because he was an inconvenience. It was a fiercely brutal attack; the only account he ever gave that contained a convincing description of the violence of murder. He told Chambers and Jay:

Summoning up all my strength, I forced him back down and his head struck the rim of the head-rest on the bed. He still struggled fiercely so that now he was half off the bed. In about a minute, he had gone limp. There was blood on the bedding. I assumed it was from his head. I checked and he was still breathing deep, rasping breaths. I tightened my grip on him again around his neck for another minute or so. I let go my grip again, and he appeared to be dead.

I stood up. The dog was barking in the next room. I went through to pacify it. I was shaking all over with the stress of the struggle. I really thought he was going to get the better of me. I returned and was shocked to see that he had started breathing again. I looped the material round his neck again, pulled it as tight as I could and held on for what must have been two or three minutes. When I released my grip, he had stopped breathing.

History of a Drowning Boy doesn't tell us any more about this attack, other than to imply that he exaggerated the above confession under pressure from Chambers and Jay.

There is no good reason to believe that, but there is cause to believe that killing in a location where, with no obvious way to dispose of the body, marked another level of psychological decline. Still, despite the situation he found himself in, once out of the flat, Nilsen reverted more than ever to his persona of a finicky and indignant complainer.

Nilsen has a number of anecdotes that, unintentionally, illustrate this. One was that, while walking Bleep one day, he found a body wrapped in a blanket on Highgate woods. Full of self-righteousness, he says he was shocked that there might be a murderer on the loose and called the police. It turned out to be a dead dog.

Further clues to Nilsen's state of mind during this period are to be found in an unsent letter Nilsen wrote to his union friend, Alan Knox. It was full of breezy chat about his new television and their shared political views. The reason for writing the letter had been to prepare for a visit from Knox; and even while Nilsen's wardrobe contained a dead body that he had no idea what to do with, he was able to cheerfully write, 'Don't let the bastards get you down.'

Eventually, Nilsen decided that disposal of Howlett's body would best be done piece by piece. Three days after killing him, he moved the body out of the wardrobe, and brought it into the bathroom. Although he covered the floor with bin liners, the main dissection took place in the bath. Nilsen put a wooden board across it and then, with the body draped over this, the soft parts of the body were cut into pieces a couple of inches long and flushed down the toilet. But this process was too slow. To speed things up, Nilsen then started to boil the flesh and viscera down to a soup-like consistency. This seemed to allow the plumbing to cope better. When the head was soft enough, he scooped the brains out and flushed them, too. The larger bones were packed into bin liners in the wardrobe with salt and padding. While separating them, Nilsen broke several knives. The smaller bones were left out for the dustman.

After Alan Knox's visit, Nilsen was able to appear relatively relaxed and chatty in company. That was how Carl Stottor found him when they met one wet May evening. Even today, Stottor's most vivid memories of the night are still the pleasant hours they spent before the attack and how Nilsen had approached him while he sat alone in Camden's Black Cap pub, nursing half a pint. He remembers being able to confide how vulnerable he had felt with his previous, violent boyfriend. Stottor told Nilsen how he had felt unable to report how he had attacked him because, until the previous month, he had been under the gay age of consent –21 – and had been scared of attracting the attention of the authorities.

Not only did Nilsen have a comforting manner, he also reminded Stottor of his very first boyfriend. The stranger seemed sympathetic and kind. Even long after the attack, Stottor continued to believe that there had been a genuine connection between the two of them.

In the immediate aftermath, though, no one seemed to believe anything he had said. The police were dismissive and, when he told friends what he thought might have happened, they convinced him that he was getting confused with an earlier attack from his boyfriend.

When Stottor later wrote to Nilsen for answers, he was still finding it hard to remember all the details of the attack. He wrote in a spirit of open enquiry but shied away from divulging the full extent of his physical injuries: how after the attack he had needed to sleep constantly for almost a week, and the problems he still had with his lungs from the drowning.

Similarly, Stottor chose not to go into detail about the emotional breakdown and suicide attempt that followed the attack. The final thing he omitted to say was the bizarre discovery he'd made that 'John the Guardsman' – whose body had been in the wardrobe that night – was the same John Howlett he'd known from his own childhood. That coincidence made the trauma all the more personal.

The afternoon after letting Stottor walk free, Nilsen's mind would have soon turned to certain welcome developments with his job. The previous October, against all expectations, Nilsen had finally been awarded a promotion. There were no immediate positions available, so he was put on a waiting list.

Friday, 25 June 1982 would be Nilsen's last day at the Denmark Street branch of the Job Centre. In the late afternoon, he was given a gold pen, a lighter and the traditional card full of friendly comments, such as 'Keep up the talking', and 'Kentish Town may never be the same again'.

On the Monday, Nilsen took the Tube three stops to Kentish Town where his new position as Job Centre executive officer put him on a salary of £7,000. The new duties involved being a finance supervisor, a post supervisor and an accommodation and premises officer. It wasn't just the salary and status that were an improvement – his immediate superior, Janet Leaman, was the only person, he says, he ever had a warm working relationship with. Everything about this new job gave him a new sense of optimism.

There was still, however, also the fairly regular outbursts of temper. Hunter-Craig described him, during this period, as being like the 'little man' in whom unexpressed anger builds up. But at work this was largely compensated for by hard work and attention to detail. It was also a sympathetic environment. The women in the office felt that Nilsen was lonely and some suspected he was gay, and probably vulnerable.

One night after staying late in the office to help mop up a flood, Leaman gave him a packet of cigarettes as a thank you.

She was struck by how he gushed about how grateful he was for the token of gratitude. Some months later, at Christmas, he told her about a phone call from his mother. It seemed he needed a mother more than most.

During his last six months at Cranley Gardens, Nilsen stopped trying to contact his mother altogether. He was now totally resigned to being a murderer. Martyn Hunter-Craig thinks that, in his own cryptic way, he admitted as such. He remembers him saying, 'I know my life will be over in the Eighties,' although at the time he'd assumed Nilsen had meant *his* eighties.

In September 1982, Nilsen found Graham Allen the worse for drugs and trying to hail a cab in Piccadilly. Allen was a 28-year-old Glaswegian known to his friends as 'Puggy'. The man whom newspapers would characterise simply as a 'registered heroin addict and petty criminal' would become Nilsen's fourteenth victim. He was tall, rugged and heterosexual, with a girlfriend called Lesley and a son called Shane. Although Allen drifted in and out of his boy's life, Shane has clear memories of him, and grew up to look increasingly like his dad. But looks, and a fondness for drugs were, more or less, *all* Puggy gave Shane. Puggy was aggressive and uncultured, but Shane is relaxed and bookish. In his thirties, to help kick his own heroin habit, Shane moved from London to a village near Grenoble in the southeast of France. He still lives there, and supports himself with casual jobs in the civil service while trying to pursue a career in writing, which in the last couple of years has included his online presence: memoiresofaheroinhead.blogspot.co.uk

It was while researching pieces for his online journal that Shane found my *Sunday Times* article, which prompted him to contact me. After an email and phone exchange, he sent me a link to an essay he'd written about his father. He wanted me to be able to see that, for all Graham Allen's faults, Puggy was still his father. The essay starts: 'My father, Graham Archibald Allen, was born on 31 October 1954 in Motherwell, Scotland. The youngest of two, he grew up with attention problems and failed miserably at school. The only thing he excelled at was football. By the age of 15, he had discovered Glasgow, alcohol and cheap prescription drugs. By 17, he was out of school, out of pocket and out of home. Having been laid off by the steel works in Motherwell and with nothing else for it, he made his way down south to London.'

After failing to find unskilled work, Shane says his father's options started running out. 'After making a few contacts, he was soon taking advantage of the lenient squatting laws of the time. With a roof over his head, it wasn't long before he was sucked into the sleazier side of city life. Cheap, strong booze and whatever pills were doing the rounds … [funding] his habit through a mixture of government unemployment money, begging, stealing and robbing tourists around London's West End.'

But then something changed in Allen's life. In 1972, he met Lesley Mead, a blonde, blue-eyed barmaid. Three years later, she gave birth to Shane. Over the next eight years, Mead spent her time oscillating between Allen and a small-time gangster called Ray. Shane's memories of growing up are of his father moving in and out of his life, and are reproduced here with kind permission from the author:

During the last five years of his life, my father was in and out of prison, in and out of rehab, and in and out of life. His living was hard and his addiction was harder – it was completely out of control … If that wasn't enough, he was also halfway to becoming a chronic alcoholic…

[On the night of Allen's disappearance in 1982] *I remember him arguing with my mother and demanding money for heroin. He was drunk and cut and she had taken refuge inside the family house.* [His] *demands took place from outside, standing on the window ledge and shouting through the glass. He was hung up their like some perverse embodiment of Christ, black blood coming out his mouth where he'd punched his own face … That was the last sight either my mother or I saw of him. Well, that and then finally climbing down before casually skipping the low garden wall and disappearing into the night. That image haunts my mother, and what haunts her even more were her very last words: 'Fuck off … and NEVER come back!'*

Shane, later, adds, 'I know the relationship between my mother and father was violent and unhealthy, but it was still love, and as we know, love is … never a logical emotion.'

Graham Allen was last seen in September 1982. Shane and his mother think that, after the scene at the window, he walked off to find drugs. They think it not unlikely that he may have had a vague plan to pay for them by mugging a gay man who'd tried to pick him up. When Nilsen found him trying to hail a cab in London's West End, his dealer had probably already advanced a large hit of heroin. He had probably also been drinking. Allen was standing at the foot of Shaftesbury Avenue with blood on his jacket.

Nilsen told the police, 'The thing he wanted more than anything else was something to eat. I had very little supply in but I had a whole tray of eggs. So I whipped up a huge omelette and cooked it in the large frying-pan, put it on a plate and gave it to him. He started to eat the omelette. He must have eaten three-quarters of the omelette. I noticed he was sitting there and suddenly he appeared to be asleep or unconscious with a large piece of omelette hanging out of his mouth. I thought he must have been choking on it but I didn't hear him choking – he was indeed deeply unconscious.

'I sat down and had a drink. I approached him, I can't remember what I had in my hands now – I don't remember whether he was breathing or not but the omelette was still protruding from his mouth. The plate was still on his lap. I removed that. I bent forward and I think I strangled him. I can't remember at this moment what I used ... I remember going forward and I remember he was dead ... If the omelette killed him, I don't know, but anyway in going forward I intended to kill him. An omelette doesn't leave red marks on a neck. I suppose it must have been me.'

Until Allen was identified through dental records from a metal plate in his jaw, he was simply referred to by Nilsen as 'the omelette death'.

At least two men survived visits to Nilsen's flat between the murders of Allen and the final murder, that of Stephen Sinclair; the first was Trevor Simpson. Simpson's interviews from 1983 paint a clear picture of Nilsen's domestic situation during his last months as a free man.

They met on Wednesday, 22 December in a Soho pub. Simpson was 20 years old and had just served six months in jail for hijacking a car in Belgium. When Nilsen met him, he was stopping off in London en route to the Midlands. After a few drinks, Nilsen invited the young man back. As with Graham Allen, there was nothing homosexual about 'Trevor from Derby'. On the first night, Nilsen slept in his room at the back, and told Simpson to settle himself in one of the armchairs in the lounge.

The next morning Nilsen told him he was welcome to stay a while. He took up Nilsen's offer for seven days, during which he was the recipient of a constant barrage of left-wing rhetoric, and suggestions they visit Marx's grave in Highgate Cemetery nearby. And, despite being struck by the smell, Simpson told police he wasn't tempted to look for its source.

Christmas came and went just like any other day. There were no cards or decorations, no special meal and no friends. On the sixth night, Simpson irritated Nilsen by being rude about a stew he'd cooked. At around midnight, Simpson remembered Nilsen, drunk, muttering about having to consult the 'professor' about whether he could stay – an odd expression that Hunter-Craig also remembers Nilsen using.

Simpson was fed up and went to sleep. At about 1.00am, he found the room filling with smoke. He ran out into the kitchen. Nilsen was nonchalantly drinking a glass of water. Back in the living room was a smouldering pair of jeans on the fire. Nilsen told Simpson he must have dropped a cigarette on it.

Nilsen's manuscript describes Simpson as the man he 'lusted over'. He goes over the thought processes by which he decided to try and asphyxiate him with the burning jeans: 'I thought of bashing him over the head with a blunt object but could not do it,' he says. 'I thought about stabbing him with a kitchen knife but couldn't do that either.' Nilsen then contemplated tying his legs together and then strangling him. But whether from cowardice or some other restraining impulse, he couldn't bring himself to attack Simpson physically. That was when he came up with the idea of the fire. Simpson stayed for another day and, when he left, Nilsen said he must come again.

Once Simpson had departed, Nilsen continued to drink heavily. It was now almost four years since the first murder. On New Year's Eve 1982, he started on the rum at lunchtime in a pub down the road. When the pub closed for the afternoon, he came home and by 8.00pm he was so drunk that he decided to invite Vivienne and Monique from downstairs to join him. Nilsen banged on their door, and slurred the invitation. The two girls politely but firmly declined.

Nilsen left, looking angry. He went upstairs and then out. Shortly after midnight, he returned. Ten minutes later, there was a commotion on the stairs. Downstairs, the front door slammed. It was a young Japanese chef called Toshimitsu Ozawa. Nilsen thinks he met him at the Green Man pub down the road just before last orders. Ozawa told police later that night that, once in the flat, Nilsen had calmly approached him with his arms outstretched and a tie in between them. Nilsen's most vivid memory was of being kicked hard in the groin. In the end, no more was made of the incident.

It was another example of how recklessly out of control Nilsen was now becoming. In his manuscript, Nilsen lists several occasions when he came within a whisker of being arrested. The closest he had come to being discovered had actually been a year-and-a-half before, at Melrose Avenue, just after the last 'mass dissection'. Because of the 'revolting nature' of the task, Nilsen says he'd got 'practically legless' on Bacardi. He then went for a drunken walk to find somewhere to put the body parts:

> *I put as much of the viscera as could fit in a space between a board and the fence near the end of the garden. The other main fleshy parts of the bodies I wrapped into smaller packages and put back under the floorboards. The stench of decaying flesh was still, even while pissed out of my mind, bad enough to cause me to throw up periodically. When recalling what I had had to go through, the reader will think it odd that I can't stand the sight of human blood (which might explain why I could not use a knife on anyone).*
>
> *In this muddled haze of booze, I took it into my mind to take Bleep up to Gladstone Park for her daily romp. There I was with the mutt on a lead tottering over to the park with a plastic carrier bag with all the surplus entrails stinking to high heavens. I left the bag, in broad daylight, by the side of a road adjacent to the park.*

The bag was found by a biology student called Robert Wilson, who called the police. The remains were seen to be in an advanced state of decay and, then, there was no easy way to determine what exactly they had been. Nilsen still, however, wants to have a dig at the police. 'Had it been subjected to a closer examination by a qualified pathologist,' he says, 'then the alarm bells would have rang loud and clear to a death probably caused by foul play. My bloody fingerprints were all over the carrier bag and these could have been matched with mine on file in a relatively short time. This omission prolonged my arrest by eighteen months and four deaths later.'

When Nilsen met Stephen Sinclair on Wednesday, 26 January, he says his 'addiction' to murder was all-consuming. Although he doesn't admit he targeted Sinclair, he cannot deny there was planning involved. A ligature made out of a tie and a piece of string was found in his flat. Nilsen says such preparation was just like an alcoholic planning his next drink. He felt powerless to resist.

After the arrest, Nilsen had said, 'I sometimes feel my sole reason for existence was the killing.' Now, he says, the 'fantasy ritual' was 'everything' to him. Even after killing Sinclair, he was finding new permutations on the same theme. He would place him on the bed and watch him slowly fall on to cushions.

A fortnight after Nilsen had been playing with the body of the young man whose life he had just taken, DCI Peter Jay, Inspector Steve McCusker and DC Jeff Butler were waiting out in the cold for him to return from work. The Duty

Officer had said something 'odd' had been discovered in a drain. When he got there, Jay says, two things particularly concerned him – the discovery of what looked like pieces of human hand, and that the blockage seemed to go up the soil pipe to Nilsen's toilet.

Jay called in the Scenes of Crime Officer. He packaged up the findings and had them sent over to Professor David Bowen, a Home Office pathologist at Charing Cross Hospital in Hammersmith. At 2.00pm, Jay drove across town to Charing Cross. Bowen had not only established these were human body parts, but had also found a piece of neck bone with clear ligature marks on it. The victim had been strangled with great force. They drove back to the flat to await Nilsen. Jay told me:

When he finally walked through that door, I walked up to this smartly-dressed man in his thirties, noted his grey suit, metal-rimmed spectacles and scarf round his neck and said, 'Hello, I'm Detective Chief Inspector Jay from Hornsey CID. I've come about your drains.'

I was almost pleased to see a wry smile appear on his face and he said, 'Since when have police been interested in blocked drains?'

I told him I would tell him more once we got into his flat and he led the way. Glancing back at me once simply to ask about the identity of my two colleagues. 'Health Inspectors?' asked Nilsen.

'No ... detectives,' I replied. [Then Nilsen opened the door.]

That awful, never to be forgotten smell of decomposing

human flesh was obvious. I looked at Nilsen and said, 'Your drains were blocked with human remains.'

And with a deadpan face, he said, 'Oh my God, how awful!'

That was his only expression of innocence because when I then said, 'Don't mess me about. Where's the rest of the body?' he immediately said, 'In plastic bags in the other room.'

That was it as far as I was concerned. I left Jeff Butler at the other door of Nilsen's flat and I drove the CID car back to Hornsey with Nilsen and Steve McCusker sitting in the back. Steve suddenly popped a question to Nilsen out of the blue: 'Are we talking one body here, or two?' he asked.

'Neither,' said Nilsen. 'It's 16!' Nilsen then offered to tell us all about it back at the station.

Looking back at that bizarre encounter, both Steve McCusker and I would say that for some odd reason we automatically accepted that he was being truthful, incredible though it was. There was an honesty about the way he spoke to us.

Nilsen carried on talking in a calm, matter-of-fact, way. He seemed totally without remorse. He told the officers that if he hadn't been caught, he might have killed hundreds. He said that when the trigger in him was pulled, a bomb blast couldn't have stopped him. Peter Jay never thought he particularly look like he cared.

The police processed Nilsen as politely and efficiently as possible. A doctor and a photographer were ordered so that there could be no suggestion of ill treatment. Then the prisoner was brought a warm meal and a hot drink. Only then, with Professor Bowen in tow, did they return to Cranley Gardens.

It was now 9.00pm. The smell seemed worse than they'd remembered – a sweet, rotten stench made sharper by the cold. Two large, black bin bags were found in the wardrobe, and in one were four smaller bags. Peeking into them, they could see two contained left and right sections of a man's torso, with the arm still attached. In the third bag was a much decomposed headless and armless torso. Finally, there was a Sainsbury's bag containing internal organs in a soup of body fluids. While it was all being bagged up, Jay stood by the door for air.

Back at the mortuary, the second large, black bag was seen to contain a man's head, boiled but with most of the hair and flesh still remaining. Another skull was found with most of the flesh removed, and another torso. Inside a tea chest, a curtain was wrapped around more bones, hands, feet and another skull. Behind plywood boxing in the bathroom was the lower half of Stephen Sinclair, clean cut from just above the waist and still intact.

Jay remembers the flat being extremely damp. Sleet was coming in the open windows, and electric fires were brought in to dry the place out. The damp made it impossible to dust for fingerprints for several days. Meanwhile, a crew was sent to Melrose Avenue. The floorboards were taken up and a tent erected in the garden. Soon, they found smashed skulls and pieces of bone. All that Forensics could determine at that stage, though, was whether the fragments were human or animal.

The police wanted as much information as they could get before making their initial charge: that of Sinclair's murder. After that, they could interview Nilsen at their leisure about the other murders. Although Nilsen says he remembers the police doing their job well enough, the more one reads his account, however, the stranger it seems. He says that, from the outset, he knew the police would 'require him to write their script'. This odd sentence seems not to be just a reference to the confessions he would give but also to how the story of the arrest would be told – that he would need to help create a story that would be told for posterity.

Nilsen also seems concerned to assert his superiority and let us know he wouldn't have made any mistakes. He finishes this section with an allegation that, before he was sent to Brixton, some junior officers asked for his autograph. He says he obliged, along with one of his 'one-liners', such as 'I don't have nightmares … I give nightmares'.

The police visited Nilsen in Brixton twice for further interviews. In total, they interviewed him 16 times for a total of over 31 hours, with 165 pages of questions and answers recorded in longhand. A word processor – the latest thing at the time – had been asked for and refused; complete sets of notes would have to be written out by hand. Each interview was between two and two-and-a-half hours and all but the first couple conducted in the presence of Ronald Moss, Nilsen's first solicitor.

From the evidence gathered in these interviews, the team set about finding the victims. Without advanced forensics, CCTV and sophisticated computer databases, the police had to rely on personal items, fingerprints and dental records.

Ironically, without DNA technology, the skeletal remains of Howlett and Allen found in the flat proved two of the hardest bodies to identify.

As in television dramas, the operations room was full of pin boards with photos and blackboards with leads scrawled over them. On one poster-sized piece of paper the investigating officers tried to fill in as many details about the victims as possible. The top row read: name; last known address; description; date missing; date of death; last seen by; how identified; exhibit numbers; statement numbers; and remarks.

Kenneth Ockendon was identified by a composite fingerprint created by the partial prints found on his *A-Z* London streetguide, and a camera light meter found in his hotel. Nilsen also recognised him from a photo. Sinclair was formally identified by fingerprints found on his leather jacket, his syringes, a tobacco tin and by his blue-and-white scarf. Billy Sutherland was identified by a photograph after his family had contacted police after seeing the news. Some of the personal items found in Nilsen's flat belonging to Martyn Duffey, such as kitchen knives, bore his name. The existence of missing boy called Martyn Duffey was soon established, but he turned out to be a different height from the one they were looking for and the search resumed.

The legwork involved in finding some victims seemed almost endless. In the case of John Howlett, the police first looked for all 'Johns' who had been in the Grenadier Guards, and then, when they realised that he might not have been in the Army, every John they could find in High Wycombe. Eventually, they narrowed their search down by finding his blood type in a strip of muscle tissue.

By the time of the trial, only seven names were filled out on the chart. The others were simply referred to by Nilsen's descriptions, such as 'the starving hippy' or 'the skinhead with the tattoo around his neck'.

10
THE TRIAL

At 4.25 pm on Friday, 4 November 1983, the state through the
agency of the judicial system made its pronouncement on me. The
anonymous jury, having gained its thrills and shocks from this theatre
of the absurd, had finally, by a majority of 10-2, agreed with the
prosecution's and judge's view of me and my past actions. The
media would take up the clarion call of me as 'evil beyond belief'.
The flashbulbs flashed and the wolves howled and in the universal
public consciousness I joined the ranks of the damned
alongside Crippen, Haigh, Brady, Hindley and Sutcliffe.

DENNIS NILSEN, IN *HISTORY OF A DROWNING BOY*

The trial of Dennis Andrew Nilsen started on the morning of Monday, 24 October 1983 at London's Central Criminal Court, otherwise known as the Old Bailey. It is an austere stone building topped with a statue of Justice with her scales and sword. As the court opened for its day's business, the clerk of the court read out eight charges against the 37-year-old defendant. These were the murder of Kenneth Ockendon, Malcolm Barlow, Martyn Duffey, John Howlett, Billy Sutherland and Stephen Sinclair, and the attempted murder of Douglas Stewart and Paul Nobbs.

Two charges were conspicuously absent – the crimes

against Graham Allen and Carl Stottor. In 1983, the media reported that the details about these offences had come in after the court indictment papers had already been drawn up and evidence gathered. The judge had, therefore, ruled that it wasn't possible to include them. But both Stottor and Allen's wife, Lesley, remain incredulous that there wasn't still time to make some provision. They feel strongly that justice was denied them. Still, the attacks were included as general evidence of Nilsen's modus operandi and Stottor would have the opportunity to tell his story from the witness box.

The courtroom was packed to overflowing. When the press benches filled up, journalists moved to the public gallery. At the front sat Mr and Mrs Ockendon; just beneath them stood the man who had butchered their son. He was dressed neatly in a grey sports jacket, light-blue shirt, and blue tie, which he had been loaned. Each time he was asked how he pleaded, he responded, 'Not guilty'.

Nilsen had eventually decided on this plea after reading through psychiatric reports arranged by his solicitor at the time, Ralph Haeems. He told me that, after his initial scepticism, he became persuaded that his earlier ideas of pleading guilty were naïve. 'There was a real diminishment of total responsibility,' he wrote, due to the 'personality dysfunction mechanisms to which I had slowly evolved from the bleakness of an emotionless child and early manhood.'

To support their plea of 'diminished responsibility', the defence produced two psychiatrists: James Mackeith and Patrick Gallwey. Mackeith had a reputation for being a reasonable and balanced man; he thought Nilsen suffered 'severely' from a number of personality disorders. He was also convinced they were, probably, untreatable, and that his grandiosity and inflated ego would render future psychological therapy futile. Gallwey agreed that Nilsen had a personality disorder, but he thought it was slightly different. He diagnosed Nilsen with a rare type of 'borderline' disorder which meant Nilsen's mind moved between a seemingly normal position and a heavily 'schizoid' state, bordering on psychosis.

The prosecution said it was murder, pure and simple. Their psychiatrist, Paul Bowden, had met Nilsen in his first week in Brixton, and visited him regularly over the subsequent months. During that time, he concluded Nilsen was a plausible, cunning murderer who had been in full control of himself at the time of all the offences.

The prosecution case was led by Alan Green, QC. In *History of a Drowning Boy*, Nilsen is pleased to point out that Green would later become the Director of Public Prosecutions and then resign when accused of kerb-crawling in 1991. Green opened his case by outlining the day of Nilsen's arrest and showing the jury photographs of the scene at the flat. He then explained more about the case they were about to hear. There would be six witnesses; the first three, he said – Stewart, Nobbs and Stottor – had all had first-hand experience of Nilsen trying to kill them. Next, there would be detectives Jay and Chambers, who had arrested and interviewed Nilsen. Finally, he said, they would hear from psychiatrist Dr Paul Bowden.

Green, wearing outsized, horn-rimmed glasses, spoke in a softly authoritative, theatrically understated manner. He began to outline Nilsen's modus operandi. He explained how he had killed men he met in public houses. They would go back to Nilsen's flat for more drink and then, at some point, Nilsen would squeeze the life out of them. He explained most of the victims were homosexual – some, in fact, male prostitutes – yet none had been killed because they were homosexual or had resisted Nilsen's advances. They were, he said, nearly all from the fringes of society and from outside of London; the kind of people whom Nilsen might feel would probably not be missed.

The murders were described one by one. The violence of the killings and indifference of the disposal were both emphasised. Particular attention was given to Malcolm Barlow – killed, apparently, because Nilsen didn't want to call an ambulance – and John the Guardsman who was strangled three times and then drowned. Green also made sure the jury knew about Nilsen's extraordinarily casual manner with the police.

The following day, the papers delighted in reporting some of Nilsen's idiosyncratic quips, such as 'I started out with 15 ties and now all I'm left with is a clip-on …' or his reply to Jay's question of how many bodies he'd had under the floorboards: 'I don't know, I didn't do a stock check.'

Nilsen's *History of a Drowning Boy* doesn't say more about the events of the trial than can be found in the press cuttings. It does tell us, however, a significant amount about Nilsen's attitude to confronting justice. One sketch he draws is full of disgust at the offensive intrusion into those aspects of his life that he had kept most private: 'The courtroom twitched nervously,' he says, 'to the sweaty gasps of guilt-ridden voyeurs hating and loving the dirt-filled revelations.' He then speculates how much more startled they might have been by the sight of 12 naked men appearing in front of them, as if he felt he'd actually experienced such a vision during the proceedings. Later, he mocks the way journalists jumped on a 'throwaway psychological cliché' he gave about assuming 'a quasi-God role'. He feels he was the only one who *really* understood what the trial was all about.

He was also highly irritated by the testimony of the first witness, Douglas Stewart, the man whom Gordon Honeycombe had met in Soho. Stewart, a 29-year-old Scotsman with thick, curly hair, took the stand looking tall and confident. In his version of events, Stewart said he had met Nilsen one November in 1980, in the Golden Lion in Soho. He had gone there, he said, not because of its gay reputation but rather because it served his favourite Scottish beer.

On the night in question, he had been one of a group chatting at the end of the bar. When Nilsen had suggested that they go back to his flat, he'd thought the invite was for the whole group, and once in the street he thought it rude not to continue on to Melrose Avenue.

Back in Nilsen's flat, they started by drinking lager. 'Dennis', Stewart told the court, then offered him vodka which he refused. 'Suit yourself,' Nilsen replied, 'I am off to bed; you're welcome to join me.' Stewart explained he 'didn't do that sort of thing'. He then went to sleep in a chair. Approximately two hours later, he woke to find his feet tied to the legs with a neck tie. There was another around his neck and Nilsen's knee was pushed hard against his chest. Stewart said he started shouting and fighting. Nilsen shouted back, 'Take my money,' as if trying to suggest that there was a robbery was going on.

Nilsen then calmly told Stewart he could kill him, even though by now Stewart was in charge. After the struggle, things calmed down. They sat in silence. Then Nilsen went to the kitchen and came back with a large knife which he held calmly, unthreateningly. Eventually, the conversation started up again, the two men shared a drink together and Stewart left. Once at a safe distance down the road, Stewart called the police. They sent a squad car over. After speaking to both parties, they concluded that it had been a lovers' tiff, made some notes, apologised to Nilsen, and then left. All the time Stewart spoke, Nilsen made notes of all the little inaccuracies in his account. Pedantically, he noted he referred to 'Dennis' and not 'Des', and mentioned vodka, not rum.

The next day, Tuesday, 5 October, the jury heard from two young men Nilsen had attacked. The first was Paul Nobbs, who had met Nilsen almost exactly a year after Stewart, again in the Golden Lion in Soho. Nobbs described how grateful he was when Nilsen stepped in and saved him from the attention of a predatory older man. He explained how, during the evening, he had called his mother twice. Having decided to stay, there was more drinking, kissing and fondling but Nilsen had declined the offer of sex.

Nobbs then described waking up after the attack. After looking at himself in the mirror, he had gone back to the bedroom. Nilsen had remarked he looked awful. 'Oh, thanks very much,' said Nobbs sarcastically.

When Ivan Lawrence, cross-examining, asked whether there'd been anything strange about Nilsen's manner during the evening, Nobbs replied that nothing in particular had worried him. The jury were left wondering if Nilsen was so out of control he could risk an attack on a man whose mother knew he was there, or whether, in fact, he was so in control that he could turn his violence on and off at will.

Similar testimony would come from Carl Stottor that afternoon. He told me when I met with him later that he had found the prospect of giving evidence an enormous ordeal. On the morning prior to his appearance in the witness box, he said that he sat in a friend's living room looking at himself in the mirror. What he saw displeased him. Having just dyed his blond hair black, he now felt he looked pale and washed out. Staring at his reflected image, he decided to apply a small amount of make-up. When he arrived in the court at 2.00pm, in an open-necked shirt with a medallion underneath, he said that he became extremely self-conscious. Suddenly, he felt very nervous. When Alan Green referred to him as 'slightly pathetic', he shrank further into himself. It was a hard job getting his evidence out.

Taking a deep breath, Stottor told the room the facts as he remembered them. When he faltered, Green helped him out: 'Is it true you told Nilsen that you weren't in touch with your family?' ... 'Did it strike you as odd that Nilsen suggested you might get caught up in that loose zip?'

Stottor told the court how he had met Nilsen in Camden's Black Cap. Stottor had come down to London to escape from an unhappy relationship. Nilsen had seemed kind and sympathetic. Despite the cut on Stottor's face, Nilsen told him how lovely he looked. Then, some drinks later, at closing time, he suggested they go back to Cranley Gardens. He wasn't pushy, and promised not to try anything on. They took a cab back to Nilsen's flat, where Stottor became more and more depressed.

When he started to feel ill from the alcohol, they both went to bed. In the middle of the night, he remembered being in a semi-conscious state and unable to breathe. As Nilsen had warned about getting caught up in the loose zip, Stottor thought the hand he felt on his neck was Nilsen trying to help. He heard Nilsen's voice saying, 'Stay still.' Then he passed out again.

Then he remembered hearing the sound of water, like a tap running. Next, he was underwater. He started to panic before passing out again. Sometime later, he woke up to find Bleep the dog licking his face. Nilsen was now beside the animal and fussing over him. He told Stottor he had got caught in the zip and probably had a nightmare as a result. Nilsen explained the water on his head was from a jug he'd poured over him to bring him to. He comforted him some more. Later, they cuddled in bed and, in the morning, Nilsen helped him to the Tube.

Stottor could only remember the evening in snapshots, but he had said enough for the prosecution to indicate that Nilsen deliberately and consciously 'chose' his victims. Counsel for the defence, however, wanted to know how Nilsen had seemed after the attack. Stottor said he seemed genuinely concerned. Lawrence suggested that this was evidence that Nilsen was moving in and out of abnormal states of mind. To emphasise the point, he told the jury how, when Chambers and Jay had asked about his manner after attacking Stottor, he'd replied, 'I hoped that these uncontrollable events would not affect our relationship.'

Now it was time for the court to hear more of what Nilsen himself had to say about his crimes and why he may have committed them. DCI Peter Jay rose to the stand with a statement Nilsen had written for them called 'Unscrambling Behaviour':

I guess that I may be a creature – a creative psychopath – who, when in a loss of rationality situation, lapses into temporarily a destructive psychopath, a condition induced by rapid and heavy ingestion of alcohol. At the subconscious root lies a sense of total isolation and a desperate search for a sexual identity. I have experienced transitionary [sic] sexual relationships with both males and females before my first killing. After this event, I was incapable of any intercourse. I felt repelled by myself and, as stated, I have had no experience of sexual penetration for some years.

In a society of labels, it is convenient for me to let others believe that I am a homosexual. I enjoy the social company of both men and women, but prefer to drink socially with men. I am not in sympathy with the state of women who are the worse for drink.

Nilsen was keen to downplay his sexual orientation, and made it sound as ambiguous as possible. His statement continued with a self-consciously confused tone:

God only knows what thoughts go through my mind when it is captive within a destructive mood. Maybe the cunning, stalking killer instinct is the only single concentration released from a mind which, in that state, knows no morality. It may be the perverted overkill of my need to help people – victims who I decide to release quickly from the slings and arrows of their outrageous fortune, pain and suffering.

There is no disputing the fact that I am a violent killer under certain circumstance ... The victim is the dirty platter after the feast and the washing up is a clinical, ordinary task. It would be better if my reason for killing could be clinically defined – i.e. robbery, jealousy, hate, revenge, sex, blood, lust or sadism.

But it's none of these. Or it could be the subconscious outpouring of all the primitive instincts of primeval man. Could it be the case of individual exaltation of beating the system and the need to beat and confound it time and time again?

Ruling out 'sex, blood, lust and sadism' as if he *wished* it could be that easy would have sounded to many in the jury as excuses clothed in fake sincerity. As for the idea he might have been acting out of a perverted sense of kindness, it was repulsive. But yet, as a whole, the statement did help to establish a gap between confessor and the crimes. As always, the author wrote like someone surprised by his actions:

It amazes me that I have no tears for these victims. I have no tears for myself or those bereaved by my actions. Am I a wicked person, constantly under pressure, who just cannot cope with it, who escapes to reap revenge against society through a haze of a bottle of spirits? But maybe it's because I was just born an evil man.

Living with so much violence and death, I've not been haunted by the souls and ghosts of the dead, leading me to believe that no such fictional phenomena, does or will ever exist. Memories of man's best friend, i.e. my dog, are already a little faded.

In the normal course of my life, I feel I had abnormal powers of mental rationality and morality. When under pressure of work and extreme pain of social loneliness and utter misery, I am drawn compulsively to a means of temporary escape from reality. This is achieved by taking increased draughts of alcohol and plugging into stereo music which mentally removes me to a high plane of ecstasy, joy and tears. This is a totally emotional experience.

This glorious experience and feeling is conjured up in this manner. I relive experiences from childhood to present – taking out the bad bits. When I take alcohol, I see myself drawn along and moved out of my isolated, prison flat. I bring [with me] people who are not always allowed to leave because I want them to share my experiences and high feeling. I still do not know the engine of my performance. The one single piece of music that I get the greatest aural alcoholic high from is 'Oh Superman' by Laurie Anderson from the Big Science *album. It has a hypnotic, trancelike effect on me. I listened to the eight-minute track ten times one night. I was compelled by it – I could not stop myself.*

In order to enlarge on [my experiences at] *Melrose Avenue and Cranley Gardens, I have made several attempts to strangle men. In some cases, the attempts were foiled by the struggle or escape of the subject. In others, I did not have the heart or desire to carry through the task. In all of the latter cases, the subject was already unconscious.*

The final paragraph sounded as if it could almost have been drafted by a solicitor: 'My remorse is of a deep and personal kind which will eat away inside me for the rest of my life. I am a tragically private person, not given to public tears. The enormity of these acts has left me in permanent shock ... The evil was short-lived and it cannot live or breathe for long inside the conscience.'

The prosecution hoped the jury would find Nilsen's statements both cowardly and brazen. The defence argued it showed Nilsen really had been overwhelmed by his alter ego. Otherwise, why had he admitted *everything*? Jay, himself, agreed he had hardly known anyone co-operate so much.

But admitting everything didn't necessarily mean Nilsen was sorry or confused. It might also have meant he was simply revelling in what he had done. DCS Geoffrey Chambers read out all of Nilsen's murder confessions. They included lines already reproduced in this book, such as: 'On the floor was a piece of string with a tie attached to it ... I know I must have killed him ... I must have made up the piece of string that night ...' and '... I looped the material round his neck again, pulled it as tight as I could and held on for what must have been two or three minutes. When I released my grip, he had stopped breathing.'

Green then brought out the cooking pot in which three heads had been boiled, the cutting board used to dissect pieces of John the Guardsman, and Martyn Duffey's knives. One person felt a profound sense of abhorrence more acutely than many others. Lesley Mead, Graham Allen's partner, had come to the trial to try to understand something of what had happened. She would tell me that watching Nilsen calmly 'play with an empty Marlboro packet, like a bored court official' simply confused her more. When she saw the cooking pot her partner's head had been boiled in, she walked out of the court.

On the afternoon of Wednesday, 6 October, Ivan Lawrence opened the case for the defence. His objective was not to dispute any of the facts that had been given but to show that Nilsen had been suffering from 'abnormality of mind' every time he had killed. This would mean he couldn't have formed the 'specific intention of murder', and therefore couldn't be held fully responsible. He told the jury that, for them to return such a verdict of manslaughter by diminished responsibility, the law merely required that he *may* have been suffering from such an abnormality. They simply had to consider him not *definitely* sane.

The three psychiatrists at the Old Bailey had a particularly unenviable task. Diagnosing Nilsen was hard enough, but guiding a jury about his state of mind when committing a crime went far beyond their usual remit. Nilsen says, 'Not to appear fully blank on the subject, they fell back on standard labels of psychiatry: "psychopath"; "explosive"; "schizoid"; "paranoid"; "psychotic"; "sociopathic"; "dissociative";

"borderline personality disorder"; "necrophilia"; "alcoholic"; "grandiosity"; and a partridge in a pear tree ...'

In truth, however, these doctors went to great lengths to express the uniqueness of this case. First in the witness box was Dr James Mackeith of the Bethlem Royal Hospital. Normally a cheerful-looking man with thick hair and a wide smile, he appeared initially subdued. He started by explaining who he was, what he did and his experience of the accused. Based on his interviews, he said he was in no doubt that Nilsen suffered from an 'unspecified' severe personality disorder. He clarified this by saying that rather than falling outside the spectrum of known disorders, he suffered from many of them.

The disorders Mackeith referred to came from the *International Classification of Diseases*. The *ICD* codifies all illnesses, and in the UK is the standard reference for mental conditions. In 1983, it was on its ninth revision, and in this version 'psychotic behaviour-types' caused by schizophrenia, bi-polar disorder and drug addiction had been separated from the range of so-called 'personality disorders'. The types of mental condition had been listed on two 'axes'. Nilsen certainly wasn't on axis one, the 'psychotic' one. He wasn't bi-polar, nor was he schizophrenic. Schizophrenics are marked by a more severe breakdown of function, such as voices in the head and bizarre delusions. They can't operate in society the way Nilsen had. And neither did his drinking affect him, for example, in the way that large amounts of LSD might have.

Many of the traits on axis two, however, sounded just like him. According to the most recent iteration of the *ICD*, the criteria for a personality disorder are as follows: '(1) Markedly disharmonious attitudes and behavior, generally involving several areas of functioning; (2) that the abnormal behavior pattern is enduring, of long standing, and not limited to episodes of mental illness; (3) that the abnormal behavior pattern is pervasive and clearly maladaptive to a broad range of personal and social situations; (4) that the above manifestations always appear during childhood or adolescence and continue into adulthood; that the disorder leads to considerable personal distress but this may only become apparent late in its course; (5) that the disorder is usually, but not invariably, associated with significant problems in occupational and social performance.'

Since 1983, courts have arguably become attuned to the varieties of mental condition that might affect a defendant. They might, for instance, be evaluated on scales like the Hare Psychopath checklist (the first items are glibness, superficial charm and callousness), and prospects for treatability are then assessed. There is also more inclination to take the findings of personality disorders seriously and not regard them merely as descriptions of character traits. Psychiatrists are now generally more inclined to attribute more than one category of a personality disorder to a patient.

James Mackeith had a reputation for being a very competent and up-to-date psychiatrist. After interviewing Nilsen for several hours, he had diagnosed Nilsen's personality as showing schizoid, explosive, psychopathic and borderline disorders. The last needs more explanation than the others.

Borderline Personality Disorder is characterised by 'black-and-white thinking, emotional instability and interpersonal relationships that flit between idealisation and devaluation, poor self-esteem, bouts of impulsivity, anger and dissociation.' It was initially called 'borderline' as psychiatrists thought such people were somewhere between neurotic and psychotic. Now the defining characteristic is seen as instability. Mackeith's pre-trial report described Nilsen as having unstable moods, impaired impulse control, sudden anger, disturbed identity, sudden need for company when alone, and futility. Interestingly, long before he knew of such psychological concepts, in his essay entitled *The Monochrome Man*, Nilsen describes himself as a man whose moods were all black and white.

Mackeith analysed his problems as starting in childhood, where he thought he had developed 'maladaptive patterns of behaviour'. These included an inability to express feelings other than through anger, which came suddenly and forcefully. This lack of emotional development meant that when Nilsen felt anxious about a failing relationship, such as that with Gallichan, he would run away – both literally and metaphorically. Mackeith had noticed in his own interviews that Nilsen's anxiety might cause him to jump to conclusions about what others were thinking.

None of this, in itself, though, was more than neurotic. Something else in Nilsen's mental development was much more disturbing. Mackeith related two stories that demonstrated how Nilsen had expressly associated unconsciousness with sex. Both stories are mentioned in Nilsen's autobiography, and have appeared in the narrative of this book. The first was walking into the sea at the age of 10 and being rescued by an older boy who masturbated over him.

The other was the story of the Arab taxi driver he claimed to have killed in Aden in self-defence. Mackeith said that these stories demonstrated an 'extraordinary' interest in the concept of unconsciousness in a sexual context.

The psychiatrist proceeded to talk about how he'd heard Nilsen would masturbate with mirrors and beside corpses prior to dismemberment. He believed this was more than simple sexual deviance. It was part of the repeated instances of Nilsen's personality breaking down.

Mackeith thought Nilsen's personality breakdowns were far more significant to the crimes than the massive quantities of drink that had also been consumed. He explained how they had come about. First, there was the so-called 'compartmentalisation' – what Mackeith described as Nilsen's ability to separate out his psychological functions 'in an exceptional way'. He thought this split in his personality, in combination with a reduced sense of identity, made him prone to bouts of 'depersonalisation', or 'dissociation'. In these states, Nilsen would have felt 'removed' from himself, as if watching someone else. These instances are strikingly similar to the 'trance-like ritual', and 'dreamlike states' which Nilsen describes.

Another constant character trait in Nilsen that Mackeith perceived was his aggression. He considered it to be especially pronounced when his point of view wasn't being met. It seemed to Mackeith that, in interpersonal situations, Nilsen was suspicious, paranoid, grandiose and craved attention. Mackeith even suggested that some killings might have been triggered when people didn't listen closely enough to him. In a written report, he said that were Nilsen to go to prison, if he didn't get enough attention he might develop a florid, psychotic mental illness or become extremely depressed.

Alan Green's strategy was to try to make Mackeith's opinions seem like imprecise waffle. He asked the jury to consider whether by attributing to Nilsen almost every disorder in the book, it actually showed that Mackeith was undecided. More to the point, Mackeith's account didn't explain *precisely* was going on when Nilsen killed. He seemed undecided, for instance, as to whether it was in blackouts or fits of rage.

Green then asked Mackeith how he knew everything he claimed to about Nilsen's past. Mackeith admitted that all he had had to work on were Nilsen's own self-reports. Green wanted to know what literal truth he ascribed to these, in particular Nilsen's drowning and Aden stories. Mackeith replied that their literal truth was beside the point; Nilsen was capable of believing quite contradictory things at different levels of functioning. What always mattered was *his* truth.

The question still remained of how one could actually believe *anything* generated by Nilsen. Green claimed he was an inveterate liar whose talking was designed just to deceive. He reminded the court how, for instance, Nilsen had told guests he was married or had seen active service in Northern Ireland. Green added that it stood to reason that, if Nilsen hadn't been so deceptive, he would not have managed to kill 15 men before being caught.

Green thought that, between night and day, he didn't so much 'separate out mental functioning' as put on an act. When strangers came back to Nilsen's flat, it didn't 'just happen' – he deliberately asked them back. Green read out some of Nilsen's statements about how he had invited victims back, and then turned to Mackeith and asked him whether or not he thought, by the evidence of Nilsen's own stories, he showed resourcefulness and cunning. Mackeith didn't think so.

Green then reminded the jury how Nilsen had allowed Duffey's knives to rust, and picked up his belongings from the left-luggage at Euston Station. As for the so-called 'depersonalisation', how, he asked, was he able to stop midway through killing Stottor? When he killed Barlow and John the Guardsman, he clearly wasn't in a trance; he did it consciously just because they had annoyed him.

Mackeith interjected, stating that just because Nilsen seemed to be saying he killed without motive, it certainly didn't mean that was really the case. Nilsen, he pointed out, had personality problems and it needed expert judgement to interpret the truth behind his statements. He remained resolute on his opinion, but he wouldn't say whether Nilsen's mental problems were sufficient for a verdict of diminished responsibility. That had to be up to the jury.

'Quite,' said Green. He read out the statute, and then asked if there was anything in Nilsen's statements that could constitute an 'arrested development of mind'. He was, after all, an intelligent and lucid man. Mackeith suggested that the definition be widened to 'arrested development of personality'. The judge agreed.

Dr Patrick Gallwey, the defence's second psychiatric expert witness, had receding hair and a professorial demeanour. Like Mackeith, he felt Nilsen suffered from a retardation of personality, but not intelligence. Unlike his colleague, however, he didn't think Nilsen's condition could be found in the *ICD* classification. He attempted his own definition, which was so complicated it ended up confusing both judge and jury. It was called 'Borderline, False-Self as if Pseudo-Normal, Narcissistic Personality Disorder'.

It was a 'borderline' disorder in that Nilsen was unstable and suffered from emotional extremes and black-and-white thinking. Gallwey called the condition 'pseudo-normal', as throughout Nilsen's adult life, he appeared to be normal, whereas he was really always on the verge of tipping into a 'false-self'. The latter was a paranoid and schizoid personality that took over during times of high stress. Being 'schizoid' meant Nilsen's emotionally blunt tendencies were intensified to the point that he couldn't feel 'normally' at all.

Even during his 'pseudo-normal' periods, however, Nilsen's emotional responses were poor. Gallwey said he constantly sought power because he felt so cut off, inferior and worthless. He also explained how Nilsen's schizoid behaviour was of the type that involved a rich, elaborate fantasy life – a trait now more commonly associated with schizo-typal cases. This, however, was generally well hidden. His narcissism was more obvious. It showed in Nilsen's constant grandiosity. He told the court: 'He really does think he is the murderer of the century.'

In response to some blank looks from the jury, Gallwey then tried to clarify the relationship between Nilsen's various mental states. Normally, he said, Nilsen was able to keep his paranoid and schizoid disturbances in check. But there was always conflict going on; psychological pressure would build up, and need release. This happened in episodic breakdowns where he was now *predominately* schizoid. Gallwey clarified the meaning of the word – it didn't mean Nilsen was delusional, but that his emotions had stopped functioning. The breakdowns were 'psycho-sexual', violent, sudden and seemingly without motive. When they happened, Nilsen wasn't in control.

Gallwey tried to explain why these breakdowns happened. He said Nilsen particularly needed close relationships to stave off his 'false self'. Life in London had been a recipe for disaster. The break-up with Gallichan may well have been the last straw. He said it left Nilsen 'drowning in his own nightmares'. With no anchor, his schizoid tendencies started taking over. These were very distinctive – of the type, Gallwey said, that 'indulges imagination for its own sake'. He explained that while such tendencies might also be found in some artists, in Nilsen they were just destructive, removing the last of his emotions. At the time of the murders, then, the victims had no meaning to him as real individuals. He was so lost in a depersonalised state that he became muddled as to their identity, and sometimes thought of them as part of himself. Nilsen echoes this when he talks about 'fantasy props' and 'dualism'.

Gallwey said he saw the murders as being entirely consistent with a 'false-self' personality finding itself in the wrong set of circumstances. Even though the killing of Malcolm Barlow and John Howlett seemed to contradict the theory of episodic breakdowns, the psychiatrist believed, in truth, Nilsen had simply misremembered his thoughts and feelings.

Gallwey thought that during the period of the murders, Nilsen would have been unable to understand what was going on. He explained how he had tried cutting back on drink but said that that could not have helped at all. But he thought Nilsen had indeed suffered from diminished responsibility, not because he didn't understand his mental problems, but because when he murdered he couldn't emotionally distinguish between reality and fantasy. That meant there could be no 'malice aforethought'. Gallwey explained that feeling was a crucial part of intent. He said that the episode with Carl Stottor, rather than showing a cold-hearted cover-up, demonstrated Nilsen had clearly gone in and out of a stage of dissociation and afterwards was 'reassembling' his personality. *This* showed the difference between the Nilsen who had emotions and the one who killed.

Allan Green put it to Gallwey that Nilsen knew exactly what might happen when he deliberately invited people back. Gallwey replied he might have factually known but he may not have *emotionally* understood what he was doing. And if he didn't *feel* his actions were wrong he would not have been able fundamentally to 'know what he was doing'. He would have known the 'nature of his acts' but not the 'quality' of them.

On Monday, 31 October, Lawrence asked Gallwey to recap. He focused on three main points. First, that the murders were part of a defence mechanism that prevented Nilsen from becoming completely psychotic by directing destruction outwards. Second, he said that if a person's emotional make-up stops working, he can be unable to attribute meaning to the things he does. And finally, he emphasised his belief that

Nilsen's schizoid tendencies had pushed his fantasy life into an abnormal and destructive place.

Lawrence then reminded the court what sort of abnormality they were looking for. He said it was one that would 'substantially impair his judgement' and was 'a state of mind so different from that of ordinary human beings that the reasonable man would term it abnormal'.

There was only one witness left – Dr Paul Bowden – again from the Bethlem and Maudsley hospital. His role was to 'rebut' the testimony of Mackeith and Gallwey. He had one big advantage over them – only he had really got to know the defendant. In fact, he had seen him 16 times dating back to Nilsen's first week on remand. He'd also spoken to others who knew Nilsen, including Cathy Hughes and Roger Farnham from the Job Centre, former boyfriend David Gallichan, and the last person to stay with Nilsen, Trevor Simpson.

Tall and moustachioed with combed-back hair, he approached the box in a cool, precise manner. On the Monday and Tuesday, he explained why he could find no abnormality in Nilsen which fitted the definition of the Homicide Act 1957. He admitted he did find Nilsen 'abnormal' in a loose, colloquial sense. But Bowden didn't feel Nilsen suffered from a mental disorder; he said he was simply a man with deviant desires who used deception to make it look like he couldn't help it. He immediately pointed to the way he would constantly revise his childhood accounts, to make himself seem more emotionally deprived than he had originally claimed.

Bowden considered Nilsen to be a man with normal mental functioning who also had extreme guilt about his own sexuality. As he felt guilty, he figured he might as well do bad things. He said the murders were conscious, deliberate acts to satisfy his desires. Nilsen's recollections, he said, were far too strong for there to be any question of the dissociation the other psychiatrists had talked about. He said he had other experience of such things and they invariably involved a long black-out.

But, as much as Bowden's testimony chimed with a 'good sense' view, his opinions soon became more counter-intuitive. It seemed odd to say, as he did, that masturbating by corpses wasn't sexual or powdering of the bodies was just a practical measure to stop them from smelling. Furthermore, it seemed very peculiar to say that Nilsen's grandiosity was merely a reaction to being caught.

The defence asked why he had first said he found no 'abnormality of mind' in Nilsen, and then later changed that to an 'insignificant abnormality'. Bowden replied he'd changed his mind. He had simply discovered more about him. It was like when he'd signed the papers to put Nilsen on suicide watch in Brixton. Nilsen had seemed agitated but, over the next few months, he felt he had got a deeper measure of him and his complaining nature.

Bowden simply considered Nilsen to be a liar and manipulator. As such, he chose to ignore many of the things he had been told by him. For example, he didn't believe the death of Nilsen's grandfather had had the damaging effect Nilsen claimed. As for Nilsen's isolation, he said he believed this was a result of, rather than the cause of, being a murderer. Finally, he felt that Nilsen had been perfectly capable of forming personal relationships, but had forced himself to objectify people. Bowden spelt out what he meant by that: 'It made it easier to kill people.' To illustrate how Nilsen deliberately suppressed his conscious, he described how when talking about the killing of John Howlett, he had to leave the room until he regained his composure.

Allen Green summed up his case over Tuesday afternoon and Wednesday morning. His message was simple: Nilsen was cunning and had used his intelligence to avoid being detected while continuing to murder for pleasure. The jury were reminded of the level of planning involved in warning Stottor about the sleeping bag zip, the preparation of the tie to kill Sinclair, and allowing Martyn Duffey's knives to rust. The fact he had been drunk was no excuse for any of his actions.

Ivan Lawrence's final address appealed to plain reason. He went through Nilsen's offences, crime by crime, and asked the court, again and again, 'Is there not anything wrong with this man?' Just because Bowden – or 'Dr No' as he called him – had failed to see anything wrong, it didn't mean that the jury had to 'ignore the blindingly obvious'. He might not have been insane 'but he wasn't normal either'.

On Thursday morning, Judge Croom-Johnson instructed the jury. He told them if they considered it *possible* that Nilsen did not understand what he was doing when he was killing, they should return a verdict of manslaughter. He closed by saying, 'There are evil people who do evil things. Committing murder is one of them. There must be no excuses for Nilsen if he has moral defects. A nasty nature is not an arrested or retarded development of mind.'

The jury retired shortly before lunchtime on Thursday, 3

November. It had been expected that they would come back that afternoon. They were, however, deadlocked at 6-6.

The next day, at 7.00am, Nilsen wrote a diary entry in his cell, which Brian Masters has kindly permitted me to reproduce here: 'I rise early, still an unconvicted man, to pen this letter. The jury is still out (and so are the Leyland workers). It will be 5 November tomorrow and society's turn to throw me on the bonfire.' At 11.25am, the judge said that he was prepared to accept a majority verdict. That verdict came through at 4.25pm – on the attempted murder of Paul Nobbs, everyone agreed that Nilsen was guilty. On every other count, the jury was split 10-2 in favour of a guilty verdict.

Dennis Nilsen was sentenced to life imprisonment with a recommendation that he serve a minimum of 25 years. He was taken down to the cells, and then off to Wormwood Scrubs. While he sat in front of the television in the hospital area of the Scrubs, his first thoughts were self-pitying ones about being 'expelled from society'. The next morning, when he woke up, he penned a letter to Brian Masters, angry about what he had read in the *News of the World* by John Lisners, whom he knew was writing a book about him. Nilsen's previously unpublished words are provided courtesy of Brian Masters: 'I arrived at Wormwood Scrubs last night. I read John Lisners' "sour grapes" as he, in his 'professional knowledge' of me summed up my life and trial. It can't be much of a book, which is largely based on fourth-hand knowledge … I exercise a great sense of relief that the trial is now finally over. I will see Ralph Haeems soon in order to discuss the merits and practicalities of appealing or not.'

11

THE END OF THE ROAD

'In a most staggering paradox, I only became
mentally liberated as a result of my arrest.'

DENNIS NILSON, TO MATTHEW MALEKOS

On 9 March 2010, the European Court of Human Rights announced their refusal to hear a final appeal by Dennis Nilsen to have his manuscript returned so that he could work on it. Nilsen had now taken his case as far as it seemed he logically could, and had failed. The European judges had made final something that their British counterparts had ruled on seven years before. This was to uphold that the Prison Service's verdict that, in his autobiography, Nilsen: (1) had nothing say in the public interest; (2) wanted to spread 'highly personal' details of some offences along with 'lurid and pornographic passages'; and (3) sought both to justify his conduct and denigrate people he disliked.

The ECHR decision was the end of the line for Nick Wells, Nilsen's lawyer for over 12 years. During that time, he had proved himself an innovative legal thinker. Changing the law in favour of a serial killer's rights, however, eventually proved too much for his abilities. Shortly after hearing the ECHR's judgment, the lawyer and his client parted company.

Nilsen and Wells' journey through the courts had started back in October 2001 with another 'rights' case. On this occasion it was Nilsen's unsuccessful attempt to get access to the gay 'pin-up' magazine, *Vulcan*. Although the bid failed Nilsen thought he had found something useful whilst preparing it – the ability to use 'legally privileged' envelopes to communicate with his lawyer. This practice made him wonder if he might also be allowed to use similar envelopes to bring in a copy of his draft manuscript.

Nilsen asked Wells about this who, in turn, asked the governor. The governor replied that as *History of a Drowning Boy* was not a legal document, it would still need to be read and approved. Some months later, however, in 2002 Nilsen asked Wells to send the manuscript in anyway.

When he did so, the book was confiscated and a letter delivered to Nilsen's cell:

The Prison Service has now read the manuscript and considered this request. It has decided not to allow the manuscript to be passed to Mr Nilsen ... The offences are an integral part of the manuscript. The manuscript does not consist of serious representations about conviction or form part of serious comment about crime, the processes of justice or the penal system. Rather it is a platform for Mr Nilsen to denigrate people he dislikes ... The withholding of the manuscript pursues a legitimate aim, namely the protection of morals, the protection of the reputation and rights of others, and the protection of information received in confidence ...

Nilsen was furious. He would later write to me: 'I understand that many of the prison revelations in the book (including the Central TV thing) will be embarrassing to the HO. I care not about this. I do not play politics, I merely write testimony of a personal life ... Although my body is imprisoned, they will not succeed in controlling the positive expressions from my mind.'

The following year – 2003 – Nilsen's lawyers decided on another tack. It was now reported in the media that Nilsen was going to take the Prison Service to Judicial Review on the grounds that certain prison rules violated his basic freedom of expression. The idea that a mass killer could take on an agent of the government on the grounds that *his* rights were being infringed sounded like the sort of thing you couldn't make up. I had almost forgotten about Nilsen's book. Now, again, I was intrigued.

I wondered if it was *just* attention he was looking for, or whether there was more to this mission to have his book published. But I couldn't judge what he was up to until I had finally read *History of a Drowning Boy*. After some deliberation I decided my best chance might simply be to write a letter and ask Nilsen, straight out, how we could make this happen. That is what I did.

Two days later, I received a reply written on his new electric typewriter and sent from Full Sutton Prison. He appeared happy to hear from me, and said he would soon put me in touch with Jonny Marling, who had a copy. On the strength of what I was going to be given access to – both *History of a Drowning Boy* and a series of essays, letters, pictures and tapes, the *Sunday Times* magazine commissioned a 5,000 word feature.

On a fresh and sunny day in May, I drove out west to see Jonny Marling in the offices of his travel business in Bath, situated at the edge of town. Marling, now in his thirties, seemed friendly and slightly intense. As he brought me a cup of tea, it was hard not to miss the large Nilsen painting by the desk.

'You must think I am very, very odd,' he said.

I changed the subject. 'How did your friendship with Des begin?' I asked.

He said he had chanced upon *Killing for Company* while browsing in a bookshop. The dust jacket revealed that Nilsen used to live in Cricklewood, where Marling, too, had lived. The coincidence intrigued him and he decided to buy it. After reading the book, Marling said he then started to become fixated with wanting to know what had made this 'apparently ordinary bloke' do what he did. He first wrote to Masters and then to Nilsen himself. The letters went well and soon they were writing weekly. Marling would visit whenever he could.

It was all very confusing. The man in front of me seemed intelligent and well balanced with a nice life. It was hard to see what place such a dark hobby might have in it. And it wasn't just criminological curiosity that had taken root in him: Marling appeared to really want Des's friendship. More than anything I was mystified why he was so ready to believe Nilsen's versions of events. Sometimes, he seemed to want to excuse Nilsen even more than Nilsen himself had done. When I asked him why he thought his friend had killed so many people, there was no hesitation – he was convinced it was the booze.

A couple of hours later, we travelled across town to collect a missing document from his home. Marling's petite wife opened the door. She welcomed me into their clean, white kitchen. After chatting about their pets and children, the conversation moved on to how she had spent weeks over the past year typing up the manuscript I was being loaned. The killer's place in this gentle domestic set-up now seemed even more perplexing than before.

In the following months, Nilsen replied to my letters in a prompt and business-like way. On request he supplied me with a list of reasons why he believed his book should be published and gave the various legal arguments that were going to be used. He told me his lawyers were looking to challenge clause '5b' of the Prison Rules, which prohibited prisoners 'sending out any material for publication if it is about their own crime or past offences.' The only exception was when such correspondence consisted of 'serious representations about conviction or sentence'.

Nilsen not only believed his was a serious work, but also that his ability to express himself was a human right. He wrote to me saying, 'A prisoner recognises that he loses his liberty as a result of a just prison sentence, but the law never recognises that he loses his basic "freedom of expression".'

But when it came to the Judicial Review it only took two days in October for Judge Maurice Kay to hear the case, and rule that the Human Rights Act had not been infringed and that he could see no other reason for the manuscript to be returned.

Despite the adverse outcome, Nilsen was pleased what I had written about the episode and the fairness of my approach. Afterwards, we kept up an ad hoc correspondence. Over a period of time, the hard-edged tone of Nilsen's letters started to soften and I begun to wonder if more than 20 years in prison was actually 'normalising' him. The continued complaints about the general state of the world were still there, but the letters were becoming more self-aware. I speculated if this might indicate psychological improvement.

While writing my magazine piece, I had asked many experts what emotional development they thought would ever be possible. Most felt his emotions and personality would probably remain fairly static. Brian Masters even told me that Nilsen only understood remorse like a 'mathematical equation'. He said 'attention-seeking' was Nilsen's 'equivalent of love' and worried that he sought to 'intellectually seduce' others' minds. But Masters hadn't seen Nilsen in more than 10 years; how could he really know?

One person who believes Nilsen has grown emotionally is Matthew Malekos. In his thesis 'The Birth of Psychopathy: the Psychology of a Serial Killer', he argues that Nilsen's creativity in prison indicates the restoration of fully-functioning emotions. He believes the murders provided an impetus for Nilsen to look into himself, and that subsequent emotional development has taken place in prison. His thesis states: 'The use of criminal actions, perversely, has made

Dennis Nilsen far stronger and more optimistic than he was at the point before carrying out his homicidal actions … he has undergone a positive personal transformation while he has been incarcerated … not because of prison, but in spite of it.'

Malekos's reasons for believing this theory start conventionally enough, but they invariably end up in very esoteric arguments. His theories encompass spiritual and mystical thinking. In particular, Malekos uses the term 'self-actualisation' – a term originally invented by the twentieth-century American humanistic psychologist, Abraham Maslow – to explain Nilsen's change. He describes it as a state 'in which an individual strives to be the best that they can be having resolved their past traumas and "inner demons"'…and says that such people '[experience] an overwhelming sense of joy from books, music and the arts'.

Whatever one makes of Malekos's theories, the question of whether Nilsen – and those like him – can change remains an important one. Prisons are meant to try to rehabilitate all prisoners. Social and religious reformers alike will tell you that whatever punishment may be required to serve justice, society must never stop caring about the state of prisoners' souls and minds. Even when rehabilitation serves no practical end – for the whole-life prisoner – a moral society should aspire towards it. This had been uppermost in the mind of Lord Longford throughout his visiting periods with Nilsen.

What, though, if change might come, not through therapy or religion, but simply through growing older? Medical literature does indicate some people with personality disorders do, indeed, find their condition subsides with time. Could this be what was happening with Nilsen? His increased self-awareness seemed to indicate so and yet a question remained of how we could trust such evidence.

Short of using lie detectors or PPGs, all we can ever go on is what people say. People like Nilsen are, however, extremely deceptive. And even though I thought I could detect signs of a changing character, every so often I would read something of Nilsen's that would frighten me. On page 312 of Malekos's thesis, for instance, Nilsen was quoted as having written in a letter: 'Yes, I am obsessed with remembering and enjoying the frisson of my sexual rituals ... what else is there [to do] but to caress [my] memories in my present social wasteland ... I do not fantasise about other prisoners, but about the past.'

Since 2003, Nilsen has remained in Full Sutton Prison. He gets up at around 7.00am and starts working at 8.30am in the workshop where he translates books into Braille. At lunchtime he eats a sandwich and work finishes at 3.00pm. His wages are about £17 a week, and with this money, he rents a portable television. He no longer has a keyboard or a budgie in his room. Nearly all his spare time is still spent on his typewriter. His autobiographical reflections on prison life now amount to 4,500 pages.

Nilsen remains on cordial terms with the other inmates on the Vulnerable Prisoner Unit, but feels little in common with them socially or intellectually. He does, however, seem to have reached an equilibrium with his surroundings. This is despite a judge having ruled in 2006, when the Home Office system of whole-life tariffs had been abandoned, that he would never be eligible for parole.

Letters I have received during the period 2003 to 2012

have continued to be written in an increasingly 'normal' manner. His favourite topic eventually moved away from prison conditions to current affairs. The last letter he sent me was about the Jimmy Savile case, which was all over the newspapers after the former TV presenter was accused posthumously of perpetrating a huge number of sex attacks over several decades. Nilsen vividly described him as 'garishly attired with long blond hair, appendages festooned with chunky gold bangles, chains, shades, and topped off by the omnipresent huge cigar, which, as well as being subliminally phallic, showed Jimmy shaking his huge cock at the world …'

Nilsen called this Savile's 'false persona' which covered up for his stunted emotional development. In adulthood, he opined that all of Savile's 'emotional interactions' were 'transacted entirely on his terms and under his control'. Then, one sentence jumped out. Nilsen wrote: 'As Savile's MO was established, he grew in confidence. Of course, he never viewed himself as "studiously evil".' Not being 'studiously evil' was the exact expression Nilsen had used when referring to himself in one of his earliest letters to me.

I wondered if this meant he, Nilsen, was about to admit the extent to which he might have enjoyed his crimes? But the letter just fizzled out. Then I remembered the emotionally inert response he had given when confronted with the full extent of the evil of his first murder. In 2005, two policemen arrived at HMP Full Sutton to show him new photographs of someone he might have killed. By the time they left, Nilsen's first victim was finally identified as 14-year-old Stephen Holmes. Nilsen casually spoke about the matter a year later in a letter to the *Evening Standard*:

In 1983, I made a full confession at Hornsey Police Station on the matter of the youth I had encountered and killed ... while I was in a drunken state near the end of December 1978 ... while I was 'bingeing' in the Cricklewood Arms pub ...

Afterwards, at Melrose Avenue, I had no idea who this youth was ... as he had nothing on him at all ... no money or other means of identification ... except, maybe, a latch key ... which was disposed of.

After my trial ... police inquiries went more or less cold. Then, in 1990, out of the blue ... while I was, coincidentally, in this prison on my first visit, (until 1991), detectives from the Metropolitan Police visited me ... for the purposes of identifying this victim.

All they had was ... a small blurred 'passport-type' 1980s photocopy of a photocopy of a small photograph ... which, for the purposes of identification ... could have been anyone ... from this scant material I was unable to make any kind of positive ID ... they departed as swiftly as they had arrived ... then, last year, a new (police) team arrived.

Carl Stottor's reaction when I reminded him about Nilsen's letter to the *Evening Standard* about the identification of Stephen Holmes was that it was a sign of his 'incredible arrogance'. He told me, 'Nilsen, is just a nasty, nasty man ... he's a nobody who enjoys the notoriety that being a serial killer has brought him.' When I told him about the full extent of Nilsen's legal battles, he rolled his eyes and said he found it outrageous he could get legal aid for his human rights case when he himself was denied victim compensation for the attack.

Stottor's appearances in numerous 'real-crime' documentaries have always shown him to be, to varying degrees, troubled. His weight has fluctuated, and frequently his voice has trembled. When I met him at his home in 2012, however, he appeared much more at peace. To draw a line under 'Stottor the victim', he now calls himself 'Kha-Ra Willis'. The name reflects his love of ancient Egypt, as does his seaside flat, which looked like cross between a museum and a bohemian hang-out. In the corner is an up-ended sarcophagus that opens up to reveal itself as a DVD rack. During our interview, a black cat called Cleopatra wandered among all the Egyptobilia and Kha-Ra's artwork.

At 51, Kha-Ra has diabetes and is HIV-positive. But still he remains optimistic about life. One of his favourite words is 'survivor'. During my afternoon with him, he used it almost continuously. He talked about how he'd survived Nilsen, drink and depression, and he intended to do the same with HIV. To put his life into perspective and to keep positive, he told me he was writing a memoir. He was keen to emphasise how Nilsen was only going to be allocated as much space as he deserved. It was clear, however, that he found just talking about him upsetting.

Nilsen's book was a particularly sore subject. Kha-Ra said he had learnt about it in 1998 from the same article that I had read. His reaction was an immediate rush of blood and panic – a sense that he just wasn't being allowed to forget about the man who had tried to kill him. Then Kha-Ra decided to do something practical. He printed up a petition and went out into the street asking for signatures. When all the sheets were full, he sent them to the Home Office.

He told me, 'This book [*History of a Drowning Boy*] is just about his desire for attention and publicity, that's all it is. Nilsen wants to cater for his monster, ego, image. He's just a monster and we shouldn't pay attention to him. We should be thinking about the victims and the ripple effect on other victims.'

Kha-Ra asked me what Nilsen had said about him. I explained how he had said that he thought he might be attributing all his problems to one night in 1982. Kha-Ra couldn't believe that, after all Nilsen had done, he could be that presumptuous. The next day, he sent me an email: 'Talk about pot … kettle! Nilsen likes to pass his victims over like they are worth nothing, just vulnerable people, waifs and strays. Nilsen's victims were blameless and innocent, something the press at the time were never kind to. The same goes for the judicial system. I think it is a great miscarriage of justice that Nilsen was never charged with my attempted murder and that I was never compensated as a victim, but that is justice for you, affordable only to those with money. All any victim seeks is justice.'

The following week, I went to see Graham Allen's former partner, Lesley Mead. Although now in her sixties, it wasn't hard to imagine her as the short, attractive barmaid her son Shane had described her as once being. But she had clearly had a hard life. Her build was now heavy and her eyes twitched nervously when she spoke. Like Kha-Ra, Mead shares her living space with a cat, a stray she found outside the community centre where she helps out.

THE END OF THE ROAD

I was here at the suggestion of Shane. I had told him I was impressed by the way he had written about his father. He suggested it might help my research to see those events through her eyes. For over two hours, I listened to Mead speaking plainly, without any artifice. She said she knew Puggy hadn't been perfect; neither had she, for that matter. But she had been enormously hurt by the way the papers had generalised about Nilsen's victims and their families. I drove home with a sick feeling in my stomach. Back in my study, I decided to re-read Shane's account of how his mother had taken the news of his father's murder: 'It all started with a scream. I heard it from the top of the road as I made my way home from school. Somehow, I knew it was my mother's pain. It was a scream from nowhere and of unbearable suffering. And it didn't stop. It was 1983 and my mother had just been informed that her lover, my father, missing for over a year, had been discovered – murdered and dismembered and stuffed in two black bin bags in the flat of serial killer Dennis Nilsen. I was seven, and Hell was on its way.'

That afternoon, two uniformed and two plain-clothes officers had arrived at Lesley's house. Shane explains how his mother dealt with learning the circumstances surrounding Puggy's death:

The months immediately after the death are vague. I hardly recall a thing. I think my mother was shell-shocked ... She stayed locked in her room, the house growing darker, and alcohol keeping her afloat.

The last sane thing, or the first insane thing my mother did, was to attend Nilsen's trial at The Old Bailey....

Post-trial, I remember my mother drinking suicidal amounts. Drunk, she would do nothing but cry and sit on the floor alongside a small stereo listening to old love songs … With the story now out of the media, the victims' families were left at home alone without even the small comfort of the nation's empathy to help absorb the event. There were no more journalists offering comfort as they scavenged the victims for scraps of untold story, and no more newspaper reports mentioning their names and telling of their plight. It was over. The murderer was in jail and other news was more important. The victims now only had the torture of solitude and silence to take comfort from … that was no comfort at all. My mother's drinking and suicidal tendencies spiralled to a climax. She could no longer take it any more. She decided that The Blackout was for her.

That 'blackout' was a suicide attempt.

I thought again about how her hand had shaken as she talked to me. I started to feel guilt about having made her relive those memories; they surely must have distressed her more than she let on.

A couple of days later, I emailed Shane and asked him how Lesley was doing. He thanked me but confirmed it had, indeed, shaken her more than she had initially realised. The scars had faded but the wound, it seemed, was easily aggravated.

Later that afternoon, I followed up a claim from Martyn Hunter-Craig that Nilsen now had a Facebook account. It sounded far-fetched, but he seemed adamant. I wondered if one of his correspondents might be posting on his behalf.

Certainly, when I looked at the page it really seemed to be his style. But as I scrolled down it became apparent that it was actually a fan using the archive of Nilsen quotes available from books, newspapers and documentaries to write in his voice.

I found it unsurprising that people on the internet should be using social media to further a fixation with serial killers. Still, it made me wonder if my own interest in Nilsen might also be helping to fuel the behaviour of such cranks. Where, I asked myself, did the line between sociological enquiry and morbid fascination exist? And, did all interest in Nilsen, ultimately, serve to flatter his ego?

I started to reflect on the last letters we had exchanged in 2012. At the time of his 'Jimmy Savile' letter he had seemed resolute he would find new lawyers and continue with his crusade to publish. He believed he could find new ways to appeal. I imagined this desire had been given added urgency since he had finally been told he would never be allowed parole.

But in April 2013, something happened that might have finally put paid to the last of Nilsen's ambitions. The Ministry of Justice announced a consultation on plans to reform provision of Legal Aid. These included proposals to reduce prisoners' access to aid other than where such access concerned a legitimate appeal over sentencing. Nilsen's complaints about the prison authorities disrespecting his human rights would certainly be excluded.

So now it appears that unless Nilsen finds a publisher willing to take on copies of his sprawling, unedited drafts in whatever form they might exist outside of prison, there really is no further for him to go. Whatever journalists and criminologists may still have to say about these crimes, to the certain relief of his victims, it seems the killer's ongoing contributions to that discussion have finally come to an end.

SOURCES AND REFERENCE MATERIAL

Aggrawal Anil, *Necrophilia Forensic and Medico-Legal Aspects* (CRC 2011)

Akhtar, S 'Schizoid Personality Disorder: A Synthesis of Developmental, Dynamic, and Descriptive Features' (*American Journal of Psychotherapy*, 151:499–518, 1987)

A Killing in the Family documentary (BBC 1999)

American Psychiatric Association, *Diagnostic and Statistical Manual of Mental Disorders 4 & 5*

Bence, Douglas &McConnell, Brian, *The Nilsen File* (Futura, 1983)

Bookmark: Monochrome Man (documentary, J Lustig/Alan Lewens production 1991)

Born to Kill, the Kindly Killer: Dennis Nilsen (documentary), (TwoFour 2011)

Coffey, Russ, 'Memoirs of a Serial Killer' (*Sunday Times Magazine* 2003)

Correspondence between the author and Dennis Nilsen

Correspondence between Dennis Nilsen and acquaintances viewed at a private crime archive

Crimes that Shook the World: Dennis Nilsen (documentary, Discovery 2009)

Daily Express: Archive reports

Daily Mirror: Archive reports

Dennis Nilsen: Gràdh a' Bhàis? (In Love with Death?) (documentary, including unbroadcast interview with Betty Scott, STV 2009)

Evening Standard: Archive reports

Kay, Mr Justice Maurice, Judgment on Dennis Andrew Nilsen v (1) The Governor of HMP Full Sutton, (2) Secretary Of State for the Home Department, (2003)

Hartnett, Peter-Paul, *Call Me* (Pulp 1996)

Honeycombe, Gordon, 'Writing Wrong's' (*Punch* 13 August 1998)

Honeycombe, Gordon, *Murders of the Black Museum* (John Blake Publishing Ltd, 2009)

Interviews with 'Rob Ferrier', 'Jonny Marling,' Brian Masters, Gordon Honeycombe, Dr Pat Gallwey, Martyn Hunter-Craig, Carl Stottor, Lesley Mead, Peter Jay, and Shane Levene (Russ Coffey)

SOURCES AND REFERENCE MATERIAL

Koren, Anna (www.annakoren.com)

Levene, Shane, memoiresofaheroinhead.blogspot.co.uk (All extracts reproduced by special permission of the author.)

Lisners, John, *House of Horrors* (Corgi, 1983)
Longford, Lord, *Lord Longford's Prison Diaries* (Lion, 2000)

Mackeith, James, Psychiatric report on Dennis Nilsen (1983)
Malekos, Matthew, *The Birth of Psychopathy: the Psychology of a Serial Killer* (Lulu 2012)
Masters, Brian, *Killing for Company* (Arrow, 1995) (All extracts reproduced by special permission of the author.)
Masters, Brian, 'Dahmer's Inferno' (*Vanity Fair*, November 1991)

News International: Archive reports
Nilsen, Dennis, 'Anatomy of an Official Conclusion' (unpublished)
Nilsen, Dennis, 'Brain Damage' (unpublished)
Nilsen, Dennis, 'Image Distortion' (unpublished)
Nilsen, Dennis, 'The Psychograph' (unpublished)
Nilsen, Dennis, police interviews
Nilsen, Dennis, *History of a Drowning Boy* (unpublished)

Observer archive reports

The Prison Act, 1952

Real Crime: A Mind to Murder (documentary, Granada 2003)

DENNIS NILSEN

'Real Life Crimes and How They Were Solved issue 38' (Eaglemoss 1993)

Rendell, Ruth, *The Reason Why – An anthology of the murderous mind* (Cape 1995)

Serial Killers: Dennis Nilsen (documentary, Discovery 2009)

Surviving Dennis Nilsen (documentary, Redback Films 2006)

To Kill and Kill Again (documentary, Brook Lapping 2001)

Viewpoint 1993: Murder in Mind (documentary, Central TV 1993)

World Health Organisation, *International Classification of Diseases 9&10*